Blister

A. SCOTT HOWE

Fourth Revision 2024
Plug-in Creations, Beaverton, Oregon, USA

ISBN: 0985076534
ISBN-13: 978-0985076535

DEDICATION

This book is dedicated to the fine engineers and scientists at work at the NASA Jet Propulsion Laboratory. I also dedicate this book to the talented individuals of the American Institute of Aeronautics and Astronautics (AIAA) Space Architecture Technical Committee (SATC) for their visions of an extraordinary future for the human race.
(see http://www.spacearchitect.org)

ACKNOWLEDGMENTS

I would like to acknowledge my wife Ingping Chia Howe for her continued encouragement. Many thanks go to retired JPL astronomer Karen Young for her expert insights, and JPL fellow colleague Tim McElrath for advice on mission planning and orbital dynamics.

PROLOGUE

Out in the cold depths of space, an ancient installation winked to life. Its convoluted surface began to shimmer with activity barely illuminated in harsh contrasting tones by the light of a distant alien sun. No sound could be heard as thousands of mechanical components moved into place and formed themselves into a large ring shape -- a perfectly circular gate framing the blackness of space. As soon as it was built, powerful forces began to course around the ring, warping the very fabric of space. The installation, called Bridgestar, had rearranged itself into a tunnel connecting two distant regions of the universe.

Without warning, a small ship emerged from the gate and made a beeline up-system toward that distant sun. The captain and crew of the ship, frantic in their hasty maneuvering, barely noticed that the ring structure disassembled itself behind them and all the little robotic squares and triangles began to disperse back to their original positions.

Unfortunately, something had followed them through the gate.

"What is that thing? I can't get a good reading on it." exclaimed one of the crewmembers.

The captain tried to shake the relentless pursuer but to no avail. He initiated a high-gee turn that plastered everyone against their acceleration webbing, only to discover that the aggressor had easily compensated and was closing in.

"Jettison the fuel pods!" the captain ordered.

Small explosions reverberated through the hull as separation occurred. As soon as the pods were clear the captain executed another high-gee turn, hoping to distract the unknown entity with the massive discarded modules. The blip on the radar didn't even flinch -- it was closer than ever. The crew began to chatter to each other in a panic. Warning lights flashed and klaxons sounded.

"It's going to ram us!" the captain shouted out as a warning.

Everyone braced for impact. The aggressive entity slammed into their side, penetrating through layers of shielding and redundant pressure lining until it sealed itself to the inner hull -- like a virus attaching itself to a cell wall. A sheared circle of metal blew inward explosively, suddenly equalizing the atmospheres of the two vessels. The high-speed collision put the combined mass of the two craft into an eccentric spin that made it hard to move about.

Something sinister crawled aboard.

"Arm yourselves!" the security officer shouted.

The crew waited as sounds of violence echoed through the hull. A hunt was on somewhere in the bowels of the ship. Screams of men and women could be heard, and strange crackling noises silenced them in the distance as if consumed by tremendous heat. Off to the side, a small boy fearfully looked at the captain as he was pinned to the bulkhead by the erratic spin.

The captain gave the bravest smile he could muster and said, "Son, remember your hiding spots? I want you to go hide and don't come out!"

The boy nodded but still looked longingly up at his father as they all crouched behind consoles. Just then the lights went out, and dim battery-powered emergency lighting flickered on.

There was movement over in the tunnel connecting the bridge to the crew decks -- a strange sort of evil black cloud drifted toward them. The boy jumped up and tried to leap into his father's arms, but the centripetal accelerations caused him to be pinned to the ceiling instead. The black cloud reacted, and the boy was sure he could see the menacing muzzle of some kind of horrible weapon pointing right at him out of the fog.

Everyone froze. The weapon wavered a bit, as if whatever monstrosity was behind the trigger hesitated to burn down a child.

Suddenly the captain jumped out, firing his weapon, creating a diversion as the boy scrambled away. The evil tube peeking out from the dark stain re-acquired a new target and sent a burst of intense microwaves cooking the man's flesh instantly. The cabin burst into a firefight as shots erupted from behind consoles and the other crewmembers joined in. One by one each crewmember was cooked alive, meeting their untimely demise. Horrible screams were silenced by single blasts to the head.

The boy looked on from behind hidden vents, as horrible "things" moved methodically through the ship, mercilessly cutting down anyone who got in their way. The dark, ghostly invaders murdered those who passively surrendered as well, including a young mother who protectively clung to her little girl.

When the dirty deed was complete, bodies were dragged off and set in centrifugal low spots where their blood was drained and collected using the spin of the ship, then stuffed in an airlock and blown out into space. It never occurred to the nightmarish entities that there was no corpse of a little boy.

The conquerors settled back with their new prize and headed home to *Blister*. Out the window, Bridgestar could be seen several clicks away. The ancient installation held in its bowels the key to dozens of solar systems -- and countless unsuspecting ships and worlds for the taking. There would be no stopping the relentless waves of invasion.

CHAPTER 1

Sochiko knew that her things were already packed and loaded, but took one last look around her chamber anyway to see if she had forgotten anything. The space was small, with barely enough room to take two short paces in any direction. One wall was filled with cabinets that had multiple hidden panels - - she could trace the outline of the fold-down desk, collapsible chairs, bookcase drawers, and closets. Above the cabinets at about eye level was a wide shelf-loft holding her bunk, all made up neatly. There were drawings, paintings, and sketches on the wall opposite, each rendered in perfect composition and balance. Some of those were hers, but Uncle Ix drew the rest.

As she looked over the room she had lived in all her life, a warm feeling swelled up inside. It was neat but shabby; since most of the original finishing had been donated to the material drives whenever there were resource shortages. This was home, and she would miss it for the time she would be away on the mission. She slowly backed out, turned off the light, and closed the door.

A middle-aged blonde woman met her in the hallway, "Sochiko, you'd better hurry or you'll miss your ride!"

"Oh Mom, they won't leave without me. Besides, I still have an hour before the pod departs." Sochiko used the ancestral time unit 'hour' often since it was the fad among young people, and all their flight schedules also used the 'hour-minute-second' time calibration.

"Sochi!" Her mom was trying hard to be a friend rather than a lecturing mother. "Remember your uncle told the pod to leave earlier -- what, a half hour?"

Sochiko froze for a moment. She looked at the attractive golden-haired female who seemed to retain her beauty and fought down the irritation welling up inside her. Mom was a genuine daughter of the Wardens, grown up in the virtual worlds of the Database. She had met Sochiko's father back in the days when the Technicians had been homeless, and had been almost the sole reason the Wardens had not exterminated the Japonican race. Blujic had been a hero.

Suddenly Sochiko realized her mother was correct -- she was running late for the most important mission of her life. She rushed over to Blujic, gave her a hug, and ran out the door. She had checked the weather forecast earlier that called for higher oxygen levels, so she snatched up her respirator but left it hanging around her neck as she set a brisk pace through the neighborhood. Only a few people she passed kept the breathing devices on their face -- like her, most had them slung back out of the way.

On her way to the pod port, she flew past apartment fronts that still had barred grillwork from the days the floating city had been used as a prison -- the pleasantly refurbished neighborhoods contrasted with the bleak cellblocks her ancestors had taken over. As she rushed down the avenues, she saw no indication of the turmoil her fathers had experienced when the city had broken up during ancient battles, lost its moorings, and drifted out to sea where it had been buffeted by never-ending storms. Forced to live for generations under hostile weather, her people had completely forgotten what the outside world was like.

"We didn't even know about the sun," her father used to say, "couldn't see it because of the tempests."

But that all changed. Before Sochiko was born, her father Mox and Uncle Ix set off in submarines to find a new place to settle, and discovered the home of the Wardens. That was when her father and mother had met. The Wardens gave them this small remnant of the floating city that still remained protected in an inland sea, as a place to resettle. They recovered parts of the main city in turn, as large sections were towed in out of the storm to make a thriving megalopolis.

As she passed a newsstand, she caught a glimpse of the headlines: 'Technician Family Ousted by Inmates' one story read. Now the city was bursting at the seams and lacking material resources for industry. Small groups of Technicians had set up settlements in the nearby forests without permission from the nomads, and almost daily there was news of someone getting hurt. Her volunteer work for the Relief Society, which was dedicated to helping unfortunates, had lately centered on finding medicine and shelter for folks who had been displaced. Sochiko saw the crowded shop fronts as she approached the pod port, and knew they had to do something quickly or there would be another war. The Technicians had already been involved in skirmishes with the land-based Inmates -- descendants of the prisoners who had originally occupied their city. Inmates were a wild nomadic people that were always looking for a fight anyway. She felt frustrated that her people had to resort to squabbles over territory. *Somehow there's got to be an answer*, she thought.

"Good luck on the flight Sochi!" a shop keeper she knew called out as she ran past, "Amazing, just amazing!"

A few minutes later another acquaintance saw her coming, "Is this the *Destiny* mission already?"

"Yes!" she excitedly called back, "We're going to dock with it."

It was hard to believe the mission was actually going to happen this time. '*Destiny*' was a light in the sky that rose and set on countless generations of worshipping Wardens. It was an ancient space station, apparently a twin to the wrecked *Origin* that had fallen out of orbit so long ago and lay in ruins out on the plains since from before anyone could remember. The Warden ancestors had climbed out of its smashed interior dazed and confused, having to begin a new life on the surface out of necessity. Where the *Origin* had become a temple of sorts, *Destiny* was still up there, intact, as a spiritual final destination of sorts. She thrilled to think that they were about to unlock another puzzle regarding Those Who Went Before, the mysterious culture that had suddenly disappeared hundreds of years before. The search for answers regarding those ancient inhabitants had consumed the Technicians, and spread to the Wardens and Inmates as well.

Sochiko worked her way through the city past one of the universities, and almost bumped into Professor Gij who had his respirator tight against his face.

"Coming to do research for the mission?" the old scholar pulled off the mask and asked.

Behind the Professor on display were mockups of the ancient vaults. The three cylindrical capsules were historic caches of information deposited by Those Who Went Before, and recovered only a few generations ago. Her great-grandfather had recovered Vaults One and Two, and her father, mother, and uncle had been among the group that had found the Third Vault. In preparation for the mission, she had spent countless hours in the library researching technology and culture of the ancients, including the vaults.

"No not this time -- today the mission begins. I'm on my way to the pod port right now." she replied.

The Professor waved goodbye as Sochi turned to go. "If I were younger, I would have done anything to be in your shoes! When you're back I want to hear about it."

"I owe it to you, Professor!" she called back.

Sochiko abruptly passed outside into the bright sunlight. She looked around and smiled at the beautiful terraced gardens that seemed to enhance the beauty of the rough, ancient structure. Her eyes followed the lines up and up as terraces framed Mother's rich blue sky, and even during the day two of the 'moons' were visible above the gardens.

The sight of the moons put everything in perspective for her. Here they lived, lonely peoples on a tiny spec in the vast universe. 'Mother' was the name they lovingly gave to their own world, Sado. The Technicians took after the Warden description of those heavenly orbiting bodies, describing them as 'moons' when actually they were odd-shaped planetoids, all orbiting the sun at a similar distance as Mother herself. From what they could observe, there seemed to be a complicated dynamic balance such that the planetoids passed by each other without colliding. In a few cases, pairs of planetoids took turns influencing each other's orbits, switching them back and forth as they traded kinetic energies. Mother also had such a partner, even though the energy traded was quite miniscule.

Mother was a small world, and if it weren't for a delicate balance between the capping effects of the ocean storms, evaporating ocean, and high oxygen-producing foliage there wouldn't have been any atmosphere at all. Sochiko fingered the respirator around her neck and thought about how her people were out of place here, requiring breathing apparatus just to walk down the corridor -- it should have been obvious that Mother could not have naturally evolved the human organism.

In her mind she reflected on countless months of training, learning highly specialized hardware, spending time suited up in neutral buoyancy tanks, familiarizing herself with endless avionics and communication equipment, vomiting in centrifuges, and even a trip into orbit. But none of that prepared her for the profound wonder she felt every time she looked up in the sky.

And she was about to touch the sky again...

The pod port was outdoors too. Sochi crossed the plaza and re-entered a small complex of warehouses that were used in conjunction with the port, then emerged onto the deck where several floating piers were extending out like a multipronged fork into the bay waters. Uncle Ix was standing on the deck of a pod waving frantically.

"I was about to call in the guard!" Uncle Ix called out with a slightly frustrated tone, but there was an amicable smile on his face.

She took his hand and jumped across the small gap between the dock and the boat. They entered the hatch and Sochiko followed her uncle to the passenger cabin that had two rows of seats running the length of the vessel, each facing outward to a line of view ports. There were several others including two of her crewmates with whom she sat back-to-back next to her uncle. An unknown person in a hood filed in afterwards and sat two seats down, leaving an empty spot.

"Sochi, you're always cutting it close!" Ix said when they finally settled in and the craft was well under way.

"Sorry, I forgot about the new departure time," she replied, shrugging her shoulders.

"By the way, your aunt says hello -- she's busy piloting with the hunting fleet you know," Ix added, "She'll be listening in with the girls."

Her uncle had married a pod pilot, and his girls had all gotten old enough to fill out a crew. Now they worked together in their own submarine to bring in swimmers during the hunting season.

Just then the unknown passenger pulled off his respirator, cleared his throat, and leaned over to catch her attention. "You're Sochiko?"

Ix jumped in and quickly introduced the stranger, "Oh yes I almost forgot. This is Merinat who will be helping out with operations."

"Warden?" Sochiko asked with a surprised expression, "I thought you guys all participated virtually." She had vaguely recognized his voice since he had worked in operations before.

Merinat pulled off his hood, revealing light brown hair. "Normally yes, but this time I thought I would try it in the Flesh."

The Wardens lived most of their lives in the virtual worlds of the Database that was a rough duplicate of the real Mother with creative enhancements. They participated in the Database world via 'rockers' that were enhanced interfaces with three-axis rotation to simulate motion. Whenever the Wardens decided to see the real world, they called it a 'Flesh kick', which was rare.

"I thought it would be appropriate on *Destiny's* visit since it was your mother who inspired so many of us." Merinat explained. "By the way, what's the story behind your name? It doesn't sound like a typical Technician name."

Sochiko rolled her eyes as if she were tired of explaining it for the umpteenth time, but a smile remained on her face revealing that she relished the attention. "Sochiko comes from the ancient Japonican. They used to name their girls with a noun or adjective attaching '-ko' on the end. 'Ko' means 'child'. Apparently, Those Who Went Before began using the simple names during the Salvage Empire era, where it was a fad to use tongue-twister syllables."

Merinat looked even more curious. "So, what does 'Sochi' mean?"

Sochiko smiled even deeper, and looked over to Ix who also smiled back. "It means 'mechanical device'. Uncle gave me the name."

Ix interjected, "Those Who Went Before typically used cute prefixes like 'flower', but something told me this one was different."

"Uncle! I didn't start out this way. You got me started -- giving me this name was just a self-fulfilling prophecy."

Ix started to defend himself but was interrupted by the warning klaxon. Their short trip was over and the sub had arrived at the floating launch platform.

The passengers all filed out of the cabin and made their way up on deck. The launch complex pod port was below Plasma level, as were all the administrative offices to protect the facilities from accidental explosion on the launch pad.

They went through the familiar routine of checking in, and each went to their separate stations to prepare for the mission.

Sochiko arrived at the crew ready room and looked for her assistants. Around the room there were multiple racks, testing equipment, tanks, and snakes of hoses and cables that filled up every visible wall space. The racks had environmental pressure suits hanging from them in various states of disassembly, reflecting how each crewmember preferred to don or doff which piece and in what order. The prize of the room, standing to one side on display, was the 'Metal Man' that had been recovered from Vault 3 during Nux's era, and then lost again for a whole generation. Those people in great grandfather's day had not recognized the artifact as a compact space suit. Uncle Ix and the other technicians had tried in vain to copy the technology and manufacturing fidelity of the suit, but did not have the proper materials or tools to recreate such lightweight outerwear.

Sochiko joined with the crew and began the long process of donning her bulky pressure suit, which was quite crude compared to the ancient one on display. Each crewmember had two assistants to help lift the bulky parts of the equipment, and to help fasten the airtight seals. Once they got into orbit it would be easier because of the microgravity, and the crewmembers would be able to help each other in and out of the suits.

"*This is it Sochi! I've been so excited I logged in hours ago!*" an electronically amplified voice called out to her.

One of Sochi's assistants was a Warden operating through a mechanical avatar. Sochiko looked over and saw the remote-control contraption holding her suit bottom. The machine was a finely wrought instrument of precisely lubricated joints, and brightly polished metallic surfaces. At first Sochiko's Warden sponsors had thought the mechanical avatars would be an ideal way for their people to vicariously visit space and eventually explore the *Destiny* space station. However, the tremendous maintenance required for its upkeep and the fragile, radiation-susceptible electronic parts cancelled that idea until better parts could be manufactured. Instead, Sochiko and her team would take along specially constructed remote mappers that would systematically record the insides of the orbital so all could experience it virtually at the same time.

"I couldn't sleep last night either," she replied as the machine helped her into the leggings, "I hope I don't fall asleep at the controls."

Once the crew had gotten into the pressure suits, they were too heavy to walk on their own since they were designed for use in microgravity. Each was helped onto a special vehicle that used a novel form of mobility -- four disks that were attached to axles at their centers and rolled the load along (Those Who Went Before called them 'wheels' -- among the Technicians wheels were not unknown, but had heretofore been used as small passive casters on push carts and toys so this new vehicle was admired as a novelty by anyone who saw it for the first time). Once the vehicle rolled its way out of the hangar and up a ramp, they were level with the flight deck of the floating launch platform and could see an unobstructed view in all directions.

"There she is -- are we really here? Pinch me!" her excited crewmate Danid exclaimed.

Though constrained by the pressure suit, Sochiko was still able to turn her head enough to see their space pod that they called *Bird Nine*. She thrilled every time she saw it -- a short and squat cluster of propellant tanks nestled into a truss structure, with a single spherical pressure cabin mounted on top.

As she looked at the beautiful space vessel and waited for the rolling machine to traverse the long approach bridge, Sochiko remembered back on the long hard road it had taken them to get to this point. They had had many failures along with the triumphs, destroying vehicles, fighting for resources, exploding fuel, and even losing lives. *Bird Five* had been lost with its crew as it exploded just after launch, Sochiko having escaped death only because of a change in the duty roster due to a faulty glove on her pressure suit. Just the previous galactic year *Bird Seven* had succeeded in orbiting Mother. Then *Bird Eight* had even approached *Destiny* to within a few nodelengths before returning the crew safely home again.

At the time, Uncle Ix had smiled at her and said, "The day we can climb aboard *Destiny* is the day we can once again shake hands with our fathers."

Curiosity had burned in her, but also caution, "Are we sure we want to go that far -- follow Those Who Went Before back to their homes?"

Ix had regarded her with a perplexed look on his face, "What are you concerned about?"

"Well, something chased them out of the sky. Are we sure we're not rushing into some terror we can't imagine?"

Uncle had shrugged it off, and even she forgot those feelings as the long training progressed. In preparation for this mission Sochiko and her crewmates had been able to study *Destiny's* wrecked twin *Origin* that was half buried out on the plains. At first the Wardens were hesitant to allow the Technicians to enter the sacred structure because of long-held taboos and religious sentiment. Sochiko's mother and father had explored the wreck soon after they first met and were later able to convince the Wardens to allow respectful Flesh pilgrimage and study. From the downed orbital they learned a little bit about how the facility had functioned, and were ready to apply that knowledge to the *Destiny* mission. The exploration of the dead space station held religious significance to the entire Warden population who would be mounted in their rockers and flying alongside them in cyberspace as the Database was updated.

As Sochiko admired *Bird Nine* sitting on the pad, the entire top of the rolling vehicle began to rise up on scissor jacks until they were level with the crew hatch of the space pod. One by one the assistants helped the cumbersome clad crewmembers through the hatch and into their seats. When Sochiko's turn came, the assistants helped her settle into the near vertical, slightly bent seat that put her back against the curved wall facing the mission commander.

Commander Tuk was a former pod captain who had spent many seasons on long voyages in small crafts, making him an ideal candidate for the space crews. Their resident licensed technician, always part of any pod crew, was Bort sitting to her left, and Danid sitting opposite was a specialist on Warden artifacts and culture, selected from the Technicians for her understanding of Warden religion and philosophy. There were also perhaps a dozen virtual crewmembers -- Wardens tied in via the rockers each had had their own workstations operating some aspect of the space pod.

"What do you expect we'll find out there?" Danid made small talk with Bort, trying to quell her nervousness.

Sochiko and Tuk went through their checklists as they waited for the hatch to be secured.

"There will be plenty of artifacts to study I'm sure, even if we're not allowed to disturb anything." Bort excitedly replied and watched the rolling vehicle outside disengage and make its way back to the sunken garage.

"There might be more than what we want to see." Tuk cautioned, but was too busy to look up.

Sochiko was also absorbed in her work even though she had wanted to relish the experience. Since she had gone through the training so many times before, her arms moved automatically over the control panel and she had little time to reflect on what was happening around her. The traditional countdown that had actually been going on behind the scenes for several hours abruptly went vocal, using Neo-Japonican. "*Ju-hachi, Ju-nana, Ju-roku,*" Sochiko began to steel herself for those few moments of pure terror. "*Ju-ichi, Ju, Kyu, Hachi, Nana, Roku,*" As pilot, she continued through the procedure and flipped switches in their proper sequence. "*Yon, San,*" Indicators showed igniters had activated. "*Ichi, Rei, Uchiage!*"

The realization of what she was about to experience hit her like a ton of bricks. She was going into space! Sochiko was surprised at the raw power of the launch, even though she had been through it before. The engines rumbled and she was pressed to her seat with explosive force, the near vertical configuration of the seat balanced just enough to take the loads but allowing her legs to stand as if she were in control. With great effort she turned her head to the side and through the view port watched clouds of exhaust billow across the water as the whole world fell away. Soon the dark blue sky faded into the blackness of space.

"Oh my!" Danid could be heard calling out, "What did I get myself into -- what was I thinking?"

Sochi turned back to see how her companions were reacting to the experience. The heads inside the helmets across from her moved in unison to the vibration of the powerful engines, and shifted this way and that as the craft reacted to slight variations in acceleration. Besides Sochiko, only Tuk was a veteran of multiple missions. He seemed calm as he looked out the view port. To her left Danid nervously gripped the hand rests as she looked out the view port on the opposite side that was embedded in the hatch.

The thrill of acceleration died down as the burn ended. Sochiko felt her body experience weightlessness as it pushed outward against the straps. She continued with her checklist and communicated with the operations crew, noticing both her uncle and Merinat's voices.

They were on the correct inclination, and Sochiko guided the craft into a rendezvous orbit with *Destiny* before jettisoning the main stage -- now their vessel consisted of just a sphere with a small rack of equipment, tanks, reaction wheels, and attitude control thrusters. She fought back a brief feeling of nausea as the crew settled back to experience the novelty of free fall, and temporarily shed some of the more cumbersome parts of their pressure suits.

Through the view ports they could see the white swirls of Mother's eternal storms -- a massive water ball suspended in the void. Bort immediately pulled out a container of water and began to squirt out drops of water from various angles, assisted by Danid, until they had succeeded in creating a miniature of Mother, a small ball of water floating in the center of the cabin, ellipsoidal and spinning just like the real one. Since microgravity is not the same as no gravity, the ball would begin to float off to the side, either through attraction to some object nearby or simply because their attempts at maintaining the ball in one spot tended to over-correct. Sochiko remembered back when she had done the same -- creating a small Mother was traditional, almost a rite of passage by new space crews.

While the two newbies entertained each other, Sochi and Tuk were going through procedures and testing their equipment. Occasionally they would draw Bort away with some question, or interact with some of the virtual crew or operations personnel. Once Tuk motioned out the view port to a bright point of light hovering above the horizon, which Sochiko knew to be light reflecting off the ambitious orbital assembly and construction project of the next generation spacecraft named '*Soarer*'.

"She's going to be a beauty!" Tuk commented, giving a thumbs up sign.

Sochiko smiled back, since she had been listed on the roster as the first pilot of the *Soarer* on the maiden mission many months hence to orbit one of the moons. She didn't know who the rest of the crew would be, but it was obvious Tuk was jealous.

It was the next wake period when they sighted *Destiny*. The crew crowded around the view ports as the shape of the ancient sphere grew more defined. Sochiko, Tuk, and the virtual co-pilot worked busily at the controls, and had to make a few course corrections the closer they got. It was counter intuitive – they couldn't just point the spacecraft toward the target and go. The gravity gradients this close to Mother were too steep. Instead, they had to trust in the nav computer that set up their thrust and moved them into transfer orbits that would gradually deliver them to the same location in space as the ancient space station. The crew cheered when they passed the point that *Bird Eight* had stopped on the previous mission, making them undoubtedly the closest anyone had approached the aged facility in hundreds of galactic years.

"I wouldn't get too excited," Tuk frowned, "That's a dead facility out there."

As she saw the curved, pockmarked surface slowly grow larger in their view port, Sochiko suddenly had a spooky feeling she couldn't shake. Tuk was right. What would they find inside? There had been hundreds of Wardens living onboard the installation back when it was operational. The refugee crew that had crawled out of the wreckage of the *Origin* had longed to be rescued by those in *Destiny*, but the seasons and generations passed and no help came. The records show that communications died suddenly at some point after that, with no clue as to the fate of those on board. Sochiko steeled herself for a visit to a tomb.

Jockeying the attitude controls and main thruster, she brought their craft in underneath *Destiny* in a slightly lower orbit that caught up with it. At about a hundred armlengths from the orbital, she slowed their approach and began sweeping sideways in a systematic survey in search of a docking port. Those who studied the wreck of the *Origin* were not able to find any ports, but *Destiny's* twin had been badly smashed and half buried.

Sochiko was awestruck. Right outside a few centimeters of transparent glass was an artifact of astounding cultural significance. The huge spherical surface seemed close enough to reach out and touch, since there was little to judge scale by. Scored and dented plates swept by as though they were flying above a textured landscape -- it was like floating over the surface of a small planet.

"What is that?" Danid exclaimed.

Abruptly there appeared a ridgeline over the 'horizon' that resolved itself into a raised field of triangular plates -- the oculus of the dome that provided a large window out to space.

The triangular shielding plates were all battened down covering the transparent panels like shutters hiding windows.

"It's going to be dark inside." Sochiko recalled that the oculus on *Origin* had faced upward into the sky after the wreck had settled in its final resting place.

Tuk commented, "I've always thought the docking ports would be on the opposite side of the sphere from the oculus."

A voice came over the com unit from operations -- it was Merinat, "*That's an affirmative,* Bird Nine. *Proceed to the opposite side of the facility.*"

Uncle Ix had theorized that *Destiny* had originally been on an orbit that continually oriented the oculus in the nadir direction, or facing toward Mother. In order to do that the station would have been set on a slow tumble that precisely coincided with the orbital period. Any docking ports would logically be near the centroid of that tumble, in order to simplify maneuvering of incoming craft.

"*We think there may be something protruding from the back side that offsets the center of mass,*" Merinat explained, "*and we haven't been able to get a clear picture of it with any of our telescopes.*"

Soon the oculus passed as Sochiko throttled the craft over the scored hull surface again. It took all her concentration to steer the pod, because the curved path they flew around the hull was not an orbit but a complex set of thrustered vectors that kept them parallel with the spherical surface. Out of the corner of her eye she could see the brilliant white and blue ball of Mother through one of the other view ports as *Destiny's* miniature horizon swept toward them. Eclipsed by the blackness of space, a harshly illuminated shape peeked over the curve.

"Control, *Bird Nine.* We see some sort of structure just like you said." Tuk commented as they watched a tower-like appendage come into view as if *Destiny* had a tail -- the dead station resembled a gigantic flower bulb with a long stem.

The tower appeared to be constructed of tubular struts with photovoltaic panels and arrays of antenna-like apparatus pointing in every which direction. As they rounded the curve of the hull, Sochiko could see a series of sphere clusters gathered at the point where the tower connected to *Destiny's* hull.

Bird Nine slowly approached the massive structure. Sochiko hovered over the base of the stem for a while as Bort and Danid snapped photos of everything and they waited for feedback from ground operations. Though the space pod was in freefall just like *Destiny*, they were actually in an orbit that would eventually converge with the massive installation, so the attitude control thrusters could be heard firing off occasionally as they worked to continually correct and maintain their distance.

"*Uh, Sochi, can you work your way around so we can see the other side?*" Uncle Ix's voice came through.

"Rodger Unc. Easing around to map the entire tower." Sochiko replied.

Each of the sphere structures, she realized, were of a scale large enough to hold one of their submarine pods. Tuk beat her to the cue as the outline of what must have been pressurized garage doors could be clearly seen facing outward toward open space, "Those must be hangars for smaller spacecraft or probes."

"Sochi, try to get closer to that one over there -- it looks like someone left the door open." Danid suggested.

As Sochiko brought them in closer, they saw that the door was opened just enough for them to get a peek inside, but there was disappointment that the garage seemed to be empty. As they mapped the entire tower, it became clear that there was no docking port.

Merinat's voice came on, "*Sochiko, we've analyzed the entire structure and think we have a solution.*" There was a pause as Marinat conversed with some of the virtual members. "*One of the garages may be opened wide enough for you to slip inside. We want you to get closer to the sphere on the third tier oriented toward nadir.*"

"Roger." Sochiko fired the thrusters and slowly moved into place over the opening, keeping *Destiny* between them and Mother.

"*Can you maneuver inside?*" Merinat asked.

The leaves of the massive door stood wide apart but it was not enough, "Negative, we won't be able to slip through." she confirmed.

"*Okay, the only way to make this work is for Bort to cut through. Tuk, you assist.*" Marinat replied.

All four Flesh crewmembers faced each other at once. Nothing was said between them, but Bort and Tuk were obviously nervous about the prospect of floating around out in the open with laser cutters, not to mention their standing orders to not disturb the ancient artifact. No one had ever done anything like it before. Nevertheless, all four got to work at pre-breathing since the entire cabin would need to be un-pressurized to let the two perform their extra-vehicular task. Each of them put on a small mask that allowed them to breathe a special oxygen mix to gradually get any nitrogen out of their systems. Since the bulky suits required a low atmospheric working pressure, the pre-breathing would prevent them from getting the bends. A few hours later they each put on their helmets, checked and rechecked the seals, and began to depressurize the cabin.

Sochiko could feel the difference as the pressure within the suit began to exceed that of the cabin. It became harder and harder to bend the arms and glove fingers because the pressure difference caused her suit to expand like a balloon, and the arms just wanted to shoot out straight from the torso. After recapturing most of the air into tanks, Tuk bled the rest out into space putting the crew into complete vacuum. Bort and Danid, though cautious were visibly excited about using their pressure suits for the first time, whereas Tuk and Sochiko had each done brief space walks before. In spite of her experience, Sochi had to admit that space walking was not something one got used to easily.

Sochiko gave control over to her virtual co-pilot, who was safe and sound in a rocker somewhere in the Warden city in front of virtual controls that appeared identical to those in front of her. She chose to relinquish the pilot seat because she was not sure how the pressure suit would impede her ability to make fine adjustments to their position, which would be critical as both spacecraft hurtled through space at 4,700 armlengths a second at mere handwidths' distance from each other.

"*Opening the hatch.*" Tuk announced through his helmet mic to the operations team as the other three looked on.

"*Tuk, make sure to approach the rent from the smooth side.*" Uncle Ix cautioned.

The locking mechanism released and Tuk pulled the entire hatch aside and tied it to a bulkhead. There were no hinges so they had to take precautions that it would not float away. At that point Tuk could be seen floating as a silhouette in front of the bright surface of the berthing sphere. After a slight hesitation, he fastened the carabiner of his safety cable to a handhold outside the hatch and gently floated out. Once on the outside, he kept one bulky gloved hand on the handhold and reached out with the other, aiming one of the 'sticky pads' toward the ancient hull, and launched himself over by gently kicking against the space pod. Sochiko could feel the attitude thrusters compensate to keep the pod from moving away from Tuk in the opposite direction. All three of the remaining crewmembers strained their heads to watch as he floated across the gap and made contact with the other surface.

It was history! The first time in living history that anyone had visited *Destiny*.

Tuk tested the sticky pad to make sure it would hold under tension, and attached the other end of his safety line to it. Fisby, the virtual co-pilot, kept the line slack to prevent undue tension forces, while Bort clipped on a pack of tools and a second safety line and sent them on their way. Tuk caught the pack and clipped it directly on the sticky pad, and installed the second safety line. While Bort readied the laser cutter and welder in the space pod, Tuk pulled out several more sticky pads and proceeded to work his way up to the hangar opening placing anchors along the way.

After Bort had sent along the laser cutter, he tentatively crept out and made his way slowly to the ancient facility by pulling himself hand over hand. Sochiko could hear the man breathing hard and nervously as the voice activated circuit kept clicking on. He was a lonely figure suspended over an unfathomable gulf in a lethal environment -- only one innocent mistake could be the end. How easy it must have been to allow one's thoughts to freeze one into immobility...

"Settle down Bort. You're doing fine." Sochi tried to calm down her crewmate.

Bort paused for a while, took a deep breath, and continued on without activating his mic. The two girls were now peering out the hatch watching the technician as he finally reached the other hull. Bort clipped the tools to his harness and followed the path that Tuk had taken moments earlier.

When the two men reached the opening, they immediately got to work enlarging it. The plan was to cut away squares on either side until there was plenty of margin for *Bird Nine* to pass through. First, they cut a hole into one of the squares and clipped in a line to keep it from floating away. Any piece of debris that escaped from them could slowly drift away from the main spacecraft and potentially become a ballistic projectile coming at them head-on at over 9,300 armlengths per second. Once they secured the clip, Bort would cut the square out and tack weld it onto the hull nearby. They proceeded around the perimeter, taking well over five hours to clear the opening of the major obstructions. When they were finished, the rim of the hole had a jagged hand-hewn appearance to it.

Sochiko was getting nervous -- she and Danid could stay indefinitely on umbilicals, but the men's suit air supplies were safety margined at six hours. The two suited men began to make their way back along the safety line one at a time, passing tools between them, with the last one disconnecting the carabiner on the safety line. By the time they were safe inside, hatch in place, and fully re-pressurized it was already a bit over six hours -- too close for comfort.

Fisby continued to watch their position as Sochiko and the others removed their gloved armlets and helmets and took care of other bodily functions. There was an odd odor in the air, and Sochiko thought the equipment smelled of gun powder. They set all the portable life support units to recharge, and Bort made sure the various gasses and liquids were refilled or exchanged.

Sochiko took over the piloting and maneuvered the space pod into place above the rough opening. Fisby and several other virtual crewmembers assisted and she slowly eased the vessel between the jagged teeth as if they were slipping into some metallic jaws. As the interior came into view, Sochiko could see what looked like a closed docking hatch and racks of tanks and other equipment against the far wall. She eased forward to hover within a few armlengths of the hatch while the operations folks studied it via onboard cameras. Keeping a hover was tough -- even though they were inside the ancient garage, they were still in an independent spacecraft hurtling through space at tremendous speeds, their center of gravity not quite coincident with the center of gravity of the station. Over an hour passed as the line filled with voices going back and forth about observations and how to proceed.

"*The first thing we need to do is check for a pressurized atmosphere on the other side of the hatch.*" Uncle Ix could be heard listing out priorities.

Cadbic, one of the Warden operations officers, offered, "*It's not entirely clear how to open that latch. The old ships must have had hardware that slipped into that socket and activated the hatch.*"

"*We'll need to get some close-ups of those sockets.*" another Warden commented.

Merinat, who was a ranking officer said, "*Okay, let's anchor down and pick this up the next wake period.*"

They anchored down by attaching three safety lines to the garage walls using their manipulator robot arm. As

Sochiko maneuvered closer to the wall, Bort carefully placed the sticky pad and locked one of the safety carabiners into it. They repeated the process two more times around the perimeter and used a winch to tighten up the last line until all three lines were taut. Sochiko was surprised at how relieved she felt to shut down the motors after the stressful long piloting duty, knowing the anchors would keep them from bumping into the ancient walls while they attended to other responsibilities.

The crew was allowed to get out of the pressure suits for the sleep period. When Sochiko awoke the next wake period she saw that Bort and Tuk were already suited up and getting tools ready. After a short meal she and Danid quickly donned their suits and the four of them checked connections and seals on each other. They depressurized the cabin and Tuk and Bort floated out toward *Destiny's* hatch to inspect it.

"*Okay, I've got the pressure gauge attached and am drilling a hole.*" Bort reported.

"*Tuk, see if you can take some measurements of the hardware.*" Uncle Ix's voice could be heard through the din of voices that came out of operations in the background.

Tuk got out a tape measure and ruled calipers and began calling out numbers. "*This is the inner door width.*" The tape measure approach had low tolerance, so if they intended to build docking ports on future space pods there would need to be plenty of compliance in the mechanism to insure a tight fit.

Bort called out, "*I'm about to break through!*"

Tuk stopped, and the women held their breath. Was there an atmosphere on *Destiny* or not? How many other pressure doors would they have to get through before reaching *Destiny's* core and main centrifuge deck?

Abruptly, Bort's arm gave as the drill bit broke through. "*It's vacuum on the other side.*"

Sochiko was a little disappointed, but the result was expected. After hundreds of seasons, and probably a dead facility, how could they expect an atmosphere?

"Okay Bort, I think you can cut your way through."

Tuk helped Bort as he used the laser to cut a hole large enough to safely traverse in a pressure suit. Sochiko and Danid began to get their gear together, including self-propelled mappers, computer taps, and bundles of tools. When the men had cut through and secured the plate, the four of them gathered around the opening and looked in.

A short tunnel disappeared into darkness. Sochiko thought she could see a floating shape and began to imagine dead crewmembers roaming about the hallways. Someone suddenly switched on their headlamp and illuminated a human figure against a far wall. Sochiko jumped as she stared back at an ancient space suit attached to a rack. There was floating debris, including tattered fabric and small unidentifiable objects.

All the other helmet lamps switched on at once. Tuk took the lead and floated into the corridor grasping handholds, followed by Bort. Sochiko waited until the two men got deeper inside before tentatively grasping hand over hand. The reality of the situation grabbed her immediately -- she was entering an ancient structure that dated back to Those Who Went Before. What were they like? How did they live, and play, and love? Were there people who never touched the ground, but spent generations inside caves of metal?

There were intersecting corridors. Short passages led to empty space berths similar to the one that held their own space pod.

At one of the open hatches, Tuk paused and said, *"Come take a look at this."*

Sochiko was right behind him. As she poked her helmeted head out the opening, she noticed that the hatch had been cut out leaving a raw, melted edge, similar to what Tuk and Bort had done earlier to the other hatch. As her gaze shifted from the cut opening to the berth interior, she noticed a big difference between this one and the others -- halfway down the domed wall a round hole opened up to space, about four armlengths in diameter. One self-propelled mapper that was being controlled by a virtual Warden crewmember drifted out of the hatch where the two waited, floated across the garage, and approached the hole. The mapper was a small mechanical ball with compressed air thrusters and a variety of lidar, spectrometers, instruments, and cameras that streamed back live telemetry and data.

"*The edges are rough and jagged -- sheared inward.*" a voice informed them over the com system.

Sochiko switched on her in-helmet display to view the images being broadcast by the mapper and saw the double skin of the inner and outer plates cleanly sheared through, with torn shards bent inward as if impacted from the outside. She watched the small remote-controlled camera float out of the hole to record the edges from another angle.

The disembodied Warden voice described the images on the screen; "*It appears as though something large attached itself to the outside. See, look how these marks on the pressure hull surround the opening.*"

It looked to Sochiko as though some metal object had sealed itself to the outside of the hull, and explosively blew a hole inward. At some time in the past someone had forcefully entered *Destiny* station from the outside...

The team explored and documented the entire berthing complex, and worked their way toward the main facility. By its shape, *Destiny* resembled a stem growth with a bulb on the end, so they developed a convention of naming the 'stem' or 'stern' and 'bulb' or 'bow', even though the station was not really designed for motion. The crew made multiple trips, keeping within their allotted six-hour suit time, and aligning their sleep periods with operations back on Mother.

They discovered that the entire facility had been exposed to vacuum, and on the second wake period they passed through unsealed pressure hatches into the bulb. It was at this time that they made a gruesome discovery. They had not yet entered the main centrifuge, which had stopped rotating hundreds of seasons earlier, but were still working their way through curved corridors and smaller cabins and offices, letting out a spool of line as they went to enable themselves to find their way back. Every volume they entered showed signs of ransacking, as if someone had looted the place. Danid had moved up one level and had discovered the main rocker ports. Accompanied by a self-propelled mapper, she decided to peek inside one of them. Her scream eclipsed all operations voice traffic.

Sochiko, who was nearby, quickly propelled herself to where Danid had found the rockers, and went inside. A decomposed corpse, fully clothed and connected to its harness hung suspended in the middle of the frame. Floating on a short tether was an engraver tool, and scrawled across the metal wall in Warden language, deeply engraved, was a final message: "I am the last, goodbye, Thelvord".

Sochiko and Danid, and likely several virtual crewmembers, bowed their heads in a few moments of respect.

One galactic hour later Tuk found the rest of *Destiny's* crew. They had been placed in body bags, one at a time, with a metal tag engraved with name and date of passing, and stacked carefully in a cold storage locker. Tuk opened one or two bags to verify, then noticed the sequential dates getting older and older the deeper one got - most had lived out their natural lives leaving only the last few to pass away in a matter of a few wake periods.

The crew held a solemn funeral ceremony for the *Destiny* victims. Operations gave them a whole wake period off as each was left to their own thoughts. Many mysteries had been uncovered, and future missions would have to take the time to search out what had happened. But there was one more task that Sochiko and the others needed to do -- recover *Destiny's* data drives.

Early the next wake period the four set out, having verified previously the way to the spindle control room. As was their practice, they let out a spool of line to help them find their way back. As they entered the control center, they once again found evidence of looting, with entire consoles evidently ripped out of their frames and carried away to who knows where.

Unfortunately, though the main processors seemed to be intact, every one of the data modules were missing, having been pulled right out of their sockets.

The crew was dejected. They had assumed the data modules to be one of the most important artifacts they could recover, but the opportunity had been lost perhaps soon after Thelvord died in his rocker hundreds of seasons earlier, as looters had picked over the spoils of war. Sochiko suspected the same violence that befell *Origin* must have hit *Destiny* as well -- some ancient space battle.

She soon changed her mind.

"*Take a look at this -- the communications receiver is still working!*" Bort expressed his astonishment.

The helmet beams that had been sweeping the room suddenly converged on the location Bort had been indicating.

Tuk floated over to see for himself, and the women followed, "*How can that be?*"

Apparently, some of the photovoltaic cells were still functioning just enough to build up a charge, and the receiving equipment switched on every few wake periods until the power drained to zero again.

"*The communications logs are still here, passed over by the looters.*" Bort added.

All four looked at each other through their helmet visors, a puzzled look on their faces. Sochi reached out to hook up one of the computer taps and began to download the logs. As she poured over the entries, beginning hundreds of seasons before, she could browse the incoming communications from the *Origin*, and then from the Wardens that had taken residence on the surface after the *Origin* crashed. The regular surface communications began to decrease in number and frequency, and finally reduced to simple queries equivalent to "*are you there?*" Then there was a gap of silence...

But as Sochiko was about to shut down the tap it became apparent that the download was still going. She gasped in surprise as a series of communications began to come up that were postmarked from a new destination called 'Bridgestar'. The messages were garbled, but carried intermittently over about five galactic years.

As she listened her fears of an unknown terror gradually returned. She began to suspect that the looting may have occurred much more recently than they had assumed. And when she saw the date of the last log she knew her fears were justified.

"Folks, we have a problem," Sochiko exclaimed, "The last transmission was only two wake periods before we arrived!"

CHAPTER 2

The Warden operations team had a seasoned virtual crewmember that specialized in software. Virginia was of course in her rocker in the Flesh, and commuted to work in the Database like all her co-workers. On the way to her post, she flew through the Crystal City with her assistant and the two of them aimed for one of the bright stars above the horizon. They passed the last tower and began to fly over grasslands and forests. Their path of flight gradually took them higher above the surface of Mother, which receded from them until they could see all the way across the entire landmass to the great wall of trees protecting them from the perpetual coastal storms. Virginia turned and watched her assistant, who was taking it all in like a curious child.

"Josh, we'll take time to study the forest later. We've got to hurry up to the ship now," Virginia began, and then wondered how it would translate in Josh's mind.

Josh was no ordinary assistant -- he was a digital entity with massively parallel dynamic neural connections consisting entirely of software. He was an artificially intelligent assistant that Virginia was raising from scratch, much more advanced than the messengers and errand runners that could be seen flying about on any given day. The Wardens had come up with a technique where they scanned the neural patterns of a donor couple to embed aspects of their personalities and psyche into a digital 'child'. The process was every bit as complex as contributing DNA to a physical child. Virginia was, literally, Josh's mother and his psychologist.

Josh replied, "The Professor is discovering useless roamers."

Virginia snickered. Through experience, Virginia knew his cryptic reply to technically mean he was trying to find clusters of third-order emergent subroutines. Or, in everyday language, 'I am looking for animals generated by the Database'. She knew when they flew over the forest that Josh was not capable of seeing trees and clouds, because he had no experience recognizing such things. Instead, he was seeing the Database as patterns of data structures. Virginia had been using a simple character named The Professor, made up to help Josh begin to create patterns and relationships. The Professor was an absent-minded fellow. He was a brilliant archaeologist, but he sometimes could be seen wearing socks of different colors or with hair standing out as if he had just gotten up. His poor grad students had to follow him around and clean up the messes he got himself into. Usually when Josh referred to The Professor doing something, he was alluding to himself, and the helpful grad students were Virginia and the other people around him. If he had said 'uncovering rocks' he would have been referring to fixed parts of the Database representing nature, and 'uncovering artifacts' were additions made by Wardens overlapping the fixed environment.

"Come along now, you remember what you'll be doing today?" she cajoled.

Josh recited the simple instructions he had been given: "The Professor will un-stack bricks and see how to assemble them again." He was to play with patterns from a source file, to see how many interesting combinations could be found. Virginia couldn't explain that the patterns were garbled transmissions broadcast from the mysterious Bridgestar, intercepted by *Destiny's* communications log. It was just barely within the AI's capacity to sort through simple patterns. In fact, Josh wasn't hearing her spoken sentences at all, nor was he actually comprehending scenarios about nutty Professors, but was only sending and receiving a highly simplified subset of patterns through filters interacting with the Database. He would learn to deal with real language later, after the operation of all his low-level maintenance routines became fully trained and unconscious to him.

"The Professor is close to the diggings." Josh replied. Of course, he was referring to the patterns he had learned to recognize within the Database, and not to any visual cue. The 'diggings' referred to the space pod *Bird Nine*, where they did their local work shifts.

Virginia responded, "Yes, that's right."

The two were high above Mother now, with the curved horizons beginning to fold into a brilliant green and white ball set in a gray background. There were two space operations in progress now -- the *Destiny* expedition and an orbital construction project to assemble a larger spacecraft for a future mission to one of the moons. But *Destiny* was receiving most of the attention of the public. Ahead of them, the ancient space station and her small companion were still illuminated points of light. The construction project shone as a third star behind them beyond the sphere of Mother. Occasionally, a Warden or two could be seen coming back the other way, and there were others in front of them also on their way to either fill their shifts or observe the operations.

The sphere of the ancient orbital facility loomed out of the gray background as they made their final approach. The space pod was also visible some distance away, having exited the space garage. These were recreations modeled in the Database, representing the actual locations of the spacecrafts above Mother. Virginia and Josh went out to the smaller craft to fill their shift.

The space pod was configured differently in the Database than it was in real life. The Technicians and Wardens had an endless argument about how real *Bird Nine* should be depicted in the Database, but since the Wardens needed to find it functional in their own environment, their argument mostly prevailed. The Database configuration included not only the spherical pressure cabin holding the physical crew, but also a large tethered frame that held a dozen or so workstations for the virtual crew to stand on the outside. The movements of the flesh crew were faithfully mapped into the Database. The operations were set up so that nominally the Warden crewmember would stay at their workstation, but could also get out and follow the digital approximations of the suited physical crew as their locations were updated in the Database in real time, like unseen gremlins carrying small remote-control units.

Virginia adapted complex programs that had been handed down for generations for use in the Wardens' extensive maintenance system of remote-control automatons. Each program appeared as an object or machine in the Database that an immersed Warden could pick up, carry, sit upon, or interact with in order to cause it to perform some work connected to the machines in the real world. The act of touching the objects triggered subroutines that drove physical hardware.

Also connected to the Database version of *Bird Nine* were all sorts of ad-hoc additions formed by civilians. As was the Warden custom, very few surfaces remained free of these artistic virtual sculptures, and many Warden visitors had left their own little additions like signatures advertising they had been there.

Bird Nine was on its way out. After having performed a final flyby inspection of the outside of *Destiny*, the crew was just getting ready to set up a re-entry maneuver. Virginia got herself situated and fed several of *Destiny's* communication log entries to Josh before getting up to speed on hanging software issues. A cacophony of voices came on the line as operations personnel interacted with the crew. The voices were not perfectly clear -- Virginia could hear all sorts of distortion as one or another operator spoke -- static, digital audio interference, splatter, or picket fencing. *Ahh, radio traffic -- the sweet sounds of remote communications*, Virginia thought as she listened in on the various loops.

About halfway through the shift the space pod was well away from *Destiny*, still approaching the re-entry burn point.

Danid's voice trembled over the com system, "*How do I forget? I see skeletons every time I close my eyes. Maybe there's some un-embodied entity out there.*"

Sochiko was trying to console her. "*There's really nothing to fear. How many un-embodied entities do you know?*"

"*Well, the virtual crew. What about the Warden virtual crew? They're all around us.*"

Sochiko replied, "*The crew are all sitting in rockers somewhere. They have bodies and a location far away.*"

Danid was persistent. She had lived among the Wardens and sympathized with their virtual reality existence. "*But what about Josh? Josh doesn't exist in the Flesh.*"

"*Nor is he nearby. He exists it is true. And we experience his presence only through the communication links set up to connect between our two worlds. But there is no un-embodied entity -- In our physical universe Josh must exist in a physical matrix somewhere. We only imagine him to be co-located with us, when actually he is safe and sound back on the ground.*" Sochiko explained.

Danid of course knew that the Database duplicated reality within its electronic circuits, but those who spent lots of time in the rockers often had a hard time distinguishing created environment from reality. It was particularly difficult to think of the real world without overlapping the added parts that people had built up over the generations.

As if on cue, Josh came onto the circuit. "The Professor pulled the string loose."

There was silence for several moments. The two Warden women to either side of Virginia rolled their eyes having heard so many of Virginia's 'Professor' psychology lectures before. But both of them apparently thought the idea of hearing a story from Josh interesting enough to lean in a bit.

Virginia got online and coaxed, "What is it Josh? Did you find a solution to the Bridgestar communications?"

"The poor Professor couldn't sleep at night, and had bad dreams."

The Warden women looked at each other in confusion. The digitized figures of Sochiko and the rest of the flesh crew, working down their list of re-entry procedures, could also be seen listening in.

"The Professor tried everything to get rid of the dreams. He heard that if you read your email and send it on to ten people you get blessings in five days, but instead he got blamed for spam."

The whole crew busted up laughing and saturated the open mics in the voice circuits. Josh waited patiently, understanding he had to allow the bandwidth to clear a bit before continuing.

Virginia asked, "What was the bad dream about, Josh? Did he solve it with the string?"

Josh continued, "Then one of the grad students asked him what the bad dream was about. The Professor walked through a misty landscape and saw numerous people on their way to various destinations. Each person had a string attached to their heart that stretched back to where they were born. Some people walked as couples or small groups and their strings intertwined, while others walked alone."

"What was the string for, Josh?" Virginia asked.

"The Professor came to an arch," the assistant explained, "It was a beautiful arch. The Professor walked through the arch and continued on his way. His heart string also passed through the opening and stayed tied to the beautiful place -- he thought back on it again and again and was enriched by the memory."

Josh paused, and then began to tell about a darker, ugly arch, "When the Professor passed through the ugly arch, his heart string was tied to that place, and his memory of it haunted him."

"Is that the bad dream?" Virginia wondered.

But Josh replied in the negative, "It was a good dream. Before the Professor went too far on his way, he backtracked to the terrible arch and walked through it again backwards. His heartstring became un-entangled with the opening -- then he simply walked around it without passing through. In time he forgot about the ugly arch."

Virginia wanted to get right to the bad dream, because she suspected the solution to the Professor's dreams would be the interpretation of the garbled Bridgestar transmission. But she also knew Josh needed to set a context that would be used in her analysis later.

"What else did he see in the misty landscape?" Virginia prodded.

"The Professor saw a person's heart string snap -- the person drifted away and was lost in the mist. The unfortunate person walked alone, so he was remembered only by his association to the places his heartstring remained connected to. But because the string had no anchor at the end, it soon unraveled and he was forgotten.

"The Professor saw another person walking through the landscape entangled to her family. When her string broke it remained tangled with the others, and she was remembered forever." Josh explained.

Interesting, Virginia thought, *a metaphor for establishing memory*. She was secretly pleased at the sophistication of the construct, even though she knew Josh wasn't actually visualizing arches and strings. She looked around and saw some of the civilians from the Crystal City had begun to take interest in Josh's story, and were floating about near the virtual *Bird Nine*.

On the radio, Sochiko's voice asked, "*What's the bad dream, and how do we interpret the transmission?*"

Virginia pleaded patience, "Josh, what happened next?"

The assistant continued, "The bad memory began when The Professor and the grad students attended an archaeology banquet at an ancient temple. He walked along a worn avenue with a drink in his hand, amazed at the carved pillars lining the way. The pillars became a sequence of arches. At the first arch he was offended by nasty writing carved in the doorway, but he walked through anyway. At the second arch there were figures of mean-looking men making scary faces, but the Professor just paused, sipped his drink, and went through anyway. At the third arch the carvings were of terrible monsters, but he just passed through wide-eyed anyway. His string still passed under all the arches. Finally at the back of the temple there was a hole in the floor. He looked down and saw far below tables set up for the banquet. Something bad happened down the hole and the Professor left, walking backwards through all the arches. The creepy arches and what happened down the hole gave him a bad memory."

Virginia got online and asked him what happened down the hole.

Josh was quite reluctant to say, but after some encouragement said, "Someone walked by down there, and the bad thing happened. The Professor fled out the door again, and passed under all the arches backwards."

Virginia coaxed even further, "What happened to the person?"

There was silence on the line.

"What was it, Josh? What bad thing happened down the hole?"

Josh, embarrassed, reluctantly answered in a barely audible voice, "He poured his drink on the person."

The whole crew roared again, and the loudest laughter could be heard from Tuk and Fisby. Josh wouldn't have known much about humor, and certainly couldn't know his remarks were the cause of the uproar.

Virginia noticed that the civilians, both Warden and Technician, were beginning to tune in almost as great a number as there was during the actual exploration of *Destiny* itself. She continued, "Josh, how did the Professor solve his bad dreams?"

Josh explained, "The Professor got his heart string untangled."

Virginia probed, "But Josh, you said the Professor went in through the portals, then went back out the same way. How could his heart string get caught in the structure?"

Josh explained, "The Professor walked to the hole, that had four columns at the corners. He walked around the hole three times and was so curious. Then he leaned over too far and spilled the drink down the hole. He was so embarrassed."

There was more laughing. Virginia could tell the whole world was also laughing too, as numberless crowds of Wardens floated a distance away from the virtual representation of the space pod in the gray void.

Virginia queried, "Tell us how the Professor stopped his bad dreams."

"He solved it by going back to visit the temple with a bigger drink. He didn't have to touch all the sequential arches, but he had to tear apart the four columns framing the hole. When those columns were wrecked and moved to the side, his heart string was released and his memory wasn't tied to the structure anymore." There was a pause, almost as if Josh were waiting for the listeners to understand the implications of what he had said.

Danid's voice came online, "So people wander around from birth with heartstrings getting entangled with everything they walk through? That's how memories are formed?"

Tuk wise-cracked, "Sounds like something that could only come from a Database junkie."

Josh continued, "Then for the first time he saw the person down in the hole was trying to eat too much cake at the banquet. First, he ate his own cake, and then he ate the cake of all the grad students too. So, the Professor was angry, poured all his drink down the hole again and left happy."

It was too much -- Josh was an instant hit. The Technicians would repeat the comical story again and again, and for the rest of the season young Wardens would clog the Crystal City with their own virtual heartstrings. Young Wardens went about pouring virtual liquids on people below, conjuring up vile stuff whenever someone crossed them in any way.

After the laughter died down, Virginia was left to try to decipher the story. While *Bird Nine* did its re-entry and performed a pinpoint landing in the water of the great bay, Virginia buried herself in the problem. At first she couldn't make much sense out of Josh's symbolic message. She was pretty sure the temple in the story was the original communication log data, which meant that most of the file was recoverable and only some key parts (the columns around the hole), needed to be deconstructed. The heart strings must have represented some temporal continuity, perhaps emphasizing the fact that *Destiny's* telecom unit had only received the message days before the *Bird Nine* crew had arrived -- was there a significance there, or was Josh detecting some deeper patterns? Virginia could not tell.

But the core of the message had to do with the person down the hole around which the structure was built, and it was a fearful message with grave implications for the inhabitants of Mother (the grad students), who would have something taken away from them. She tried language recognition routines and sound filters, and even tried a variety of unusual approaches such as visual wave interpreters and color filters but to no avail. Josh had taken the raw data and instead of inferring typical crypto analysis, had fit it all to a mathematical function, and then arranged it to the archeologist psycho-scenario.

The interpretation came gradually, where Virginia had to take parts of the story and crosscheck it with other known scenarios to find the meaning. In a few cases she had to construct new scenarios to first verify independently, then crosscheck with Josh's story. When the answer finally came, the result was astonishing. Someone or something at a place called 'Bridgestar' had sent a message to *Destiny* only days before the crew arrived -- timed to intimidate Sochiko and her colleagues, and by proxy, the inhabitants of Mother.

Over and over again, the transmission repeated, "*No one will survive. Will take all. Will cook your flesh and obtain your ownings.*"

CHAPTER 3

Several months later Sochiko walked out of a presidential hearing in disgust and headed home. She absent-mindedly strolled the narrow passages from node to node while her mind raced. *They've lost their vision*, she thought. The whole leadership had somehow become shortsighted. First news about the Bridgestar threat had sent shockwaves through both the Technician and Warden communities. The unknown terror that She had suspected had suddenly gone mainstream, and everyone was frightened about what might be lurking out in the cold depths of space. If that wasn't bad enough, after the *Destiny* expedition interest in space flight seemed to have waned. The Wardens had mapped the orbital so their citizenry could make pilgrimages to both their sacred shrines, but the virtual ways of the Wardens didn't require any further investment in actual hardware.

Among the Technicians there were those who said that the resources being 'squandered' on space technology would be better spent on Mother. Even her colleagues in the Relief Society didn't seem to understand the long-range benefits. Sochiko tried to argue that with a little investment in space infrastructure they could gain access to the minerals available on the moons. Also, some of her technician colleagues were claiming that their world Mother might have been too small to keep a stable atmosphere, and eventually it would all boil off. But the counter-argument was always for 'patience' -- the time would come someday to do space research, but first they had to solve their own problems at home. It was that shortsighted Tapital, the salvage lord who argued until Sochiko was on the verge of tears.

As Sochiko walked in the door, her mother greeted her, "Hi dear, how did it go?"

"The president was threatening to pull our funding, Tapital yelled at me all day, and I couldn't think of an argument clear enough to convince the staff of the importance for expanding our operations."

Sochiko saw a hint of anger creep into her mother's expression. Blujic had always been a rebel, and had been Sochiko's most ardent ally. In particular, the older woman had become outspoken on exploring the moons, with the eventual goal to set up mining operations. After all, how many resources could they continue to extract from the dissolved liquid deep in the Mineral Strata?

"The moons are solid minerals, no need to process," she would say, but to no avail.

Blujic took a breath out of the respirator to calm herself and replied, "They never move unless threatened. It took major quakes to get them to dive down under the thrash tide and take a look at Mother's Heart -- we could be recycling all those piles of refuse by now."

The story of the thrash tide and the gigantic object that hovered beneath it, commonly known as Mother's Heart, was one of the more mysterious tales Sochiko had ever heard -- a massive wreck of a spacecraft thought to be caught in magnetic fields at Mother's core, orbiting below the surface on a course determined by tidal action from the moons. The sunken derelict was home to thrashing billions of fish, and every season or so its passage would bring abundance to the hunting fleets. Sochiko's mother would often talk endlessly about recycling all the mountains of refuse that had collected over the seasons on its hull.

"Mom, the threats are right in front of their eyes, there's an unknown enemy at Bridgestar, and still they can't see."

Sochiko's father Mox was away on assignment so the two of them had dinner alone and took turns ranting about politics. After they both repeated the same arguments at least four times each, they decided to call it a night.

Sochiko didn't feel like sleeping so she brought out a book she had been reading about Defender politics. The Defenders were a small group of Technician ancestors who could be called the last of Those Who Went Before -- they had preserved the knowledge and genealogy of their fathers and hid records away in the three famous vaults of Grandfather Nux's day. The Defenders were finally all killed off when chaos reigned and thrust the people into hundreds of seasons of darkness. For many generations her people had forgotten even the basic nature of their world, never having seen the sun or experienced a calm day without storms.

Sochiko eventually drifted off to sleep and dreamt about the next, and probably last mission -- to fly around one of the moons. She saw the trusses, tanks, pressure modules and major subassemblies lifted off one at a time and assembled in orbit as the great centrifuge of the *Soarer* came together. She dreamed that there were hundreds of spaceships orbiting among the planetoids, and a boy was out there trying to contact her. They began sending messages to each other across the void. He could talk to her heart like no one else...

A few days later Sochiko found herself on orbit in a twin to *Bird Nine* outfitted to carry eight crewmembers. The compact, spherical cabin of *Bird Ten* was more spacious than she would have imagined, because none of the crew wore the bulky pressure suits. They were approaching the newly constructed spaceship *Soarer* that would take them on a swing-by around Abb, one of the misshapen planetoids that interacted with Mother around their host star.

"Unk, we've acquired *Soarer*." Sochiko informed Ix who was listening from operations.

The fully outfitted *Soarer* consisted of a linear superstructure with two perpendicular side booms. A ring was spinning around the superstructure axis such that the cabins at each of the ends of the booms made up an artificial gravity centrifuge. On the forward end of the superstructure were microgravity cabins and the docking port, and the aft end held the propulsion system.

"*Okay, proceed to overtake.*"

Soarer lay on a Mother polar orbit with its axis of rotation parallel with the line of travel. The most efficient way to approach the massive spaceship was to chase it from behind and insert *Bird Ten* right in front of the docking port that was on the spin axis. Sochiko pulled up to within ten armlengths of the port. Slowly, with both vehicles synchronized, she eased the two closer.

A big challenge for docking two vehicles in the harsh vacuum of space was the extreme temperature differences between the two craft -- surfaces exposed to direct solar radiation tended to be hundreds of degrees hotter than those surfaces in shadow. If the two met together too soon the expanded hardware on the hot side would not fit the shrunken material on the cold side. Only handwidths away, the docking mechanisms made contact via a small thermo conductive extender and Sochiko waited until the two equalized in temperature before making the final handshake.

After equalizing the pressure with the *Soarer*, the crew opened the hatch and moved into the larger vessel. *Bird Ten* would remain docked to the *Soarer* the whole mission, and would provide them a way to return to Mother at the end of the voyage while the *Soarer* stayed in orbit.

The two centrifuge booms were each identical, holding living quarters and labs. The tube that connected each boom held a counterweight lift that was computer-controlled to estimate the mass of the person entering, and counterbalance the same mass in the opposite boom to maintain a perfect balance. So when each crewmember entered a lift at the microgravity core and began descending one of the tubes, an equal counterweight would move down the opposite tube at the same rate. When two lifts were being used at the same time the counterweight system compensated automatically.

At first it was difficult to get used to entering a lift in microgravity that gradually gained the illusion of weight as it moved outward toward the booms, but the eight crewmembers soon got accustomed to it. They divided into two groups and moved four into each boom, which they affectionately named 'arm' and 'leg'. Both 'arm' and 'leg' were encapsulated in a thick, double-walled tank filled with water -- the two meters thickness of water shielded the cabins from galactic cosmic radiation on long-duration missions. Most of the water in the tank was frozen, but a complex circulation system kept a ring of liquid around each cabin for the crew to swim in.

The next day Sochiko initiated a burn that would put them on a trajectory toward Abb, which was nearing its closest approach to Mother. It was the first time any vessel had left Mother's orbit, and their window allowed them to take five galactic weeks to reach the planetoid and return again. Once Sochiko got the ship on course, all she had to do was perform minor course adjustments until they reached Abb. The crew settled into their various routines and research projects.

Two days later Sochiko was having a meal in one of the galleys with Worlith, one of the Technician crewmembers. To Sochiko, 'Worlith' was one of the funniest sounding names she had ever heard, following the Technician tradition of choosing hard-to-pronounce syllables. In Neo-Japonican, there was no provision for pronouncing 'r', 'l', or 'th' consonants, so Worlith always had to correct others.

"The sun doesn't appear to be a perfect sphere. There's a bump on one side that we don't understand." explained Worlith who was an astronomer monitoring the numerous telescopes on the *Soarer*.

"How did you find out about it?" Sochiko asked.

The other woman squinted her eyes and screwed up her face in what looked to Sochi like a tight, shriveled ball, which was a peculiar expression the woman often made when she was puzzled by something. "We blotted out the circle of the sun to study its corona by using a disk -- we created an artificial eclipse."

"What does that look like?"

"It has the appearance of a brightly illuminated finger ring. But to one side, there is a very small, dark bump, like a stone set in the ring."

It was a small oddity, but to a layperson like Sochiko many of the phenomena observed in the heavens were just as strange. After that the conversation shifted and she forgot about it until five days later when she was once again eating in the galley, this time with Bort who had also followed her on this last mission. Abruptly, Worlith rushed in quite excitedly and interrupted the meal.

"It's a planet! I can't believe we didn't see that."

Bort and Sochiko looked at each other in a puzzled glance, and then waited for Worlith to sit down next to them.

"The bump on the sun is Mother's twin! There is another planet hiding behind the sun," she explained, breathlessly.

Sochiko suddenly remembered the conversation they had had a few days earlier. "I don't get it -- how can a planet be protruding from the sun?"

The shriveled face balled up again, and Worlith continued, "Since we are moving out of Mother's orbit plane, we're able to get a different perspective. The bump on the face of the sun has resolved itself into a tiny disk. It appears to be another planet on the same orbit as Mother, almost directly opposite the sun!"

Worlith explained that the planet should be visible using telescopes from Mother -- now that they knew it was there, they should be able to detect the planet a little lagging the sun when Mother was in perihelion, and a little ahead of the sun when Mother was in aphelion. Sochiko and Worlith sent a message back to operations to get the astronomers looking for the new planetary disk.

As the days went by Sochiko developed a daily habit of donning mask and tanks and doing laps in the ring pool. She would swim around the circumference of 'arm' whenever she had something to worry over, such as the possibility of a new mysterious planet that may harbor aggressive space invaders. The whole crew excitedly followed the progress of Worlith's observations. Faddard, another Technician crewmember who was working the array of telescopes, pointed several of the cameras toward the new planet, and Sochiko pointed one of the three communications antennas toward the distant disk. She, like the others, was beginning to suspect this new planet might be the mysterious Bridgestar.

The *Soarer* caught up with Abb, and entered orbit around the long, misshapen planetoid. Since the moon was fairly small, they were easily able to maintain a low orbit allowing their instruments to obtain close-up views of the surface. However, because of the elongated nature of the rock, Sochi had to use propellant just to keep the orbit stable whenever they passed over the poles, because the effective density of the moon changed dramatically along its short and long axes. Near the equator the Technicians had landed a small robotic instrument package only months before that had steadily been collecting data.

"I've got a signal from the probe." Sochiko informed operations.

Faddard pointed all the spectrometers at the surface and they aimed telescopes and cameras at interesting features. All eight crewmembers gathered in the galley on 'leg' to pour over the various data feeds. There were some virtual crewmembers in attendance, but the time delay of the signal was getting longer so very little real time communication with the Wardens was possible.

"Take a look at those structures!" Stox, a geologist, indicated some natural feature on Abb's surface.

Sochiko studied the up-thrust crust and thought there was a pattern that seemed too regular. The surface appeared as though it had parallel lines etched on its face, yet it had a natural, rough, fractal feel to it.

"I think those grooves seem to cover the entire surface." Stox noted.

One of the physicists, a fellow by the name of Buutz, poured over data being downloaded from one of the instruments on the lander probe. "There appears to be a strong magnetic field. The moon may be a natural magnet."

Stox said, "Can you tell where the magnetic poles are? I wonder if they coincide with those swirls just offset from the ends." He indicated a place where the parallel surface grooves came together in a whirl.

"Yes, I think you're right. The surface must have been molten at some time and cooled with the fields fixed, orienting the molecules of the crust."

Two nights later they were on their way home again. Sochiko had finished her swim and was sitting at the dimly lit communications panel all by herself, having just sent a report back to operations. The cabin was filled with shadows. As she got up to head for her bunk after a long day, the familiar tone sounded signaling an incoming carrier wave. Tiredly, Sochiko sat back down again, put on the earphones, and listened to the transmission.

At first, she didn't understand what the message was saying. There was an excited rush of garbled verbiage in a deep, aggressive voice, interspersed with static. She thought she recognized her uncle trying to warn her about something, but the voice seemed too young. There was a familiar accent that couldn't have been Ix. And the words, though phonetically similar matched little of what she could understand.

The message ended and repeated twice. Sochiko listened to the recording over and over again, to see if she could pick something out of the garbled jumble of syllables. What was it that seemed so familiar yet alien?

The answer occurred to her gradually. In those late hours under weak reading lights, she suddenly remembered Josh, the Warden artificial intelligence and that silly story about The Professor. Sochiko looked up and began to imagine ghosts hiding in the shadows -- she was listening to the same voice she had heard on the previous mission to explore *Destiny*. The ominous warning that had been received on *Destiny's* com unit only days before they had arrived.

The transmission had come from space!

Nervously, Sochi checked the postmark, dreading what she would see -- and involuntarily gasped as she saw Bridgestar. She hesitantly tied into the computer and ran the message through the translator. Thankfully, Josh's entertaining story had given them the key to deciphering the language, which turned out to have some similar vocabulary to the Technician's language, but differed in particles, conjugation, and accent.

The translation came back immediately, "*You will be destroyed. Are on the way now. Are almost at your hatch. Will kill all and own your ownings.*"

The warning hit Sochiko like a solid wall -- they were in danger now? Was there a mysterious invading force making its way toward them from Bridgestar that very moment?

Panicked, Sochiko typed out a reply on the same frequency, taking time to translate her words into the language of the invader. "What do you want? Why do you intend to kill?"

Her hand hovered over the 'send' key and she hesitated -- should she transmit or not? Was there really some aggressive terror out there waiting for them? Could the enemy trace the signal back to their current location?

Suddenly she got an inspiration -- she could route the message through the robotic probe sitting on the surface of the moon Abb. Quickly she narrowed the beam and aimed the transmission toward Abb, and configured the carrier to retransmit in the alien frequency, then hit the send key.

After sending off the message, she knew the time delay would result in a lag between her broadcast and any reply, so she quickly went to wake Worlith. The older woman got up promptly and listened to Sochiko's description of the events.

"Sochi, I don't know if that was a good idea. What if the transmission was simply broadcast widely, and whoever they are don't even know we're here?" Worlith reproached.

"I think they've been monitoring our radio traffic all along." defended Sochiko, "Do you recall how The Professor accidentally spilled his drink down the hole and got the person wet? Virginia confided with me afterwards how that represented our accidentally giving ourselves away."

"But doesn't The Professor represent Josh? If we gave ourselves away, it would have been the grad students who spilled the drink."

Sochi frowned, "I considered that too, but apparently there are some nuances in the story that point to our virtual communications as being the culprit, and in this case The Professor represents that as well."

Worlith screwed her face into a ball in that peculiar gesture, "At any rate, they know we're here -- what can we do about it?"

"Worlith, have you been monitoring telescope images of the new planet?"

"Yes, they've been getting clearer the farther away from the sun we go."

Sochiko urged the woman to bring up her most recent data. Worlith followed her to one of the data stations and brought up a series of images. In the photographs the planet appeared as a faint disk brightly eclipsed by the nearby sun. Sochiko flipped through the images slowly, carefully examining them one by one, back and forth in sequence.

She settled on one and pointed, "There! What are those?" She was indicating two faint spots away from the disk that could have been artifacts of the camera, or a pair of stars.

Worlith flipped back and forth herself, and discovered the spots in other frames -- they migrated in relation to the planetary disk.

Surprised, Worlith excitedly exclaimed, "Those are satellites of the planet, and big ones at that!"

"Could they be invading spacecraft? Coming from Bridgestar?" Sochiko worriedly asked her companion.

Worlith looked up at Sochiko in deep thought but didn't say anything.

For some reason Sochiko didn't really believe there would be a reply -- after all who would have thought there could be communication with someone from outer space? Just the thought seemed ridiculous. And as the minutes and hours passed, she felt justified at being skeptical.

However, a reply did come, only much later than she would have thought. The two women had dozed off in their chairs and when the incoming tone sounded it was already early morning. Sochiko snapped to attention and stared at the com unit in disbelief. She checked the postmark and confirmed it was from Bridgestar, then recorded the message and ran it through the translator.

"*This one not invader. This one warns of invasion. Spread like cancer, infect every ship relentless tide.*"

Sochiko and Worlith looked at each other for an instant as fear gripped their insides, then Sochi realized the impact of what had just happened -- they had made contact with intelligence beyond Mother!

"It's a warning! Someone is trying to warn us!" Worlith exclaimed.

For some reason, Sochi remembered the dream she had had about the boy out among the sea of ships. She thought about the warning and began to wonder -- had the previous transmissions also been in warning rather than in hostility? The two women broke into grins and smiles and stood up and hugged each other.

Just then Bort wandered in to get breakfast and see what the commotion was about. "What are we celebrating?" he asked.

Sochiko excitedly explained about the two-way communication with the unknown intelligence that may have been friendly caution. "But the news may not be good. There appear to be artificial satellites around the planet, and they may be heading our way. The message tells of imminent danger."

As she presented her theory, the rest of the crew began to wander in and were astonished. The evidence was sobering -- the crew pondered the idea of ruthless invading armies on their doorstep.

Without warning the alarm sounded as another incoming message interrupted their thoughts. In unison all turned their heads toward the receiver, wondering if the alien voice would come with even worse news. Sochiko sighed with relief as Cadbic came on.

But her relief would not last long.

"*Sochiko, I've got a message from Tapital. Stand by.*"

Tapital was the aggressive lord that had argued with her before the mission, and almost drove her to tears. She waited patiently as Lord Tapital got online and began to speak.

"*Sochiko, I know we have had our differences. I have argued against expanding space operations, in spite of your admirable advocacy.*" Tapital paused like a politician, waiting for the complement to sink in.

He continued, "*But something has changed all that. I've come to ask you to consider how we can develop our mining and capacity for acquisition of raw space materials and manufacturing to build a fleet of space pods.*"

Sochiko sat dumbfounded. "What happened?" she implored, "What has happened to change your mind?"

Tapital waited an unnatural period of time due to the time lag for Sochi's words to reach him. He began slowly, using grave tones, "*Two wake periods ago we lost contact with a joint deep ocean Technician-Warden field station. We tried to contact them using various repeater networks but to no avail. Finally, just this morning we sent a pod to discover what had happened. The crew found this ...*"

Suddenly Tapital's face was replaced by a video. The video showed a pod suspended in the Plasma ocean with divers swimming about. Above, a natural ceiling of roots and hanging growths could be seen, showing that the location was in one of the caverns below the Warden land mass. The view shifted to the left and a large spherical hull could be seen, tied off to nearby growths via anchor lines. Sochiko recognized one of the fixed field laboratories that had been established in various remote locations, but something seemed wrong -- the lab seemed to be hanging by the lines rather than tugging them upward through buoyancy.

The view shifted again as the diver slowly approached the lab. Nearing the center of the scene, a near-perfect circular hole with rough edges could be seen, as if a giant ball had punched cleanly through the hull. Another diver swam into view holding a tape measure, and measured the diameter at several armlengths.

After pausing to record the measurement, the diver holding the video recording device drifted through the hole, which apparently should have opened into an internal air-filled space. A gruesome scene assaulted their eyes, with bloody corpses drifting about in a wrecked room.

"*We were able to hold off the corpuscles and recover all the bodies.*" Tapital's voice could be heard over the top of the video. "*Every soul had been brutally murdered, and the place ransacked. Sochiko, do you recognize the culprit?*"

Sochi understood immediately. The circular hole matched the entry penetration left by the marauders in the hull of *Destiny*. The mysterious invading force had attacked the station. Somehow, a far-away menace had come too close to home.

CHAPTER 4

In a distant star system, a man prepared to leap out of a large disabled space freighter into the void. Grasping one handhold after another, he used powerful arms to pull himself along the corridor leading outward to the airlock. All of the hatches were open. By the time he got to the outer hatch he had built up quite a bit of momentum and shot out of the open doorway. He had no environmental suit on, and was unconcerned about temperature extremes or air supply -- he simply took a breath whenever he felt like it.

In this region rows of wrecked ships had been tethered to each other to keep them from drifting away. As Kret floated across the gap toward another ship, he scanned sideways in all directions to make sure he was not being followed. To his right he could see a smaller powered craft moving in the distance, perhaps three or four kilometers away, but it wasn't likely that the occupants would have taken notice of him. He could also see other farmers and scavengers, like himself, that were leaping from ship to ship in search of something to sell for their next meal.

He landed on the second ship flat against the hull, and quickly wrapped his fingers around handholds to keep from bouncing off. Hand over hand he pulled himself around the curve of the vessel until he could see the partially disassembled remains of a third ship beyond. For a few moments he paused in order to scan for enemies. Pressing his back against the hull and spreading his arms in an iron cross, Kret faced his body outward toward the vast interior of *Blister*.

Hundreds of kilometers across, *Blister* was a gigantic bubble of air orbiting the local star on the edge of the habitable zone. In front of him there was nothing but atmosphere for several dozen kilometers. Hundreds of small ships, wrecks, and unidentified objects floated, scattered about in freefall. Occasionally pieces bumped into each other in their unique orbits, only to slowly be nudged off on different trajectories. Beyond that, the great partially transparent barrier that separated his world from the cold, hard vacuum of space stretched out in all directions, deflecting collisions of junk against it. As he swept his head from side to side, he could barely see the curve of the barrier as it wrapped around behind him through the haze to form the vast pressurized freefall environment. He saw vessels in flight, but again none of them were close enough to take notice of him.

Kret launched himself toward the third vessel. As he neared the other ship, he scanned the sides for movement. This one was halfway dismantled, so outer plates and hull had been stripped away leaving beams and girders exposed like the bones of a huge creature. He knew the ship, and knew that a particularly grouchy old man claimed it as his own and disliked visitors. Sure enough, Kret caught movement toward the stern, and sensed the wretched fellow flicker from one hiding spot to another on an intercept course within the bowels of the rusting hulk. Fortunately, Kret calculated that he would reach one of the beams before the welcome party arrived.

Kret extended one arm and set himself to grasp the beam, avoiding sharp edges and torn metal. At the same instant he located a large hanging electronics box nearby, and snipped it off by its hanging wire the moment he made contact. He quickly tucked the box between his legs as he spun around looking for a way out. In these situations, it was more efficient to use powerful upper limbs for propulsion and dexterous legs to cradle the goods.

Kret rounded a girder and lost track of the old man. He stopped floating and backed himself tightly against a partially dismantled bulkhead, eyes intently scanning the ruins around him for movement. He sensed that the old one might be getting into position for a leap to cut him off at some point, so he ducked backward and worked in the opposite direction from what intuition would have dictated.

Kret spied another ship beyond and quickly assessed a good launching point. He made the final push, intending to deflect himself onward to the new destination but suddenly the old man attacked out of nowhere.

"This is my cache! Stay away!"

The old man impacted Kret just enough to send him in an unintended direction, clearly away from the ship he was aiming for. At the last instant the old man reached out and tried to pull Kret back, but ended up slowing his drift instead, stranding him out in the void with no propulsion system.

As he drifted away, Kret looked back and saw the old man sneering at him, as if he had gotten his revenge. Kret pulled up the electronics box that had been tucked between his legs and held it up, sneering back.

"Give it back! That's mine!" the old man yelled, staring at him with eyes full of hate.

The farther Kret drifted away, the more dangerous it was -- he needed to make a decision fast or be adrift for who knows how long. There were people who had starved to death because they had drifted too long between islands of wreckage. He could take the electronics box and heave it away at just the right angle so that the reaction would send him toward his goal. But the mass of the box was quite small so it might take him days to cross the small gap.

Thinking quickly, Kret called out with the intent of striking a nerve, "Too late smuzzard brain. It's mine now. Why don't you come and get it?"

In a rage, the old man leaped out with precision, aiming at the held-out box. Kret had been calculating, and just before the old one connected, he tucked in and spun around ever so slightly, bringing his legs cocked up behind the box. When the other grabbed on, he immediately relinquished the object and kicked off, using the reaction of the old man's momentum to propel himself faster. The resulting direction of travel was not ideal -- Kret found himself passing over a wider gap than he had originally intended, toward even less welcome hosts -- he was drifting toward the Tensakian base.

"Darn it! Not over there again..." He frowned.

But at least there was a destination. As he reached the hull of a smashed-up derelict and grabbed an outthrust antenna, he looked back and saw the old man drifting slowly toward a cluster of ships in the other direction, probably doomed to spend a night or two out in the open. Kret sneered again and spun around to avoid the old man's curses.

Propelling himself over to an open hatch, Kret stared into the dark hole and hesitated. Should he go inside or not? The wreck he had landed on was part of a massive wall of space junk that had been cabled together in ancient times. Over the centuries, rockets, spaceships, fuel tanks, and platforms had been stacked side by side until the barrier grew, began curving inward, and ultimately wrapped around to meet itself in a gigantic hollowed out junk heap. The resulting shell protected the spacious volume inside from wandering refuse, and had over the centuries been used as a hangar, vehicle assembly plant, smuggler's warehouse, viper's den, and half a dozen other functions as it was bought, sold, torn down, built up, taken over, invaded, and occupied. And, Kret noted with a sigh of frustration, the deeper one got the meaner they came -- its current owners were no friends of his.

Kret frowned as he imagined those highly organized Tensakian units launching off in their attack ships, wave after wave, relentlessly hunting his family and scattering the farmers... What if he could get back at them somehow, and perform some kind of sabotage? *I must be crazy to even think about going in there,* he thought.

Grasping the handholds and protruding frames, Kret could occasionally feel the vibrations of impact as the huge garage complex played a slow pinball match with the countless debris drifting loose inside *Blister.* He looked down the hole and thought, *I don't have to do this; I can just turn around and push off for somewhere else.*

But he had already made up his mind to do mischief. With one decisive yank, he propelled himself into the dark opening. The key, he considered, was how to get oneself through the wreckage without being detected. This was no hermit's barge -- the Tensakians would not be so kind. Kret's history with that ruthless army went way back, his first encounter being when he had been a young boy. If they found him, they would kill him without hesitation. With caution, he found a service conduit and got inside, using a variety of cryogenic sprays, digital noise, and full-spectral jammers to erase his signature from any electronic snoops.

Kret took stock of what he had on hand. Sulfur pots, cesium, suction grippers, and a spring-loaded winch he had found earlier that he had intended to sell to finance his next few days of foraging. The winch was one of those kinds that would wind up the spring as you played out the cable, and when the cam was released, the spring would reel the cable back in extremely fast. But he needed something else -- something to launch the sulfur pots and some method for getting out of a tight spot.

With years of experience under his belt, Kret got to work. He made his way slowly along the interstitial space between the old crew cabins and outer skin, poking at bundled pipes, conduits, junction boxes, equipment bays, and engine compartments for something he could use. Once he had scoured the first wreck, he found a discreet route over to the next one, and so on. Several times the gaps between ships were too exposed, so he pulled out a cutting torch and created his own passageway through the crumpled bulkheads and girders. More than once he had to pause and cover himself as patrols passed by within armlengths.

On about the fourth wreck, Kret recognized the layout as being a vessel type he knew, which gave him an idea -- that particular model had small kinetic mass driver tubes for sending off nanosat probes. He wriggled through the service space toward what he remembered being the bow of the ship and sure enough, found several tubes lined up in a row, having been stripped long ago of any remaining precious electronic satellite cargo. In no time he succeeded in loosening the bolts of one of the tubes and quickly figured out how to cock the mechanism and insert a sulfur pot. The launcher was small enough to be carried on his back -- perhaps he could also find heavy ballast among the junk piles that could be thrown away in the appropriate direction to steer himself through freefall on a getaway...

But as Kret foraged among the wrecks, he knew that propelling himself with a mass launcher would not be enough -- the Tensakians were sure to have jet packs and would easily be able to catch him. With these thoughts in his head, it was on the seventh derelict that he made the luckiest find of the day -- behind an airlock bulkhead was a huge air tank, still fully pressurized. With a supply of supercharged compressed air he could do anything...

Kret found the remains of several backpack life support units near the airlock and stripped out four air tanks. Using the compressed air he filled each tank to capacity, and rigged them all onto a frame. Then he loaded four sulfur pots into the launcher and picked up a large bag full of spare nuts and bolts he had collected along the way. With all the equipment together, he looked on with satisfaction. *It's show time*, he thought.

After finishing a quick meal, Kret put on a crash helmet, strapped the ungainly air tank frame onto his stomach, and mounted the high-torque spring-loaded winch onto the front of the unit. Then he prepared several water-soluble containers of pure cesium and collected up the rest of the equipment.

He exited the compartment fully with security in mind, backing out in a long process designed to both detect and discourage any possible stakeouts. The bulky bundle roughly equaled a full load of scavenged goods, so the added eccentric mass and off-balance momentum were well within what he had trained himself for. As is always the case in a microgravity environment, momentum could be your worse enemy, but controlled properly could also be your greatest advantage.

Outside, the filtered skin of *Blister* began to choke off the light of the local star. The night cycle had arrived, and artificial illumination began to burn on faraway floating islands. Kret made his way through the wall of wrecked starship interiors along makeshift passageways. He used no headlamp, but reached for handholds in the absolute blackness in a carefully choreographed trajectory that amounted to not much more than redirecting the forward momentum of both himself and his massive load.

Along the way he took time to peek out of open hatchways toward the interior of the protected space. A pair of spotlights had been mounted on either end of the vast space, and the Tensakian army was sweeping their beams back and forth. The largest Tensakian vessels were suspended in the middle of the huge garage via cables, but the smaller air cruisers were left to drift and employed automatics to make small attitude adjustments via air thrusters. Kret knew the Tensakians had only three cruisers, and two of them were right in front of him.

He pulled out the suction grippers and strapped them on his hands and knees. The grippers were simple suction cups that had levers for breaking the seal on the fly, so he could effectively crawl along smooth surfaces like an insect. Checking to see no one would notice, Kret took a leap toward one of the big space-faring vessels, and barely avoided a spotlight as he collided with a bulbous structure protruding from the side of the vessel. The suction grippers held. As he clung to the structure in the dark Kret began to understand the nature of what it was he was clinging to -- he looked up and saw rows of identical pods attached to the mother ship and felt nausea as he realized he was holding on to one of the marauder capsules used by the bastards to raid outlying farmer communities and forcefully rendezvous with ships. There were a half dozen of the capsules docked nose inward, all lined up along the larger vessel's hull.

He grimaced as he removed his equipment and lashed it to the inside of one of the capsule thruster tubes. *I wonder if there's a way to disable these beasts*, he thought, but quickly hid behind the tube as the spotlight swept past. They had murdered his family! Hate seized his breast as he seethed with anger toward those inhuman monsters.

Kret took the cesium and bag of nuts and bolts and hung them from his belt. He left his equipment cached in its hiding place and made another leap straight for one of the cruisers, keeping himself just below the curve of the hull. He touched down as lightly as he could and scrambled along the smooth surface toward the antenna stack.

When he reached the radar mounts, he brought out a tool and lifted the small dome covers on each, inserting some of the nuts and bolts so they would float around freely inside. Having deposited half the pieces, he replaced the covers and carefully leapt over to the next cruiser, and repeated the process until the nuts and bolts were all gone. He kicked back and giggled as he imagined the racket those loose connectors would make in zero-g when the Tensakians started the radar spinning. He ducked as a spotlight illuminated the cruiser for an instant.

Next, Kret worked his way toward a maintenance hatch near the stern of the cruiser. He used his tools to loosen the bolts and slipped inside the cramped maintenance space. The cruisers were equipped with microgravity restrooms. Zero-g water tanks had a baffle system that maintained water pressure even when there was no gravity to drain them, but Kret knew how to open them up without making a mess. He was careful to keep the noise down because he could hear Tensakian bastards in heated conversation out in the corridor. He slipped the cesium into the tank and figured he had about a half hour before the water-soluble containers dissolved. Pure cesium reacts explosively with water...

Careful to cover any evidence he had been there, he went back to the access hatch, made his exit, and crossed the gap to where he had stowed his equipment.

The next part was going to be tricky -- he had to make a diversion. After securing the equipment to his stomach, Kret scrambled along the hull of the big starship past the row of marauder modules until he found the main crew hatch. Then he brought out the launcher. Pop, pop, pop, pop, four sulfur pots were sent on their way into various open ports in the distant wall of wrecks, right under the noses of the spotlights. He observed the impact sites to make sure each had ignited and were generating their acrid fumes.

Before the smoke became too obvious, Kret hooked a carabiner onto one of the handholds under the hatch, and reeled out the thin cable of the spring-loaded winch. He crawled all the way around the circumference of the large starship, depositing cable like a spider spinning a web, until he almost made it back to the hatch again. Each length of cable that came off the winch wound the heavy-duty spring mechanism tighter. Just out of sight from the hatch, he clung low to the hull and waited.

Soon there was excitement along the wreckage wall. The Tensakian officers were whooping and hollering and switching on more spotlights as the sulfur smoke began to thicken. Somewhere a klaxon sounded, and more voices shouted. As expected, the starship hatch flung open and several of the distasteful figures emerged and made their way toward the direction of the cruisers.

When Kret heard the hum of the cruiser motors start up, he slowly crept toward the open hatch. Peeking inside and finding the passage clear, he slipped in, still winding out the thin, almost invisible cable. He snickered as he heard from outside the sound of dozens of nuts and bolts rattling about under radar domes.

Kret worked his way down the corridor, counting cabin doors as he went. At the third door he paused, suspended in the middle of the air, trailing the thin cable. Easing the panel open, he verified that no one was there, and that the ship's com unit was ready and waiting.

He thumbed the unit, patched into the deep space antenna, and began his message, "You must arm yourselves to defend against the pirate invaders. They'll kill you all! We are peaceful farmers."

He knew the message would make its way to Bridgestar, pass through the gates on the interstellar repeaters to over a dozen star systems, and make its way up-system to anyone who happened to be tuned in.

Kret heard a muffled explosion. He figured there was enough cesium to blow out the entire side bulkhead of the air cruiser. Too bad he couldn't be there to see the fireworks...

He quickly switched frequencies and began broadcasting on the local network, "Hi all, guess where I am?" Behind him, he could hear his own voice being amplified outside on the loudspeaker across the vast hangar. Surely the Tensakians would have figured his prank was a diversion by now. "I'm right in the middle of the Tensakian nest. Stupid Tensakians! Goodbye."

Kret backed out the door, anchored himself on a handrail in the corridor, and slipped the winch cam. As soon as he saw a figure silhouetted against the open hatchway coming after him, he cut the anchor. The high-performance spring proceeded to wind up the cable and catapult him along the corridor. He tucked up in a ball just as the cable slammed him against the frame of the hatch and propelled him out the opening. Somewhere along the line he collided with at least two Tensakians and probably knocked them silly.

The cable whip lashed him around the girth of the starship. He could hear shouting as the Tensakians pursued him in vain.

Kret knew one of them -- they had had altercations from way back. He snarled as he heard that dreaded voice call out,

"Kret! Come back here! I should have killed you when I had you in my sights!"

Kret yelled back, "No way Rusty. I should have got you back when I had the chance!"

When the cable brought him halfway around, he figured the others would probably discover the carabiner end anchored right in front of their noses. Sure enough, someone cut the line and he rocketed tangentially away from the hull out into the void. He tucked into a ball as the cable snapped back and nearly sliced through his crash helmet. The winch reeled it in and continued its rapid rotation until the spring lost all its potential.

Kret shot out into the void toward the wall of wrecks. There was smoke everywhere and a smell of rotten eggs. He could see the disabled cruiser drifting off to one side.

Suddenly the second air cruiser was upon him in hot pursuit. He waited until the vehicle was almost within capture distance, and fired off the valve of one of the tanks. The compressed air shot out and wrenched him to one side, changing his course so suddenly that the cruiser couldn't follow. By the time the cruiser swung around and made-up lost ground, Kret fired off a second tank.

To a certain extent he was able to steer the compressed outflow by rotating the tank with his hands, but only to make minor course corrections. He used the jet from the second tank to aim for the back of the vast hangar. When the Tensakians thought they were close to cornering him, he fired off the third tank directly toward one of the dismantled wrecks. The force of the blast sent him between the skeletal beams and blew him right through three partition walls.

Kret knew where he was. He shook off the pile of debris, pulled himself down a short corridor and stepped out into the dark open sky of *Blister*. The fourth tank rocketed him off into the distance. By the time the Tensakian cruiser got itself turned around, crossed the protected void, exited the garage, and worked its way around Kret was long gone.

CHAPTER 5

A galactic year later the *Soarer* was heading out on another flight. This time it was going to be a long one.

"*We've got friends out there.*" Sochiko had proclaimed in defiance of the scaremongers who dwelt on the threat of invasion.

Typical Sochiko, Virginia thought, always sticking up for her friends. Even those she hadn't met. But no one was disillusioned to think that the Technicians and Wardens had better firepower than some unknown advanced space faring civilization.

This time the eight-person crew was on their way to visit the unknown planet directly opposite the sun from Sado-Mother, whom some claimed to be the mysterious Bridgestar. Their course would backtrack Mother's orbit, which was shared by the other planet, and cut across the ellipse to meet it as it came around the back of the sun.

"*With our guns blazing if need be...*" Sochiko had said as they left orbit.

A few weeks later Virginia was tiredly listening to a debate about why their lander probes had failed on the last two robotic missions to Abb, one of the moons. Bort, who was serving as one of the physical crewmembers on his third mission, was on the team that designed and operated the landers, so he was required to patch into all the discussions aimed at developing a third probe. The rest of the crew were not directly involved, but often listened in if there were gaps in their responsibilities.

The time delay with the *Soarer* was getting longer, so trying to hold a real-time conversation with the crew was testing Virginia's patience. Bort's long-winded monologs were monopolizing the circuit, and it was impossible to interrupt someone who still had five seconds of hot air yet to arrive.

"*Both missions had identical payloads and failed at the same point in the excavation sequence.*" Bort concluded, finally.

"They never even began the sequence," countered Merinat.

There was a pause as the message went all the way to the *Soarer* and Bort formed a reply. "*We don't know that. All we know is that the landers didn't send back verification!*"

Merinat seemed at a loss, and didn't say anything. No one said anything. The landers were supposed to drop off excavation rovers that would dig a few holes and analyze the diggings for mineral content.

Virginia thought she saw a flaw in Bort's argument and began to speak. At the same time Bort, Merinat, Cadbic, Sochiko, and several other voices spoke up as well, competing to be heard.

Suddenly a familiar voice carried over the com, and everyone else ceased talking immediately, "The Professor got out of the hole." Josh, who had been analyzing the problem said simply.

Again, there was silence. They had been working the issue for days, and she was hopeful the artificial assistant had been able to spot patterns that could help solve the problem.

After a while Virginia got on and tried coaxing him along. "What did the Professor do?"

"He walked out of the hole."

"Josh, can you tell us what happened from the beginning? How did he get in the hole?" Virginia pried.

"The Professor went to a strange moon with his grad students." Josh explained, "They found a deep hole constructed by unknown ancient engineers, the opening was quite wide across. When they stood at the top, the Professor could see scaffolding around the edges going down several levels. They looked down in the hole and couldn't see the bottom."

"How did the Professor get down in the hole?" Virginia repeated.

"The grad students went down a ladder, and when no one was looking, the Professor dropped a rock in it."

"What happened to the rock?"

"It fell but there was no sound of it hitting the bottom. Then the grad students were calling him so he went down the ladder." Josh explained.

When Josh paused, Virginia encouraged him some more, "So the Professor got out of the hole by climbing the ladder?"

Virginia was thinking the 'hole' must symbolize the problem of the failed landers, and the 'ladder' must have been part of the solution. She was amazed that the new story and their own dilemma were set in similar environments, and renewed her hope that his scenarios would begin to converge with reality as he gained more experience.

"No, he went down further. There was a vending machine on the scaffolding, and the Professor wanted to buy some juice. So he got some coins and started putting them in the machine. But he dropped two of the coins and they rolled over the edge before he could catch them. The Professor watched them fall and waited for them to clang when they hit the bottom."

"Did they make a noise?"

"They never made any sound. So, the Professor got his juice and opened it up as he followed the grad students. When the students walked into an ancient room carved in the wall of the hole, the Professor was going to follow them but he

71

dropped his juice. The can fell at the edge and it all poured out. He watched the juice fall into the hole." Josh explained.

"Did the juice make a sound?" Virginia asked.

"No, and when he accidentally kicked the can into the hole it didn't make a sound either. So the Professor went in the room to see the carvings on the wall."

Josh paused for a long time. He seemed embarrassed.

Virginia tried gently to pry out the rest of the story, "What happened next Josh?"

"The Professor started thinking a bad thing."

"What was he thinking about, Josh?"

The artificial intelligence stayed quiet for a long time, while Virginia tried all sorts of ways to phrase the request. Finally, Josh relented, and offered a little more, "He couldn't help but think about it. He was so curious."

Virginia, given an opening, pressed for the rest, "What was he curious about?"

"The Professor couldn't stand it anymore, so while the grad students were discussing the carvings, he snuck out and looked down the hole again. Then he did the bad thing."

Again, Josh was silent, and Virginia gave him some space and didn't press him. Finally, he admitted, "The Professor peed down the hole."

Some of the crew couldn't help but snicker, even though they thought they saw it coming. Virginia sensed the entire operations team beginning to join in and listen.

Josh recovered, and continued the story, "The Professor looked down and saw one of the coins on the lowest deck -- it hadn't fallen after all, but had been stopped by the catwalk platform. So, he climbed down more ladders to retrieve the coin.

"The lowest platform cantilevered out over the hole, and in order to get the coin he had to crawl out on a narrow beam and reach across a wide gap. When he reached the spot, he found he was only a handwidth short of being able to reach across."

Virginia was only dimly aware that a 'crowd' had gathered. There were background voices on the comlink, and Warden citizens could be seen milling around in the Database. The brilliant assistant was proving to be a hit as before.

Josh continued, "The Professor thought that if he could shift his weight out to the ledge where the coin lay, he would be able to reach it. So, he cantilevered himself out as far as he could go, then leaned forward to tip his center of gravity out over the hole, effectively forming a bridge. He was easily able to retrieve the coin. However, no matter how many pushups he did, he was not powerful enough to push his center of gravity back over the gap again.

"The Professor was terrified of what might happen if the grad students caught him bridged over the gap, so he tried to put one leg across. Unfortunately, this made him drop the coin. He lost his balance trying to grab for the metal disc and fell into the hole after it."

By this time Virginia could see her companions caught up in the story, and the crowds had gotten larger. It was apparent no one was thinking about lost landers anymore.

"The Professor kept falling, expecting to hit the bottom any instant. He soon was in total darkness as the circle of light that was the mouth of the hole shrank above him to a point, and finally winked out. He switched on a headlamp and soon saw a cloud of small items coming up at him out of the hole. As they whizzed past him traveling upward, he thought he could identify a variety of small objects ranging from an old shoe, someone's lost sock, a missing set of keys, old jeans that don't fit anymore, stale French fries, and a note with Sally's phone number on it. He even saw a skeleton in a closet."

Sochiko could be heard letting out a muffled giggle.

"He soon heard a rushing sound coming up out of the hole and -- smack! A small object flying up at a high speed glanced off him. Smarting from the pain, he wondered if more objects would fly out of the hole.

"Sure enough, a small silvery object whizzed up out of the hole and passed fingerwidths from his face. So, he expected more bombardments.

"But instead of another object, next came a shower of liquid that shot up at him and soaked his face and clothes. The dripping substance smelled like juice.

"And then another object, an empty juice can, came up and glanced off his side.

"Finally, after falling another half hour with no more objects, another shower of liquid came up out of the hole and soaked him again. This time it was..." Josh broke off, then tried again, "This was..." but couldn't finish.

Virginia stepped in and asked what it was. She had to rephrase the request several times.

Josh reluctantly continued, "It was pee."

Sochiko and the whole crowd burst out laughing.

Josh continued, "The Professor was soaked in pee and was upset. Then he looked below and saw the coin that he dropped falling ahead of him -- and the distance between them was narrowing. He also saw a small point of light below. For some reason he felt his fall began to decelerate. As his rate of fall continued to slow, the point of light below him got bigger and turned into a circle. The circle got bigger and bigger and amazingly, he could see what looked like sky and clouds through it.

"Suddenly the circle resolved into another hole -- he had fallen all the way through the moon and the circle was the hole on the opposite side.

"The coin in front of him slowed to a stop and began to come toward him. He reached out to grab it but missed as it flew past, this time falling down the hole in the opposite direction. The Professor also slowed to a stop and reversed direction.

"He fell for a long time again and once more shot past the cloud of forgotten items.

"Soon he could hear a rushing sound coming up from below, and barely missed the rock as it flew up out of the hole.

Next the silvery object flew up and bruised his arm as it flew past. Then a shower of juice came up at him, followed by an empty can.

"He realized that all those things that had hit him as he was falling were things he had dropped into the hole in the first place, that were now orbiting back and forth straight through the center of the moon. The cloud of forgotten items were things dropped by curious visitors over the centuries, that had lost their momentum and had become suspended in the middle of the moon, which was the low point of the gravity well. And he dreaded what would come next..."

Josh paused for a while and then continued, "He was soaked again by the nasty fluid.

"This time, the circle he could see below him getting larger and larger was the mouth of the hole he had fallen in. He began watching for the coin that was just ahead of him in it's own orbit, and also kept an eye on the scaffolding built around the opening.

"Suddenly he heard his name being called. The grad students had come looking for him. 'What are you doing?' they called out. The Professor saw the coin slow down, stop, and start falling again toward him. He also began slowing to a stop, and answered, 'I dropped my coin,' and reached out and caught it as it began to fall past him. The Professor slowed to a stop out in the middle of the hole, suspended in space, face-to-face with the grad student. 'Got it!' he calmly said, and promptly fell back into the hole again."

The crowd roared with laughter. Virginia couldn't keep from giggling, and the comlink capacity was exceeded. Josh paused as the overload continued on for several minutes.

Finally, when the noise on the link died down, Josh continued, "The Professor knew he might lose momentum eventually, and as he flew past the suspended cloud of lost items, he realized he might become another skeleton in the closet. So twice more he endured pelting rocks, coins, cans, and juice showers, and twice more he had to fall through the urine.

"But on his next approach up to the mouth of the original hole of entry, he quickly undressed and made a rope of sorts with his clothes. He tied his shoelaces onto the pant leg that connected to his coat that tied arm-to-arm with his sweater that tied to his shirt, which end he hung onto. He called up for the grad student to catch the rope, and got ready to toss the shoe to the student. Finally, as he slowed to a stop, he saw the students and tossed the shoe. At the same time, he saw the students toss him a real rope. He caught the rope and had to let go of his clothes, which found their way down to the cloud of forgotten items."

Virginia listened as he explained how the Professor then climbed up the ladders, out of the hole, and went home in his undies.

The Wardens were ecstatic, and once again Josh's fan base was zooming all over the place in glee. Soon thereafter several 'holes' could be found in the Database with young Wardens diving in and out. Even some of the younger Technicians wondered whether it would be possible to dig a hole all the way through one of the moons for recreation.

With that episode over, the crew spent the next few days in a lighthearted mood, optimistic about their mission, even if they encountered the pirates.

It was just two days later when Virginia was able to go online with a solution for Josh's Professor story. She extracted Josh's analysis from parallels between the story and the reality of the situation.

Merinat took a guess, "I suppose our shielding for the motors and electronics was not sufficient -- the orbit through the moon of the Professor must mean reverberation in the com signal, that somehow prevents the signal from escaping the strong magnetic field?"

Virginia countered, "No, that's not the case. The grad students represent *us*. *We* are down in the hole somewhere near the top, studying only the surface layer -- the problem is much deeper than we have realized. The Professor represents Josh, who must fall into the hole to understand its extents.

"Josh experiments with various analyses, by dropping exploratory probing into the problem. The last is an act of desperation that eventually backfires and comes back at him. His probing reveal nothing, until he goes in deep and cycles through several iterations, each time revisiting the previous probing as he passes them going up or down.

"Josh benefited most from the analysis represented by the last coin, which he was able to capture in the end. But the final solution required him to lose the clothing of preconception, and choose between it and the rope of safety and enlightenment. Losing the clothes also allowed him to come clean from his earlier over-enthusiasm."

When Virginia paused, Merinat asked, "Then what is the interpretation?"

Virginia explained that every subtle part of the story carried meaning, such as where and how the rock or coin glanced off him. But the most striking symbolism was attached to the cloud of lost items suspended in the middle of the moon. The problem did not start with the Technicians or Wardens -- it stretched back for ages. Each encounter has left its artifacts, lost and forgotten, including skeletons of victims who never were able to climb out of its pull.

Virginia explained, "The bottom line is that the landers are digging and testing the soil as designed, but their antennas are pointing toward Bridgestar. An unknown party has somehow taken over."

The crew was alarmed once more. Even over the comlink tension could be cut with a knife. Who were these invaders?

Virginia compounded the mystery, "I don't know how to explain this, because Josh doesn't know either. The artifacts are mainly of Technician origin. But so is the hole."

Sochiko, who had been chastised for sending a transmission to aliens without permission, apologetically came online in a timid voice, "*Is it because of me? Did I show them where the landers were when I routed the signal through them?*"

"Perhaps," Virginia stated matter-of-factly, "but the Technicians are intimately involved with the culprits somehow."

CHAPTER 6

One morning Sochiko was sitting in the lounge and her thoughts started to wander. Her mind had just begun to imagine how a pirate could land on Abb and reprogram a lander when she was startled by an incoming communication from Bridgestar. Her heart began to pound and she stole a quick glance at the forward monitor that still showed a small twinkle of light that was to be their destination. *Is that where we're going*, she thought, *is that planet out there the mysterious Bridgestar?* She slipped on the earphones and listened to the message, then ran it through the translator. The translation programs had improved, so the messages were higher and higher fidelity.

"We are looking forward to meeting you someday. What is your home like? The armies may find your world and cause trouble. Have you prepared weapons? What sort of weapons do you have. We are trying to keep them occupied, but there are too many."

Sochiko immediately packaged up the message and its translation and sent it along to Merinat and Cadbic. Having gone through the painful experience of cross-culturally misunderstood motives among themselves only a generation previously, the Technicians and Wardens wanted to avoid trouble with angry cosmic neighbors.

"*We'll take a little time and craft a good reply.*" Cadbic's response came after a little delay.

Sochiko pictured the lonely boy in the sea of ships, "We've got to develop some kind of trust with them."

"*Even if they are friendly, if we describe our weapons couldn't the invaders be listening in as well?*" Cadbic pointed out.

Unfortunately, Cadbic's worries appeared well grounded. Four hours after sending off the first Bridgestar transmission, another message from Bridgestar came through. Sochi put it through the translator.

"*Be careful about describing your weapons. The armies want to know what they are up against. Beware the death pods. They are small spacecraft that ram the victim ship and attach to its side before taking over. Destroy them on sight.*"

Sochiko considered the second message for a while before sending it off to Cadbic -- something seemed odd about it, as though the garbled sentences were more refined or educated, or even computer generated. She couldn't be sure, but the voice might have been from a different individual than any of the previous messages. Was there more than one communicator on that far away world?

The next day Cadbic came back with a benign reply, carefully worded to avoid giving away information, while at the same time having a cordial feel.

"*We're all set to route this through one of the deep space satellites so you don't disclose the* Soarer's *flight path. Send this on a narrow beam.*" Cadbic rattled off some coordinates of the current orbit of the satellite.

Merinat added, "*There may be two separate groups out there, and everyone back home is wondering whether the Technicians are scheming about something.*"

During the previous week the general Warden public seemed to have gotten wary of the Technicians because of Josh's analysis. '*The Technicians are intimately involved with the culprits somehow'*, Sochiko thought. Some of the Wardens wondered if the submarine people were actually doing more than just peacefully coexisting out on the perimeter of their domain. Even some of the Technicians were beginning to wonder if there were secret subversive groups out there rivaling each other like the Rebels and Defenders.

Sochiko was dumbfounded, "Do they think Technicians are fabricating the messages? Who would be capable of what we've seen? Some group who can achieve spaceflight can't be hiding among us!"

The mixed crew who knew the inside functioning of the partnership had no such doubts about each other, and continued to work well together. However, that still left the possibility of a renegade group, and they tried to figure out why Josh would make such an accusation.

"*It sounds ridiculous I know, but the connection is real. About that I have no doubt. You have to remember that Josh is taking patterns from all sorts of places, and not merely isolating the case of the malfunctioning landers.*" Virginia opined.

Ix jumped in, "*Perhaps it's simply a comparison of language. Our friends out there and the Technician languages seem to have come from the same Japonican source. At least they are closer related than that of the Wardens.*"

Merinat's voice came over the link, "*Well, we still need to learn more, especially since there may be more than one group out there, with at least one of them extremely hostile.*"

Sochiko turned to Worlith, who had been assigned with her on the *Soarer* mission to the new planet, "Any news on those orbitals? Does it look like we'll have any unwelcome company?"

The operations crowd stayed silent as Worlith gave her latest report, "They certainly are huge. But neither one has left orbit. And there may be more than two -- I've been able to detect traces of what may be smaller objects."

"Can we tell if they are artificial or not?" Sochiko asked.

"We're still too far away to tell. But though they are large, they're not massive. My intuition says they are hollow."

There was silence on the line as everyone contemplated what would happen if they had a confrontation with an advanced alien hostile race. The unspoken worry on everyone's mind was whether or not the ship was flying right into the middle of the enemy's nest.

Two weeks later the isolated point of light in their monitors had grown into a small disk, and Worlith's telescopes could begin to distinguish the shapes of the orbitals. The larger one had a long profile with a length to width ratio of seven to one, and the smaller one was roughly spherical.

"I'm convinced the smaller one could be a close triplet to *Origin* and *Destiny*," she began one morning over breakfast, "but the larger one could swallow it whole."

"And they still haven't left Bridgestar?" Bort asked.

They had gotten into the habit of calling the planet 'Bridgestar', but Sochiko wasn't sure anymore.

"No, none of the satellites have changed from their original orbits. It also appears there are several smaller ones that only show reflection from the sun at certain angles."

Merinat, in a delayed reaction, joined the conversation, "*We'll need to send two of the probes to investigate the orbitals. Sochi, have we refined the approach trajectory to stay discreet?*"

Sochiko had been working on various scenarios for several weeks, "No, there's no solution that will keep us hidden from both the orbitals. But we can do an ellipse that dips down once every few days -- it may give us an advantage in case we have to run for it." She didn't add what should have been obvious: *If we can see them, surely they can see us*, she thought.

After another delay Merinat replied, "*Okay, let's avoid the larger one as much as we can. If we trust that the smaller one is identical to Destiny we will not have to worry about weapons or propulsion systems.*"

Day by day the *Soarer* approached the planet and more and more features could be distinguished on its surface. Faddard and Stox began to put together a picture of the world as being rocky, barren, and having little or no atmosphere. It was somewhat of a disappointment, but at least the planet didn't fall into the misshapen magnetic planetoid category like all the moons. They estimated the mass to be roughly identical to Mother.

Worlith soon was able to identify the larger orbital as being approximately cylindrical. "And it has blinking lights!" she explained with excitement. "It has an active power system, and appears also to be equipped with a propulsion system."

"And the smaller one?" asked Bort.

"Is as we suspected. An identical orbital facility to *Destiny*." Worlith replied.

The *Soarer* made its final approach and launched the two probes in the process. The entire crew was on the alert, and every new sighting of orbiting space junk got everyone in a panic. On the one hand they were curious about each little artificial satellite, but they also dared not waste fuel, time, or energy investigating when they had to be constantly looking over their shoulders for an aggressor.

"*The small satellites are probably communications and global positioning hardware anyway.*" Uncle Ix suggested.

Sochiko was still wary, because some of the objects were large enough to have an occupiable volume. "And they could be loaded with instrumentation as someone's eyes and ears..." she fretted.

The crew had trained for dozens of scenarios with aggressive spacecraft approaching the *Soarer*, but Sochiko felt unprepared when the first genuine encounter occurred the following day. Suddenly out of nowhere they realized that they were being followed. An unknown vessel was closing in from underneath, and actively maneuvering to match their trajectory. Sochiko and the other crewmembers looked at each other in alarm.

"Can you see it? Description please!" Sochiko called out.

Faddard had quickly trained one of his telescopes on the vessel and began describing what he saw, "It's a short, squat cylinder. I can't tell what sort of propulsion system it uses."

"Is there a round hatch in one end, the forward end?" Sochiko shouted in desperation.

"I don't see any from this angle."

"Bort! This may be it. Arm the missiles and await my command." Sochiko ordered.

Bort was already strapped down in the central non-rotating spindle core between 'arm' and 'leg'. He quickly faced the weapons panel and acquired the target, hand hovering over the trigger.

Just then the alarm went off indicating an incoming call. Sochiko switched the message onto loudspeaker. To everyone's surprise, the voice that came through was in the Warden language.

"*Hello, this is Everwebber Port. Will you be remaining in orbit or landing at the facilities?*" the voice asked.

Sochiko didn't know what to say. Should she tell them their intentions and risk invasion? She must have paused longer than expected, because the voice repeated.

Sochiko stammered, "We... We will be staying in orbit."

The voice replied, "*Thank you. Please follow me and match our orbit. This will be your parking orbit for as long as you stay at Everwebber.*"

The craft came up from under them and began to veer off to a slightly different inclination than she had planned. She called out, "Bort, keep your hand at the weapons station, but don't fire unless I say."

The crew braced themselves for major accelerations as Sochiko steered the *Soarer* onto a course that followed the small vessel. *So this is how they strike*, she thought.

"Steady, Bort."

"I'm locked on and ready." he replied.

Sochiko tentatively worked to stabilize the ship, always keeping her eye on the little vessel. Could it be leading them into a trap? Is it bait drawing their attention until others can swoop in from the side? "Any secondary vessels out there?" she asked.

And there was another worry -- would any of their missiles hit their targets when they needed them? How many duds would they have to shoot off before one connected? Sochiko wasn't very confident in the new weapons.

"All clear." Worlith answered.

When Sochi calculated their new position, she was impressed -- they couldn't have been in a better place. The new orbit was identical to the big ship but just over the horizon from it. They would be able to keep out of sight and still get the signal from their probe. Once the *Soarer* settled into her orbit, the small vessel flew off and was soon out of sight.

Sochiko, recovering from the surprise welcome, got on the com system and tried to raise the voice again, asking all sorts of questions. But there was no response.

Stox expressed what was on everybody's mind, "It must have been a recording. The vessel was a robotic pilot boat."

It was sometime later when the two probes did a rendezvous with their respective targets. Stox got the first images in from the sphere-shaped smaller orbital, confirming that it was identical to *Destiny* -- a facility meant to remain parked in a permanent orbit. The curved hull loomed out of the darkness, with the harsh direct sunlight illuminating only some of the surfaces. As with *Destiny*, the orbital showed evidence of forced entry.

"Take a look at those holes. Looks like they struck in numbers." Stox commented as the crew gathered in the 'arm' to watch the incoming images.

Sochiko could see multiple round-sheared openings in the hull of the orbital where the looters must have forcefully invaded using the death pods.

Besides the holes, large sections of the stem and sphere were missing, and Sochiko imagined someone might have cut the structures off and towed them away as loot or salvage. However, in spite of the signs of violence, the dead orbital hinted that there might not be anyone in the neighborhood who cared whether the station was inoperable -- perhaps no one cared whether they visited or not.

A few hours later, images from the second probe came in. They watched in amazement as the gigantic hull of the other vessel got closer on the view screen. The probe continued to show a steady stream of imagery like no one had ever seen. They seemed to be approaching the vessel from the rear, and observed what apparently was part of a massive propulsion system that used technology no one could identify. And there were lights -- exceptionally bright patterns of lights showed out into the blackness of space. The ship was apparently alive.

"Take a look at that!" in one of the shots Faddard pointed out a small object floating off the rear of the massive ship. It was another short cylinder similar to the pilot boat, but had a slightly different design. As the probe got closer, they saw that the hull was blackened and scorched from excessive heat -- it was a burned-out wreck.

Sochiko had a bad feeling about this. The wreck seemed to be adrift behind the big ship in roughly a similar orbit, like a shadow or ghost. She could imagine the charred remains of the crew still strapped in their seats, forever following the giant vessel.

"Stox, I don't think we should draw attention to ourselves. Something tells me the big one destroyed the little one -- maybe we should have the probe back off a bit?"

Suddenly, as if to confirm Sochi's fears, the probe received an incoming call. In an archaic form of the Warden language, a voice boomed over the com system, "You have entered a secure area. You have sixty seconds to present your security clearance." Followed by an audible countdown klaxon that began sounding out one-second intervals.

Stox frantically reversed thrusters and tried to back away but it was too late. The countdown ended and a flash of light erupted out of a tower protruding from the side of the ship. The probe feeds went dark.

The crewmembers gathered in the 'arm' all looked at each other in shock. It was the first sign of aggression they had personally witnessed. There was no doubt about it -- the large ship was armed and dangerous.

Over several days they monitored the big ship but it did not budge from its orbit.

"The invaders met their match," Stox proposed, "I think that burned out wreck drifting behind the big ship was the remains of one of the death pods. They couldn't get past the automated security."

Maybe so, Sochiko thought, but kept the crew on alert anyway. On the other hand, there was excitement from the crew as every hour or so their equatorial orbit passed over a complex of unknown structures built on the surface. From the distance of their orbit, it was impossible to pick them out with the naked eye, but Faddard and Worlith faithfully trained their telescopes on the target and tracked it all the way to the horizon each time they passed.

"That must be Everwebber. The robotic pilot boat probably directs spacecraft into orbits that maintain line of sight with its ground stations." Bort commented.

"Take a look at those circular patterns. Do you suppose they could be spacecraft berths?" Stox commented.

Sochiko was intrigued by the extent of the interconnected domes, tubes, and cylinders that seemed to be patterned on a grid. It was unlike anything on Mother -- the Technicians thought in terms of triangles since they grew up in *The Continent*, and the Wardens' physical structure amounted to simple bermed pyramids. She wondered if they were about to meet their alien friends -- or should she say 'encounter'?

"But there doesn't seem to be any action going on. The spaceport appears deserted." Stox pointed out after a prolonged session on the telescopes.

In addition to the 'town', there were signs of scarring and excavation at a few spots on the lower latitudes -- evidence of mining? On one pass Faddard thought he detected radio signals, so everyone pointed their instruments at one of the sites. By the fifth orbit it was confirmed -- there was definitely digital radio traffic in what appeared to be a major operation.

Worlith looked at her monitors, "There's something moving down there, but I can't make it out -- like an army of little vehicles..."

Everyone looked up at the word 'army', an uneasy look on their faces.

The rest of the day Sochi got the crew busy on prepping the lander, and made assignments for the first descent. They had decided that the active mining operation would be their first target. Initially, she would take Faddard, Stox, and Prech, then give the second trip to Heln, Bort, Worlith, and Buutz. Unfortunately, the crewmembers would need to wear the bulky pressure suits, so Sochiko and the other three began running around in oxygen masks doing the required pre-breathing as they readied the equipment.

The lander got under way the next morning. Sochiko guided the small craft to separate from the *Soarer* and do a deceleration burn that would cause it to fall toward the surface. Suddenly a Klaxon sounded warning of another vessel nearby. Faddard quickly armed the missiles and all four were frantically looking out the view ports to try to get a visual. Stox spotted it first, a squat cylinder speeding toward them, attempting to match their trajectory.

Then an incoming transmission interrupted Sochiko's concentration. "*Hello, this is Everwebber Port. Will you be remaining in orbit or landing at the facilities?*"

The voice was in the Warden language. Sochiko relaxed -- it was the robotic pilot boat.

She answered, "No, we intend to land elsewhere on the planet."

Sochiko wondered if it was allowed, or if she would have to designate the coordinates in some unknown positioning protocol. Was there a security code for other sites similar to the big ship?

Her fears were laid to rest when the pilot boat answered, "*Thank you. The area outside the spaceport does not fall under Everwebber jurisdiction. However, Everwebber maintains emergency and safety facilities should you need assistance. Please do not hesitate to call the spaceport.*"

The pilot boat then headed off and was soon out of visual range. Sochiko steered the approach toward the mining operation that Faddard had identified, and slowly thrustered to reduce altitude. At first the area showed no distinguishing features beyond the battered and cratered natural landscape, but as their altitude decreased, they began to see markings and stains on the ground that gradually resolved themselves into roads and diggings. Soon they were able to see glints of reflected light that indicated possible machinery.

Sochiko was excited, and she could read the same anticipation on her colleagues' faces through the bubble helmets -- they were actually going to set foot on another planet! Even after studying the moon planetoids over the last year, no one had actually gone to the surface since there was still worry about the strong magnetic fields. What would it be like?

She aimed for a spot several dozen nodelengths away from the diggings, yet still traversable with the un-pressurized rover. Much of the mining operation appeared to be staged in a flat valley where a concentration of structures acted as a nexus for incoming ore deliveries, but all the diggings were in the highlands round about. Sochiko chose a landing site in the valley floor that had a small hill between them and the operation.

"*Soarer*, we're down to 1000 armlengths." she reported.

Sochiko searched for a spot that was free of boulders, and performed some side thrustering.

"Down 500." she continued to give their progress, which was relayed on to operations. "Approaching 100."

Back on Mother, the entire Technician and Warden population monitored their progress with enthusiasm. Even some of the Inmates who had ties or dealings with the

Technicians wandered in from the forest and watched with interest from community viewing areas.

For an instant the whole universe stood still. The reality of the experience hit Sochiko all of a sudden and she wondered how she had gotten into this fantastic situation. Then the big moment arrived, and Sochiko chose a reasonably flat spot to set down. The large craft spit up a cloud of dust and touched lightly on its landing legs. She powered down the engine and shut the system off. They were on an alien planet.

"We've landed." Sochiko announced, and could hear applause in the background.

She looked up at the others and saw the thrill on their faces. Stox, their resident geologist, was so excited he could not sit still. After all, no one had ever set foot upon rocky surfaces on Mother either, since the entire landmass consisted of floating growths. This would be the first time anyone had an opportunity to observe hard ground up close.

The crew hurried with the various post-landing procedures and buttoned up the bulky pressure suits. By the time the cabin had been depressurized Stox was almost pounding at the hatch, and Sochiko and the others were not far behind.

They slowly opened the pressure port and moved the heavy hatch aside to reveal an alien landscape of harsh barrenness all the way to the distant mountains. Since 'Bridgestar' (or whatever this planet was called) was roughly the same mass as Mother, they did not feel any differences in gravity, so moving around in the bulky pressure suits was quite cumbersome. Fortunately, the suits had slimmed down a bit since Sochiko's first trip to explore *Destiny*, or she wouldn't have been able to move around at all.

One by one the crew vacated the hatch and stood out on the lift. When all four had gotten in position, Prech operated the winch that slowly lowered them to the surface. Once lowered, the lift platform would become a work porch only one handwidth above the surface. They all locked arms, approached the edge, and on the count of three simultaneously stepped out onto the planet surface. From then on, the names of Sochiko, Faddard, Prech, and Stox would go down in history as the first persons to walk on another world.

The crewmembers each had their own tasks to begin right away. Stox began walking around the perimeter looking for potential samples that could be brought back to Mother for future analysis. Prech and Faddard began deploying the rover from its storage rack on the side of the lander, and Sochiko started up the bulky, self-contained mappers that would be remotely operated by the Wardens. They had a dozen mappers for this purpose, six each to be deployed and left behind at each of the two landing sites they would eventually visit. Prech was more than a little distracted by the proliferation of dust that got kicked up and clung to the machinery, and Stox soon became stained dark gray because he couldn't stop playing in it.

When the rover was ready, the four climbed aboard and began the slow journey over the low rise separating them and the mining operation. As they topped the rise, a wide panorama of activity became visible to them. To the left on the distant highlands, some equipment was moving around on terraced slopes, and Sochiko supposed the machines were participating in excavation and carrying ore. A line of loaded ore hoppers was making their way down the mountain, passing empty hoppers on their way up.

In the center of the valley, jumbles of structures were receiving the ore, and outputting stacks of some product that Sochiko couldn't identify. The stacks grew to a certain size, then seemed to grow wheels and mobilize themselves across the valley to a paved tarmac, and attach themselves to what appeared to be a rapidly growing tower.

When she looked at the various pieces of equipment in telescopic viewers, she could see that every vehicle or structure seemed to be constructed out of a similar set of modules that reconfigured and morphed into whatever shape it needed at the time to do the work at hand. Sochiko was astounded -- she did not see any sign of life, at least nothing that resembled life as she knew it.

As the rover continued to descend the slope, she panned across the valley with the viewer, and her screen was suddenly blocked by something quite close. The telescoping mechanism took a few seconds to readjust its focus to a wider angle, and centered on a menacing-looking machine moving across the plain right toward them.

"Faddard, stop for a bit. Get ready for violence folks." Sochi ordered.

They activated weapons mounted to the rover and trained them on the approaching machine. Seconds later the menacing machine slowed to a stop in front of them.

A voice in Wardenese sounded in the helmet com units, "*Please do not approach any closer. This is a dedicated mining operation closed to public access. If you require assistance, please contact ...*"

The voice then rattled off meaningless numbers and syllables. After finishing its message, the sentry moved back to a point several nodelengths away and stationed itself between them and the ore-processing center.

"Merinat, are you getting all that?" Sochiko relayed through the *Soarer*.

After a delay, the reply came back, "*Yes, we've also been watching video from some of the mappers. Whenever one of our machines gets too close, some modules from the working mining equipment detach themselves and reconfigure into a security guard.*"

As she watched the self-mobile stacks make their way toward the tower, Sochiko was surprised when they began to stop their parade and loiter at a point several nodelengths away. The attaching exercise ceased and the tower stood still.

Suddenly the tower lifted right up off the surface and flew straight up into space, with no visible means of propulsion.

"*It's a cargo ship!*" Stox gasped through the suit com.

Thinking quickly, Sochiko sent a message to the *Soarer*, "Heln, track the spacecraft that just took off from our location."

After a few minutes Heln answered, "*Okay, got a fix. It's not stopping for orbit, but breaking straight out of the gravity well.*"

Worlith jumped on the line, "*I got a visual, but it's moving at a high rate of acceleration -- we'll lose it soon.*"

"See if you can reverse calculate its trajectory, and find out its destination." Sochiko added.

Worlith replied, "*Okay, working on it.*"

There was another pause, then Worlith came on all excited, "*I'll have a trajectory soon, but you should know we just detected another small craft heading your way! It's going to land in your vicinity.*"

Sochiko asked for clarification, "Is it an empty cargo ship?" But she knew it could not be so because she watched the self-mobile stacks of parts move out on the tarmac again and begin to assemble into another cargo ship.

"*No, it's much smaller, and it's heading directly for you!*"

Sochiko was again alarmed. The four suited crewmembers shifted their attention to the black sky and tried to look upward -- no easy task in the constraining helmets. They twisted around, trying to scan the horizon.

Prech spotted it first, descending toward the crest of the rise behind them, a bright star rapidly approaching their location. The crew scrambled to get their weapons aimed at the newcomer as the object decelerated. Again, Sochiko felt sick with a dull pain in the pit of her stomach as she considered a potential confrontation with hostiles. *Here we go, finally a visit from the invaders*, she thought.

When the spacecraft got into visual range, she saw that it wasn't shaped like the squat pilot boat, but had more of a streamlined shape, as if it were designed for atmospheric travel as well. Or underwater -- her fear intensified as she recalled the images of the butchered Technician crew in the looted underwater outpost that Tapital had sent. She started the video camera rolling.

She motioned for Faddard to drive the rover back toward the lander but it was already too late. The strange craft set down on the top of the hill between them and the craft that was their ticket home.

The crew waited in silence with their weapons pointed at the newcomer. Sochiko recalled Ix's stories of how they first encountered the ferocious Inmates, and none of their weapons had been effective at first. Was that the case this time? Were there invaders sitting in that ship laughing at their primitive weapons, getting ready to kill them with one sweep of some high-technology ray?

The hatch in the side of the vessel opened. A helmeted figure stepped out, followed by a second. Here Sochiko got her first shock, and she could hear the others gasp in the com units. The visitors' environmental suits could have been identical replicas of the ancient suit they had found in Vault 3 so long ago, the 'Metal Man' of Nux's time that they had tried in vain to replicate. The suits were very light and compact, made from jointed metal rather than soft material. Neither figure carried anything that resembled a weapon, but who knew what sort of technologies a determined techno-pirate might possess?

The figures slowly walked down the hill toward them and the crew waited. Sochiko and her team were surrounded -- the silent sentry on one side, and the two visitors on the other. About ten armlengths away, the helmeted figures stopped. Sochiko marveled at the fine quality of the details and workmanship of the pressure suits. But even more so, she was amazed that right in front of her there was a person, hostile or not, that was not born on Mother!

The universe stood still again. Little did she know that these strangers would hold significance for untold generations of Technicians.

They faced each other in what seemed like an endless lapse of time. Then one of the strangers reached up and pulled back the visor on his bubble helmet, revealing the face of a kindly old gentleman through the clear material. The easy-going countenance disarmed her at first, until he began speaking in the same dialect she had grown to fear. She switched on the translator and listened to the message inside her helmet com.

"*Hello. We have need of repairs on our ship. We back traced the departure point of the cargo crafts and saw your mining operation and thought you might be able to synthesize a part for us.*"

Were these creatures the aliens that had sent warning messages, or were they part of a fearsome invading army? Was this a ploy to get them occupied with some task, only to strike when they weren't expecting it? Sochiko didn't think so, but she decided to act on the side of caution anyway. It was true they had compact numerical control mills that had the capacity to machine some types of solid parts, but all that equipment was on the *Soarer*.

She replied, "We are just visitors here too, observing the robotic operation. However, we do have the ability to synthesize some types of parts. What do you need?"

The stranger turned abruptly and looked out on the horizon behind them. Sochiko turned and saw that another of the robotic cargo crafts had assembled itself and lifted off, shooting up unto space toward an unknown destination.

The stranger replied, "*We need a beryllium alloy part machined.*"

"Beryllium! We don't have any beryllium. Can we use titanium instead?" Sochiko asked.

"*Titanium may do temporarily I suppose, enough to get us back through the gate.*" the stranger mused. "*Please follow us.*"

Sochiko hesitated. If she followed the strangers, would she be placing herself in mortal danger? Once they got the help they needed, would they turn around and attack? But the thrill of meeting a person from another world overcame any hesitation she may have had. She knew she couldn't put the others in danger, so she left Faddard in charge with strict orders to keep his finger on the trigger, and labored in her bulky pressure suit up the hill after them.

Operations caught on to what she was about to do on the other end of the time lag. Cadbic begged her to reconsider. "*Sochi, you have no idea how this would stress your uncle.*"

"I know, but I've got to do this. I don't think there is any malice here -- these people are isolated travelers in need of assistance. They even thought we were natives!" Sochiko replied, feeling more and more confident.

As she approached the ship, she realized it was quite small. In fact, it could have been a distant cousin to one of the smaller six-person submarine-pods the Technicians used to navigate Mother's Plasma. The elder man stepped onto a platform and entered the airlock, then motioned for her to join him. Since there was only enough room for the two of them, the companion waited outside, presumably to wait his turn in the small chamber.

"*What is your operating air pressure?*" The man's voice translated in her com unit as he looked at her through his clear faceplate.

Sochiko was at a loss. They had been able to translate the language, but units of measurement were so subjective between different cultures. The man was apparently concerned with her welfare -- if the inside of the ship had a lower pressure than her suit she could get decompression sickness, or the bends. Fortunately, she had a gauge on her chest that measured outside pressure just for that purpose. She showed him the gauge and waited for the pressure to rise.

"*Sochi!*" Uncle Ix had gotten word of her interaction with the strangers and yelled at her through the helmet com. "*Remember micro-organisms. You have no idea what sorts of bacteria or viruses they may carry.*"

"What do you mean Unk?"

The time lag made a dialog impossible, but several minutes later Ix explained, "*We have no idea how many hundreds or even thousands of generations our two peoples have been apart. Bacteria and viruses that are harmless to you may devastate them -- or vice versa.*"

Sochiko could tell Uncle Ix was worried, but he was just as intrigued as she was about the visitors and where they came from. He added, "*Sochi, their space suits must have common heritage with the ones used by Those Who Went Before -- perhaps they can give us some clue about our ancestors. I'll need to show these images to your father.*"

Sochiko tried to explain about the idea of biological containment to her host, and he nodded in agreement. When the airlock reached cabin pressure, he removed his helmet and opened the inner door, but she kept her suit sealed. There was a short corridor with doors opening off of it, and he led her in her bulky outer wear to what must have been the bridge, full of monitors and banks of controls. There were four people there, two men and two women, who looked as though they had been through a war. Haggard looks and bags under the eyes, Sochiko thought these people must have had their share of hardship.

Through a hand mic (so she could hear through the helmet) the kindly gentleman introduced himself as Masamune Hughes. "*And this is Dr. Hiroyuki Toshige, his wife Dr. Emi, and Jiro Kitamura. You are on the* Towa Maru."

Masamune showed her a bit of the control room, using some terms she didn't understand. "*We're so glad to find you! We've been wandering all over and have seen nothing but robotic systems.*" he said

From the direction of the airlock a partly suited woman wandered back -- the companion they had left outside. Behind her a second woman followed, full of smiles.

"*This is Dr. Kitamura's wife Beth, and my wife Dr. Sachiko.*"

Sochiko was quite surprised at the similarity of the name. She began speaking but realized no one could hear her. When she motioned that she wanted to talk, Jiro jumped up and switched on what Sochiko assumed would be a speaker system.

Sochiko set the translator to capture her voice in real time, and excitedly said, "My name is Sochiko! I can't help but feeling we are cousins somehow."

Sochiko had so many questions that she wanted to ask, but had to take care of business first. She spoke through her mic to the colleagues she had left behind on the surface.

"Faddard, I'm alright. We are approaching five hours suit time, so you'll need to take everyone back to the lander for recharge. Hughes and his crew have a way to fill my air for me."

Masamune brought two small metal parts, one of which was cracked in half. "*This one was broken, and you can see it is a mirror of this intact piece. Can you scan in the geometry and cut a new one for us?*" he asked.

Sochiko took the piece and turned it over in her hands. It wasn't complicated -- she could have Bort do it in about an hour. They had the titanium alloy needed to make the part, but with their limited ability to harvest the metal from the Mineral Strata in Mother's Plasma, a block that large would cost the same as three whole pods. She turned to Hughes and asked, "Can we get to orbit? Our mother ship has the right equipment."

Masamune answered in the affirmative. She told the crew and operations that she would ride with the strangers to orbit and rendezvous with the *Soarer*. "Bort, get someone into a pressure suit to meet me at the airlock, and have a portable sterilizer handy."

They seated her in one of the acceleration seats and in no time had reached significant thrust. The trip to the *Soarer* happened in about half the time it would have taken her own lander. On the way the always-present Everwebber pilot boat showed up and escorted them to the target orbit. Masamune showed surprising sufficiency in the Warden language, which he called a 'butchered dialect of English', so Sochiko spoke with the crew in mixed Wardenese from that point on since the translator left gaps.

The *Towa Maru* pulled within a few armlengths from the *Soarer* hatch. In the airlock, Sochiko clipped on a tether and jumped across the short gap to the other open airlock where a suited up Worlith was waiting. She handed over both the intact and broken pieces.

As they bathed each of the parts in the radiation from the sterilizer, Worlith said, "*I tracked the cargo ships out beyond. At first I thought they were heading completely out of the solar system, but there seems to be a faint reading of radio traffic out there on the edge.*

During the observation, a burst of radio waves came from the location, and at the same time we got another message from 'Bridgestar'! Sochi, I think we found the source!"

Things had taken on a complicated twist. Sochiko thought back to her image of the boy in the sea of ships -- were the crew of the *Towa Maru* from the same group that had been sending them warnings?

"So our friends do not live here in Everwebber, or on this planet?" Sochiko thought the big ship in orbit was still a mystery, but it didn't appear to belong to the pirates, and didn't seem to be an aggressor unless threatened.

Worlith took the pieces inside and Sochiko followed the tether back to the stranger's vessel. She had a flood of questions to ask Masamune, and while Bort did his work on the parts she aimed to get as much out of him as she could. Hughes had been suited up with her in the airlock, and brought her inside the cabin again.

"Who are you? Where do you come from?" She asked.

"We're from Kasei. It's a long story, but I'll just say that we've been trying to prevent a planet-wide disaster from destroying our home. But we went through the gate and got lost. We've been wandering ever since."

Sochiko did not understand what the 'gate' was, but pressed on with her questions. "Have you been sending us messages?"

"No, we saw you for the first time near the mining operation and thought you were overseeing it."

"What about Bridgestar. Have you ever been to Bridgestar?" Sochi queried.

"I don't know what that is. Is Bridgestar a planet?" Hughes replied.

"We don't know either, but there is evidence of extremely hostile pirates that may come from there. Do you know anything about pirates?" she asked.

Masamune was surprised, and answered in the negative. He said they would be more cautious in the future.

Sochiko asked, "Tell me more about the 'gate'."

Masamune explained, "*You don't know? It's an orbital facility out on the edge of the solar system that allows ships to pass through a wormhole to distant stars. Kasei is far away, my dear, orbiting around a star named 'Sol'.*"

Sochiko was astonished. She never would have imagined such a thing. She asked, "How did you engineer the gate?"

Hughes replied, "*We just stumbled on it. And unfortunately, we have no idea how to aim it or get back.*"

"How long does it take to get out there from here?" she asked.

"*The* Towa Maru *can get there in just a few days -- she's quite fast.*"

The gate intrigued Sochiko. Her imagination was fired up and she could not get it out of her mind. "Do you have any video of the gate?"

Hughes brought her over to a monitor, and she bumped around in the heavy suit until she could see the screen through her clear faceplate. The images he showed were fantastic. A massive structure mostly obscured by absolute darkness, with only a few surfaces dimly lit by the far away sun. Powerful spotlights from the *Towa Maru* illuminated the side as they swept back and forth. The surface was alive, teeming with small objects or vehicles moving back and forth along the wall. Sochiko recognized one of the cargo vessels that had taken off from the mining facility -- it approached the huge space station and melded itself to the surface of the hull, only to disintegrate as all the modular stacked pieces animated themselves and crawled onto the wall, scattering in every direction. Sochiko realized the whole structure was teeming with them, going about doing repairs, inserting themselves into the fabric, or pulling out dead modules to carry them away.

The view shifted and the *Towa Maru* entered a garage of sorts, then emerged again.

"*Then we were here again. We keep going between two solar systems as though the mechanism is stuck. We can't get back to Kasei.*" Hughes explained.

Sochiko delivered the parts about an hour later, and the *Towa Maru* delivered her back to the lander on the surface. She had many more questions to ask, such as finding out about Kasei, their culture, their economics, and especially their technology. But the other team was rushed and needed to leave.

"*We'll visit Mother if we can learn to aim the gate, and if we solve our planetary dilemma.*" they promised.

Sochiko could not have known that they would never see them again, but that they would learn about Masamune from a different source, and that the story would defy all imagination.

They all waved as the poor wandering strangers took off and headed once more to the gate, following another cargo vessel.

She got her crew ready, and they loaded all the samples on board. They lifted off and let the Everwebber pilot boat lead them back to the *Soarer*. Sochiko got online with operations and the *Soarer* and reported what she had discovered.

"I think the 'gate' is Bridgestar." she explained.

Worlith agreed, "*The broadcasts come from there also -- we've confirmed that.*"

In a few minutes, Merinat spoke up, "*Well, we've been calling the planet 'Bridgestar', so I propose calling it 'Minato'. That's an ancient way of saying 'port'.*"

The nomenclature stuck. Everyone began calling the world Minato, but suddenly the attention was out there at the edge of the solar system. Everyone wanted to get to the real Bridgestar, but such a vast distance was well beyond what the *Soarer* could possibly handle.

A few days later Heln and the other three readied the lander for the second trip down, this time to visit Everwebber. They reloaded six new mappers, and performed the zero-g refueling operation.

Sochiko watched the monitors as Heln separated the lander for the second time and began the descent. It was only minutes later that the lander crew got an expected visit.

"*We've got company,* Soarer." Heln went on to describe the robotic pilot boat that had appeared again. "It's asking if we intend to land at the spaceport."

Sochiko replied, "Go ahead and answer in the affirmative. Follow its instructions, but stay alert -- there may still be some occupants down there, and we don't know the security systems. What happens if the automatics demand berthing fees?"

Everyone snickered.

Heln reported the details of the descent. The pilot boat continued to lead them down.

Suddenly, He got on the line, "Soarer, *we're getting a confusing echo. The pilot boat's message is repeating.*"

Sochiko looked up in surprise. "Heln, what do you see?"

"*The pilot boat is coming at us! I'm trying to maneuver -- it looks like it will ram us!*"

Sochiko called out, "Heln, release the missiles! Destroy it!"

But there was no reply. Silence reigned on the line.

CHAPTER 7

Ix was out in a pod again. He was using the underwater voice phone to talk to his twin brother Mox, who was all excited about something.

"*Ix, you've got to take some time when you get back. There's something odd about the video Sochi sent back. It can't be real.*" he said.

"What do you mean it can't be real? I'm sure it's genuine." Ix took a quick breath from the respirator.

Mox continued, "*Is it possible someone inserted a false data stream?*"

Ix was mildly worried, but had to get off the line. "Okay bro, it's not likely, but we'll look at it later. I'll call you as soon as I arrive."

Ix hung up the phone and let out a deep sigh. He was always worried about Mox, who served as Advisor One and president's assistant occasionally, but had to use a stand-in whenever his amnesia returned. Now he was ranting on about a video. When he was well, he was focused, but when the sickness struck it was hard to tell if he was serious or not. Ix thought he'd give it a few days, and if his brother still had the video on his mind, he would listen to what he had to say.

Ix was also worried about the lander crew that had gone missing. The Technician and Warden public were concerned, and expected some resolution of the issue soon. Did the craft crash because of human error? Was the failure mechanical? Had they met hostiles? He had no idea what to do.

And if that wasn't enough, some factions of Wardens had begun accusing the Technicians of collaborating with the unknown invaders. Both sides were uneasy, and Ix wasn't sure about how to calm the people.

Ix turned his attention back to the job at hand. He was on a larger steel-hulled transport sub this time, as part of the command crew. There were several squads of deep Plasma divers on board, as well as remote robotic drone teams. They were heading out to rendezvous with Mother's Heart, in hopes of raising the great ship that brought Those Who Went Before to Mother so many thousands of seasons ago. Raising the wreck!

Ix thought back at all the complex events that brought them to this particular mission. When Sochiko had given her report of the meeting with the aliens, and what she discovered about the 'gate' on Bridgestar, the public had gone wild. Ix had never seen so much support for the space program from both Technicians and Wardens alike, in spite of the lost lander. The consensus was to build a spaceship that could manage the vast distances out to the edge of the solar system, where the wealth of space faring civilizations could be had. All other programs were given second priority. There was a flood of enrollment into space pilot and technician programs -- even the major Inmate families sent some of their children to join.

The first priority had been to learn about interstellar travel. How did Those Who Went Before do it? If they succeeded in raising the great ship, would they be able to reverse engineer the powerful propulsion systems that could build up enough speed to make such a journey practical?

He looked over toward the navigator's shoulder and saw that the needles were going haywire. At another station the sonar scope showed a waveform that indicated an artificial bulge in the Plasma ocean surface. It was a sure sign that the thrash tide was nearby, hiding the mysterious vessel on its strange orbit inside Mother.

"We're approaching the swimmer cloud." The navigator reported.

The sencho said, "Say goodbye to the hunting fleet, boys." The Neo-Japonican term 'sencho' was the title they gave all their pod captains.

Ix could see the situation monitor that showed all the positions of the pods in the area. Many of the blips that represented submarines accompanying them began to divide up and move to the flanks of the great thrash tide where a billion fish seethed. Only the three salvage vessels stayed the course of penetration.

The sencho ordered, "Initiate the screech."

"Yes Sir," was the reply from one of the men.

The screech was a sonar signal especially prepared in its frequency and strength to chase away most swimmers. The image on the monitor began to show a marked dent in the tide as the salvage vessels headed in and the navigator called out depths.

"We'll be nearing the target in fifteen minutes." the navigator looked back and reported to Ix.

Ix looked up and nodded to the admiral, then headed off the bridge. He went back to the mess area where the diving squad hanchos (section chiefs) were having a discussion and quickly called in, "Fifteen minutes!"

He paused just enough to see the hanchos stand up and scatter to get their men ready, and continued on to the drone operator stations.

Gij, the head pilot and son of the university Professor of the same name, was just reaching up to organize a set of manipulator implements when Ix walked in.

"Fifteen minutes," he repeated, then walked with Gij to the small 'war room' where the drone operators would plot their area scans.

The rest of the team was lounging there, and snapped to attention when Gij entered. He began to go through a pre-mission checklist.

"What is the status of the compressed air storage?"

One of the men answered, "Two of the tanks were leaking and have drained off some of the pressure, but the other one hundred twenty-eight are holding. There's also one bad tank on the other pod."

"Are we fully charged? We may have to drop the umbilical in some spots."

Another operator answered in the affirmative.

"What about the controllers. Are we hot?"

"We've kept the drones booted up since this morning."

Gij went over a few other items before reiterating the steps for the umpteenth time. "We'll be staying deep for a few days. Our first task will be to find out how the crew scuttled the ship. We'll need to identify all the holes before entering the hull. Next, we map out all the main structure elements, and determine an approximate mass for the ship. If we can identify a small number of very large cavities of the right volume our job will go a lot quicker."

Another man spoke up, "Sir, I've never understood Mother's Heart. I understand how it could be pulled this way and that by the moons, but how does it stay so near the surface? Every calculation I make says the Plasma ocean is nowhere dense enough to keep the wreck from sinking to the exact center of Mother."

Ix jumped in, "Let me get this one," and turned to the technician, "That's one of the things we'd like to find out. Do you recall the images of Abb and some of the other moons? We have a theory that the Heart is a very long and slender structure, like a highly magnetic twin to Abb whose center lies at the center of Mother, and the wrecked ship sits on one of the ends. Perhaps anciently Mother's Heart was another moon that fell into the ocean. Those Who Went Before evidently knew their ship would not sink completely out of reach -- they may have been hoping to recover it after the war crisis passed."

"Maybe they were trying to hide something." a technician near the back suggested.

A few hours later the drone team was gathered around their monitors watching the video feeds from the drones. The eerie images of a dark wall barely illuminated by the drone spotlights sent shivers down Ix's spine. He recalled his feelings many years ago when he first saw the vessel, and remembered the row of blank portholes and the imagined ghosts staring back out at him.

"The ship is resting on magnetized iron, Ix. I think you were right about the Heart being the remnants of a moon." Gij called back.

Ix smiled, "And you can probably bet that the mounding phenomenon of Mother's Plasma over the thrash tide is due to tidal effects off the end of that long mountain of iron."

Up close the hull was not smooth. The wall was occasionally broken by unidentifiable protrusions and indentations, and the drone team faithfully explored every one.

Thankfully, the ship's hull was not magnetized, nor was there much corpuscle activity. The drones were able to get close and scrape the surface at times without the fear of getting stuck.

As they moved along, the drones would catalog the exterior and do ultrasound readings of the interior. This allowed the mapping of internal densities to help find large cavities or heavy structure, both of which would be useful to know when they determined lift points.

By the end of the day the team had used the two drones to circle the entire ship. Even though he was prepared for it, Ix was astounded by the ship's size -- it could contain their entire city easily within its interior. There were no apparent breaks in the hull at all. The ancient crew had apparently sunk the vessel by opening all the hatches wide open, including some big garage bay pressure doors that must have allowed large volumes of Plasma to flood in quickly.

The next morning the technicians and machines rested while they put together the previous day's maps into collages representing the overall ship. The ultrasound density maps showed large cavities or low-density zones at both ends of the sunken vessel, and Ix calculated that the volumes might be enough to lift the wreck if filled with air.

"We'll need to send the drones out to find passageways into those cavities." Gij remarked.

One of the men pointed out the large open pressure doors, "It looks like the fore cavities might be garages."

"Yes, and we can probably keep the drones tethered through there. The conning tower is right above that so we may have time to branch off and explore." Ix proposed.

Ix was nervous about seeing cabins and passageways occupied long ago by ancient crewmembers. But it was exciting to consider that his own ancestors once lived and worked on board, and the more they penetrated its secrets the less of a ghost ship it seemed.

"Ix, take a look at this. There appears to have been repairs done to this part of the hull." Gij noted.

The image showing on a monitor was a photograph taken high on the hull earlier in the day by one of the drones. A pattern of patchwork traced out a circle on the metal clearly visible under the layer of growths. A follow-on image showed the growths scraped away, and the scar prominently exposed to open Plasma. At some point in the distant past there was a circular hole that had been patched.

"Curious," Ix replied, "how big is that circle?"

Gij put the size of the patched area at a few armlengths across. "Looks a bit like those holes found in the *Destiny* orbital."

Ix said nothing but remained in deep thought.

By early afternoon Ix followed the technicians down to the staging area. The transport pod had a diving well that made ingress and egress easier than an airlock. Ix walked into the staging area and noted the flurry of activity. He saw the two drones sitting in special crane racks on the opposite side of the well, all booted up and waiting for their next assignment. A large group of divers were suiting up in special deep-sea gear that included helmets and heavy-duty gill collectors.

Other squads were pulling folded membrane bladders and large compressed air tanks out of the storage hold and setting the packages on the edge of the well. Several of the divers had already entered the Plasma and were standing on an underwater metal platform, and began pulling the bladder packages into the pool.

Ix threaded his way through the crowd on the heels of Gij and two of the technicians. The men pulled each of the drones off their racks and set them in the water, getting a little help from the divers. As the technicians readied the robots, Ix watched the video feeds on nearby monitors. The video showed the scene underwater. The platform was a porch of sorts hanging directly below the diving well, with all four sides exposed to dark, open Plasma beyond. Ix could see the divers standing on the deck, with head and shoulders protruding out and truncated by the water surface. Underwater lights lit up the whole porch. Some of the folded bladders and tanks were being stacked underwater on the platform, waiting to be moved over to the vessel.

The drone began to move and the scene above the platform shifted. Spotlights attached to the drone created a long beam of illumination as it pierced the darkness, punctuated by small floating particles caught in the glare. As the drone pressed forward, occasional glimpses could be seen of divers who were to swim alongside the drone stringing brightly colored cord to mark the path to the entrance.

The drone spotlights captured the hull gradually, where the pitch-black Plasma faded to gray and resolved itself into a circle of illumination crisp against the rough growths found everywhere on the metal surface. The scene edged sideways for quite a while, then abruptly the wall stopped. The light showed into the interior of the lost space ship.

Momentarily the technician steered the drone backward until the entire opening fit inside the spot of illumination. It was a large circular hatch big enough for a small pod to enter. The great pressure door could be seen displaced to one side in a pocket built into the hull, encrusted with layers of growths.

Two divers swam into view and began to attach the cord onto a frame just inside the opening. When the line was secure, the divers backed off to the side and turned to hover, facing the drone. The technician steered the machine forward past the men and crept into the darkness. The spotlights illuminated a wide passageway that continued only about fifty meters then abruptly ended at another open hatch in a vast floorless cavern.

"Paint the surfaces with the lights. We need to get a good feeling for this space. I'm sure this is the bow cavity that we detected." Ix whispered.

The technician replied, "Okay, here's a tour of the facilities, folks."

The drone first made one round of the vast space, and Ix noted a variety of structures protruding from the walls, ceiling, and floor that may have been docking gantries, complete with boarding bridges. The gantries showed no preference for orientation, giving Ix an impression that they were to be used in microgravity. However, it was clear that the vast garage could be pressurized, since the large tunnel they had used as an entrance had been a gigantic airlock with both inner and outer hatches flung open.

The drone came across three other vessel-sized airlocks -- one directly across from their entry point, one directly downward opening onto the growth encrusted magnetic surface of Mother's Heart, and one directly overhead that had a faint greenish light filtering in.

"That one is going to be a problem," Gij noted, "We'll have trouble keeping air in this chamber with that open."

Ix suggested, "We can begin filling bladders at both ends of the cavity, and have a crew figure out how to shut those doors. Otherwise, we'll need to build a bridge across the hole to keep bladders from slipping through."

Ix and Gij lingered a while longer, and then shifted their attention over to the other set of monitors where the second drone was slowly progressing along narrow corridors free from its tether.

One of the technicians on the second team said, "Okay, place a repeater right there. Let's take the passageway to the left."

"Any luck on finding the low-density area in the aft portions?" Gij asked.

The technician turned and reported, "Yes Sir, but so far we haven't found a large cavity, just dozens of medium-sized rooms, perhaps cargo holds."

They watched the video scene as the drone followed a corridor, then turned left through a large door opening up into a big room. There were stacks of crushed containers jumbled on the floor that had been abandoned thousands of seasons before. Apparently, some of the containers had been secured to tie-downs that appeared at intervals on all the surfaces, including walls and ceilings.

The drone backed out and continued its search. Several hours later, after negotiating numerous corridors and smaller spaces the second drone passed through a heavy bulkhead and had to turn back because of a low battery. It was apparent that contrary to the monolithic vast garage at the fore, the inflatable bladders in the aft would need to be individually placed in multiple smaller chambers in order to effect buoyancy.

The diving teams began ferrying across folded bladders and tanks over the next few days. Ix, Gij, and the technicians verified the load paths through bulkhead structure and divers began placing the bladders with as much precision as they could.

One by one valves were opened and bladders began to fill with air. The technicians worked out a sequence so no single location would get too much lift before any other, or else undue strain would be placed on the ship's structure. The diving squads in the vast garage near the front of the ship worked at a slower pace, because it took so much time to place the bladders in the maze of cargo holds in the rear.

One morning, since the placement of air bags was on track and the diver crews needed less and less supervision, Ix, Gij, and some of the technicians decided to take one of the drones to explore a little deeper into the ship. Ix had been thinking about the circular scars (there were several) that had been patched by the ancient crews, and wondered if the holes had any relationship with the invasion by pirates. Could it be conceivable that the hostile aliens had been around that long? Had the ship been attacked and the invaders repulsed, after which their ancestors did a repair job to patch up the damage?

Ix watched the monitor as the drone found its way back to the large open hatch and into the vast garage. Lights had been mounted to a few key gantries, flooding the space with illumination. Seeing the great space all lit up stressed the size of the vessel, and Ix estimated the entire sphere of *Destiny* could fit inside with room to spare. It was amazing how that ancient crew could have landed the ship intact on Mother's oceans!

The drone entered the space, and Ix could see the giant bladders plastered to the ceiling, partially filled with air. Teams were systematically filling empty bladders and aiming them to float up to target gaps. The technician steered the drone toward one of the gantries and into the open hatch on the end of a boarding bridge. The bridge was like a tube lined with handholds, which could be flexed into a tight fit against the hull of whatever small craft happened to be docked at the gantry. The drone proceeded slowly down the tube and found itself in a wide collection area on the end. Several boarding tubes converged on the space, and Ix imagined it to be a reception area that welcomed new passengers. Ix could envision Those Who Went Before floating along the tubes into the reception hall and funneling toward the end where there would be a large banner welcoming them aboard.

As the drone pointed its spotlights up the space, Ix almost gasped as he saw the welcome sign just as he had imagined it. The sign had a layer of growth so it could not be read immediately, but the technician steered the drone closer and began to scrape away the layers with the robot manipulator. The archaic Japonican characters revealed themselves one by one.

"Tansaku Kakou," Gij read the first line.

No one had a clue what it meant.

Surprisingly, the second line turned out to be in another language that they knew well, but the meaning still escaped them. In a crude form of Warden, the sign read, "*Axiom*: Tensakian Processing."

A few days later the great sunken interstellar ship '*Axiom*' was slowly rising above the surface of Mother's Heart. There was just enough air to achieve positive buoyancy, with air pumps in place to quickly make adjustments as needed. They were setting up to tow the vessel to the inland sea near The Island, and hoped to keep it just below the surface until they could guarantee that the ancient hull would not quickly oxidize after being exposed to the atmosphere.

Ix had a few minutes and hooked up with Sochiko who was on her way home to Mother on the *Soarer*.

"Your father says he saw something unusual about the videos you sent. They haven't been tampered with, have they?" Ix asked.

"*Unk, of course not. What's wrong with them?*" Sochiko asked after the communication delay.

"I'm not sure. I haven't had a chance to see him yet. By the way, have you ever heard of the name 'Tensakian'?"

There was astonishment on the other end. Sochiko replied, "*I just got a message from our friend at Bridgestar -- he says that the hostiles are called the 'Tensakians'!*"

CHAPTER 8

Kret still had his armor on. The Tensakians were on the prowl again, and this time they were out in force, searching the various Farmer strongholds for a certain piece of stolen equipment. Kret patted on the hull of the small vessel and smiled -- they'd never find this one!

He turned to Davo the Farmer and said, "Take off the protrusions and supplementary equipment but try to keep all the subsystems intact. We especially want to see how those missile systems work - they might have chemical explosives!"

Davo was a hard-looking character, quite tall with gnarled hands. The Farmer led a difficult life, trying to carve out a living with artificial gravity, seeds, sunlight, and a few chemicals. And today they were banding together to repel the Tensakians.

"Do you want to keep the propulsion system in one package, or can we pull out all the tanks and piping? This thing's huge!" Davo replied.

"We've got to take that one apart. What happens if those Tensakian rats penetrate this far, they'll spot that thing right away!" Kret paused, and continued, "But keep all the parts together and label everything you disassemble so we can put it back together again."

"And the pressure vessel?"

"You can cut that up as soon as you digitize the design. It's not much good with a hole in it."

Kret had to leave. He was all set for battle and his Farmer unit was waiting in the zero-g staging area. He stepped toward the door and paused, turning around to take a look at the room. He thought about a girl far away whom he had never met, who'd probably be worried sick about now. One more thing...

"Make sure you hide that stuff under the corn." He said, then rushed out.

At the end of a short corridor Kret stepped out into the garden. The sight was beautiful. He looked up where the huge centrifuge arched overhead, and the rows of lettuce started off as curved lines of green at his feet and raked up the spin-ward side until they faded into a soft carpet on the wall. The patchwork of crops blanketing the inside of the drum were broken here and there by chemical plants, hydroponics tanks, sheds and other structures, and Kret could see various bits of machinery and farm implements. That was where they hid the most valuable stuff, particularly if it could be disguised as something useful -- just that morning Kret had hauled several canister-like machines that had been attached to the stolen vessel because they looked like fertilizer enhancers. As soon as things settled down a bit, he intended to take one of them back to his lab and figure out what they were for.

Kret turned slowly and walked the other way, anti-spin-ward through the tomatoes. The closest elevator spoke was twenty-five degrees away, so he began walking up the curve of the wall, but as is the case in all centrifugal artificial gravity environments, his perception told him the gravity vector was always 'down' under his feet.

The wheel was open on both sides to the vast *Blister* interior. To his right Kret could see a series of other great wheel farms, strung out in the distance and partially eclipsing the sun shining through *Blister*'s wall.

To his left, Kret could see more wheels among the vast sea of wrecks and flotsam and jetsam slowly drifting and colliding. The wheel had an automatic avoidance system that used a clever gimbaled set of thrusters in the core to slowly power away from potential hazards without upsetting the rotation and angular momentum. Unfortunately, if too many things came at once the system couldn't keep up, and the Farmers weren't always able to keep the debris away -- every few weeks perfectly good patches of crop were flattened.

Suddenly, Kret heard a ruckus behind him in the distance. He turned too quickly and the coriolis effect gave him momentary vertigo. He could see a Tensakian cruiser approaching a neighboring farm with a bullhorn blaring, and shouts from angry Farmers carried even this far. From this distance Kret could not make out what the bullhorn was saying, but he was sure it could only be the typical banter and propaganda the Tensakians tended to use. A second bullhorn started up, as the Farmers on that distant wheel began arguing back.

As Kret ducked into the spoke elevator lobby, he saw several Tensakian shock troops fly toward the hub and heard the concussion bombs. That was interesting -- both parties usually refrained from destructive weapons, preferring microwave or precision lasers to avoid harming the hardware. And chemical explosives were so rare no one would thoughtlessly waste them on just any raid. *The Tensakians must be furious this time*, he thought. But Kret smiled inside -- there was going to be a battle.

Kret met up with his battle group in the hub, most of whom were floating around getting their weapons ready. He looked around and found the boss, and propelled himself over.

"Did we get the Surians to listen to reason?" He asked.

The Surians were another Farmer group who often sided with the Tensakians. There were a lot of ragtag groups out there. Kret had heard of most of them, and he and his friends were making some headway convincing the others to join them.

"The bastards. They killed Mikor last week!" Boss answered.

Kret seethed. His fists clenched spasmodically. He vowed to make the Surians pay someday, and get rid of the Tensakians who were so much trouble.

A few minutes later, the rest of the stragglers showed up and boss started the fans on the Black Stallion. Each of the Farmers leapt over, and found a spot where they could tie on and point their weapons. Boss powered the fans and slowly pulled away from the gantry, heading for the open garage door. As soon as the craft cleared the opening, they could hear the action going on two wheels over. Kret saw three Tensakian cruisers, several Farmer vessels and even some of the big Farmer salvage ships had joined in. The bullhorns were blaring away. As the Stallion got closer, Kret could hear the Tensakian threats.

"*Turn the stolen ship over immediately,*" the bullhorn blared," the perpetrators will be destroyed!"

"*You Tensakian bastards! Go back to your hole!*" one of the Farmer bullhorns shouted back.

A flameout grenade blew up somewhere and there was a lot of shouting. As the Stallion got closer, Kret launched one of his own grenades at the closest Tensakian cruiser. As expected, the grenade was deflected and burst in a fireball in mid-air. However, Kret's attack brought two grenades heading their way, and the men easily deflected those as well.

Kret could see the other Farmer group trying to repulse the shock units. Someone from the other group saw the Stallion and called out, "Kret's here! Hey boss! Need some help."

Five of the Farmers on the Stallion jumped off and used their momentum to leap toward the fray, while boss redirected the fans in a slow power turn to allow Kret to train the grenade launcher on the ships. Kret cut loose several units that got deflected.

The Farmers on the wheel were pushing the shock troops back. Kret sent off three more grenades that flamed harmlessly in the gap between ships. He noticed that one of the cruisers had a scar on the side that appeared to have been patched up recently, and gave out a chuckle as he thought about cesium in the zero-g toilet -- definitely one of his better ideas!

Kret swung the launcher around and had it pointed in the right direction just as a knot of Tensakian foot soldiers pulled ahead of the pursuing Farmers. Kret smiled and lobbed a single grenade right into their path. It flamed flawlessly, sending the rats flying in all directions. Kret watched as they regrouped and manipulated their wounded fellows toward the nearest cruiser.

Suddenly eight concussion bombs came at him at once -- five from one cruiser that he deflected, but three more came from the opposite direction and landed in the frame of the Stallion.

"Time to bail boss!" Kret shouted and the two leaped away in various trajectories.

The Black Stallion shattered into a hundred pieces, with struts, motors, and bent fan blades still spinning intact in every which direction.

Kret landed on the side of the wheel hub and clung on. He turned around to see who had launched the grenades and saw one of the big Tensakian space-faring ships coming toward the wheel. He watched as two death capsules detached from the ship and backed away from the main hull. Kret watched with a heart full of raging hate as the capsules rotated on their thrusters and began to accelerate in his direction.

Kret used a series of handholds on the outside of the hub to pull himself across the hull. The capsules approached at a high speed and Kret turned around and watched as each of them collided with the hub garage wall not far from him, one after the other. The shock vibrated the metal plates where he clung. Kret knew what was going on. In his mind's eye he could see circles of hull blown inward, and Tensakians pouring out with heavy microwave impactors, cooking flesh and mowing down all resistance.

Helplessly, Kret seethed in rage, and vowed to never let this war end until all Tensakians had paid the ultimate price.

A short distance away in a neighboring wheel, unknown to Kret a mysterious machine winked on. Sensors and cameras rotated on a turret, and found itself in the middle of a vineyard of walnut trees. The turret spotted five others of its own kind, all dented and non-functional. The machine tried to rise using its thrusters, but found a peculiar form of glitch sent it sprawling to the ground again several feet away. When it tried to rise again, the same thing happened. Four times the machine made an attempt to rise off the ground only to be swept sideways, further and further from its fellows. The fifth time it adjusted its thrusters to aim in the opposite direction, and with some tricky maneuvering succeeded in rising off the ground and maintaining a hover. With a little experimentation it was confirmed -- somehow, in one direction it could relax and with very little thrustering could get where it wanted to go, but in the opposite direction it had to push against an unseen force to make any progress.

The machine labored back to its non-functional fellows and began an inspection. None of them could be made operational, but the batteries could be scavenged. The machine did a quick survey of its surroundings and broadcast the data, then went into a sleep mode to wait for a return signal.

CHAPTER 9

Ix sat on the floor of Mox and Blujic's residence and looked up at the monitor. There were also two avatars that had accompanied Ix, small spherical machines hovering above the deck that were being controlled by Merinat and Cadbic from rockers in the Database. Blujic and Mox were standing on either side of the screen.

"Watch this one." Mox said as he pulled off his respirator.

The view was from a camera mounted on the un-pressurized rover on the surface of Minato. The video went through scenes showing the security robot guarding the automated mining facilities, to Sochiko and Stox in their bulky pressure suits with harsh Minato landscape behind them, to sequences showing the alien encounter. Ix watched as Sochiko had a discussion with Hughes, then followed the two up the hill to their ship. Hughes and Sochiko entered the airlock first, then after a while the alien woman entered and the ship lifted off.

Mox stopped the sequence and started a different video. "Now watch this."

This time part of the scene repeated itself from a different angle. There was a view of the un-pressurized rover, with Sochiko and the other three looking toward the camera. The mining operation could be seen in the background. The two suited aliens walked into the view with their backs facing the camera and began the discussion with Sochi. Suddenly in the background one of the mining cargo vessels finished assembling itself and lifted off into space.

Ix was surprised. "That's a view taken from the alien ship *Towa Maru*. I didn't know they had given us their video."

Mox also had a puzzled look on his face. "This is the strange part, why the first video could not be genuine. The aliens never sent us their video."

Ix was confused, "Then where did this come from?"

Mox looked at Ix in a sober stare, slightly nervous. Blujic also had a serious look on her face.

"This video came out of the Third Vault. It's hundreds of years old."

Ix's mind was racing as he made his way through *The Island* streets toward the pod port. There were several videos they had found in the Third Vault, and every one of them had either the old man or his spaceship the *Towa Maru* in them. The one Mox showed them apparently also had Sochiko and her landing crew in it, but in truth even though the suited individuals wore characteristic Technician-designed pressure suits, there was no way to see their faces and Ix supposed some other race hundreds of years ago could have coincidently designed similar equipment for similar environments. So, supposing they had Sochiko's verbal account on hand, it could be that someone had deliberately hijacked the video portions of her broadcast and switched in doctored sequences based on those scenes from long ago. But why would anyone go to such elaborate lengths for a hoax? And if the perpetrators had enough skill to manufacture such a video, could they also simulate Sochiko's voice?

Ix had arrived at the pod port but stopped in his tracks. Suddenly he was alarmed -- could Sochi be in danger? Had the Tensakian monsters captured her -- or worse -- and devised a hoax that tried to convince the Technicians she was safe?

Ix boarded the shuttle pod and rode it out to the research facility for interstellar propulsion where the great *Axiom* from Those Who Went Before had been towed and now lay anchored just below the surface.

He went through the motions of going over the day's targets for survey with the salvage teams, and mechanically watched highlights of the previous days' attempts to reverse engineer the secrets of the ship. But his mind was not all there and anything of worth found in the ship was badly decomposed or corroded anyway.

And nagging on his mind was the Tensakian sign and other more recent evidence that their own ancestors were somehow involved with the Tensakians. Was there indeed still a faction within the ranks of the Technicians who colluded with their outer space colleagues and who had access to the videos in the Third Vault?

At midday Ix suited up to participate in the opening of what the technicians were calling the 'engine room'. During the scuttle operation so long ago, the ancient crew had opened all hatches throughout the ship except where crew were not meant to go. The 'engine room' appeared to be one of those places that were sealed, maintained entirely by automated means. The chambers were flooded nonetheless, and the technician team felt that the heart of the propulsion system seemed to be behind those sealed bulkheads.

The research center was a sprawling complex floating on the inland sea adjacent to the space launch center. A series of platforms on the surface traced the outline of the ship just below the surface, and permanent pontoons had been built that ran the entire length of the vessel. The intention was to eventually raise the vessel out of the Plasma using its own buoyancy once they determined that hatches could be sealed or that the hull would not fall to oxidization when exposed to the atmosphere.

Ix stood on the platform suited up and ready to go with the other officials who would be participating. He peered into the Plasma and could see a massive dark shape just below the surface. It was an ominous sight, and reminded him of the days when the Heart was a thought to be a creature, and huge dark shapes under the water struck fear into even the most courageous. When the security detail indicated an all clear, the group jumped into the Plasma one by one.

Ix floated in the netted safety area until the guide indicated where to swim. Looking toward the vessel, he could make out part of the hull that was so huge that it faded into the distance, obscured by low visibility. The guide gathered everyone together and had the group swim single file into one of the rear hatches. They proceeded down a series of corridors marked by brightly colored ropes and arrived at a wide staging area bathed with underwater lights. Numerous Warden mappers and avatars also were in attendance, in addition to the Technician representatives. A crew of salvager divers had set up their equipment ready to cut through the bulkhead as soon as the ceremony concluded.

This was the first time Ix had been able to see the ship up close, and not through a remote screen. As he drifted in the micro currents, he looked closely at the growth encrusted metal wall, and let his eyes wander to where the wall met the ceiling. The thought that thousands of seasons before technological beings drifted up and down these corridors hit him with great impact. He was astounded that someone could navigate the vast distances between stars. He was overwhelmed that his ancestors could construct and steer such a behemoth. His mind went around and around with the Tensakian sign, the hijacked Abb landers, the looted *Destiny*, and the elaborately crafted videos. What was going on?

Ix barely registered as the crew cut through the bulkhead and the first views of the 'engine room' came to light. He hardly paid attention that the machinery and electronics beyond the wall was so far gone that no amount of reverse engineering could figure out what principle Those Who Went Before used to power their ships. Ix was so deep in thought he didn't even notice the spherical avatar that had eased up in front of him and was trying to get his attention.

"*Ix!*" a voice was saying out the fog of his mind, "*Ix, I have something urgent to talk to you about!*"

Ix shook his head and the whole room came back in clarity. He focused on the little machine.

"*Ix, this is Fisby. I need to show you something.*" the voice said.

"Can you tell me what it is now?"

Fisby replied in the negative, "*You need to join me in the Database.*"

"Okay, I need to get back topside and find a rocker." Ix replied, and the two of them wove their way in and out of the crowd and swam back down the colorful rope-lined corridors. Behind them, two other avatars followed -- Merinat and Cadbic?

After climbing out of the Plasma, Ix headed for the showers and quickly changed into his street clothes. A row of high-priority rockers was installed in the administration center. Ix climbed into a tactile suit and rode the small lift up to the exact center of the sphere. He connected the harness and waited as the real world faded out and he found himself in the vast departure hall. He shoved off and floated high above a sea of translucent eggs, each with its own occupant experiencing some corner of the Database, and followed the lighted markers to the exit.

Fisby was waiting for him in the lobby of the space tower, a crystalline transparent jewel floating at the end of wispy bridges and catwalks.

"I don't know how to explain this, but something fantastic has happened." Fisby began, "Merinat and Cadbic know about it, but we haven't told anyone else."

"What is it?" Ix asked.

"Follow me."

The two floated Warden-style through the glistening corridors to the mapper stations. Row upon row of cockpits held Warden workers seated at the controls of mappers, remotely directing the far-off machines to turn this way and that and continually add to the Database.

Ix thought that somewhere in the room, six Wardens drove mappers that had been left on the surface of Minato, studying the automated mining operation and capturing the natural landscape. Two of the mappers had even begun the journey overland toward the distant Everwebber Port town, since the machines intended for placement there had been lost.

Fisby brought him to a special section cordoned off from the rest. Marinat and Cadbic were there, having just attended the same 'engine room' opening ceremony Ix had via avatars. Ix looked and saw twelve workstations. Six were occupied, but the other six were empty. Briefly, Ix thought of the lost crewmembers of the fated Minato lander and bowed his head in a silent salute.

When he looked up, Merinat was pointing at one of the six empty cockpits indicating for Ix to get inside. He sat down on the simulated seat and felt it firmly grab his posterior. Ix had operated a mapper before, having gone through the course that was offered by the space institute, but it took some reminders from Fisby to remember all the controls.

"Remember this is one of the time-delayed mappers. You won't get instantaneous response off of this one, but will have to give it instructions, then wait till the command and result goes all the way out through space and back." Fisby explained.

"But isn't this one of the missing machines gone down with the lander?" Ix asked, but as soon as he said it he began to nurse a slim hope that perhaps one of the machines had survived.

The blank cockpit walls dissolved and Ix was surprised that he was surrounded by foliage. The video signal was weak and jerky, as if many of the frames were dropped in transit. A fine snowy static occasionally obscured the view.

The little mapper was hovering above a small clearing, and even though it was standing still, Ix could see the readouts showing its thrusters screaming -- it was fighting to maintain its position. He looked around the clearing, turning his head around the full-surround view afforded by the cockpit, and saw rows of trees and the glint of more metal off to one side.

Curious, Ix directed the mapper to steer itself over and observe the metal pieces, and waited for the time delay as his control signal crossed the vastness of space and the video result returned to display in the cockpit.

"You have to be patient with this one -- it seems to be farther out than anything we've sent before" Cadbic noted.

The response took more than an hour, and the four chatted about their latest theories about the sunken *Axiom*. When the video returned, the scene shifted as the mapper traversed the clearing to reveal five of its fellows, dented and mangled, laid out in the weeds. There was no sign of the rest of the lander.

"Ix, look upward." Merinat suggested.

Ix turned his head upward in the cockpit but could only see a covering of leaves and branches. He spotted a hole in the cover and directed the mapper to hover under it. As the static-filled video signals came in, he was astounded at what he saw. There overhead perhaps half a kilometer above was a green-carpeted ceiling with more trees -- growing downward!

Merinat explained, "It appears the mapper has found itself inside a vast garden centrifuge. It's a great cylinder spinning to create artificial gravity similar to the inner drum of *Destiny*. It can't hover properly because of the centripetal vector induced by the rotation."

"What is this place? How did the mapper get here?" Ix asked.

The virtual version of Cadbic scratched its chin in the universal sign of perplexity. He proposed, "I don't think the lander crashed. I think the Tensakians captured it and brought it here -- wherever 'here' may be."

Fisby said, "I think providence has given us an extraordinary opportunity. Who knows how this mapper can transmit all that distance by itself, but somehow we have a window onto their world that we can trust."

Cadbic agreed, "Fisby, take care of this personally. Use all the techniques you use for stealth on Mother and stay hidden."

Merinat, who had also been at Mox's residence before the 'engine room' opening ceremony, added, "There's more. Steer the mapper down that row of trees."

Ix sent the command to move down the row and they waited in silence. After a while a jerky sequence of frames came back as the mapper moved up into the tree branches in stealth mode, and followed the row of trees. Soon it came upon a large camouflaged structure partially buried in the deck. The structure formed an enclosure protecting a large object of sorts. The mapper moved forward as it detected no heat signatures of live occupants. It slowly and cautiously floated into a gap in the structure and focused on the object.

Ix gasped in surprise. The object was a small spaceship that Ix recognized immediately. All those suspicions and worries that had been plaguing him the last few days came crashing down in single blow. There in front of them was the *Towa Maru*, the spacecraft piloted by Masamune Hughes in all the videos that came out of the Third Vault! And what was worse, Ix suspected it was probably the same vessel that functioned as a prop in the doctored videos supposedly sent by Sochiko.

Ix began to doubt even the authenticity of the Third Vault. How big was the hoax, and who had masterminded it?

CHAPTER 10

The *Soarer* was due to arrive back in Mother's orbit in only a week. Virginia thought, if the Tensakians were planning some attack, and were perpetrating a hoax to cover it up, then the timing of the *Soarer's* return ought to bring some big surprises. The Wardens, Technicians, and even the Inmates had mobilized in hopes of arming themselves against an unknown, technologically superior foe.

On the other hand, most of the excitement in the local neighborhood centered on the exploration of the great ship salvaged from Mother's Heart. Even though the equipment was cankered, ruined, corroded, and unworkable, the technicians were still making headway on understanding some of the basic subsystems.

Virginia and Josh were working together on deciphering data and patterns coming in from various observations, hoping to extract deeper meaning out of what was apparent on the surface.

She looked up at the virtual wall where various sketches, models, and data were grouped in huge hierarchical tree structures and relationship diagrams. Tracing one branch, she could understand the gigantic superconducting linear motors that drove the rotation of the huge artificial gravity centrifuge drum, and the counter-rotation mechanism that kept the entire ship from spinning. On another branch, the various automated lines for moving small packages and supplies from place to place within the ship was described.

Virginia sighed. The big ship had passenger cabins, but the major purpose appeared to be for cargo. She could reverse engineer the major life-support elements, but the propulsion system still eluded her.

"So far, all we can tell is that there were two systems -- one for local space that must have used a nuclear energy source, and another unknown system for long distances." Virginia explained to everyone online.

Merinat, floating across the room asked, "Can't you tell what sort of fuel the long-distance system used?"

Virginia replied, "No, something is missing. There are three empty cavities near the stern where some large equipment used to be. It's almost as if they jettisoned the equipment before even reaching orbit around Mother."

Virginia used the latest three-dimensional model of the ship to show where the cavities were located. The model floated in mid-air in front of her in the Database, and on monitors for all those folks online.

The discussion began to center around the possibility of developing a nuclear propulsion prototype inspired by the corroded remains found on the ship, and specifications found a few generations earlier in Vault Two. A nuclear system would already cut down the time to get to Minato by a significant amount, even if they couldn't figure out the main propulsion system yet.

Suddenly, a familiar voice came online. "The Professor returned to normal." Josh said.

There was silence on the line. Everyone knew there would be a profound interpretation of a current dilemma.

Virginia waited a bit, then began to encourage the details out, "You mean he was not normal?"

Josh replied, "He was small."

"Do you mean he was physically small?"

"Yes, he was a tiny size."

Virginia paused as she thought about how to proceed. She continued, "Josh, tell us about what happened. How did The Professor get small?"

And so, Josh began his fascinating story, "They found a technological artifact and wanted to see how it worked. It was a kinematic engine. But they didn't know how to take it apart."

"So how did the Professor get small?" Virginia coaxed.

Josh explained, "The grad students made a matter expander so they could enlarge the artifact and see how it works. If you turn the knob to the left, it gets big, but if you turn it to the right, it gets small again. Righty tighty lefty loosey."

"So, what happened, Josh?"

"The Professor was washing his hands and his ring fell down the drain. He looked around, but the grad students were discussing about the artifact. He thought about getting a wrench to take the pipe apart, but then he saw the matter expander."

Josh paused as if to let the idea sink in, then continued, "The expander was a coffin-shaped frame sitting on the counter next to the sink. It created fields that changed the distance between the electrons and the nucleus. So, the Professor made sure no one was looking, got up on the counter, and sat on the pad under the frame. Then instead of turning the knob to the left, he turned it to the right to 1:100 scale and laid down in the frame.

"Soon he began shrinking until he was only about seventeen millimeters tall. The first thing he noticed was all the colors looked funny, since the size of his eyes matched up with certain wavelengths that shifted along the spectrum. He took a breath, and didn't seem to have any trouble with larger air molecules but had to breathe more often to get enough. Then he stood up and took his first step. Just setting his foot down catapulted him up in the air about a hundred millimeters, and he landed on his side -- his muscles were still configured to propel a hundred-and-seventy-centimeter body and he forgot. Carefully he began walking across the pad, which was made of machined aluminum. Each step left a little dent in the aluminum that he hoped the grad students wouldn't notice. When he got to the edge of the pad and looked toward the sink. The pad was about twenty millimeters thick, so he easily hopped down onto the stainless-steel countertop. Unfortunately, eighty kilograms of weight sitting on two small points left even bigger dents, even though it was metal.

"The Professor carefully walked over to the sink, leaving little dent footprints along the way. When he got to the sink, he slipped over the edge and slid down the curved slope, landing near the drain. Fortunately, the sink was strong enough to take the tremendous point loads of his tiny feet. He stood at the edge of the drain hole and looked in. He refrained from spitting or peeing down the hole, because he knew he would have to jump down there. And he did.

"Unfortunately, there was water in the trap, and his tiny arms did not have enough surface area to tread water and keep his eighty kilograms above the surface. Also, his body density had changed -- the volume of water his tiny body displaced was not even a gram, so there was no way he could ever gain buoyancy from swimming.

"Fortunately, as he sunk to the bottom of the water in the trap, his full weight hit the curve of the pipe and it failed. The water, the ring, and The Professor crashed through the bottom curve of the trap and fell the distance to the wooden shelf under the sink.

"Unfortunately, the point load of The Professor's tiny body crunched through the wooden shelf and made a hole, and the Professor ended up chipping the concrete underneath, right smack in the middle of a family of mice. The crash made a huge racket, but again his small ears were sized to different wavelengths than he was used to so it sounded a little strange. He looked up and could only see light coming down the drain, through the broken pipe and hole in the wood he had made, but he had lost the ring somewhere up on the shelf. So, he jumped up the hundred millimeters or so back up through the hole to see what he could see.

"The first time he jumped up, he couldn't see the ring, and crashed back down to chip more concrete. So, he jumped again. Over and over, he jumped up and down, each time turning himself slightly to see a different angle, crashing more of the wood, and chipping more concrete. Finally, he found the ring, jumped over toward it, and grabbed hold as he crashed through the last time.

"Just then the grad students opened up the cabinet and saw the wrecked pipe and shelf and looked at each other with puzzled expressions.

"The Professor, holding a ring that was bigger than he was, crashed through the wooden baseboard of the cabinet and rushed out to the middle of the floor, chipping concrete at every step. The grad students, thinking he was a bug, stomped about trying to get him. One of the students was a good shot, and slammed his foot right on top of him. The Professor braced for the impact, but his body was so dense that the force of the single kick distributed over his entire seventeen-millimeter length and barely smarted. The student on the other hand, wearing thin sneakers felt like he had stomped on a sharp protruding bolt and let out a yell.

"The Professor looked around for a place to hide and saw the artifact on a small tray on the floor. It was about twenty centimeters long, and big enough to hide under. He escaped under the artifact but had to drop the ring in the process. The grad students picked up the ring while the Professor looked out from underneath."

Josh paused again. Virginia noticed that the Warden crowds had begun to gather again. Young fans were eagerly listening to what he had to say, and many of them were speculating about the ultimate meaning.

Josh continued, "The Professor, hiding under the artifact, looked up at the engine and saw all sorts of holes that were big enough for him to peer inside and even enter. He remembered that he had the same mass and weight, but higher density, so he carefully explored the inside of the engine and learned how it worked, without destroying delicate parts.

"Suddenly, the artifact shook as the students tried to pick it up. The students were surprised that the small item had somehow gained eighty kilograms. Several of them got together and lifted the engine and set it onto the pad inside the matter expander frame with the Professor still inside.

"The Professor quickly climbed back out of the hole and ran out onto the pad. He looked over onto the counter and saw his ring sitting there. He ran over to grab the ring, then rushed back to the pad waving his arms and trying to make noise.

"The grad students suddenly saw him and realized what had happened. They removed the artifact from the pad and had the Professor lie down in the middle. Just as they adjusted the knob to expand a hundred times, one of the students pulled the ring out of the enclosure, and the Professor was returned to normal."

As was always the case, Josh's Warden fan base went wild. The story wasn't near as comical as the previous ones, but for the next few weeks Wardens of all sorts of scales could be found all over the Database. Microscopic and miniature young people flooded the crystal city. There were even a few cases of giants walking around, and once a huge monster trod through the major avenues.

Virginia was quick to get an interpretation, and got everyone online a few days later, just hours away from the scheduled return of the *Soarer*.

"As you know, every small detail of the story has symbolic meaning." she said.

Merinat guessed, "I suppose he has figured out how to reverse engineer the main propulsion system?"

Virginia shook her virtual head, "Not directly. Even though the subject matter was trying to see how an engine works, the actual reverse engineering of the system was not something he could symbolize. Instead, he has told us how to get into the ship."

"Get into the ship! We already know that." Merinat complained.

Virginia continued, "We know how to get into the ship, yes. Just like The Professor knew his weight and mass before he started on his adventure. So how much did he weigh after he shrunk?"

Cadbic and several others answered at the same time, "The same as before. Only the density changed."

"Yes, before starting out, the Professor thought becoming small would give him advantages over being large, but most of the disadvantages remained, and were actually multiplied." Virginia looked around at the faces gathered in the Database conference room.

"First there was a personal problem that needed solving. The issue didn't have anything to do with the more important challenge of learning how the motor works. The Professor had lost his ring down the drain, and there was a danger that he never would see it again. He was frantic to figure out how to solve the problem, and resorted to dramatic means in spite of the fact that simpler tools existed to solve the problem. But taking the risky route resulted in a solution for the more important challenge."

Cadbic asked, "So what does the ring stand for?"

"The ring stands for a problem Josh had to solve first before he got to the real problem. And at some point, he has to pass it on to us to solve. Recall that the ring had to be snatched away from the matter expander before it grew to be a problem a hundred-fold bigger."

Ix was online too, and asked, "*What about when the grad students tried to stomp him out?*"

Virginia smiled, "There will be a time when we don't recognize Josh's efforts, and will try to stop him."

"Okay, so what exactly did Josh solve this time?" asked Merinat, "What did you mean about knowing how to get into the ship?"

Virginia looked at each of the officers sitting virtually in the conference room. "The Professor's mass was the same before and after being shrunk. The *Axiom* that Those Who Went Before scuttled is an identical twin to the big ship orbiting Minato!"

CHAPTER 11

Ix, Mox, and Blujic were together again at the space institute, studying videos and trying to put some pieces of the puzzle together. The new revelation that the large ship orbiting Minato was the same type as the great ship from Mother's Heart put a new light on things. First of all, Ix again wondered if the videos received from Sochiko were real, or cleverly crafted fakes.

"Play that part back." Ix indicated to Blujic, who had the controls.

The scene taken by the fated probe showing a massive hull from the propulsion end still didn't seem to match what they knew the *Axiom* looked like, but it was close. The big ship in orbit appeared to be the same except for some additional massive modules attached around the perimeter of the stern.

"If we follow the line of reasoning that these images were fabricated, then we have to assume someone had seen the sunken ship early on." Mox pointed out.

Blujic fiddled with her respirator, "And that could be why there are slight differences."

Ix looked at her and asked, "What do you mean?"

She explained, "Well, how much detail did we have about the ship at first? We only had cloudy impressions of it, taken underwater with low visibility. If someone were to take all our early images and try to piece together a model of the ship, they would have had to fill in some gaps."

Ix was reminded of gray areas in the Database that had not been fully mapped -- the Wardens had the capability of filling in blank areas with fictional detail, and indeed often did so. But on accurate surveys they left gray patches so the observer knew which parts were real.

Ix said, "So what you're saying is someone among us may have supplied the Tensakians with the images, so they could fabricate fakes?"

Blujic retorted, "I'm only saying so in order to follow that line of logic. It's a disturbing possibility that may have repercussions in other areas. For example, did our folks ever even leave orbit? If someone is clever enough to fool us with video, when did it start? Did we actually sit down with Sochiko and watch any of her videos with her between missions? It could be that she has been satisfied that we watched her transmissions as she had sent them, when actually they could have been hijacked and gradually altered along the way, even on earlier missions."

Ix thought the idea incredulous. He let his skepticism show, "Let's not let conspiracies get out of hand. Someone would have caught something like that, even if it were as simple as Tuk going back to show the videos to his grandkids. There's a limit to where we can consider the start of the fakes, and I say it only could have been possible on this last mission. And most of that will be either verified or debunked tomorrow when the *Soarer* returns to Mother's orbit."

"*IF Soarer* returns to Mother's orbit." Mox quickly interjected.

Ix changed the tune a bit, "Okay, so what if the videos are all real? What assumptions can we make from that extreme?"

Mox objected, "The videos can't all be real, because that puts us into the position of having to explain Sochiko and her party appearing in ancient video from the Third Vault."

Blujic considered, "But even the imagery from the Third Vault might be a plant if we consider that the vault could have been tampered with before we found it."

Ix recalled how Mox and Blujic were with him on the survey mission where they had found the Third Vault floating among the flotsam and jetsam of one of the inland bays. Who knows how long it had been drifting out in the open.

He observed, "True, the Warden mappers could have found it many seasons before we even came across it. And the Wardens might be the only ones clever enough to craft fabricated video."

But Blujic stood her ground, "No, that can't be. Remember that the videos had depictions of your Technician ancestors, Those Who Went Before, well before we Wardens even knew your race existed. And how could Sochiko and her crew be in the videos when she wasn't even born?"

"*IF* that is Sochiko's crew and not a falsified scene." Ix corrected, "But for argument's sake, we can consider that some of the video might be real, such as the encounter of the probe with the big ship in orbit."

Blujic agreed, "Yes, I had the impression it was a military ship, still functioning on automatics after all these generations. But now we know it is just a cargo ship, so the defenses are probably self-protection from perceived collision threats. Do you suppose the burned-out craft tailing the big ship's orbit could have been pirates trying to attack it?"

Ix snapped off his respirator so his entire face glowed with curiosity, "Maybe. Josh has given us hints about how to find holes in the security shield, just by analyzing the sunken vessel from our ancestors. I think we should assume this even if we still entertain the idea of a fabricated version for caution's sake."

Blujic stated the obvious, "If we can indeed find a way past the big ship's defenses, we'll be able to study a working example of an interstellar engine!"

In the afternoon, Ix got in a rocker and called on Fisby to see if he had made any progress. The two went to a nearby conference room and routed all the image data to display on the walls.

"The time delay is a killer. We have to depend on the mapper's own automated stealth mode, and often it ditches passersby in priority over our navigation commands." Fisby began.

Ix asked, "Have you been able to widen your range yet?"

"Yes, I've explored much of area around the clearing, and have gone through the complex of camouflaged buildings. But the best observations so far have been hovering at the tops of the trees pointing cameras all around the curve. Look -- I've made it all the way to the rim."

Ix looked at the snowy, noise-filled imagery displayed from the latest downlink and could see the mapper was up in a tree next to a high wall. In spite of the poor quality of the data, the entire curve of the drum could be seen, and it was even possible to see over the wall to the beyond. The view was the most amazing thing he had ever beheld -- large numbers of shadowy shapes of what he presumed to be spacecraft, rotating wheels, and unidentifiable objects drifting in the distance. The more distant shapes lost their resolution and were hard to discern over the general noise and static in the images, but the scene fired Ix's imagination.

Fisby explained, "This agricultural wheel seems to be occupied by a group who does mainly farming. But they have some very interesting hardware hidden in those warehouses."

Ix nodded in agreement, "Sochiko has reported all along that there are probably two groups out there, one of which is extremely hostile and dangerous, while the other may be trying to combat the first group. It may be that these farmers know they need to hide anything valuable from the pirates."

Fisby affirmed, "The camouflaged buildings have trees on their roof. It would be impossible for anyone to see them from the air."

Ix mused, "But there's something that bothers me. Why would our mapper be in their vineyard, and why would the farmer-types have possession of Hughes' *Towa Maru*?"

Just then, the mapper's vision swept out over the vast void outside and spotted a large cloud of debris not too far away, migrating along some unknown vector, and Ix had an idea, "Did you say the mapper had trouble hovering and maneuvering in the centrifuge because the floor deck is constantly rotating?"

"Yes, the mapper gets confused because the ground is not a stationary gravity vector." Fisby explained.

"What about in orbit?" Ix asked.

Fisby smiled as he caught a glimmer of what Ix was thinking, "This is the same model we used to float around the inside of *Destiny*. Zero-g microgravity is no problem."

"Okay, I'm thinking we can take a look around a bit. See that cloud of debris? Maybe we can lose ourselves in there and hitch a ride!"

Fisby complied immediately. He aimed the targeting feature and requested the robot thruster out to the drifting trash heap.

"One more thing," Ix added, "Keep track of this pinwheel. We still haven't located the rest of the remains of the lander or our missing crew members."

Early the next morning both the Technician and Warden communities were in a state of high alert. Warden telescopes had detected two objects coming in where there should only have been one. The Technicians had fabricated dozens of explosive missiles, but couldn't prepare as many as they had hoped due to resource limitations and the time they took for manufacture. Another worry was missile accuracy -- three out of five of the weapons tended to curve off course.

The citizens had all armed themselves as well. The Wardens had all their remotes out in force, with a sizeable group defending the central buildings in the Flesh, and the Technicians had hand-held electrical prods similar to the tools divers used to chase off corpuscles. Some of the Technician families had purchased bows and arrows from the Inmate families, even though the weapons likely would not stand up to space-faring hostiles.

Ix, Mox, and Blujic waited at the space center as the two craft approached, accompanied virtually by Merinat, Cadbic, and Danid who had come to see Sochi. They were frantically communicating with Sochiko to discover the nature of the threat.

"But Unk, we don't see any other craft!" Sochiko argued.

Ix and Mox looked at each other. Was Sochi's voice being synthesized somehow to try to cover an attack? Fortunately, there was hardly any time lag, meaning the transmission was from nearby.

"We see it plainly on the telescopes. The Technician network has just picked it up too."

Sochiko paused, apparently to check her instruments, *"All of our scans show nothing!"*

Ix suggested, "Sochi, send out a pulse or something, both radio and on visual frequencies so we can see if there is a difference between the two."

The incoming stream of images promptly showed one of the points of light pulse in a quick pattern. However, the second object pulsed soon thereafter in the exact pattern. Could it be some sort of echo or artifact in the system? Or was there a hostile trying to imitate the *Soarer*?

Ix was about to tell the Technicians to zero in on the second craft, when suddenly the pulse pattern began again on both vessels in reverse order.

Ix and Mox looked at each other again with puzzled expressions.

"Unk, we initiated a pulse pattern. Did you pick it up?"

Ix answered, "Yes, we saw the pattern both times, but the other vessel also pulsed."

Sochiko's voice came on, alarmed, "*That can't be; we only pulsed once!*"

Ix was shocked. Both Mox and Blujic also showed their surprise.

Cadbic's voice came on the line, "*The vessels are maneuvering into orbit. We have indications that Soarer has initiated a burn.*"

A chatter came on the line as commands were issued through various channels for defense teams to get ready. Cadbic gave a series of updates as the ships followed each other into the same orbit.

"*Sochi, the unknown vessel is either behind or ahead of you. We show the position should be above the horizon -- can you see it?*" Merinat asked.

"*No, nothing. We can't detect anything in either direction.*"

The three Technicians squirmed uncomfortably. Ix verified that the telescopes were providing two profiles that each matched the *Soarer*. The vessels followed each other across the sky. Suddenly one of the ships moved out of line and began to sink toward the planet. Alerts could be heard online in the background as various departments mobilized their personnel for a possible invasion.

The unknown vessel began to do some strange maneuvers that did not seem possible. Rather than move smoothly into transfer orbits to change altitude, the craft would suddenly do right turns at tremendous speeds and completely change directions, throwing off all telescope and weapons locks.

Ix ran the calculations and shook his head -- the amount of forces in each of the turns must have exceeded thousands of gravities, much higher than any known material could withstand. And yet the vessel continued to come.

The unknown object passed over the top of the Warden continent, and abruptly dove into the Plasma ocean just off shore, disappearing from all their instruments. Ix knew that any normal structure would have shattered by the impact.

He contacted one of the admirals immediately, "We need to send some crews to the location and find possible wreckage."

The admiral answered, "*We have two pods in the area already. They're heading toward the point of impact now.*"

"Have the crews also check for tsunami or other signs of disturbance." Ix cautioned.

Ix also checked the deep radar readings to see if anything had come in yet. Traces of a hard object could be seen in some of the readings, but the noise in the data was too great to pick anything out -- variations in density of the Mineral Strata left too many ghosts.

For the next few hours, the entire population of Mother was in confusion. Reports of sightings came in by the dozen as the panicked citizenry, meaning well, accused their neighbors and described all sorts of imaginary suspicious phenomena.

The Database was even worse. Concerned young Wardens would invent some kind of protective armor to wear, and would go about reporting each other as they were shocked by each other's appearance. Many of them were still confused about the difference between what they could see in the Database and the reality of the Flesh.

The various official agencies and personnel soon were overwhelmed as they checked out countless reports, only to find legitimate persons and occurrences.

In the midst of all this, Sochiko and her three fellow space travelers were still trying to get home. Ix, Merinat, and Cadbic had to leave a lot of the search for invaders to the local agencies, and turn all their attention to tracking and recovery of the *Bird* re-entry vehicle.

Ix, Mox, Blujic, and a dozen others finally let out a sigh of relief when Sochiko, Faddard, Stox, and Prech walked through the hatch of the recovery submarine safe and sound. The crew was quite haggard and very excited to be back home. Ix hadn't been sure up to the last minute whether they would be seeing her or some imposters. He was so overjoyed that he forgot all about the situation with invaders -- for a time.

The crew went their separate ways with the intention of getting back together in a few days for debriefing. As they walked through *The Island*, they overheard excited chatter among citizenry regarding the latest sightings -- it was a madhouse but Ix was too caught up in jovial company to take much notice. Ix followed Mox, Blujic, and Sochiko back to their apartment and the four of them celebrated late into the night.

The next morning Sochiko stepped out to go meet with some friends. Ix had stayed in their living room since his wife was away commanding a Pod crew anyway. He and Mox were going to head over to the space institute again to see if there had been any new developments.

"Future, don't forget tonight we're having dinner with Sochi and her friends." Blujic called out as they headed down the corridor.

Blujic often used 'Future' as a name, which was the temporary moniker Mox had chosen for himself when he had first gotten his amnesia many seasons ago. Ix was looking forward to the evening's dinner, because they would finally have the chance to show Sochi the fabricated videos and get her reaction to them.

The twins caught the shuttle pod across the bay and as soon as they stepped out of the hatch a messenger was there to meet them.

"Ix, there has been some strange activity around the ship. Please come down and take a look."

Ix and Mox eyed each other and rushed toward the dock at the research facility for interstellar propulsion, following the messenger. They stepped into the mapping room built over the top of one of the massive pontoons, where the majority of the interface with Warden mapper crew and computer modeling was coordinated. The messenger, whose name was Dal, directed them to gather around a monitor. As soon as they were settled in, Dal began to show them security images taken earlier.

The submerged massive hull of the ship could be seen extending deep below the Plasma on the left, with shadowy outlines of the pontoons and other structures and sub-Plasma equipment visible around the edges. Ghostly vestiges of passing objects could be seen burned into the images, as if something passed at tremendous speeds.

"Take a look at this Ix, what do you suppose these marks are?" Dal asked.

Mox studied the frames for a while then observed, "It looks like multiple streaks interacting with each other. See how they swing wide from each other, then come close? This sparking pattern occurs at the closest point."

Ix concurred, "Yes, almost as if there were a battle between two extremely fast unknowns."

The three studied frame after frame taken from security cameras at various locations around the ship and found the same pattern again and again.

"This set of traces has a particular signature," Ix concluded after studying the images for over an hour, "it makes its path toward the ship, and suddenly another one comes out and blocks its way. I think we have more than one visitor."

It was late in the afternoon by the time they made the realization that the 'invasion' was purely digital. Reports back from the pods investigating the point of impact showed negative on tsunami or physical traces. The Technicians went back and compared the incoming data from the telescopes and found some alteration had taken place by the time it got to their screens. The processing was systematic -- an entity in the Database had registered itself inside, and pushed outward to impress itself onto the physical sensor data streams.

At first the Technicians were relieved because there was no physical threat. But when some of the Warden automatons began attacking Technician hardware, they began to suspect the enemy was real and had succeeded in hijacking the piloting of the robots. Wardens frantically sent out their agents in the Database to track down an increasing number of stolen workstations infected by a virus that handed control over to an unknown master. The situation was even worse when some of the newer steer-by-wire pods began to plot their own courses.

"Take a look at the pattern of occurrences. Everything is centered on the great ship. It's like dueling -- whenever one virus sets a machine on a course toward the ship, another one comes out and counters it." Mox observed, with Merinat and Cadbic online with President Andak, Tapital, and several other Technician and Warden officers.

"*Have we traced the source of the virus -- do we know how it is spreading?*" Chief Warden Hasnac asked.

Cadbic, who had been in security before switching over to the space institute said, "*No, but we think there is a perpetrator within the Database.*"

"Who or what is fighting the aggressor?" questioned President Andak.

"*We don't know that yet either, sir.*"

Ix was listening to the conversation, and contributing where he could. However, since he had no background in security all he could do was answer questions related to the 'invader' that had 'followed' the *Soarer* in. An incoming call indicator kept lighting up on his communicator set, but he continued to brush it off, annoyed that someone would call at an important time like this.

Mox, who had been on the President's errand ever since the *Soarer* had reached orbit said, "We have reason to believe that the aggressors are tapping in from the outside."

"*But someone on the inside is moving around as well --*" Cadbic explained, "*we are close to tracing the original invader.*"

Ix noted that the insistent caller was still at it again. He ignored the com set and listened to a poor theory being put forth by one of the Warden security people.

Just then Danid, who was working with the Wardens, caught his eye. She leaned over to him and whispered, "Ix, Faddard and Stox have suddenly gone missing. They can't find them anywhere."

Ix shrugged it off, "I'm sure they're out with their friends."

Danid, with a worried look replied, "They both have missed several appointments with their friends."

"Are any of the girls missing too?" Ix winked.

Danid, frustrated, sat back in her chair and pouted.

Tapital spoke up, and Ix diverted his attention to the salvage lord's interesting news, "We've just discovered there may have been artifacts built into more of our data. It has concerned me that the Tensakians could land on Mother and terrorize us, so I had a full investigation made into the underwater outpost invasion incident that happened way back at the beginning."

Ix looked around, and the whole room was gripped by Tapital's discussion. The com set light was still blinking, but Ix hardly noticed.

Tapital continued, "It seems as though there was indeed an unfortunate incident at the outpost. The crew had spotted something, and reported an approach by an unknown vessel. Soon after that all communications stopped. The crews we sent out apparently broadcast back this video that you have all seen."

Tapital pointed and portions of the video showing the circular holes in the hull and the grisly discovery of the raided outpost played on a screen.

"After the investigating pod crews returned, no one thought to show them their own video as transmitted, so some very peculiar details went unnoticed until recently.

"During our subsequent investigation, we sent another crew out to retrieve the raw data from the security cameras. Watch these two images side by side."

On the screen, the left image showed a shadowy streak of an unknown craft approaching at very high speeds. The right image showed similar features in the environment, but the streaks were missing.

Two videos began to play side by side. Ix recognized the left video as the one where the diving team approached the spherical outpost hull and highlighted the telltale round hole where the Tensakians had supposedly invaded. But on the right, the later crew had videoed the same scene from a similar perspective, and a more ragged hole was visible, with edges turned out as if something had exploded from the inside.

Tapital continued, "We called in the original crew to try and find out what the discrepancy was. None of the original investigators recalled seeing the round hole on the left, but were surprised the true ragged hole didn't show. Furthermore, after investigating the cause of the explosion, we are now confident it was due to an explosion of an oxygen tank, caused by a software error!"

Everyone in the room gasped. There had been no physical attack on the outpost. Instead, the enemy had apparently been testing the ability to tap into the Technician and Warden networks from that early stage, and caused an explosion using the Technicians' own equipment. Ix was not really surprised, since he and Mox had been stumbling on the other fabricated video streams. Were any of the pirate attacks real? Did the space crews really see those circles in *Destiny's* hull? He watched as one of Tapital's advisors came up and whispered something into the salvage lord's ear. Tapital listened in earnest, and his eyes got wide. When the assistant sat down again, the lord got everyone's attention again.

"Everyone, I've just been informed of some alarming news. Prech and Tuk, who participated in previous space missions, have gone missing. Our investigators tried to locate them today to ask them about any discrepancy between the videos we received and the scenes they witnessed, but their families have reported them missing since yesterday!"

Alarmed, Ix looked over to where Danid had been sitting, but she wasn't there.

Tapital added, "In fact, we can't find any of the crews that supposedly saw the physical evidence of the pirates, even since the exploration of *Destiny*!"

The whole world sank in on Ix. Sochiko was also on those crews! He looked down at the desk and saw the light flashing again. He went to pick it up but knew already what it was about.

Blujic came online in an exasperated voice, "*Ix, I've been trying to get you or Mox all afternoon. Sochiko is missing!*"

CHAPTER 12

Compact patterns of code crunched out a series of shelled objects impervious to penetration. The objects assembled into a virtual fighting machine that moved aggressively forward out of the obscure background with blinding speeds. Kret was almost taken by surprise again, but managed to confront the enemy with a well-aimed counter virus that matched both the speed and intensity of the attacker. So far, his guards held out, and the enemy had not been able to approach him. Kret watched as the enemy machine dissolved and dissipated into a useless cloud of hardened digital components.

Kret smiled and considered how difficult it had been to crack the networks of the water world. The Farmers could have laid low and no one would have been the wiser. But the Tensakians had gotten there first, and he intended to cause as much trouble as he could. Three other Farmers had joined him in full immersion and they all had their hands full. They roamed the countryside blasting trees and glass towers to smithereens as the enemy attacked again and again in ruthless fury.

The Farmers knew it, and the Tensakians knew it -- the prize was the great sunken ship and all the data describing its weaknesses. It was the key to commandeering the intact interstellar in orbit above Everwebber! Once inside the water planet's database, all one needed to do was to approach and enter the ship and her secrets would be obvious. And Kret was determined to keep the Tensakians away.

Kret dipped below the surface and made a lightning loop around the virtual ship. In three spots enemy fighters appeared out of nowhere and relentlessly engaged his agents. From the perspective of the natives, it must have appeared as though streaks of lightning clashed and tangled.

Turning a corner, Kret came across a submarine. He quickly dashed over and began probing the machine, looking for a way in. The propulsion and steering systems were straight forward, so he commandeered the craft and set himself up to override the navigational commands given by the live crew.

Just then an enemy agent streaked through the deep and attached itself to the hull of the submarine. Kret steered the craft in circles and tried to shake the other off. The two fought and struggled, alternately gaining command of the helm and causing it to go every which way. Once Kret succeeded in throwing the other off, but the controls were so vulnerable the enemy jumped right back on.

It soon became apparent that the fight for the submarine would remain at a draw. Kret got his agents working on it and moved on to his next target. He streaked through the liquid and passed Davo on the way. The two paused quickly for a quick exchange.

The water people went into great care about the appearance of their avatars. But Davo was down and dirty, simple and effective. His avatar was just a collection of sinister-looking ambulatory mechanisms with a variety of tools attached. Kret raised one of his own virtual arms and saw a high-performance claw with integral snips -- he probably looked just as formidable.

"I just spent time setting up agents around the ship. What's the progress in the image manipulation department?" Kret quickly asked.

"The Tensakians have never been so relentless. It will be hard to keep a clean edit for long. And the water people suspect manipulation." Davo answered.

Suddenly a sphere zoomed in and parked itself between the two avatars. Before Kret could take action, the sphere exploded and shattered all his senses.

Kret woke up in the real universe, blinking his eyes, connected to dead immersive equipment. At first, he forgot where he was because his immersion had been so long and so real. Kret thought perplexedly, *what the hell happened?* Next to him on the floor, Davo was also stirring and began to moan. He was all wrapped up in a nest of wires that had been part of the hack workstation.

"What was that?" Davo asked, rubbing his forehead.

"I have no idea. I've never seen anything like it before." Kret answered.

He looked up and saw the other two Farmers still immersed and engaged in battle -- they were twitching involuntarily while their nerves received stimulation from the activity that was at the same time being dampened so their real limbs didn't flail about. Suddenly one of the men exclaimed and fell backwards as his arms and legs flew about wildly. It was as if some invisible force had knocked him off his seat. Kret and Davo watched as Torga writhed in pain for a few moments.

As soon as the initial shock wore off, Kret got angry. He swore to himself that he would break back in, and completely destroy those cursed Tensakians completely out of the network.

Davo and Torga got themselves a meal, and took care of bodily needs long deprived of them in the virtual environment. They reconnected themselves and immediately went through the long, drawn-out process of extracting the multiple rotating ciphers along a gauntlet of security features employed by the water planet's network.

Kret didn't move back in immediately. He began analyzing the series of events recently recorded of their mishap, and tried to reverse engineer the nature of the weapon. Over and over again he immersed himself and replayed the sequence up until just before the painful moment of personal shock and disconnect. The sphere streaked into place so fast that even the fine resolution of the analog step imager caught only a fine ghost of a motion blur in just the last millisecond. Kret tried to trace its direction of approach but discovered that it had spiraled in at the last instant -- a perfect stealth weapon.

Kret tried to analyze the sphere from its code content. He was able to extract arrays representing position and orientation matrices of simulated water particles, and the dense set of numbers that were the boundaries of the avatar geometry. He also discovered that the sphere had two morphologies -- an initial seamless shell that suddenly decomposed releasing millions of smaller viruses in all directions. But the viruses were impenetrable until the instant of impact, and anything remotely in the position to capture a glimpse of the code within was already exposed to its maliciousness.

Kret puzzled over this, as he watched in slow motion the little modules disintegrate Davo's avatar arms and limbs. Suddenly he realized -- the virus ate through the avatars but left native simulated particles unscathed. Somehow the weapon was able to differentiate whether an object was native or was being remote-controlled from the outside.

He had no idea how to reproduce the weapon, or how to stop it. But knowing that it targeted outside agents made all the difference for prevention.

Feeling confident, Kret once again lined up with his colleagues and hooked up. Instead of breaking into the water world network right away, he immersed himself in the *Blister* community and found himself floating virtually above the very spot his body sat. He caused his mind to soar out of the wheel and into the empty void between drifting relics. As he surveyed the various rotating gardens, he noted that they were all sewn up tight with sophisticated encryption protocols that even his team couldn't crack. Unfortunately, the Tensakian nest was even more impenetrable. But today he was heading for the Free Market.

Kret pushed his mind to cross the great void in haste, and searched for the gigantic airlocks along one of *Blister*'s massive walls. There were four clusters of eighteen airlocks each, lined up in cardinal points around the perimeter. Most of the locks were non-functional and had long been converted into zero-g warehouses or garages by anyone who was strong enough to hold on to them. But two of the huge chambers were free by common consent, and were referred to as the Free Market.

Kret found the gigantic pressure doors and noticed the increase of activity. Even though he was there virtually, the Free Market was a crowded place in both worlds. For the most part, the immersed condition matched that of the real world. Kret saw how some of the inner airlock doors had been frozen open in various positions, their mechanisms cannibalized over the centuries. He smiled as he recalled his own participation taking apart the massive valves and pumps of one of the locks in order to repair another still in working order. The marks and scouring, including large dents and scars where pieces were cut away, were true to his memory of them in the real world.

At the ninth and tenth door all sorts of floating vendors and market goers drifted about in every which orientation. Customers and traders poured in and out of the locks, which were rigged as three-dimensional street fairs. The Free Market was the nexus of trade and center of merchant activity. Numerous avatars hawked wares that could be inspected before actually going there, and deals could be made using the strictest crypto-security.

The market had its vile side -- in one quarter numerous young women and men were displaying themselves, and everyone knew what they were advertising. For an instant Kret thought he saw someone he recognized among the faces, perhaps the woman from the water world craft who had been sold into slavery, but when he looked again the face was gone and he had more important things to do anyway.

"Going my way Farmer?" one of the blindingly beautiful avatars asked.

"Not today sweetie." Kret brushed her off and continued inside, knowing the real thing was never as good-looking as the representative.

He moved forward past dens and bars where all sorts of vile liquids were consumed, and strange mind-altering smoke could be had. The virtual versions were a bit awkward -- in real life it would have been much worse. After passing a game arcade and two weapons dealers, Kret floated into a narrow passage and slipped under a brightly lit sign.

A young black clad man sat behind a desk in a zero-g chair. Two women and another man lounged about connected to wired helmets. They were A-eyes getting enhancements.

The man in black stood up and walked on the wall. There was a fluidity to his movements that suggested great agility. Kret immediately sensed the capacity for lightning speed and reflexes in a capable opponent.

"Hi Kret, haven't seen you in a while. How can I help you?" the man greeted.

"Hi Stan. I'm looking for an A-eye to do an interesting job."

"Oh? You're always getting me into trouble. But never had a better time. What sort of skills do you need?" Stan asked.

"I need someone to go outside *Blister*." Kret explained.

"Okay, been there done that. You got a ship coming in?"

"No, this is outside the system." Kret calmly suggested.

Stan's eyes widened, "Did you find Mars! Is their network really as big as the legends say?"

Kret frowned, "No, Mars is hopeless. That gate has apparently been disabled. It would take several hundred years to get there through normal space."

"Come on Kret, I'm going insane. *Blister* is too small and I'm going island crazy. You know all the interesting stuff happens in the real world." Stan paused, then grabbed a glass vase sitting on the floor, "Watch this!"

He hurled the vase against the wall and it shattered in a million pieces. The physics-based subroutines caused the shards to bounce off the walls just as if it had been in a real zero-g room, and a large portion of it sprayed the nearest A-eye.

"Hey watch it!" he called out from under his helmet.

Stan brushed it off, and winked at Kret, "Now watch this."

He waved his hands and suddenly all the particles began to come back together again. The shattering effect, like a video run in reverse, played the whole scene backward until the vase formed itself again and returned to Stan's hands, intact.

"You see, there's no entropy here. Cause and effect are simulated, and everyone knows if you get it wrong you can just recall the backup sequence and do it over again without consequences." Stan pouted.

"You wanna trade places?" Kret asked.

"I would in a heartbeat. You guys come in, enjoy all sorts of deadly games and dubious activities because there are no consequences. Do you realize what that does for those of us living here? Anything imaginable is possible but it's so antiseptic and sterile. There's nothing to overcome. There's no challenge. There's no danger. There's no necessity!"

Kret thought that sounded like paradise. "Well, you know what can happen in somebody else's database? You could get deleted!"

Stan smiled wide, and Kret knew he had a volunteer.

"What are you going to do about your little operation here?" Kret asked.

Stan nonchalantly put his hand on his hips, "Oh, I'll go alright. But part of me wants to stay."

Stan snapped his fingers and immediately cloned himself.

One of the copies turned to the other one, "Sorry to leave you like this, but it's your mess now."

The other one said, "Have a good trip, I'll be just as bored when you get back."

Kret, amused, floated out the door, and turned just briefly to watch one of the clones follow him. Instead of heading back to the wheel, Kret went to the nearest Free Market virtual network stall. There were plenty of them around, since there was a high demand for logons that couldn't be traced back to a physical location. Also, Stan was on hire and Kret didn't trust him enough to allow him to look over his shoulder while he worked through the crypto-maze to access the Farmer's stronghold. He did trust him to do the job as his onsite agent, because he planned to strand the A-eye on the other side, only allowing him back when he finished the job, and Stan hated the Tensakians just as much as Kret did.

At the terminal Kret logged on and worked his way gently through *Blister*'s network. *Blister* had an automated antenna system that picked up small broadcasts, amplified their signal, and bundled them up in a single powerful beam to Bridgestar. Bridgestar acted as a repeater, and took the signals through the various gates and sent them along. Incoming signals worked the same way such that any interstellar transmission would have several hours transmission time lag at the most as long as they had an operational gate between them -- signals simply propagated normally at the speed of light.

Kret and his colleagues had a clever way to beat the time lag using agents and compressed or expanded time, which was easy to do in a computational environment.

Once he opened up the pipeline, he and Stan flew through the interstellar corridor and appeared in the water planet network. For Kret, an agent was formed directly under his control that was smart enough to make quick decisions while his mind was out of synch with the rest of the universe. But Stan's entire data structure was moved to the new location as his subroutines were copied and deleted from the *Blister* network -- he went native.

They found themselves under the ocean in the guise of two multi-armed machines ready for war, probably not far from where Kret and Davo had been exiled out. Kret began showing Stan around, and describing their operation. As they approached the massive sunken wreck, they again encountered enemy fighters and Farmer agents doing battle. Kret joined in and showed Stan which tools worked the best -- except that he noticed the fighter subroutines were getting tougher, and it was clear that Stan would have to improve on the armory a bit.

They left the scene and Kret led the way to the forest at lightning speeds. Their presence attracted enemy viruses along the way so their progress had the appearance of a zigzag trail that sped from encounter to encounter. *It will be harder and harder to stay here*, Kret thought.

"I want to introduce you to someone." Kret said as they floated through the trees.

They came upon a virtual maze with walls of trees and shrubs. Kret taught Stan a series of codes that got them deeper and deeper into the maze, which shifted its walls as they passed. As they made their way through the maze Kret transformed his avatar into an attractive, well-dressed man, and Stan followed suit. Finally, they came to a large clearing that had a beautiful lake and small meadow. A cluster of people were milling about the meadow and looked up as Kret and Stan approached.

Two of the men in the group looked threatening and aggressively came at them. Kret calmly folded his arms and sat back in mid-air as the men aimed a barrage of questions at him.

"What's going on here?" one pressed.

"We demand to be released! How long do we have to stay?" the other one complained.

A woman floated over from the other end of the clearing and said, "Kret, is that you? What's happening?"

Kret got up and moved past the two exasperated men and addressed the woman, "Sochi, it's good to see you are alright. There's a terrible battle going on out there."

"Why do we have to stay here?" Sochiko asked.

"The Tensakians are after you -- all of you." Kret answered calmly.

"But why would they be after us? We demand to be released!" one of the men cut in.

Sochiko turned and calmed the man, "It's okay Tuk; I'll handle this."

Kret explained, "They are after the secrets of the sunken ship your people found. They've been manipulating video from your transmissions, and you are all witnesses that the video is incorrect."

Kret looked at the men, then said only to Sochi, "I need to talk to you, privately."

Sochiko nodded and started heading for the trees, but the two men intervened.

"I'll be alright. We're in the Database, remember? What could possibly go wrong?"

When they were far enough away, Kret looked at her for a few moments. She was quite beautiful, but avatars tended to overemphasize attractiveness -- Kret still didn't know what she really looked like.

"I've wanted to meet you for so long." Kret said finally.

Sochiko smiled, "Me too," but a feeling of doubt came over her face, "Can I really trust you?"

"Yes, have I ever done anything for you to think otherwise?"

Sochiko didn't say a thing, but just looked back at him.

Finally, she began, "Kret I have so many things I want to ask you about. I need to find out more about you, and about the Tensakians."

Kret put his hand up to her cheek and gently hushed her. Though the avatars were not real, his move had the desired effect -- Sochiko responded like a baby to its mother's touch.

"There will be plenty of time later. First there is a battle to be fought." Kret explained, and began to head back to the group with Sochi in tow.

Kret feared the new weapons that could ferret out externally controlled agents. Even though they were safe inside this sanctuary, the area outside was probably teeming with the enemy already, waiting to pounce as soon as he exited.

"I'd like to introduce Stan. He'll be checking back on you from time to time, even if I can't." Kret explained to the group.

The man Sochi referred to as Tuk was angry, as were several others, "You can't keep us here like this!"

Even Sochiko was concerned, "How much longer will it be? We'll be of greater help on the outside!"

"Don't worry it won't be much longer." Kret assured them.

Then he and Stan left the group and passed into the maze.

Kret turned to Stan and said, "Let some of them escape if they can. But don't allow Sochi to come to harm under any circumstance!"

They transformed themselves into fighting machines, and braced themselves for battle. Just as expected, a barrage of viruses and fighters came at them. Kret and Stan whirred and spun, slicing and stabbing at lighting speeds. The opposition crumbled one by one. The fighting went on and on, as more and more of the enemy appeared. But they were making progress -- the numbers got less and less.

Finally, the two of them surrounded three of the fighters who gathered together in a group, back-to-back. They were about to clean up the last few attackers when a sphere came out of nowhere and landed on the far side of Stan. Kret watched in slow motion as the shock wave tore through Stan, the three attackers, and finally reached him and the lights went out.

Kret found himself rolling on the floor in pain. Davo and the other two were standing over him, grinning.

"We thought you'd be joining us soon." Davo said.

"We can't get back in. We're shut out completely." Torga added.

"Damn!" Kret exclaimed, and pounded his fist on the floor. The action caused his head to throb even more and he winced in pain.

But Kret thought back and smiled. He recalled the explosion, and as the shock wave moved past Stan, he could still see the other, clear as day, untouched by the impact! His hunches were right -- they still had a man on the inside.

Yet Kret had a troubling thought. In his mind's eye he could see the two fighters, and he remembered the shock wave passing through leaving them intact also. They were not Tensakians!

CHAPTER 13

Everything and everyone was insane. Space operations officer Cadbic watched as haggard Wardens dragged back to their workstations in the Database after minimal breaks to eat or catch a little sleep. The whole citizenry was mobilized -- some crewed the fighters, while the vast majority, lacking in ability to react fast enough to engage the enemy directly, spent their time building stronger and stronger fortresses. The crystal city was in shambles.

Cadbic heard reports of pods going in circles in the real world, and of all sorts of Technician machines malfunctioning, in addition to Warden equipment. It wasn't just a problem confined to the Database -- no one was safe.

He doggedly stuck to his post, on the slim hope that one of his crew would find a clue to the madness. Arriving at the space mapper section, he saw the room in ruins, as walls and partitions fractalized into broken polygons and solids. But the workstations held.

A tired Fisby monitored the strange world of the Tensakians, and looked up as Cadbic floated over. The fatigue couldn't mask the enthusiasm on his face.

Fisby made eye contact, and motioned to the screens showing views from far away *Blister*, "Take a look at this! It's techno heaven."

The immersive screens of the workstation showed a hazy wall of wrecked spacecraft completely surrounding them, forming a gigantic cavity. It was dim with several bright points of light illuminating the twisted plates and metal shards making up the wall. On the far end was a gap in the barrier, through which a vessel was slowly entering from the vast bright space beyond.

"It's a garage for space ships," Fisby began, "One of the squabbling groups keeps this as their base. See? There are spotlight and weapon mounts here and here."

Cadbic saw the static-shrouded silhouettes of figures at each of the posts, and thin pencils of light sweeping back and forth.

Fisby continued, "These guys are well-organized. They even have uniforms."

"Can you tell who they are? What sort of activities do they engage in?" Cadbic inquired.

"I'm not sure. But they appear to be decent -- might be worth getting to know them."

Cadbic cautiously rubbed his virtual chin, "Well, keep the mapper under cover for now. What else have you found?"

Fisby switched off the live feed, and began to play back a series of previously recorded videos. Cadbic saw several battle scenes, where two clearly distinct groups engaged in chasing and scattering each other. In one scene the uniformed group prevailed, fighting among the huge rotating gardens. In another scene the uniformed figures were dispersed and scattered. It seemed as though not all the rotating wheels were farms. Several of them were crammed with buildings that were so numerous it was hard to distinguish one from another -- huge spinning metropolises with countless inhabitants moving about on their various business.

Cadbic asked, "Have you made an analysis of their weaponry?"

"Yes, they seem to use a lot of incendiary devices that create large balls of flame, but no real explosive power. They also have beamed weapons that are capable of killing a person from a distance. To me it looks as though everything is designed to have maximum kill power without harming any of the physical facilities." Fisby paused, and switched the video again, "Take a look at this."

The mapper appeared to be drifting among a cloud of debris. The nearby pieces of wreckage and junk were intriguing in their own right, and had they not been charged with a critical mission, Cadbic would be satisfied performing a close analysis of the discarded pieces. But more impressive than that, the vast interior of the mysterious *Blister* environment spread out beyond, with countless rotating gardens, floating islands of wreckage, and various sized vessels moving back and forth on their own errands. The massive wall that formed a boundary of the vast space could be seen as it curved out of the atmospheric haze and formed a barrier only what seemed like a kilometer away on the opposite screens of the workstation. The wall appeared to be constructed out of a complex web of structural members barely visible through the partially transparent surface. Sunlight was streaming in, presumably in a controlled manner to prevent too much trapped heat.

Cadbic also saw what looked like insects or wall-hugging vehicles, slowly moving across the surface.

"Those must be maintenance machines." he said.

Fisby concurred, "That's what I thought too."

As Cadbic surveyed the magnificent piece of engineering, he swept his gaze down along the massive barrier. At one point there were openings or portals in the wall, surrounded by increased activity.

"What's going on down there?" Cadbic asked.

"I don't know for sure, sir, but there appears to be a market of sorts." Fisby replied.

"Can you get down there and look around?"

Fisby rubbed his chin as if the task was a little too much, "Well, this video was taken a long time ago, as the mapper drifted along with the debris field. I can steer the machine to investigate, but there may be no convenient hiding spot -- we'd have to cross vast distances out in the open."

"I think it could be important. The traffic around here seems to come in all shapes and sizes so the mapper may blend in that way. Let's take the risk." Cadbic decided.

Suddenly in their own Database world a ghostly streak crashed through the wreckage of the workstation partition -- in lightning speed a pair of undefined somethings chased each other in fierce battle. Cadbic and Fisby ducked, but the strange troublemakers were already gone.

The two looked at each other and Fisby rolled his eyes, "It's been like that for the past few days."

An hour later Cadbic was sitting at his own workstation operating a mapper avatar, dodging virtual projectiles at the research center for interstellar propulsion. He could have visited the facility in the Database, but the avatar afforded him a big advantage -- it allowed those in the real world to interact with him.

As he hovered over the Plasma of the inland bay, the battle scenes in the Database overlay the imagery of the real world, giving it a chaotic effect. Streaks of passing objects maneuvering and accelerating at tremendous speeds appeared as ghostly trails, punctuated now and then by sparking explosions where they confronted each other. More than twice, he had to quickly steer his own avatar to miss projectiles and passing fighters, but his reaction time was so slow he wasn't doing as well as he would have liked. Once a wispy tendril circled around him several times and suddenly a horrible-looking multi-armed fighting machine slammed into him and tried to wrest the controls of the mapper away from him. But just as it was about to take over, another fighter came out of nowhere and rammed the first, knocking it away, and the two went off at high speeds tumbling, tossing, turning, and sparking each other with virtual blows. Cadbic continued on a little stunned, trying to keep from hyperventilating.

It was quite clear that the submerged *Axiom* was the center of the battle.

He made his way to the control shack on one of the pontoons above the *Axiom* where Ix and Merinat were waiting. Like Cadbic, Merinat was in a Database workstation controlling a sub-Plasma mapper. As Cadbic settled in beside Ix, who was actually standing there in the real world, he saw that the self-contained data drive was in place, ready to go.

Ix turned to Cadbic's avatar and asked him to rehearse what they needed to do, "*Cadbic, please explain how this will help.*"

Cadbic went through the security procedure, "This is how we back up very important stuff in the Database. Essentially, we make sure all the important data is isolated into the self-contained hard drive and then simply cut it off from the Database. No one will be able to access it because it will only exist here in this shack, in the Flesh."

Merinat jumped in, "*The ship is now completely enclosed by the black-out barrier.*"

Cadbic explained, "The barrier is a data wall that exists only in the Database. Once the enclosure is complete, we associate all objects inside the wall to the self-contained drive."

"*We're working on that right now.*" Merinat informed Cadbic.

Briefly, Cadbic switched over to see the view coming in from Merinat's mapper. In front of him the massive bulk of the *Axiom* stretched on into the gloomy waters, strangely overlaid with a gray wall. In real life there was no barrier, but in the Database the gray wall completely surrounded the ship.

"*It's done. All data has been isolated.*" Merinat reported.

"Okay Ix, cut the connection."

Ix pulled out the cable that connected the drive to the network. In the Database, the gray wall suddenly vanished. There was no trace of the ship at all.

"Guard that drive!" Cadbic stressed.

Ix looked somewhat perplexed. It all seemed too simple. *"But the ship is still there."*

Cadbic explained, "It's gone. We can't see it anymore."

As if to stress the fact, a pair of battling fighters zoomed right into the vacuum left by the ship, leaving traces of their lightning-swift passage.

Ix repeated, *"But the ship is still here. What if the mappers pass by again? The information would be restored."*

Cadbic thought for a moment, "True. There may be some exterior portions restored to the Database. But remember, we have instructed our mapper operators to stay away. And none of them are working now anyway. The key is the interior."

Abruptly, Merinat's mapper went wild and began to move swiftly toward the ship. It aimed for one of the open hatches and sped through the Plasma at top speed. Just as suddenly the avatar came to a stop, and slowly made its way back to where it had been originally.

"Sorry guys. One of those demons just took over for a bit. Had to fight it off." Merinat explained.

Ix looked out over the vast protected area under which the dark hull of the submerged vessel could be seen as a shadow below the surface, and said, *"We'll need to double our protection in the real world. They can still get in by commandeering our hardware."*

Just then a messenger in the Database rushed up and got Cadbic's attention, "Sir, two more have been found!"

Cadbic stood up, alarmed, "When?"

"Just now in the rocker port. Please come with me, sir."

"Two more what?" Ix asked.

Cadbic took leave of the others and quickly followed the messenger through the battleground back to the land of the Wardens. They proceeded to the rocker port and he went through the process of docking himself, and the painfully slow decoupling sequence that brought him down to the small locker room below deck. In the Flesh again, he quickly changed into street clothes and rushed outside. The messenger popped out into the hallway at the same time, and they walked up the corridor to where a crowd had gathered. Cadbic spotted some high-ranking faces among the group, including Chief Warden Hasnac.

He turned to his companion and asked, "Who is it?"

The man replied, "This time it is strange, both of them are Technicians."

"But don't Technicians usually logon from *The Island*?" Cadbic noted, puzzled.

"There's something else sir. Chief Warden Hasnac asked for you because you know them."

They caught up to the crowd and Hasnac saw him approach out of the corner of his eye. He turned to Cadbic and said, "Take a look inside. It's not a pretty sight."

Cadbic turned to where the Chief Warden indicated and saw a rocker door propped open. He poked his head inside and immediately his nose was assaulted by a rank odor -- it smelled as though the automated waste handling system for urine and feces disposal had been overloaded.

Cadbic immediately thought of Wardens who had in the past gone off the deep end and stayed in the Database too long -- their bodies begin to take sustenance from rocker coupling, and all their physical needs are burdened on the system. It was not uncommon that older folks and infirm individuals had simply passed away, spending their last living moments in an environment that didn't care about weak physical bodies. In fact, all the elderly he knew had gone that way.

Cadbic eased inside the small locker room and saw that the lift was down, leaving a gaping hole above. He almost dared not to look, knowing what he would see, and kept his eyes downward until he stood right underneath.

Slowly he looked up and was startled. A contorted face, eyes still open, hung upside down in the frame just handwidths above him. Suddenly he was weak and felt himself begin to buckle in the knees. He looked away again and held onto the lift frame, forcing himself to stay calm. Once again, he steeled himself to look into those lifeless eyes, and the impact of what he saw played out in his mind. He knew they had a problem -- the deceased was Prech, one of the missing space crew, a healthy young man with no reason to die.

Cadbic rushed back out to the waiting crowd and breathlessly inquired of the Chief Warden, "Who... Who is the other one?"

Hasnac frowned and bowed his head. Then he slowly looked up and answered, "It was Tuk! Poor Tuk -- looks like he was fighting for his life!"

Cadbic looked at the others in confusion. Merinat was there too, having just arrived, and was enraged. Cadbic backed up against the wall, and suddenly feeling exhausted slid down until he sat on the floor. The missing crewmembers were all there somewhere, in rockers, trapped in the Database. Something must have drawn them there and forced them into danger. They had to do something quick, or none of them would get out alive!

CHAPTER 14

Sochiko floated between two Database trees, not really aiming for any place in particular. She'd never been so bored in her life. Besides the meadow and small lake, a tight circle of trees was all there was. If she tried to get past the trees, the forest fooled her again and again and she always found herself eventually coming out onto the meadow back to where she had started. Once she flew into the sky, and got higher and higher. She got high enough to see the entire Warden landmass, and aimed out over the countryside. But when she chose a spot far away to set down, the Database forest fooled her again and she ended up descending on the same meadow, with her trapped colleagues.

Sochiko had already gone through the messy process of relieving herself in the virtual world, and it was not pleasant. She was reminded of emergency training for pressure suit operation, where they had to relieve themselves in diapers while working in a vacuum, and go through the process of clean up afterwards, all the while enduring the re-pressurization process in a simulated airlock. And mealtime in the Database was not very enjoyable either.

In her absentmindedness she suddenly stumbled upon Danid, who was entertaining herself forming small block-like structures. Since Danid had spent her life studying the virtual people, she had picked up a few skills from them.

"Hey that's interesting. Can you make anything more complex than that?" Sochi asked.

Danid looked up as if noticing Sochiko for the first time. "Bigger, but not more complex. I'm afraid it will keep you occupied for only a few hours."

Sochiko drifted down and started to give it a try herself.

"Have we heard anything from Tuk and Prech after they entered the lake?" Danid asked.

"No, nothing." Sochi replied.

It had been a whole day since the two men had dove into the lake to look for a way out. Sochiko was still hoping they had gotten away and could inform someone.

She still had mixed feelings about whether to trust Kret or not. On the one hand, every time the man showed up her heart began to flutter. She didn't know what came over her. She had never been in love before, so she couldn't tell whether this was some sort of infatuation, particularly since Kret came from another planet -- how amazing would that be?

And yet all her alarms were going off and telling her to stay away. Was it because she was shy? Was she always due to be the geek, destined to stumble and awkwardly step on potential partners' toes? Or was she fated to icily approach every relationship with cool engineering clarity, only to get flustered when something does not compute?

Danid showed Sochiko how to use hand movements that presumably got the subroutines in the background to produce visible geometry. "I can't do this any longer, Sochi. Even with all my experience, I've never been able to stay in the Database this long."

"Just hold out a little longer. I'm sure Tuk will come through for us."

As the two women occupied themselves with simple block structures, they noticed a stir out on the meadow --

Faddard and Stox could be seen with a third figure. It was Stan. Sochiko thought having reservations about Kret was a natural thing, probably experienced in every social situation where attraction of the sexes occurred. But her loathing of Stan was absolute -- she dreaded even looking at the man, and if it weren't for the fact that Kret had introduced him, she would have rebelled long ago.

Sochiko and Danid got up and floated over to see what was the matter. Faddard could be seen arguing with Stan, and the two of them could have been close to blows had they been in the real world.

"What do you mean we have to stay longer?" Faddard yelled.

Stan, in a lithe manner Sochiko associated with a ferocious animal, took a stance as though he was about to pounce. The two squared off with hate in their eyes.

Sochiko jumped in quick, "Cool it guys. What's up?"

Faddard, never turning his face away from the other snarled, "He says Tuk and Prech escaped but were killed by the Tensakians!"

Sochiko hadn't expected that. Her heart went up to her throat and she could barely choke out a "What!"

Stan kept his pose of a crouching animal and said, "Kret warned you to stay put. It's too dangerous out there!"

Faddard lunged at Stan and Sochiko was able to intervene at the last moment.

"You son of a... I'll bet you did it. You killed them!" Faddard spit out.

Stan hadn't flinched, but growled, "Why don't you give me a try, spaceman?"

Sochiko looked at them in confusion, "How could this happen? We're in the Database! How could anyone get killed in the Database?"

Stox joined in, "I'm sure they're not dead, they were just logged off somehow."

Sochiko barely noticed Danid backing away in despair.

She turned to Stan, "Tell us exactly what you know."

173

Stan explained, "The Tensakians have better technology than you have. Can you imagine what a well-aimed virus could do if it got into the harness system and life-support hookups in the rocker?"

Faddard was ready to tear Stan apart, "Why are we in here in the first place. We wouldn't be helpless in the rockers if we hadn't been drawn in."

They were all called into the Database under a variety of false pretenses -- answering an invitation from a friend, making an official inspection, doing a media appearance, etc. Soon after logon their hosts had disappeared right in the middle of a battle, and one of Kret's agents had plucked them out of danger and brought them here.

Stan countered, "It wasn't us who called you in. The Tensakians counterfeited someone you knew and got you into a vulnerable position."

The argument could have gone on but Stan took his leave again, having delivered his warning. Faddard was still fuming, and Stox wasn't too far behind him.

It wasn't an hour later when Sochiko realized Danid was missing. She could not be found in any of the spots in the Database they had access to. The three of them searched the entire meadow, forests, and even in the lake but none of the barriers were open to them.

They would have begun searching from a higher elevation, but they began to notice traces in the sky that they had not seen before. Streaks of ghostly white showed the passage of speeding objects just outside their ability to capture clearly.

Sochiko began to worry that the Tensakians had broken through, and the forest illusions faded away. Suddenly an army of Wardens descended down and surrounded the three.

"Sochiko! Are you alright?" Cadbic cried out.

Sochiko was in tears. She looked up and saw Merinat, Hasnac, and even Uncle Ix! She couldn't describe the feeling of comfort that came over her. They took the three back to the rocker port at the space institute where they had hot showers and a meal (the three of them had logged on from Technician rockers).

An hour later Sochiko sat with Ix, Stox, and Faddard, discussing the incident. Danid was there too, bundled up in a warm blanket.

"How did you get out?" Sochi asked Danid.

"I went through the lake like Tuk and Prech. As we were building the block structures, it dawned on me that the exit key might have been a form function, and any Warden could have figured it out right away." Danid explained.

Stox was shaking his head, "But you could have been killed!"

"I knew it was dangerous, and I didn't want any of you to get hurt."

Ix filled in his side, "After we isolated the ship data, the enemy seemed to disappear and the fighting dropped of significantly. Danid came wandering back and told us where you were, and how to get in."

The three crewmembers thanked Danid profusely -- she was the hero of the day.

"What happened to Stan?" Faddard asked. His cheek was flushed showing he was still apparently angry.

"I don't know who that is." Ix returned, "But such a character may have been fictional. There was a lot of illusion, apparently. We're starting to think that Josh may have been involved."

CHAPTER 15

The next evening Ix, Mox, Blujic, and Sochiko were gathered at Ix's place, relaxing after a day of recuperation. The day's weather had called for unusually high oxygen levels so everyone had their respirators in their laps. Ix's wife Holina and daughters Fukako and Enko were on one of their rare trips home together so they made a big party of it. The three women ran their own submarine pod in a three-person crew that Ix occasionally joined, when the space institute duties allowed.

Mox and Blujic, who had gotten heavily involved with the research of the *Axiom*, recounted some of the things they had found, and Ix had been discussing the recent attempt to steal the sunken ship data. Josh was isolated for the time being, and consented to stay under voluntary 'house arrest' at least until they got to the bottom of the events.

"It was Cadbic who suspected there might have been someone on the inside." Ix explained. "We still don't know if there were others involved or not."

Sochiko could not believe she had been the victim of a carefully orchestrated fraud, and the motive escaped her. "But how do you know it was Josh?" She asked.

Ix went through the steps. The Database recorded everything, so they could analyze each encounter in detail later on.

"We traced each encounter back to its origins and found Josh had been in the vicinity each time, moving from place to place almost instantaneously within the computational environment." he said.

"What about Kret? What about the Tensakians?" Sochi eyed her uncle with an incredulous look in her eyes.

"All illusion, apparently."

A disappointment clearly showed in her countenance. Ix couldn't tell if it was because she had been tricked, or something else -- a crush maybe?

Mox jumped in, "Now that we have you home safe, you can look at the fabricated video and tell us the difference from what you transmitted on your mission."

"First of all, just for the record, you DID visit *Destiny* and Minato, right?" Blujic came in from the side.

Sochiko looked at her mother with hands on her hips, "Mother! You sound like a doubting Tapital or something. Of course, I was there!"

Blujic added, "And you did meet those aliens?"

"Yes, of course -- why the interrogation?"

Mox began, "Take a look at these." and proceeded to play the two underwater outpost videos side by side. "Josh, or someone, has been tampering with our video streams in real time."

The sequence on the left showed the telltale circular hole indicating pirates had raided the outpost, but the right-hand image indicated a rough hole, apparently from an internal explosion.

Mox explained, "The one on the right is the correct video, corroborated by witnesses on the scene. However, the one on the left is, as you recall, what we received from the transmission. The explosion was apparently caused by a software malfunction -- something had invaded their system, found a weakness, and caused the failure."

Blujic added, "But Tensakians were never there physically. Some people in the space institute don't even think they exist. They think all the pirate broadcasts were a fabrication."

Ix mentioned a few other concerns, "Some people are saying that *Destiny* might not have had any holes either, or the Minato orbital."

"Some don't believe you even went at all." Blujic interjected.

Sochiko had a hurt look. But Blujic quickly reached out and held her hand and gave her a look that said, *but we believe you.*

"Well, she can tell us if the sequences we have are correct or not." Mox began to show the videos of the *Destiny* encounter.

Sochiko faithfully watched each of the clips with a smile on her face, nodding and laughing, frowning or shaking her head as she recalled the circumstances surrounding each shot. When the last clip finished, everyone sat back and looked at Sochi.

"That is exactly how I remember it. How did I ever get there? It's hard to imagine the four of us floating down those halls -- but we were actually there!" Sochiko reminisced.

Blujic carefully queried, "But what about the condition of the station. Is it accurate?"

"If you are referring to the evidence of the invaders, yes, we discovered the holes and found a ransacked station."

Mox put another video on -- it was the scene showing the approach to the massive ship orbiting Minato. They watched as the scene showed the burned-out wreckage of the smaller ship, and the aft end of the large vessel before ending with a flash.

Blujic noted, "We've discovered that the vessel at Mother's Heart may be almost identical to the ship in orbit around Minato. If we could figure out how to enter the Minato starship through study of the *Axiom* it might open up a road to the stars!"

Mox explained, "We based some hope on this sequence being real, and have studied the ship in detail. But we didn't know whether the video was genuine or doctored."

Sochiko smiled again, "Of course we weren't there physically, but this appears to be the same as the sequence we saw transmitted from the probe."

Ix and Blujic smiled at each other and began to engage in excited chatter about a possible mission to Minato to study the ship and mining facilities. Just then Holina, who had been busy working as chef (which she often did as a therapeutic activity on her time off), came out with a tray of snacks.

Holina said, "The next mission will have to be big, Ix. You won't get by with just a crew of eight you know."

Ix reached over and picked up one of the treats. "Well, the *Soarer* has only been back for not much more than a week, but she's modular, and we can strap on more drives and pressurized modules. Many of the pieces are already in orbit."

Mox was hanging back, and hadn't joined in the conversation. There was something on his mind troubling him. Ix had already attached more modules onto his imaginary enhanced *Soarer* and began verbally designing several new ones when Mox spoke up.

"Wait! We haven't resolved everything." he said.

The whole room went quiet, and Ix's design remained unfinished. Everyone looked at Mox as he put on another video. They watched the screen as images of Sochi and the others planeted on Minato's surface near the mining facility and began zooming in on various operations. The security robot moved up and set itself a respectable distance away. The scene showed the alien spacecraft *Towa Maru* land at the top of the hill and the two suited figures emerge.

Sochiko was smiling and nodding. When the sequence was over the whole room was looking at her with solemn expressions.

Sochiko looked at everyone in turn, and said, "I haven't been debriefed yet. We haven't had the chance to talk about what it means to have set foot on another planet!"

No one said anything, but continued to stare.

"Don't you see how astounding it was? We were there! We walked in the dust; our faceplates separated us from hard vacuum. We reached out and touched another world. And we met folks who had never set foot on Mother before!" Sochi continued.

But the others continued to stare.

"What? What's wrong?"

Mox, with an incredulous look on his face, asked, "Is this the video sequence you sent? Did you notice anything strange about it?"

Sochiko reacted to the stonewall put up by the others and began to be alarmed. "Yes, this is what we sent. What's happening?"

Mox calmly set the other video on the screen, the one supposedly taken from the Third Vault. They watched the whole scene from the perspective of the aliens, as Masamune Hughes faced a group of suited individuals with mining activities occurring in the background.

"That's Sachiko, Hughes' wife. Mother -- her name is almost identical to mine! We must be cousins or something..." Sochi began, but trailed off as she saw the shocked look on the others' faces.

"Sochiko, do you recognize this scene?" Blujic asked.

"Yes, of course. I was there!" Sochi replied.

Blujic shook her head. "No Sochi. you couldn't have been there. This video was taken from the Third Vault before you were born!"

Sochiko didn't know what to say. She stared at the others and couldn't believe what she was hearing. "No, that can't be. It can't be. I was there! I walked the corridors of the *Towa Maru*. I met Masamune, Sachiko, and the Toshiges and Kitamuras. This can't be from the Third Vault!"

A gloom descended on the group, as they realized they had only solved part of the funny business; the mystery was as deep as ever. Ix immediately thought of Josh, or whoever had doctored up the underwater outpost videos, but realized it couldn't have been. Even if Josh had been around and even if some rogue Warden group had planted the videos, and set up the Third Vault for 'accidental' discovery by the Wardens, it still did not explain how Sochiko could have been in the video or remembered it having happened.

Ix knew about an ancient principle called Occam's Razor, which required one to abandon all complex or unlikely explanations and embrace the simplest possible cause. If Occam were applied here, Ix hated to admit it but Sochiko must have been delusional. Either that or Mox's copy of the Third Vault video had been tampered with.

The next day Ix made a call to Virginia to see if she had found out anything.

"I tell you Ix, Josh is not capable of these things. He has gotten very good at juggling patterns, but he couldn't master the subtlety that such image processing would require." Virginia defended.

"Yes, but what about the virtual battles?" Ix countered.

"Well, that might be possible. But who was he fighting?"

"He wasn't fighting anyone as far as we can tell. Just showed up and made a ruckus." Ix explained.

Virginia seemed puzzled, "But I thought the fighting died down when the data about the ship was isolated. I can't understand the motive for going after the ship's data."

Ix was puzzled too. After talking with Virginia, he and Mox went to the university museum to try and locate a pure copy of the video. The university had multiple copies that could be checked out by interested persons. The twins watched every copy they could get their hands on, verifying the dates the copies were made -- most of the storage media and recording dates pre-dated the mission to Minato, and one or two versions had been made before Sochiko was even born. Each recording showed the exact same sequence that Mox's copy had.

Ix went as far as to look up who had checked out the copies all the way back to before the mission, and was surprised to discover some of them had not been touched at all.

In the late afternoon Ix hooked up to a rocker and visited the Warden main library, and watched their version as well. Neither Josh nor Virginia was on the list of patrons who had viewed the files.

The next day Ix was needed at the space institute, so the issue had to be put on hold. The Warden employees were all excused for the week because of all the damage they had suffered from the digital invasion. The Wardens were all busy repairing their city, or downloading backups of the various damaged buildings and facilities.

The preparations were being made to enlarge the *Soarer* for another mission to Minato, for a longer term. The mission would be to make a detailed study of the mining operation, explore Everwebber, and the greatest prize of all, attempt entry of the massive, intact orbital twin to the sunken *Axiom* anchored at the research facility for interstellar propulsion, using the knowledge they had gained from the wreck.

Parts of such a mission had been foreseen, so their plans for constructing modules and increasing the size of the *Soarer* had already been under way even before the ship returned.

Ix spent the next few days managing the engineering department and observing the manufacture of some of the components. Ix noted it was quite frustrating that every bit of raw material had to be extracted painfully from suspension in the Mineral Strata as powder feedstock, and it was apparent that the manufacturing lords and all their crews were motivated by the possibilities that unlimited resources could bring -- many civil projects went on hold or held lower priority to the space program. Ix was thankful for the turnaround, and was happy that even Tapital and other long-time opponents to the space program had caught a vision and were now their greatest supporters.

Ix found it amusing that the turning point for Tapital was the supposed attack on the remote sub-Plasma outpost, that had subsequently been shown to be fraudulent, and yet the salvage lord was as supportive as ever.

Another thing that occupied Ix was the memorial for the crewmembers lost in the digital battle. Several of the Warden staff had also been found dead, but the loss of the two respected Technician crewmembers had been a second blow after the downing of the lander on Minato. The whole space community was in mourning, and Ix visited with Tuk's grandchildren and other family members.

One afternoon Ix visited the research facility for interstellar propulsion to see what progress had been made.

"From what we've been able to gather from the records in Vault Two, Those Who Went Before had two efficient means to travel the vast interstellar distances." Del the Technician began, "One was this mysterious gate, or Bridgestar -- for some reason they were able to create a tunnel between two points in space."

Ix had been thinking about the gate ever since Sochiko had transmitted her report about her meeting with Hughes. Apparently Bridgestar was not a habitable destination in itself, but a gateway to other solar systems. Each star had an identical Bridgestar station that safeguarded the gates to other systems -- a network of shortcuts for quicker travel. If they could cross the vast distances of their own solar system to reach the gate, what worlds of opportunity awaited them?

"The second form of propulsion, apparently used by the *Axiom* out there, generated a bubble around itself -- it shrunk the very fabric of space in front while expanding it behind." Del continued.

"So how did this make travel efficient?" Ix asked, "We know there seems to be a universal speed limit -- nothing can exceed the speed of light. Even if we could go the speed of light, it would take several years to reach the nearest star, and some of the worlds Those Who Went Before visited, such as Kasei, could be hundreds and thousands of light years away."

Del explained, "The advantage of expanding or shrinking space is that the spacecraft doesn't need to move at all. It will need a secondary propulsion system to get clear of massive gravity wells, such as a planet, but once it gets to the jumping off point, it won't violate the universal speed limit."

"How fast -- what speeds are possible?"

"We don't know -- it might be dependent on how much energy is available. Something is missing from our sunken ship, that the ancient crew jettisoned before scuttling her. I think it may have been the power plant." Del suggested.

"Okay, what kind of power are we talking about?"

"Well, I figure it must be the equivalent output of a small star."

Ix was floored. "What! What kind of power system could produce the energy of a small star?"

"I don't know, but that may be the reason they jettisoned it."

Ix considered, if there was a massive power plant jettisoned by the ancient crew, it might still be out there somewhere. He made a note of informing the astronomy section to look out for it.

Later in the week Ix watched the debriefing of the three remaining crewmembers of the Minato mission. He was worried about Sochiko, and was concerned that the long mission might have stressed her out. Occam said she was delusional, but corroborating evidence began coming in that supported her position.

Ix found a break in the debriefing schedule and pulled Faddard and Stox aside, individually, and showed them the same video sequences Mox had shown Sochi the previous week. Both men confirmed that the video was genuine, and wondered how it was that Ix had gotten a copy of the video recorded by the *Towa Maru* occupants. Their testimony confirmed Sochiko's.

Ix was not comfortable with the conclusion. There was a causal discontinuity in the way all the facts tied together.

Though he would never have believed it, unless there was some massively orchestrated fraud that included people he trusted deeply, it was apparent that the video clip somehow reflected two events separated by hundreds of years!

CHAPTER 16

Virginia gradually worked her way along a path, having slowed the recorded sequence down enough to observe all the data patterns in every direction out to about a hundred meters. The voxels along the path were disturbed, but even if she slowed the sequence down to a standstill, a clear shape would not materialize. It was only when the sequence reached a burst of activity that the multi-ambulatory creature blinked solid for an instant, and then faded again as it headed off on a new trajectory.

"Say that again in plain Wardenese" Cadbic implored.

Virginia explained, "Josh was moving so fast his avatar was a blur. It only showed itself whenever there was a collision."

Cadbic was confused, "But doesn't the Database represent entire patterns? how could his data structure be so blurred?"

"As an artificial intelligence, his patterns are much more complex with a higher granularity than what the Database is capable of showing -- he exists at a lower level independent from what we can see."

Cadbic was still confused, "And why did you call it a collision? I thought Josh was all by himself."

Virginia considered for a minute, then explained, "That's what I thought at first. The Database represents air particles in a convoluted grid-like pattern so that it can realistically simulate wind patterns. These are called voxels, or three-dimensional pixels. The Database then runs a finite element analysis on the voxels using a physics-based algorithm, and simulates realistic wind flowing around objects."

"I'm not sure I understand." Cadbic seemed even more confused.

"Well, just think of them as particles that fill up space."

"So, what does that have to do with a collision?" Cadbic asked.

Virginia continued, "The pattern of particles should be unique everywhere. Now watch this."

Virginia set a subroutine going, and waited for the result. Suddenly two parallel curving swaths of bright purple overlay the scene.

She pointed and said, "I just did a search for identical matches of particle spread, which shouldn't exist. But the particles along these two parallel paths match each other perfectly, offset by about thirty meters. Notice how one of the paths intersects with Josh's route every time there is an altercation."

"So, what does it mean?"

"It means that someone has consciously sampled the data thirty meters out there, and copied it over here, erasing whatever might have been here in the first place. Someone has edited out the evidence of a second party." Virginia concluded.

Virginia and Cadbic looked at each other, and Virginia recalled the interpretation from the last time Josh had told that silly story about the shrink machine.

"Do you remember when Josh foretold that we would doubt him -- the grad students stomping on a miniaturized Professor? I think this is it. Poor Josh has been frantically trying to protect us and we thought he was the enemy program gone haywire!" Virginia pointed out.

Virginia spent the next few days documenting all the confrontations, and seeing if she could trace the deleted paths back to their source. Many of the altercations linked together, but some of them disappeared into regions that hadn't been fully backed up or recorded properly -- the data had been lost.

Josh was still under house arrest, but only as a formality until both the Warden and Technician leadership were all on board. Virginia had him help with some of the more difficult traces because of his recent memories of the confrontations. But they still couldn't get anything useful out of him regarding the nature of the invaders.

One morning Cadbic came to check on her progress, and several others were present. Merinat and Ix were there, and Sochiko was on the outside calling in on voice only, still traumatized by the recent captivity in the rockers.

"*Kret and Stan must have been real,*" Sochiko began, "*they spoke of the Tensakians.*"

Cadbic had doubts, "We haven't been able to find any evidence of their presence."

"*Perhaps their traces were deleted too.*" Sochiko opined.

Virginia suggested doing another search, "We could widen the parameters and look for traces where two deleted paths interacted with each other. Maybe Kret and Stan were fighting the Tensakians too."

They all agreed that was a wise choice.

But just then a familiar voice came online, "The Professor got caught by all the women."

Silence reigned online as all those in the vicinity shifted their attention to Josh.

"Now that sounds like real trouble." Cadbic joked.

Virginia was amused, and encouraged the digital prankster to continue, "Josh, tell us from the beginning."

Josh began, "The grad students wanted to walk among the natives and observe their craft, so they borrowed some stealth beanies."

Merinat asked, "A stealth what!?"

"Josh, explain the beanies." Virginia repeated.

Josh continued, "A stealth beanie polarizes the atoms in a field and induces quantum curvature to space by bending each atom around its pole."

"Why do I even ask..." Merinat mumbled in the background.

Josh continued, "The degree of curvature can be micromanaged so light bends around the wearer."

Josh paused a moment as if waiting for his explanation to sink in.

"I think I know what he's saying," Ix took advantage of the break, "the person wearing the beanie becomes invisible."

"But there's two kinds of beanies," Josh added, "there's the male type that you just turn on and the curvature is fixed and light goes around until it leaks out, and there's the female type that has all sorts of adjustment possible and you can control the light in subtle ways."

Virginia pushed Josh a little further, "So someone who wears the beanie becomes invisible. What did the Professor do? What about all the women?"

"I think I know where this is going, is this Professor fellow a peeping Tom?" Merinat could still be heard mumbling in the background.

Virginia began to hear others as well -- as usual Josh's fan base started to gather and news of a new story spread like wildfire.

Josh continued, "The grad students precisely adjusted the female beanie to bend space around one person so that light approaching one side would curve around and exit the opposite side as if the wearer were invisible. But they had to program eye holes."

Fascinated, Sochiko asked, "*Why does the beanie need eye holes?*"

"Because if all the light curved around, none of it would reach the wearer's eyes -- the environment would be completely black devoid of illumination." Josh explained.

When he didn't continue, Virginia coaxed, "What happened next, Josh?"

Josh hesitantly continued, "Unfortunately the Professor dropped his ring again, and it rolled out the door. He went out chasing the ring as it rolled down the corridor, but just as he was about to snatch it up, it rolled under the door into the ladies' room."

Merinat mumbled again, "I knew it..."

Josh continued, "The Professor stood outside the door not knowing what to do. Just then Pamela came by and walked into the restroom, giving him an angry glance.

"Then he remembered the beanie and snuck back to the lab. But when he got to the lab bench, he couldn't remember which beanie was which so when no one was looking the Professor grabbed one of them and slipped out into the corridor. When he put it on everything went dark, and he couldn't find the eyeholes -- he had accidentally picked up the male beanie. It was like having on very dark sunglasses."

"Why can't they program in eye holes for the male beanie?" Ix asked.

Josh's response was almost like a frustrated adult explaining something to a child, "Because, silly, the male is pre-programmed to just turn on or off -- you can't mess with his ego."

Sochiko snickered -- *men are all like that*, she thought.

"And to anyone who looked carefully, someone wearing the male beanie would look like a transparent dark blot floating in the air." the digital assistant added, "So the Professor stumbled down the hallway by feel and accidentally ran into somebody. Whoever she was screamed and ran down the corridor to escape the invisible monster."

From somewhere Virginia heard giggling as crowds gathered and listened in.

"The Professor nervously entered the ladies' room, but hesitated when he heard Carla and Stephanie as well as Pamela. So he got down on his hands and knees and began feeling around on the floor, trying to avoid the women. Pamela left the room, then Carla, leaving Stephanie by herself. Unfortunately, he couldn't hear where she was, so he accidentally grabbed her foot, sending the poor woman screaming out the door. Alone at last, The Professor was able to scour the entire floor."

When Josh stopped talking, Sochi asked, "So did he find the ring?"

"No," the artificial intelligence replied, "the ring wasn't there."

"Josh, what did the Professor do next?" Virginia coaxed.

"He went back to the lab, and when no one was looking he swapped the male beanie for the female one, and walked invisible into the offices where the women worked. First, he quietly went to Carla's desk and tried to peek into her purse. But in his maneuvering, he accidentally bumped the woman and knocked the purse off the table. Carla screamed so he had to escape.

"Next he found Stephanie's handbag and thought he could look inside. Unfortunately, Stephanie looked up just in time to see him look at her -- two eyeholes floating in the air! She screamed and he got away.

"Soon all the women in the office were running around with brooms, umbrellas, and various objects swatting anything that looked slightly suspicious, including the nearest confused fellow who happened to be handy.

"In all the confusion the Professor spotted Pamela's bag sitting on her desk as Pamela herself wildly chased spooks around the room. He ducked and leaped and avoided flying objects until he found himself next to the bag. But this time he somehow mistakenly adjusted all the knobs on the beanie so light would bend ninety degrees -- everyone who looked at him saw what was happening to their right as if it were straight ahead."

Again, there was a pause in the monologue. Virginia noticed huge crowds had gathered and were intently trying to listen, and some were already play-acting the events.

"Did he get the ring?" Cadbic asked.

Josh continued enthusiastically, "Unfortunately the Professor saw everything to the left -- when the bag appeared in front of him it wasn't really there. All he got was handfuls of frenzied women, and they were closing in on him.

"When he adjusted the knob again, light from one direction passed on through making him invisible, but light from the other direction made the women invisible! The Professor had to alternately shift and turn to keep the ladies guessing, and ran away as fast as he could.

"The women saw him phasing in and out and began to chase after him, wondering why the man couldn't make up his mind. But the Professor knew it was that female beanie's fault.

"Finally, the women caught up with him in the corridor just as he passed the ladies' room. All that estrogen piled on top of the poor fellow so he couldn't move. And there right in front of his eyes he saw his shiny ring on the floor just out of reach. The grad students came out to save him but it was too late -- someone kicked the ring before he could collect it and it rolled right under the door of the ladies' restroom."

The crowd gathered in the database applauded their favorite storyteller, and for weeks thereafter young Wardens could be seen filtering their avatars to be half invisible, with floating eyes, limbs, or creepy dis-embodied heads.

Several days later Virginia had come up with a solution, but it was as confusing as ever, "The ring stands for the same problem as before -- the grad students haven't solved it yet so the Professor has to try to do it himself."

"Does it have to do with deleted traces of Tensakian visitors?" Cadbic asked.

"*Or Kret, or Stan?*" Sochiko added.

Virginia replied, "I'm not sure. But apparently the women represent something like that. Notice how the women aren't included in the grad students, like Technicians or Wardens, but are strangely involved with their work somehow, like out on the periphery."

"Could it be Inmates?" Cadbic suggested.

"No, Inmates are out -- might as well group them in with the grad students."

Ix wondered, "*So did Josh solve it?*"

"Apparently not -- in the end the problem got away. Is there something lately that you've been struggling with, that doesn't seem to make any sense?"

Sochiko knew it and Ix knew it, along with several others, but no one said a thing. They had been struggling with the issue of mysterious invaders, and the much sought-after wreck submerged just below the surface in the inland sea. But they all knew that somehow the strange dilemma with the videos from the Third Vault was the key to everything.

CHAPTER 17

Sochiko looked out one of the view ports as the hull of the rebuilt *Soarer* drifted past only a few armlengths away. There were now four main pressurized centrifuges, each rotating on its own to simulate artificial Sado-Mother gravity.

"See how each section rotates opposite from its neighbor? The intention is to cancel each other's angular momentum." Sochiko explained to her six passengers, "It's actually more stable than the original design."

Her family was all there. Mox, Blujic, Ix, and Holina had all been assigned to the mission as specialists, and had gone through minimal training. Ix's girls had found a replacement for Holina and elected to stay behind to run the family pod operation.

"And those are the equipment bays?" Sochiko's mother asked, pointing to large volumes clinging to the central spine forward of the rotating sections.

"Yes, all packed and ready to go. And she's heavily armed..."

The mission to Minato had quickly escalated to be much larger than even Uncle Ix had imagined. In the past few years Sochiko noted how the *Soarer* had doubled and quadrupled in size, and a twin called the '*Stellar*' had also been started. Each ship had been designed to carry thirty crewmembers each. The entire population sacrificed, scrimped, and saved for the benefit of the operation, knowing the economic payback would be quite soon.

The main purpose of the mission was to set up a mining and material processing operation that shot a steady stream of ore and material carriers back to Mother, which would be caught and processed in orbit. The pair of ships was equipped with portable factories to maximize the use of in-situ resources. Once they arrived, they would first set up the extraction of fuel and consumables to make sure water and air production were self-sustaining. Then they would manufacture simple carriers and begin mining, material processing, and transportation operations.

A secondary mission to which Sochi's parents were assigned was to try and crack the security system of the massive ship orbiting Minato.

Sochiko was amazed at how far her people had been able to progress so much in so short a time. Only a few years before and she had been hovering over the deck in *Bird One*, just trying to keep the craft airborne. But when she thought about it, surprisingly enough the technology and infrastructure to seed such a major space operation had already been in place for a generation. Package factories and manufacturing had been established and perfected from before the time of the great exodus from *The Continent*, and molecular extraction of minerals from Plasma had been on-going for generations before that. Even living and working in a pressurized environment had analog parallels in the enclosed and confined submarines, chambers, and passageways of *The Continent* and *The Island*, and there were precedents for operating factories on board some of the pods -- especially for the production of consumables.

It was intended that the *Soarer* have a mission duration of three years, whereupon it would return to Mother for refitting. A third vessel under construction would take its place and join the *Stellar*, which would be away for five years. It was hoped a significant permanent base could be established during that time, perhaps re-establishing a facility at Everwebber, which was apparently unoccupied -- only one of the mappers they had placed lived long enough to approach the space port, but it had lost power on a highland overlooking the town.

"Prepare for docking." She warned, but the passengers were already belted down.

The small craft, almost identical to *Bird Ten*, maneuvered under the bow of the *Soarer* and Sochiko eased in sideways. On the central axis of the larger vessel a short node had been added with four docking ports. Three of them already were occupied -- Sochi was bringing up the last bunch.

Once the outside temperature equalized and the mating mechanism showed complete handshake, Ix opened up the hatch and secured it to one of the bulkheads. The group happily drifted through to join the welcome party on the other side. Soon they had all dispersed and had gone to their separate cabins in the artificial gravity sections of the ship.

Sochiko noted with mixed feelings that the old name plates 'arm' and 'leg' still hung over the first two lifts, but six more names had been added -- 'salt', 'pepper', 'hikari', 'kage', 'peak', and 'hole'. In a moment of silence, she thought back on the triumphs and sacrifices that had gotten them to that point. She couldn't get over losing the four crewmembers, which she counted among her best friends. Now she owed it to them, and to Tuk and Prech, to strike out again and overcome the odds. She swore the Tensakians would eventually pay for the pain they caused. Sochiko only lingered for a few moments in reverent thought before making her way to her old cabin.

The *Soarer* left orbit a few days later. There was much more pressurized volume in the new *Soarer* than before, that made the long journey a lot more bearable. The crew went through countless training exercises, disassembled and reassembled equipment, and servicing the fleet of vehicles. Those who were qualified did numerous space walks, particularly to the equipment bays to service the equipment there, and the pilots did occasional local jaunts with the four *Birds* docked on the bow.

Ix and the others were not qualified for extravehicular activities, but kept busy nevertheless. One of the most enjoyable things about having family on board was the entertaining off-hours. Ix and Mox would get together and tell stories that would enthrall the whole crew.

But there were disadvantages -- in spite of the fact that Sochiko was ship captain, her mother was still mother and always chided her about various domestic details, not the least of which was the subject of marriage. Blujic would pick out a random member of the crew and ask if Sochiko might be interested, or would try to set up situations where the two of them were alone. Fortunately, Sochiko lived on a different arm of the rotating community or her mother would drive her crazy.

They got word that the *Stellar* had left Mother's orbit about a month after them. The word came right on the heels of good news that Worlith, one of the four crewmembers of the fallen lander, was still alive. But the situation was grave -- she was being held captive in a market-like place on *Blister*. Fisby had been able to drive their operational mapper right into the marketplace on the heels of several other automated messenger machines and no one seemed to notice. As with the other machines, the mapper was able to wander the market without attracting undue attention. Worlith was spotted with a group of other battered women, apparently being held as domestic servants and possibly prostitutes. Fisby knew it had been Worlith because the woman also saw the mapper and recognized it, and did all sorts of delaying tactics to keep the machine in sight in spite of the brutal prodding of the human traffickers. Fisby was able to get the mapper to flash a signal, in code, that Worlith acknowledged. The woman, who had begun with a dejected look, straightened up and took courage after that. Cadbic had ordered the woman to be top priority, and had Fisby follow her after that.

After hearing the news, Sochiko donned mask and tanks and took a long swim in the volume of water surrounding the hab module. When she got out, she ended up with her family and several other crewmembers around the table in the 'Kage' galley, trying to make sense of everything.

"Well, obviously the lander didn't crash after all, but was forcefully taken by the pirates." Mox began.

Ix noted, "Of course we knew that already -- we had the mapper there as evidence. If Worlith is still alive, perhaps the others..."

"Fisby still hasn't been able to get close enough to actually communicate with her, to get her side of the story." Faddard, who had also been assigned on the *Soarer*, pointed out.

Sochiko was angry, "This means we have to do all we can to figure out this interstellar puzzle. We have to rescue her!"

The whole group sat around in silence, and every one of them knew how remote and hopeless that possibility was. When it came to understanding the piloting, navigation, and physics of the great interstellar ship, they would be like a backwoods primitive inmate stumbling on board a modern high-tech submarine, knowing vaguely what the machine was for, but having no idea how to run the thousands of gauges, knobs, switches, and other controls just to start up the motor. But they were determined to try -- a slim hope was better than no hope.

But first they had to figure out a way to break into the ship.

Ix had a theory, "Two identical ships of the same type stranded in the same remote solar system seems too much of a coincidence. Suppose both ships were from Those Who Went Before?"

Several of those around the table looked up, surprised at the thought.

"What do you mean?" Faddard asked.

Ix explained, "Say there were two refugee ships, pursued by an unknown enemy. One breaks down and needs repairs. However, the spaceport is unmanned and the automatics at the port don't have the capability to do the job. Since they are in a hurry, they transfer the crew from the disabled ship over to the functional one and continue on their way to Mother."

Mox was excited, "Hmm. The ship at Minato could function as a decoy so they could get away."

Ix added, "So that would mean they probably set it up as a booby trap with a back door. If they intended to recover the sunken vessel, they probably also meant to eventually recover the Minato vessel."

Sochiko considered the possibility of both ships belonging to their ancestors. They already knew how to approach the orbiting ship from their study of the *Axiom*. Perhaps the security code was already in their possession, lurking in the lore and history of Those Who Went Before!

During the voyage Sochiko got two transmissions from *Blister*. Sochiko's heart got into a flutter when she went to answer the first one. But it wasn't from Kret, it was from the other communicator -- the one with the overly refined language, she thought.

"*The pirates know where you are going, and they will stop at nothing to get your prize.*" the voice said.

"Who are you? Are you Tensakian?" Sochiko suspiciously prodded.

When she had asked before, the voice had stayed silent, but this time, after a suitable time delay due to the distance, it answered in the affirmative, "*Yes, the Tensakians are a peaceful people. Your ancestors were Tensakian.*"

"I don't believe you! Why have you abducted our officers? Release Worlith immediately!" Sochiko angrily demanded.

The voice started to protest, "*We don't have any space-worthy vessels. That's not...*" but the transmission ended.

The smooth voice echoed in her mind and made her sick.

Shortly thereafter the second transmission came in. It was Kret. It shocked her how much relief she felt.

"Kret we missed you. After you were blocked from the Database the assault ended and we were able to go home safely."

There was a delay as the signal went all the way to *Blister* through Bridgestar and back, "*I'm so glad you got out of there.*" Kret said.

Again, Sochiko was amazed. She was talking to an alien! She couldn't believe she was having a conversation with a human who had never before set foot on Sado.

"*Did you get to see your uncle? How is your family?*" Kret asked.

"Everyone is doing fine. They're here with me now --" Sochi was about to say 'on the *Soarer*' but thought better of it, since the Tensakians might have been listening as well.

Kret changed the subject and his voice changed to a sober tone, "*Sochi, the Tensakians know you are on the way to Minato. They're after the big ship. Be careful -- they'll try to contact you and get you to tell your secrets.*"

"Yes, I just got a message already. Those bastards have one of our crewmembers!" Sochiko complained.

"*There are so many things that need mopping up. I wish we could get in there to free the whole lot.*" Kret lamented, "*It takes all our energy just to keep them out of our farms!*"

The journey went without major incident. The *Soarer* arrived safely in orbit around Minato several months later, shepherded by the Everwebber automated pilot boat, whereupon the crew immediately got to work preparing for a long stay. One of the first orders of business was to do a detailed survey from orbit with spectrographic telescopes to find out where mineral concentrations were. Another major task was to prepare vehicles and self-contained habitats that would become permanent outposts on the surface.

One morning Sochiko gave the go-ahead for the first mission down to the surface. Mox and Blujic were assigned to the artifacts team, who had the task of exploring Everwebber with Stox and one of the pilots. Since her parents were not trained for the bulky space suits, they were to remain inside the pressurized rover to monitor the outside activities of the other two.

Sochiko stayed close to the com unit, nervously listening in as the team made their way to the surface guided by the automated pilot boat to one of Everwebber's landing pads. The video feeds showed the descent from various angles, and she must have held her breath as she watched the planet surface approach ever closer. When the pilot finally indicated a safe landing, she was able to catch her breath again.

Immediately there was movement out on the periphery of the camera's vision.

"Soarer, *we may have company.*" Stox's voice came through on the loud speaker. "*I'm arming the missiles.*"

Sochiko, nervously recalling the last time she let a crew leave for Everwebber, warned her colleague, "Don't take any chances!"

Mox and the pilot could be heard puzzling over what they saw.

"*Are those people out there?*" Mox asked.

The Pilot responded, "*Something's coming, but it isn't people. Looks like some vehicles of sorts.*"

"*No, look out there near those buildings. Aren't those figures standing out there?*" Mox asked.

"*Oh, I see. I can't make it out.*"

On the monitor, Sochiko could see small white specks a great distance away, as if white-suited figures milled about. On another screen, small dark-colored vehicles approached the lander.

"Soarer, *I think we are safe,*" the pilot reported, "*it looks like there are several small maintenance vehicles coming out to meet us. Appear to be robotic.*"

Sochi repeated, "Just don't take any chances. Keep your weapons trained on them."

Several minutes later the pilot reported, "*There's a message coming in. They're asking us if we need any fuel or power recharging.*"

"Tell them no need -- wait! Ask what selections of fuel are available."

A few minutes later the pilot came back on, "*There's a long list, most of which I've never heard before. But I'm pretty sure chemical propellants were on the list -- liquid oxygen, hydrogen, methane, kerosene, tetro, monometh, hydrazine, plutonium, plasma --*"

Interesting. Sochiko thought the spaceport resources may prove to be an added bonus to their consumable supplies, over and above what they could produce themselves. It depended on how Everwebber got its inventory -- was it imported? Were the machines serving from a nearly depleted storage that hadn't been renewed for centuries? Did they get their resources from the automated mining camps, or were they unrelated?

"Decline for now. Eventually we should get someone to test the quality and mixture." Sochiko concluded.

The lander consisted of two vehicles -- a descent / ascent spacecraft with a pressurized rover slung underneath. The ground crew transferred down into the rover via a pressurized tunnel. While Mox and Blujic monitored the video feeds, Stox and the pilot went through pre-breathing and got into the rover airlock. They put on their pressure suits and went outside to make an inspection and observe the surroundings.

"*The robots are still waiting around,*" Mox noted as the two got ready, "*be careful.*"

Stox walked around the lander and began poking at the pavement. "*Seems to be sintered Minato soil. We'll have no trouble with dust around here.*"

Then he walked right up to the robots and began looking them over.

"Stox! What are you doing!" Sochiko demanded.

"*It's alright, I got this. I'm the only one who can do this.*" Stox began, his helmet cam showing the machines from various angles -- well-maintained caterpillar treads, insulative body, antenna and gimbals. "*I'm interrogating the robot.*"

After a short pause Stox reported, "*It only has limited capacity, but it has access to maintenance records. There's been no landings for more than a year.*"

Curious, Sochiko thought. "Does that mean something landed in the past few years?"

"*Not sure. But it says there is a record of refueling and power draw from about that time.*"

Sochiko calculated back. It could have been about the time she had seen Masamune Hughes and the crew of the *Towa Maru*. Or someone else...

"*I think these machines are programmed to stay as long as the lander is on the surface, anticipating any assistance that might be needed. They're in very good shape.*" Stox commented.

The pair finished the inspection and got back inside the airlock. Fifteen minutes later the rover was on the ground, pulling away from the lander that they left buttoned up on automatics. They began driving toward the buildings in the distance. Sochiko had one of the security people remotely keep weapons in the lander trained on the maintenance robots in case they were not what they seemed.

As the video came in, it was clear that scales were deceiving. The 'figures milling about' ended up being a collection of gantries for servicing spacecraft. One of them was moving back and forth over an unidentified piece of equipment, with several maintenance robots swarming around it.

Sochiko watched in fascination as the robots removed and replaced components, cut and welded from nearby stacks of materials. In one of the screens, she saw a robot approach the rover from one side.

Stox's voice came on the line, "*There's another incoming message. They're asking if we have any crystals for lasers and electron beam cutters.*" Then there was a pause and he continued, "*I think the whole place is equipped for self-maintenance, but there may be a few hard-to-manufacture special components that need to be imported. They must have run out of crystals.*"

Ix, who had been working on the *Soarer* to get the package factories ready, came online and said, "Ask them what the specifications for the crystals are. Maybe we can manufacture something for them."

Stox got the information and the rover moved on. It was just as Stox had said -- robotic maintenance facilities in low, un-pressurized buildings that seemed to be knocking out parts or repairing other equipment. There was a whole world of wonders their technicians could explore.

Once or twice the rover came across ore carriers that were coming in from the highlands. Everwebber appeared to be a living mechanical organism living off the land.

"Why don't we just use this?" one of the technology people asked. "We don't need to set up a thing."

"Maybe eventually." Ix countered, "But we can't get dependent on something we don't understand. Take it slowly girl. We could begin by trading simple things and relearning the old technology. This was all ours, and we have forgotten."

Stox asked one of the robots where there were facilities for humans, and got directions to a ramp that led deep into the ground between high berms of regolith. At the bottom was an entrance to a tunnel that led several hundred armlengths to a large metal bulkhead. A hole had been cut into the wall.

Stox and the pilot suited up again and entered the facility while Mox and Blujic remained in the rover, relaying the signal back to the *Soarer*. They watched as the helmet cams of the two crewmembers showed empty room after empty room. The place had been long deserted, and probably looted on top of that. There was nothing of value remaining.

"*It will take a lot of work to get this habitable again. We'll have to figure out how to route power down here and pressurize it.*" Stox noted.

Soon the two were back in the rover on a return trip to the lander. Sochiko welcomed them back to the *Soarer* the next morning.

By the time the *Stellar* arrived, two habitat outposts had been established -- one on the Everwebber landing pad and another in the nearby mountains where they began to do some test drilling and excavation. For a people who lived generations of their lives floating on water, the digging and hauling of regolith proved much more difficult than they had imagined.

Also, the factories didn't work as well in vacuum as they had expected. The problem was in the lubricants they had chosen. The substance they had tested in vacuum chambers evaporated in full solar exposure, so they had to rig up shields and sheds to keep the equipment running. Unfortunately, that only prolonged the evaporation and they soon began running short on supply.

In both instances they found a solution in the Everwebber operations. The solutions for various excavation techniques could be observed, and they were even able to trade some crystals for a couple of the excavator machines that worked much better than their own. Ix got the technicians to employ one of the purchased machines to do the work, while another crew broke down the second machine with intention to reverse engineer it using their own electronics and protocols. They even traced the Everwebber material processing and assembly lines for the excavators, and learned how to harden the alloys and precision fit parts, in ways they hadn't mastered yet.

The crystals also bought a generous supply of a super lubricant that worked well in all the temperature ranges. Ix again cautioned against getting too dependent on the stuff, but for the time being they had to compromise.

Unfortunately, the trading reduced their supply of crystals. The proper minerals couldn't be found on Minato, but were gleaned from the mineral strata deep in Mother's Plasma. Merinat, who had gone on a Flesh kick and assumed command of the *Stellar*, put together a barge full of processed aluminum, beryllium, silicon, and other rare minerals and sent it on its way back to Mother with a request for more crystals. The manufacturing process for crystals was elaborate and expensive, but by the time Merinat's care package arrived a large batch had been produced and, along with food and other logistics, were packed into the carrier and sent right back out to Minato.

Ix and the technology crew had much more success with processing consumables. They were able to get small batch plants going that output a supplementary supply of oxygen, hydrogen, water, and nitrogen, and were able to process the highly toxic monopropellant hydrazine. They traded some with the Everwebber facility to obtain samples of the fuels produced there, and determined them to be high grade and good quality. They also discovered that all the chemical fuels were manufactured locally, so along with their own production they were able to meet their entire supply needs without importing anything from Sado.

Of greater interest were the autonomous operations Sochiko and her crew had stumbled on during the first mission. From Sochi's testimony regarding what she saw on Masamune's video of the 'gate', they assumed that the reconfigurable, morphing machines were part of the maintenance chain of Bridgestar. They watched as countless modules were manufactured and assembled themselves into carriers that launched toward the outer rim of the solar system.

The Bridgestar and Everwebber operations were completely unrelated. And the interesting part was that the Bridgestar technology made Everwebber look like backwoods Inmate efforts by comparison. The efficiency and cleverness of the system was a thing of beauty. Unfortunately, the Bridgestar operation security force was always there, and Ix and his technicians could never get close enough to figure out how it worked.

As far as security was concerned, on the local scene there was nothing but good news. Sochiko and Merinat had dedicated security details, armed to the teeth, which kept constant watch on all operations. The security division had their own ships and remote probes that patrolled endlessly.

There were one or two incidents where they thought they had stumbled on security threats, only to discover as yet unknown satellites that had activated for one reason or another. They watched the spacecraft until it powered down again, always vigilant. It appeared that for the time being, they were secure in their operations -- no sign of Tensakians at all.

However, Sochiko got another transmission from Kret, who warned her that the Tensakians were sure to be in the vicinity.

"We've got five heavily armed gunboats patrolling our operations. I don't think we'll be caught by surprise." Sochiko explained.

"*They might not need surprise --*" Kret began, but Sochiko inadvertently interrupted his thought.

"Isn't there anything you can do to help?" she asked.

"*About all I can do is tell you their movements as we see them -- they've already left.*" Kret said.

About six months after their arrival, Mox and Blujic who headed up the artifacts team decided it was time to take on the big ship in orbit. The Technicians had prepared six probes to help with the job, and their specialists began to set up a plan for breaching the security of the vessel. Mox believed Ix's theory about Those Who Went Before, and was convinced they would be able to come up with the command codes.

If all went well, the technicians would guide the probe on a course that would intersect the ship's orbit orthogonally, and meet up with one of the massive doors leading to the vast garage, precisely when the orbits crossed. It would be a tricky maneuver, but every technician that studied the problem was convinced it would be the only way to get past the particle beam tracking from either end. The only problem was that they would need to come up with the right code to open the hatch at just the right instant, and they also had to perform a very quick deceleration maneuver to keep from crashing or passing right on out the identical large hatch on the other side.

For the security code, they had six well-known phrases that Mox had put together out of lore from Those Who Went Before, and if it took more than that they would have to manufacture new probes.

To keep it from crashing, each probe had a large engine with enough propellant to slow it down considerably, after which inflatable bags would cushion the actual impact.

On the first try, the technicians steered the probe toward the rendezvous point. The video feeds began to show the distant vessel coming over the horizon, slowly at first, then increasingly fast as the two objects approached each other at nearly a half dozen kilometers a second. Suddenly the vast wall of the ship was upon them. Autonomously the probe initiated its deceleration burn and began to approach the great hatch.

"*You have entered a secure area. You have sixty seconds to present your security clearance.*" a warning message in Warden came in on a transmission.

Mox sent off the first code word and waited for a response. Unfortunately, there was a flash of light and all video feeds went dark. The probe was blown to smithereens.

After that they tried two more probes using the same approach but with new phrases, only to see them both lost as the first.

That evening Mox, Blujic, Sochiko, and several technicians got together for dinner to discuss the day's failures.

"I think we ought to come in from a higher orbit and dive down to the upper hatch. It'll be easier to control that way." one of the technicians suggested.

"That's a good idea -- all of the probes would have missed the hatch even if it were open. In fact, I can't find any solutions that could hit the hatch right on at such high speeds." another added.

Blujic was worried. "Why would the warning be in Warden if it were a Technician vessel?"

There were assenting voices as everyone agreed that there might be an inconsistency.

But Mox was adamant, "Those Who Went Before parked the vessel over a Warden facility. Surely they would warn anyone using the facility in their own language."

"Dad, you have to admit how far-fetched that sounds. Maybe you should consider a different strategy." Sochiko pointed out.

"And do what? Which phrases should we use in Warden? Or do you suggest we blow a hole in the door before we get to it?" Mox asked.

They all looked at Blujic suddenly. But Sochiko's mother appeared to be at a loss.

Blujic offered, "We have a scenario that could give us possible codes from the Technicians -- phrases from Those Who Went Before that were carefully preserved from generation to generation that possibly might have been planted to help them recover the ship. But what scenario could there be that would give us any clues in the case of a Warden-owned vessel?"

Everyone looked at each other expectantly, but no one had an idea.

Blujic continued, "If it were a Warden vessel, who's to say it wasn't some merchant captain that just intended to go down to the surface for a local meal, and used his wife's name as a password, but got interrupted by the war?"

"And if we tried some other approach, such as to blow a hole in the door, don't we have proof out there someone already failed at such an attempt?"

Blujic was referring to the burned-out pirate vessel who hadn't succeeded in forcing entry.

She concluded, "I propose we continue with the current plan. If we fail, that ship has been in orbit for hundreds of years, and a few more years wait won't do a bit of difference."

"But what about Worlith? We need to rescue her." Sochiko crossed her mother.

"Dear, think about it. Even if we get into the ship, do we have any illusions that we could drive the thing?" Blujic posited.

"No, I guess not."

Mox faced the group again, "Are we all on board to continue?"

One of the technicians voiced his dissent, "I don't agree, but I don't have a better plan. I suppose we'll have the capacity to manufacture new probes soon enough."

The next morning the group watched as the fourth probe dove down from a higher orbit. It was the right choice, and the technicians verified that the trajectory would allow the craft to slip right into the hatch if it were open. They all turned to Mox, who sent off the fourth phrase.

Again, the probe video feeds went dark after a flash of light.

But the fifth try was the charm. Mox could have kicked himself as he realized their most regarded phrases should have been moved up to the top of the list. As the fifth probe dove toward the hatch and the warning sounded, 'One Eternal Round' resulted with the hatch opening wide. Unfortunately, a glitch in the inflation system caused the probe to glance off the side of the tunnel and destroy itself before ever entering the garage.

But now they knew Mox's persistence had paid off and they had one more probe. Sochiko didn't want to take any chances, so she had the team plan for security measures in preparation for when the booby trap was disarmed. For the final probe, Mox and Blujic and the entire technical team boarded a shuttle and set up their operations following the great ship from a safe distance, flanked by three of the gunboats.

As before, the technicians guided the probe in a dive from above, and Mox delivered the phrase when the warning came. The hatch opened and the retro rockets roared. The probe slipped precisely into the center of the hatch and instantly the bags inflated. The probe flew down the tunnel and bounced around a bit inside the garage as it lost kinetic energy. Finally, it drifted slowly in freefall. The bags deflated and were discarded.

The scene that piped through the video feeds was partially expected, since they had seen its twin underwater many times before. But this time not all the docking gantries were empty -- there were several smaller craft attached to boarding bridges that hadn't been disturbed for hundreds of years.

"*Welcome home. Would you like to turn off the security system?*" a voice came back, this time in archaic Japonican, similar to the language of the Tensakians and Farmers.

"*Yes!*" Mox replied.

By evening the shuttle had entered the ship and docked to one of the gantries. The three gunboats remained outside, diligently watching for intruders. Danid and another trained woman on the crew donned pressure suits and entered the airlock.

"*There's a pressurized atmosphere.*" Danid reported as the airlock equalized with the gantry tunnel.

Sochiko monitored the video as the women cautiously exited the airlock into the connector bridge.

Sochiko transmitted, "Test the air pressure and mixture."

"*Okay, testing now.*"

Danid's helmet cam showed the testing equipment while the other woman continued on down the tunnel. At the end of the tunnel several passageways, presumably from other gantry tunnels, converged on a larger space. Just like in the *Axiom*, but without the layers of corrosion, a sign in both archaic Japonican and old Warden read, '*Vector*: Tensakian Processing'.

Sochiko had heard about the sign from her uncle, but still didn't know what to make of it. Did it originally process criminals?

"*We've got a name for this tub -- the* Vector. *The air is a good mixture of oxygen and nitrogen, quite clean and sterile.*" Danid reported, "*The pressure is a bit higher than what we're used to on Mother, but not by that much.*"

Mox could be overheard asking the ship questions. "*Is the life-support operational?*"

"*Life-support is operating within allowable tolerances,*" was the reply piped over the radio to Sochiko.

Mox asked another question, "*Do you have maintenance logs for the past two hundred years?*"

Sochiko snickered to herself -- only her father would ask such a silly question and expect a serious answer. But answer it did.

"*All maintenance logs have been kept since the construction of the ship.*"

Sochiko listened as Mox was able to verify that Everwebber had periodically serviced many of the *Vector*'s systems, keeping them viable over the centuries. The ship had been in constant communication with the port, and had requested for orbital servicing after every so many hours of operation, depending on the particular system's factory service recommendation. Everwebber had complied, penetrating the *Vector*'s security through the maintenance loophole.

Sochiko was relaxing, listening to her father's amusing dialog with the ship and noting the progress of Danid and the other woman, when suddenly there was an emergency call coming in. She answered it immediately.

"*Sochiko, we've picked up an unidentified spacecraft approaching the alien vessel.*" it was from one of the gunboat security teams.

Sochiko reacted quickly and got all the gunboats on the line. Two of the vessels were in a position to intercept, while a third vessel was on its way. The other two were occupied with the mining and manufacturing enterprise but also responded in case they were needed.

She watched the monitors as the intruder accelerated toward the ship. Without warning a pair of projectiles launched from the aggressor and shot toward the two gunboats. The first one hit in a ball of flame.

"Patrol Two, are you there? Come in Patrol Two!" Sochiko called frantically.

There was a pause during which Sochi feared the worst. But a voice came on, "*We're okay. All systems go. It was just a fireball -- got singed around the edges a bit.*"

The other gunboat had time to maneuver and missed the second explosion.

Patrol Two sent out two missiles of its own, both deadly on target. Just before impact, the monitors showed the intruder break into multiple bodies -- was it a pirate mother ship launching its death pods? Something among the cloud of blips exploded in a direct hit.

A report came in from Patrol Two, "*We've confirmed a direct hit on the mother ship, but all the death pods have been launched.*"

A video feed showing a blown-out hulk came in as Patrol Two swung by the wreckage. A long hull with rows of empty sockets, punctuated by holes with twisted metal drifted on a black velvety background. The video began tracking a smaller object off to the side and the ship maneuvered to follow it. The gunboat fired another missile that traced its way across the scene toward the distant target. It impacted with a discernable spray of debris that fanned out in all directions. The crew cheered.

Again and again, the two gunboats, soon joined by the third, tracked down and destroyed the invader targets. Cheer after cheer rose through the transmissions as crews congratulated themselves on their good aim.

But something seemed wrong. Sochiko sensed that even though they were succeeding, there didn't appear to be any resistance. A star-faring civilization, especially one that made its living preying on others, should have had more formidable weapons.

The answer came only thirty minutes later, when Sochiko realized her mistake.

"*Sochi, the* Vector *has stopped responding.*" Mox complained.

"What do you mean?" she asked, "Has it stopped volunteering data?"

Mox replied, "*It won't even acknowledge my queries to the old questions.*"

Faddard, who was on *Soarer* at the time with part of the science team, broke in, "Sochi, there's a change in the orbit of the *Vector*. I think it is moving to a higher orbit."

The video feeds of Danid and her companion confirmed it -- the two were pressed against one of the bulkheads in apparent acceleration.

"*Sochi, we have unknown accelerations here,*" Blujic came on.

The big ship was moving away, and the gunboats were elsewhere chasing invaders. Or were they?

"Faddard, see if you can get a probe somewhere to get some close-ups of the bridge of the ship." Sochiko quickly directed.

Soon an image came back from a probe in geosynchronous orbit, showing the ship silhouetted against the bright crescent of the planet. Sochiko zoomed in on the bridge until the image was grainy. She panned it back and forth until she found what she was looking for.

"Hey Unk, take a look at this." A panicking Sochi beamed the image to Ix who was in the zero-g core of the *Soarer*.

Ix, who had been following along anyway, immediately looked at the image and gave his opinion, "Honey, I'm afraid what you suspect is correct. That bump on the side is a death pod. The pirates have taken over the *Vector*."

CHAPTER 18

Hideous black cloud-like entities hovered above the control panels, and settled into place at various workstations. One by one cloaking devices switched off, dissipating the mist effect and leaving fully armored figures decked out in sensors and weaponry. One imposing figure lovingly caressed the sleek console and was pleased that it responded to every command. The pirate captain smiled, considering how well the decoy had worked. They had piled the entire crew on board a large death pod, and approached the ship from the opposite direction as the mother ship was sacrificed -- and it was a worthy sacrifice indeed!

Several of the captain's companions scrambled between stations in order to pilot the massive vessel, as they set a course for Bridgestar. Their training and understanding of the operation of hundreds of spacecraft allowed them to quickly take on the daunting task of basic maneuvering, where the more advanced operations would need more time. Unfortunately, they soon became aware of a problem.

"We have attitude control, but the main engines for local maneuvering seem to be malfunctioning." one of the pirates reported.

The leader commented, "We suspected such, which is why it was abandoned. How long can we depend on attitude control for forward vectoring?"

The pirate replied, "They'll take continuous use, but the specific impulse is very low -- it will take us months to get to Bridgestar at this rate."

The captain turned to another, "What about the interstellar drives?"

The second invader answered, "The interstellars are in a higher orbit -- we'll need to pick them up on the way out. They seem to be functional, but they can't be activated near a gravity well or the navigation will be distorted."

The captain smiled again. The ship was the key to wealth and power. Using the interstellar drive, they would be able to reach Kasei without Bridgestar -- and that great civilization would be accessible for plunder.

Another pirate reported, "Sir, the water world folks have begun pursuit."

The captain asked, "The small gunboats?"

"No, I don't think the smaller vessels have enough specific impulse to catch us. One of the larger ships is on its way."

That Sochiko! The captain had given her fair warning, and they had won fair and square. "How long until she catches up?"

"Probably not until tomorrow -- they are on the other side of the planet."

The captain asked, "How long until we can dock with the interstellars?"

"It will be at least several hours, sir, using the thrust from attitude control."

The captain frowned, "We'll skip Bridgestar and go straight interstellar. I want the operation of those deep space drives understood in two days." The captain paused then turned to one of the killers, "Go down and find the woman's family, and set them out to drift -- that should delay her for a while. Kill the rest."

CHAPTER 19

Blujic panicked as she heard Sochiko's dreadful words over the com unit, "*The pirates have taken your ship!*" Then the signal was jammed and all they could get was scrambled bits and pieces.

She and Mox stared at each other, and Blujic's mind began racing. The invaders could be on their way down from the bridge any moment now. They would immediately begin searching the shuttle. How soon, if at all, could they expect a rescue party?

"Danid," Blujic yelled, knowing her voice would be picked up by the cabin mic, "We've got unfriendly visitors. The pirates will be around any minute now! Come back immediately."

Danid's voice came back weakly, "*Got it. I've already heard.*"

Suddenly an aggressive voice came on the line, heavily accented from the Tensakian-Farmer dialect, "*We know you're here. Give up and you won't be harmed.*"

All four of the cabin occupants looked at each other in shock. Gij the pilot reacted first and rushed over to snap off the radio. They would have to maintain communications silence.

"Can we fly back out?" Blujic asked.

Gij checked his instruments and replied, "No way out. The hangar doors have shut."

The three men looked around for anything they could consider a weapon. Blujic began scouring the shuttle for things they might need, and started putting together a backpack of sorts.

"Take as much food as you can, along with the prep unit. I'm going to stay here with the shuttle." the pilot said.

Mox protested, "You can't! It will be suicide!"

"I'll have an advantage. The shuttle is armed, but only against aggressive spacecraft. I can pull away from the gantry and fly around inside here -- should be able to hold off the invaders unless they have heavy portable armaments." the pilot explained.

Little did he know just how long they would be fugitives.

Blujic and the others agreed it might be a good strategy, and thought it would protect the landing party.

"Whatever you do, don't let them know you are here. Maybe we can convince them everyone is on board the shuttle." the Pilot warned.

Thirty minutes later the three of them floated just inside the gantry tunnel. Blujic noticed a peculiar musty odor as if the air had not been disturbed for a long time. She looked through the window in the hatch to watch the shuttle undock and back into the center of the vast garage, then all three turned around and made their way down the tunnel.

Looking ahead into the dark, Blujic thought she caught some movement eclipsed by the figure of her husband ahead of her. As she kept her eyes trained toward the end of the tunnel, she was startled as something flitted past the round opening.

"Future, did you see that?" she whispered.

"Yeah, there's something out there. I think they are machines." Mox answered.

The tunnel opened onto a corridor that ran behind the massive garage bulkhead from which the gantry protruded. The three spilled out into the larger passage and shot on various trajectories toward handholds they each had aimed for. Blujic looked up and down the corridor and spied the machine she had seen earlier -- it was apparently clinging to the wall performing some sort of cleaning or polishing as it crept along and did circles around handholds, hatches, conduits, ducts, and other fixtures breaking the otherwise smooth surface. As the wall cleaner disappeared into the darkness, another small machine powered by bursts of compressed air came hovering down the center of the passage. The three backed up against the wall as the machine slowly drifted by. Blujic tried to observe what the machine was for, but was not able to discover its purpose -- she couldn't help but recall the Warden automatons and mappers that crisscrossed the Warden facility performing all sorts of maintenance tasks.

As they made their way through the corridor, the age of the place settled on Blujic gradually. There were a large number of hatches lining the walls, floors, and ceiling that led to who-knows-where. Though well maintained, the ancient bulkheads seemed to hold secrets she didn't want to discover. She began to wonder whether it was the right choice to leave the shuttle that might actually have been the safest place for them.

They came to the location where the Tensakian sign marked the passage beyond, but as they drifted into the convergence of passages, Blujic saw more movement down one side corridor. She expected to see other small maintenance robots, but was startled to observe a large human figure coming toward them. The three grounded their momentum by sliding feet under sidewall restraints and pulled out clubs and sharp instruments, ready to use the primitive weapons on whoever came at them. It was with great relief that they saw the two suited women on their way back toward the garage. Both the women had taken their helmets off,

Danid letting hers drift along behind her back on the end of a short tether. Jevn, the other woman, had clipped hers to the front of her chest harness.

"Glad you decided to join the party." Mox commented.

The girls nervously smiled and moved to join the group.

Blujic began to notice a pattern in the lighting system of the ship. Though there was illumination immediately in their vicinity, the *Vector* appeared to sense their movement and turn lights on whenever they entered a corridor, shutting them off behind them. The smaller maintenance machines they had observed didn't seem to have the bulk required to trigger the motion sensors. Blujic suddenly had an awful feeling that perhaps the pirate masters had ways of tracking the group just by tapping into the sensor activity.

Explaining the problem to the others, Blujic asked, "Does anyone remember if there is a way to get off the main corridor?"

Kerf, the other technician, spoke up, "There are two service conduits that extend down to the power plant -- one of them is not too far from here. But it will be a tight squeeze -- no way those girls are going to fit with their pressure suits."

Kerf had been with the project from the beginning, and had been among the drone operators exploring the *Axiom* on Gij's team. Blujic was relieved to have someone with them who had explored every corner of the sunken vessel -- it was knowledge they could put to good use. Mox also had dove the ship on numerous occasions, but in her research, Blujic had only studied the data that had been collected.

She smiled and looked at the two bulky pressure suits. "That's okay -- I think I've got an idea."

Kerf led them through open hatchways and a maze of passageways, avoiding various kinds of maintenance robots along the way, until they arrived at what appeared to be a main avenue of sorts that must have run the entire length of the ship. Kerf paused in the intersection to catch his bearings, in a move that may have saved their lives.

Each of the party clung to the walls of the small side passage as they waited for Kerf's signal to proceed. Without warning Blujic began to feel an unknown force working on her body from the side. She was pressed against one wall of the passage, and those clinging to the opposite wall found themselves hanging over empty space -- the *Vector* had begun to maneuver, and the resulting accelerations were pressing them against the bulkhead. All they could do was hang on, and hope the forces wouldn't tear them away from the wall. It was especially difficult for Blujic, who had started with a massive backpack of zero weight that had suddenly gotten very heavy. She fought the pack's momentum as the acceleration vector changed direction and caused the passage enclosure to change roles, from floor to wall to ceiling and back to floor again.

After a while the shifting accelerations stabilized in a single direction. The forces acting on their bodies resolved into a weak gravity of sorts, giving a local 'up' orientation to the corridor. Blujic assumed the constant acceleration would back off soon, so she braced herself for more changes. She would later find out the light gravity would stay consistent on their long journey to hell, as a byproduct of the stellar singularity drive.

Had Kerf herded them into the wide avenue earlier, they all may have fallen to their deaths because that great passage had become a bottomless shaft. Blujic clung to one of the handholds for fear that she would fall into the pit. Several medium-sized 'floaters' -- the compressed air-driven hover machines -- moved up and down the shaft, and seemed to take the accelerations into stride. The ship's lights made an island of illumination that lit up the walls for several nodelengths upward and downward, but beyond that the shaft faded into darkness.

"Okay let's get moving. Mox, if you look over to your right, you'll see a hatch. Inside that room there's a small maintenance panel that opens directly onto the duct." Kerf explained.

Mox had to leap across the shaft in order to get to the hatch. Fortunately, there were plenty of handholds available. He stationed himself beside the panel, locked his legs into the nearest restraint, and began fumbling with the handle. Though they had figured out how to open the pressure hatch at the docking gantry, no one had occasion to try one of the doors leading to a typical side cabin. The hatches in the sunken ship had all been fixed open, and their mechanisms had long corroded solid.

While Mox worked at the door, Kerf and Blujic helped the women doff the pressure suits and strip them of useful equipment such as magnesium space flares and other tools. They took each piece of the pressure suits and reassembled them as per Blujic's instructions, until the two girls were standing free next to fully assembled empty suits.

"Now watch this." Blujic winked.

She took a tether attached to the top of one of the helmets and waited until a floater slowly rose from below. She wasn't sure if the plan would work, because she didn't know the carrying capacity of the little robots. But she leaped across and hooked the tether onto a lug protruding from the bottom of the machine, while at the same time using her momentum to clear the pit and land beside her husband.

Blujic turned around and watched the little machine struggle with the added weight. At first the pair began to sink, but the thrusters kicked into overdrive and slowly, much more slowly than before, the robot compensated and moved upward again, pulling along the empty suit. The group watched as the suit obscured its carrier, and appeared to be a human figure floating slowly upward. As Blujic expected, the motion sensors responded to the bulky suit and the illumination switched on as it made progress up the shaft.

By that time Mox had figured out how to open the hatch, and Blujic slipped inside to set down the pack she had been carrying. It was a very narrow chamber, and Blujic noted with relief that the light hadn't come on inside. The two of them switched on headlamps, and Mox began removing the maintenance panel Kerf had described.

Blujic turned back to help the others. Across the way, she saw that Danid had gotten the second suit ready to go. Kerf spotted a floater descending from above, and helped her prepare to attach the tether. As the floater approached eye level, Danid eyed the lug, and leaped out to hook it on. The tether attached, but as her momentum carried her across, she realized the lower gravity had caused her to misjudge her coordination in respect to the handhold. Blujic reached out in an attempt to draw the woman in, but was unable to catch her as she slipped by. Danid bounced against the wall and fell into the abyss, passing the suit-laden floater.

Blujic stared down in horror. Danid's passage activated the lighting as she went down, and Blujic saw that the woman was flailing about, trying to grab onto handholds as she flew past. Fortunately, at one point she was able to kick away from the wall and propel herself into a side corridor. She slammed into the floor and disappeared from sight. The floater carrying the suit continued to slowly sink past the point where Danid had disappeared.

"Danid!" Blujic called downward and briefly looked over to see sullen-faced Kerf and Jevn peering down with worried looks on their faces.

"Danid! Can you hear me?" she repeated.

There was no response.

Blujic turned back inside and reported to Mox, who had succeeded in getting the panel partially removed, "Future, Danid has fallen! I've got to climb down and see if I can help."

"There's no time! Someone could be here any second now!" Mox replied.

"Dear, I've got to go. I'll find another way in."

When Blujic got back to the door Jevn was clinging to a handhold having just leaped across. Blujic swung herself over the edge and began to climb down.

"Kerf, I'm going to get her. Is there another way into the conduit?" she faced the technician who was preparing to leap.

"There is, but it's not as easy to find as this one. I'll go down with you." Kerf volunteered.

The climb in light gravity was actually quite easy, and was much more intimidating due to the height than it was dangerous. Blujic found there were plenty of handholds that could be used as a ladder. She scaled quickly down the shaft with Kerf following. Somewhere, she suspected, there were lifts or carriages meant to move up and down the shaft, but there was no time to find out where, or to figure out how to call one.

The side passage that Danid had fallen into turned out to be a short vestibule that functioned as a staging area for a large cargo hatch. Blujic saw a crumpled figure lying against the far bulkhead and rushed over.

"Danid! Are you alright?" she cried as she approached the figure.

Danid let out a moan indicating she was still alive at least. Blujic carefully looked over the girl to check for injuries. The obvious one was a broken leg that was unnaturally curled underneath her. From what Blujic could guess, Danid must have launched herself off the side of the shaft and momentum flipped her around so that the right leg took all of the landing force. There was no way to tell if there were internal injuries as well.

"Danid, move your fingers for me." Blujic said as she worked to make the girl more comfortable.

Danid was able to move the fingers on both hands and arms as well. The inner clothing worn by crewmembers underneath the bulky pressure suits was soft and comfortable. Blujic removed the bootie from the girls left foot.

"Okay, wiggle your left toes."

"I can't feel my left toes. I can't feel anything down there." Danid replied.

Blujic feared the worst, that Danid might have sustained damage to her spine. But there was no foreseeable way to treat the girl until they were able to get back to the *Soarer*.

And the situation was even more desperate...

"Someone's coming!" whispered Kerf, who had arrived on Blujic's heels and had gone back to check the shaft. "We'll have to go through that door."

Kerf immediately headed for the large cargo hatch and looked for the mechanism that would open it, while Blujic frantically tried to figure out a way to comfort the injured girl and lift her at the same time.

"Give me your weapon." Danid said. "I'm staying here."

"Don't be silly. I'm getting you out of here." Blujic protested.

Kerf managed to trigger the mechanism and the large hatch slid noisily into a pocket to the side. Blujic vaguely saw mountains of crates and other equipment as she struggled with the injured woman. Kerf came over and the two of them carried Danid to a clear spot on the floor just inside the hatch. Kerf quickly jumped over and activated the mechanism. The three of them watched as the door closed shut, a little too loudly for their comfort.

Blujic breathed a sigh of relief. The lights in the cargo hold had switched on when they entered, but with two pressure suits floating around who-knows-where, they still had a chance -- if the pirates were monitoring the motion sensor data, they would be getting three readings simultaneously.

"Quickly, let's get Danid away from the door." Blujic suggested and looked around at the interesting assortment of unidentified equipment and cargo that filled the chamber.

Blujic could have spent days exploring that room. But her mind was occupied and she couldn't do anything about it then. She spied a stack of metal containers that might be climbable, particularly in the light gravity. They carefully carried Danid over and worked out a method for slowly making their way up the stepped pyramid-like pile. They found a narrow spot protected on two sides, but there was only enough room for two people to lie down flat.

"You girls stay here, and don't move a muscle no matter what. I'll find another hiding spot." Kerf said.

Danid was fading in and out of consciousness and had gone into shock, so Blujic began treating the woman's injuries while Kerf pulled some of the containers out and restacked them to span over the top in a roof of sorts.

"This should shield you from the motion sensors." he said, then climbed back down.

That was the last time Blujic ever saw him alive.

A few minutes later the lights went out and Blujic cautiously turned on a small headlamp as she pulled off her jacket and tore it into strips. Then she used the strips to bind the broken leg with her improvised spear, sending Danid into unconsciousness from the pressure. Ironically, Blujic rolled her eyes as she realized the 'spear' she had been carrying was from the shuttle medical kit meant for use as a section of pole in a stretcher. When she had done everything she could, she lay back and tried to get some rest.

Sometime later Blujic tensed as the sound of the hatch sliding open echoed through the chamber. From her perspective under the pile of containers she could not see the door, but could hear footsteps that made a hollow clang like metal against metal.

Suddenly she heard a heavily accented voice, "Come out -- I know you're in here."

Blujic held her breath, not daring to even let the passage of air through her lips betray their whereabouts. Next to her, Danid began to stir but Blujic held the woman still.

She was startled by the sound of a scuffle. Blujic heard Kerf's voice cry out and imagined him trying to pommel the stranger with his primitive club. She cowered as she heard the fighters slam into the stacks of cargo. Blujic hoped Kerf would have a fighting chance, but her hopes were in vain as the struggle ended quickly, and soon only the distinct stranger's footsteps could be heard.

She closed her eyes and kept herself wrapped around the wounded woman, burying her head in the other's side. The footsteps walked around a bit, and she could hear the stranger poking and prodding at various pieces of equipment. She mentally followed the footfalls back to the main hatch, and noted with relief that the invader left the hold and closed the door.

Blujic waited long after the lights went out and at some point, fell asleep. Danid stirring next to her awakened her.

"Water," came a hoarse whisper.

Blujic brought out a small container and held it to the woman's lips.

"They'll be looking for me." Danid said.

"What do you mean?" Blujic whispered.

Danid began to explain, "They'll find the empty suit and know that we tricked them. They heard my voice and know 'Danid' is still out there somewhere."

"That's okay -- we'll keep you safe." Blujic replied, "How are you feeling?"

"My leg hurts." Danid offered.

That was good news. She had Danid wiggle her toes on both feet and confirmed the movement.

"You'll be okay. We just need to keep you down for a while till rescue comes."

Blujic began thinking about what to do next. They were probably safe as long as they didn't trigger the motion sensors, but they had brought only emergency ration bars that were almost gone. The bulk of their food Blujic had loaded in the pack she had deposited with Mox. She also didn't know how Kerf was doing. Had the technician suffered harm -- or worse? Once the empty suits were found, the invaders would search all over the place. Fortunately, the pirates didn't know how many were in the landing party.

Blujic called out softly to Kerf but got no response. She made up her mind to take the risk and climbed out of the niche that was their hiding place. Immediately the illumination ramped up to full brightness and Blujic was able to switch off the headlamp. They would have to hurry -- the lights coming on could bring down the hostiles again in short order. She helped Danid crawl out and the two of them climbed down the stack in the low gravity.

At the bottom Blujic began to look through the stacks for Kerf as she dreaded the worst. Her fears were confirmed when she came across signs of a struggle. She involuntarily gasped when she found the lifeless body of Kerf sprawled out face down in a pool of blood and began feeling weak in her knees. She knelt down and examined the body, holding a cloth over her nose and mouth. Blujic squinted as she gently lifted and prodded with her free hand, trying to keep her emotions steady. *Curious*, she thought, the bleeding had come from a non-vital leg injury. However, patches on the torso took on the appearance of cooked flesh as if subjected to intense heat. She felt light-headed and fought off a fainting spell.

Blujic noticed the man's hand was tightly clenched. As she peered closer, it was apparent that he had died holding on to a piece of writing media. She dropped the cloth covering her nose and used both hands to work the fist open.

The crumpled sheet was a note Kerf had scribbled on while in hiding after he had prepared the niche for the women. 'Locker back panel' was all it said. Blujic was sure the note was for them, perhaps giving them some scrap of information that would help them avoid the invaders.

What could they do? They could not just leave the body there -- it would be undignified. On the other hand, if they disturbed him, the pirates would find out. But what if Kerf crawled out by himself? Blujic began to get the glimmering of an idea that might allow Kerf to perform one more service, and give Blujic time to ferry Danid safely away.

She stood up and carefully pulled Kerf's arms in order to drag the body toward the main hatch. But instead of doing a smooth drag, she jiggled the body a bit, trying to make it look as though a bleeding injured man had crawled along, dripping some of the blood on the floor. When she got to the hatch, she found Danid standing on her good leg, ready to go. Blujic propped Kerf's body in a dignified manner near the hatch mechanism, against some flammable containers, making it look as though he were ready to face any enemy that walked through the door. She tore away at the remnants of the blood-soaked pant leg and tidied him up a bit.

They opened the hatch carefully and Blujic had Danid slip outside. She pulled out a space flare that they had salvaged from one of the suits and rigged it so that once the hatch was closed again, reopening it would set off a causal chain that would ignite the hot magnesium and encapsulated oxygen and turn Kerf's resting place into a funeral pyre. Finally, she set the trigger -- a tall object she found stored in one of the stacks. She held the object at an angle and had Danid shut the hatch. When the door slowly closed enough to support the leaning object she let go, and the hatch shut. At the last instant she slipped one corner of the torn pant leg into the slot near the bottom, so the closing hatch clamped it against the jamb. When they were finished, the fabric appeared as though it had gotten caught while someone crawled through, tearing it away from its owner.

Blujic and Danid paid their respects in front of the tomb. They knew they didn't have much time, because the ship's illumination was on a timer and had Kerf been alone, setting up his own booby trap, the timer would have begun its countdown as soon as the hatch closed and his movements ceased triggering the motion sensor.

Blujic had Danid wrap her arms around her neck in piggyback fashion. She was sure it would be easy to carry, climb, and even jump with the woman on her back in the low gravity. With Danid secure, she stood on the edge of the shaft.

Blujic wasn't sure what to do next to keep up the deception. All she could think was to hide out in a side chamber until Kerf's 'funeral' was over, and delude herself that she may be able to somehow jump the stranger from behind while the other was distracted by the fireworks.

She peered over the edge and found precisely what she was looking for -- a small hatch just below the platform on which they stood, set into the far wall. She leapt across the gap with Danid on her back, grabbed onto exposed handholds and protruding conduits, and quickly opened the hatch, all the while working through heroic plans of how she would sneak back out and cross the abyss, and climb up from underneath to surprise the enemy. The women found themselves in another small, dark chamber lined with panels of some sort. There wasn't time nor was it advisable to switch on the headlamp, so she could not get a good glimpse of the room. Fortunately, the lights did not trigger, meaning they didn't have to deal with motion sensors.

Blujic quickly shut the hatch most of the way, and left a hairline crack through which she could peek outside. The small gap allowed a dim light to leak into the room, until a few moments later when the lights outside automatically turned off, and the women waited silently in the dark.

The wait seemed long, even though Blujic suspected it could not have been more than half an hour. Her fear intensified as the moments passed and she could not keep from shaking uncontrollably. Why was she doing this to herself? The heroic plans to defeat the dreaded Tensakian started to seem like grand illusions that had no basis in reality, and in retrospect, she could not believe she could have missed so many considerations. She had made all sorts of ridiculous plans, trapped herself and Danid in a dead-end hole, and somehow assumed that she could be a hero. What was she thinking?

Illumination in the shaft shook Blujic out of her thoughts. Something large enough to trigger the lights had moved into range. She nervously crouched next to the slot to get a view of the hatch vestibule. Whatever illusions she had about playing a hero were swept away when she saw two hideous shapes descending the shaft via unknown means. What was she seeing? All she could think of was that evil incarnate had taken on the form of dark billowing clouds that drifted down the passageway. As her eyes focused, she could see shadowing figures, or something inside the foggy substance, brandishing some sort of apparatus or weapon. *They must have some sort of cloaking field around them*, she thought.

One of the partly transparent figures alighted on the ledge, while the other remained suspended in the shaft farther up. Briefly the heavily armored figures came into focus.

Blujic was too nervous to take a breath, and tried to concentrate on the enemy. She knew that if she could possibly help it, she would never put herself in such a situation again. Just the sight of the figures decked out with arrays of deadly implements struck terror to her core. Each figure was unusually tall, with plated scales that covered the entire body, designed for maximum freedom of movement. In spite of the heavy plating each figure moved in quick, fluid motions that reminded her of a well-muscled creature bursting with disciplined energy. There were numerous devices mounted to their helmets, chests, backs, arms, and legs that seem to be imprinted with protrusions or unidentifiable etchings that gave her the impression of finely manufactured machinery, perhaps microelectronics. Blujic had no doubt the terrible strangers were protected by a full suite of sensory technology across a broad spectrum, and there would be no possibility of sneaking up on one of them.

How much of the attached equipment related to weapons she didn't know, but each of them embraced a long black wicked implement that they seemed particularly engaged with. At one point both of the attackers moved their entire concentration along the lengths of those awful tools, aiming them in unison at something directly below. The cloaking mechanisms instantly switched on but Blujic could still see deadly muzzles aimed downward. A tense moment or two passed as they tracked the unseen target that turned out to be a floater rising from below. When the Tensakians determined the floater was not a threat, their helmets and weapons roamed the perimeter as they took in all the possible angles an attacker might lurk.

Blujic began to fear that the two invaders would open every hatch nearby just out of rote practice. She turned to look at a barely visible Danid who had fixed her gaze on Blujic, apparently trying to figure out what was happening by reading

Blujic's facial expressions. She was sorry she couldn't give the woman any comfort.

The pirate hovering in the shaft continually whirled about, aiming the evil weapon while the companion focused on the hatch. All the instruments of destruction pointed toward the hatch as the invader moved in to trigger the hatch mechanism. Like clockwork both figures moved in unison to the side and backed against the wall as the hatch opened, ready to inflict death on anything that emerged.

Blujic's booby-trap worked only too well. From the angle she was observing, it was possible to see telltale flashes on the walls and hear the sparking as the space flare ignited. The combustible material she had placed around Kerf's body burned better than she would have hoped, producing a fireball that traveled out into the shaft. But the pirates calmly pressed themselves against the wall, watching the inferno with impassioned neutrality. When the flickering had died down, the invaders slowly moved into the hold and left Blujic's field of view. Blujic and Danid bowed their heads in a moment of silence in farewell to Kerf.

The pirates' calm demeanor renewed Blujic's worry -- what would happen if they saw through the deception and came rushing out, realizing there were others nearby? They would surely look in all side compartments right away. She fought the urge to run, remembering back in her Flesh kick days avoiding inmates and mappers, that running usually drew attention, but a good hiding place increased one's chances of not being discovered. Patiently she waited, hoped, and prayed that the two terrible monsters would conclude that Kerf had crawled out and set himself up as a booby trap.

Machines began to arrive, probably called automatically, and Blujic could hear a rushing sound as compressed gasses or chemicals suppressed the flames.

It seemed like a long time before the two figures emerged again, aiming their instruments of death in calculated search patterns. Blujic froze with fright. The two fluidly avoided the fire suppression operation and stepped off the ledge, one aiming downward and the other upward along the direction of travel as they rose up the shaft. Soon after they had disappeared the lights went out. Blujic gently slid the door shut and leaned back against the wall, finally able to take a breath. They were safe for the time being, and in all the excitement she hadn't noticed how tired she was. She was physically and emotionally drained, and finally allowed herself to succumb on the coattails of an adrenalin high.

Blujic awoke several hours later, and was confused about where she was in the dim light. The strange gravity acceleration was still there, pressing her to the floor. She groggily looked over and saw that Danid had her headlamp on, snacking on emergency rations, and remembered they were still in a dilemma. They were as good as dead if they had to stay put, and how far could they get if they ran?

Blujic switched her own headlamp on and looked around the small room. One wall was lined with tall metal doors or panels. She went down the row of doors opening each one, and rummaged through rotting fragments, tools, and unidentified objects that had been sitting undisturbed for hundreds of years. There were a few potentially useful items, but nothing that was portable. Certainly, there was nothing that would serve as food or a weapon.

The last door was wider than the others, and had characters etched onto its face. Blujic could not understand what the characters meant. However, the door was locked and she could not figure out how to open it.

"We're below the entrance Mox and Jevn used to enter the service conduit. Maybe it parallels the shaft down." Danid suggested.

Blujic stared at the locked door, "That would put it right behind this bulkhead." she said.

Suddenly she remembered the written note Kerf had been clenching at the time of his death.

"Locker back panel." she repeated from memory.

"What?" Danid asked.

"Kerf left us a message, 'locker back panel'. Maybe this is what he was talking about." Blujic explained.

She began to tap and push on the door, seeing if she could find a pressure-sensitive release. She pounded on both edges, beginning at the top and working downward.

Blujic was startled when there was an answering knock from the other side. She stepped back away and stared warily at the panel. The knock repeated itself, and there was a metallic noise.

Suddenly the door popped open and Mox stood there with a grin on his face.

"Future, you stupid -- " Blujic began and rushed up to give him a hug.

"We found a great place to hole up in. You'll love it." Mox began, "Then I got so worried when you didn't show up."

"How did you know we were here?" Danid looked up from her spot on the floor.

Jevn peeked from behind Mox and looked down at the injured woman.

Mox continued, "I went back out and peeked down the shaft just as those two bullies flared up the neighborhood. I was worried sick, and thought you were in trouble. When the pirates left, I went back down the conduit and tried to find a way to get closer to the cargo hatch. Then I found this panel and heard you pounding -- I was so happy, I knew it was you."

"Mox, Kerf is dead." Blujic said with a solemn tone.

Mox and Jevn both frowned. Blujic explained that the pirates knew at least two people were on the loose because of the empty suits -- and one of them was a female named Danid. Since Kerf was caught, they would deduce Danid was still on the run.

"Okay, we obviously can't confront them directly. But I guarantee Danid the fugitive is going to be a pain in the rear." Mox gave them an evil grin.

CHAPTER 20

Fisby sat at his virtual workstation and immersed himself in the mapper's full-surround video feeds. Because of the jerkiness and high static content, he had to take frequent rests to avoid getting headaches or nausea. He paced his breaks to occur during the time delay, while waiting for his instructions to reach *Blister* and the mapper's responses to return to Mother.

This time he was really nervous. He had taken a chance and was betting a lot on a few meager preparations, while the life and well-being of a poor girl on the other end was at stake. The mapper was carrying one object in its gripper that Fisby had picked up in a trade -- and he was risking both the mapper's autonomy and the life of the girl by delivering it to her.

The story of how he obtained the item was quite interesting on its own merit. Only two years before he would not have even remotely imagined being in such a place, or doing such amazing feats. It began a week before as he was driving the mapper around, exploring the market place of that strange zero-g culture. He had watched Worlith from afar, as the slave masters herded the shabbily dressed women back and forth between what was probably their sleeping quarters and the various posts where they served as barkers, waitresses, cleaners, and undoubtedly slaves of the flesh. Fisby had no idea how they decided the duty roster, but it was fortunate that they had tethered Worlith to a booth that sold zero-g drinks. The woman was forced to serve lewd customers everyday, and her masters came around in the evening and beat her for not doing things properly.

Fisby had watched for patterns in the customers, and made note of how often the masters came around. He finally thought he saw a short period where the mapper might approach Worlith with less risk. But he figured there would only be one chance, and he would have to get her away quickly and smuggle her out to the perimeter farms. What he needed was a torch that would cut through fingerwidth metal shackles.

During the times he was not watching Worlith, Fisby sent the mapper around looking at the various stalls, looking for some kind of tool that would do the job. He sent the machine on fake errands that mimicked the way other robotic messengers were behaving, and noticed the traders as they came in.

Once he followed a group of scavengers out into *Blister* proper, and observed how they picked over derelict spacecraft and junk heaps. He also made note of which sorts of machined parts or electronic gizmos brought in the largest trades. If the scavengers noticed the mapper, they inevitably would make an attempt at either capturing it or chasing it away -- an action that Fisby interpreted as protecting territory.

Finally, on one of his rounds exploring the market place, Fisby turned the robot into a narrow alleyway that he had avoided previously, afraid someone would ambush and steal the machine. To his delight the way opened up into a wide spherical space lined with equipment booths. All sorts of tools, hardware, and construction materials lined the zero-g cabinets. It was no time before Fisby spotted a series of heavy-duty shears that he thought might be just right for the job.

That very afternoon he set the mapper out to scavenge for parts, knowing the main bulk of traders would be heading back with their finds looking for a trade, and the junk heaps would be nearly empty of scavengers. Because of the mapper's small size, it was easy to squeeze into places where the typical scavenger couldn't fit, so in no time at all he had located a fine piece of electronics that he released from its housing by gingerly snipping at the flat wiring harnesses with its end effectors. Fisby had sent the machine home, prize in hand, to its usual hiding place for the night.

Today was the day. Fisby had awoken the little machine early and headed down to the market place still grasping the electronics piece. He didn't know what to expect, because the mapper had never been programmed for communication directly with humans except through the remote control and video feeds. He had thought up a series of routines that would cause the robot to respond to humans in a way they could understand, such as point, shake sideways for no, nod for yes, and a few other actions. However, the machine wasn't capable of recognizing human actions, which posed a problem because of the time delay -- how to perform a complex trade with a human using entirely pre-programmed actions.

He came up with a feeble solution that he hoped would do the trick. He programmed a sequence into the mapper that would have it go up to the booth proprietor, show its electronic piece, and quickly zip over to the zero-g shelf and point to a set of humungous shears. If all went well, the robot would leave with the shears in its gripper, but if there was a misunderstanding and the electronic piece was lost, he would have to go out and scavenge again for another piece.

Fortunately, the sequence went remarkably well, and Fisby watched it unfold as the video signals came in. The proprietor, evidently used to dealing with remote proxies for customers, showed great flexibility in her interpretation of the little robot's gestures. Just as expected, the mapper left the booth with the shears in hand.

Fisby sat nervously in the virtual workstation. Now the machine was hovering across the way, watching Worlith for the right opportunity. He saw Worlith search for the little machine, and watched the woman experience pleasure at the comfort of knowing the machine was there again, like a mother watching over her daughter.

Fisby timed the arrival of the slave masters, and watched customers turn their heads as one of the brutal men beat her for some unknown reason. He watched them leave, and rejoiced when he saw the battered Worlith look up at the mapper and smile. He counted off three minutes and moved in.

Worlith looked at the machine in wide-eyed wonder, not knowing what to expect. But when the mapper reached up with the manipulator and displayed the shears, a worried look came on her face. She looked around to see if anyone was watching and reached out to take the shears. A couple of customers took notice and began to watch the drama unfold.

Fortunately, no one moved in to stop her. She took the shears and worked through the shackle cables as she floated around in a strange sort of acrobatic dance, the momentum of her every move translating back to affect her absolute position.

Unfortunately, the cable was much stronger than Fisby had thought. It was only halfway cut by the time the masters were supposed to come around again. Fisby had the machine grasp the shears away from Worlith and quickly moved off into the distance just as the ugly fellows hovered around the corner. Fisby noticed that Worlith had draped a cloth over the cable and tied it on where the partially cut gash was located.

The customers stared at the slave masters and waited to see what would happen. The more brutal character looked for another excuse to beat Worlith and noticed the cloth tied to the wire. He reached out to pull it off but suddenly one of the customers floated over and got the man's attention. Fisby held his breath, positive that the onlooker would give her away. But to his delight the customer spent several minutes keeping the brutal fellow occupied, and the motley group left without laying a finger on the girl.

Fisby had the machine move back into place and Worlith finished the job. The customers who had been watching all waved goodbye as Worlith quickly flitted away from the drink vendor and followed the little machine out.

Unfortunately, things didn't go as planned. The slave masters came back early, and even though Worlith was able to duck to the side and avoid them as they floated by, the two immediately discovered the severed cable and gave chase. Fisby had foreseen such a possibility and programmed a battle maneuver into the little machine -- he entered the two targets, set the mapper to track them, and executed the command to make stabbing and slicing motions with the gripper that was holding the shears.

Worlith made her escape as Fisby helplessly watched the little machine do something it was never designed to do. The machine thrust and slashed, keeping the two men occupied, but just as often one of the fellows would get through and slam into the little robot. Some of the blows caused the machine to momentarily lose its calibration, or cause the video signal to blank out briefly. The machine would lose a few precious seconds recalibrating and one of the men would get around it. The machine would then rush to head him off, and the battle would begin anew.

Fisby was sure the mapper wouldn't be able to keep up the defensive posture for long, and wondered how he would ever be able to get Worlith away to the safety of the farms. They cleared the market place and barely shot out into the open when the end came. Fisby would remember back in satisfaction the moment the little mapper somehow stabbed the shears through the stomach of the brutal slaver, even though he was sure it was merely a shallow flesh wound. However, at the same instant the other fellow had used the wide-open area to sneak around the robot's back and send a disarming blow that completely disabled the manipulator. A second blow spun the little machine around, and Fisby would thereafter be haunted by the last scene as the video feed blinked out for the last time -- he saw Worlith getting away from her captors, only to have her momentum shoot her straight into a large platoon of Tensakians swooping in from a distant ship.

CHAPTER 21

A strong-armed rescue seemed within reach as Sochiko worked to bring the *Soarer* on the tail of the lumbering giant. Ix and Faddard, who had been on board at the time, half-heartedly complained that it might be unwise to follow, but knew there would be nothing stopping her. Faddard clocked the trajectory and found that the pirates must have timed the attack with a window to Bridgestar.

"I want to head them off. Is there any way to get in front of them?" Sochiko asked Faddard when they just peeked over the horizon from the other craft.

At first it seemed as though they would catch up with the lumbering giant in a day or so, but the pirate crew seemed to find ways of supplementing their thruster systems.

"At this rate it will take at least a week to catch up, assuming they stop accelerating. But that doesn't look promising." Faddard returned.

Sochiko thought for a bit, then remembered a scrap of information that she had read regarding Those Who Went Before.

"Are there any moons nearby?" she asked.

Faddard consulted his charts, "Yes, several. There are at least five encounters with Minato in the next two days."

"Have you ever heard of a gravity sling?" Sochiko asked.

Ix, who had stayed silent knowing how strong-willed his niece was, spoke up, "I've heard of it. But no one has ever tried it before."

"We've considered gravity slings as a short cut to get ore back to Mother, but it didn't seem very feasible." Faddard added.

"Why aren't they feasible?" she asked.

"Well, the way the gravity sling works is by approaching a planet, and using it's gravity well to accelerate. The spacecraft would trade its potential energy into kinetic energy. If you do a burn at the right spot, it would allow the vessel to significantly borrow kinetic energy from the planet to increase its velocity."

Sochiko frowned, "Find me a solution that will get us ahead of those monsters."

A few hours later Faddard came up smiling. Sochiko sat him down and listened to what he had come up with.

"Not only have I got a solution, but I think we have two opportunities in case we don't get it right the first time. But it will be very risky." Faddard explained.

Ix rolled his eyes.

Sochiko beamed, "Okay, let's have it."

Faddard hesitated, getting signals from Ix. But it was too late -- Sochiko wouldn't be stopped.

"If we perform one burn in an hour from now, it will put us toward Ko. Ko is out of the way but it will give us a tremendous boost, and if we aim ourselves right, we'll be ahead of them."

"Okay, do it!" she said with a tone of finality, "What's the other opportunity?"

Faddard paused again, unsure about whether to proceed. He looked to Ix, who appeared to have given up.

"Well, that will also put us in the neighborhood of Abb, which will shoot us around back to Minato. Then if we slingshot around Minato, we'll have enough velocity to reach Bridgestar in four months." Faddard said quietly.

Sochiko almost fell out of her chair, and Ix groaned. Both of them stared at Faddard for different reasons.

"Are you serious?" was all she said.

Ix spoke up again, "Sochi, let's think through this rationally. Maybe we can sling around Ko, but we've never done such a maneuver before. If you take the *Soarer* all the way to Bridgestar using gravity assist, how will you slow down once you get there?"

Sochiko said nothing, but just stared at Faddard.

Several hours later they were on their way to Ko. The burn had been successful, and the crew was busily getting ready for their first real gravity assist. Merinat got online and pointed out that the first mission around Abb had also been a form of gravity sling that sent them back to Mother, so the maneuver already had a precedent of sorts. But the trajectory Sochiko was planning would be much more difficult. They checked and rechecked the calculations.

Two days later the *Soarer* fell into Ko's gravity well. Ko was the farthest of the moons from the sun, and had a similar density and mass as that of Sado and Minato. Faddard trained their telescopes onto the icy planet as their spacecraft screamed by at a mere fifty kilometers above the surface. As Sochiko watched the images streaming in, she suddenly had a disturbing thought -- Ko could have been Mother that just happened to be a little too far from the sun. She wondered -- if they had been equipped with ground-penetrating radar would they find an oblong magnetic heart?

The *Soarer* performed its burns perfectly, and shot out the backside on a course to intercept the big ship. Unfortunately, bad news came in only a half hour later.

"The *Vector* has slowed its trajectory. It looks as though there was a rendezvous with an unknown satellite." Faddard reported.

Sochiko was concerned, "Is it a second pirate ship?"

Faddard shook his head, "I don't think so. The satellite seems to have been there a long time."

"Do we have any information on the satellite? I wouldn't guess that they would be stupid enough to stop and steal a spacecraft when half the solar system is on their tail." Sochiko asked.

"The orbit is quite a ways out there." Faddard began, "I've never seen it before."

Ix suggested, "It's the stellar drive. It's too massive to park very close to Minato. There's one of those circling Mother too, we think. Those Who Went Before jettisoned it before scuttling their vessel."

The next day there was more bad news. The big ship completely disappeared without a trace. *Soarer* was heading for a rendezvous with empty space.

Sochiko pounded her fist on the table trying to vent off her anger. The invaders had sidestepped her every move. Where could they have hidden that monster?

Uncle Ix deduced that the pirates had probably figured out how to aim the stellar drive, and somehow, they had launched themselves at tremendous speeds toward *Blister*'s home star.

"We think the ship uses exotic forms of energy to form a bubble around itself." Ix began, "The drive may even consist of a pair of black holes, spinning at relativistic speeds."

"Does that mean it is capable of exceeding the speed of light?" Sochiko frowned.

Ix explained, "No, that isn't even possible. In the direction of travel the drive shrinks the fabric of space, and expands space behind it. In effect, the ship never moves at all."

"How long will it take them to get there?" she asked.

"No one knows. It could take months, or only a few hours."

Sochiko thought the entire episode was quite overwhelming. If the ship had already rushed on its way toward *Blister*, how would she get her parents back?

Frustrated, she excused herself and went to her private quarters. It was apparent on the faces of the crew as she passed that they were all nervous -- they had never seen her in such a combative mood before. Sochiko donned a mask and tanks and headed for the ring pool to do some laps.

There were several issues to solve, and she needed to think clearly. It hadn't occurred to her that the enemy would be capable of bypassing Bridgestar altogether. Faddard had said it might be possible to get to the station in four months -- but how would they decelerate once they arrived? Running through the calculations, she figured at their velocity they might be able to get themselves in a long elliptical orbit around Bridgestar if they used all their fuel in a deceleration burn, and if the station exceeded a certain threshold density. But no one knew anything about the orbital facility. Would they have a robotic fuel depot like Everwebber? There were so many risks -- was it worth it?

Sochiko thought of her parents who may already be mistreated by the evil Tensakians. She thought of poor Worlith who had evidently been forced into some sort of slavery at *Blister*. Was it worth the risk to save the ones she loved?

Sochi considered her duty. If the *Soarer* passed out of service for a spell, would the vital mining operation suffer? She didn't think so -- the critical parts of the operation were set up and approaching self-sustainability. She was sure the crews would be able to supplement any resources with items they could trade for in Everwebber. Merinat's ship the *Stellar* was there in case they needed to evacuate.

What of the alternative? If *Soarer* stayed, would they be better off?

The next morning Sochiko called a meeting of the entire crew. She knew there would have to be complete unanimity on the decision. She spelled out the risks, explained the unique opportunity that they had, how the *Soarer* was stocked for a few more year's journey.

Merinat called in from the *Stellar*, "*Sochiko, you can't do it. Come back here and let's figure out a less rash approach.*"

To Sochi's surprise, Uncle Ix defended her, "I think we should do it. If we head into this with our eyes open, knowing we may never return, we'll be prepared for whatever danger lies ahead. But think of what we will gain if we succeed?"

Faddard also sounded positive, "Mother is in good hands. Our fellow countrymen Technicians, Wardens, and Inmates alike are on the threshold of an economic revolution no one can even dream of."

Virginia joined in from Mother, after a short time delay, "*Josh says you should be able to do it.*"

Sochiko stood up and looked at everyone in the cramped room, "Well, what do you think? We can pass around Abb at a higher altitude and slow ourselves down enough to jump right back into the same old business on Minato. Or we can go lower and sling ourselves to eternity. Are you with me?"

Ix and Faddard raised their hands. Then Holina and a few others. One by one the rest of the crew stood in support. There was not a single dissenting vote.

Sochiko smiled, "Bridgestar, here we come..." she said quietly.

CHAPTER 22

Mox leaned back against the wall and relaxed for a minute, with his backpack hung almost to the floor next to him. He tended a small wall hugger robot as it meticulously polished the surfaces around conduits, ducts, and hatches, and was careful to move along when the robot made progress down the passage. To his left and right the corridor faded away into darkness, and in his immediate vicinity the corridor was brightly lit, responding to the movements of the little robot.

Without warning, the illumination flickered on a distance down the passage to his left. He eased himself backward behind a pipe and kept a wary eye in the direction of the newcomer. He carefully slipped his hand into the backpack and pulled out a pair of field glasses, which he raised to his eyes. There in the viewfinder was a medium-sized floater, slowly working along the corridor performing whatever inspection it was programmed to do. Mox relaxed again and watched the machine trigger more lights as it made progress down the hall.

It had been a few months since the *Vector* was taken over by the pirates, and the four of them had evaded capture, engaging in small acts of sabotage whenever they could. Mox had become an expert of the lighting system, and had found ways of manipulating the system from distant junction boxes, control panels, and conduit raceways that required the invaders to come down personally to trace malfunctions and make repairs. Among his exploits were the great blackout, where he shut off all the lights for a time, and the great whiteout where the entire illumination system stayed on for an entire week, draining power from everything else.

Mox's latest brainchild was to manipulate the sensitivity of the motion sensors so they would respond to fist-sized objects. He had only last week watched with satisfaction as the fruit husk he tossed down the corridor triggered the sensors all the way along its path.

The invaders were slow to react. Occasionally they would tap into a loudspeaker system and say, "*Danid, we know you are there. Come out and we'll guarantee your safety.*" or "*Danid, join us! We can use someone of your talents.*"

But sometimes it took them days and even weeks to send someone down to look for the problem spots. Mox suspected that the operation of the stellar singularity drive required more hands than they could spare, so they could only take advantage of breaks in the operational schedule to send anyone out. Fortunately, this gave Mox and the others a degree of autonomy to move about as they pleased.

Over the weeks Mox had identified several modes of egress from most parts of the ship, so it was possible to avoid capture even if the enemy sighted one of them. Mox reached back and felt the fire suppression tank on his back to make sure its nozzle was clear of obstructions. On several occasions one or the other of Mox's colleagues had had to use the compressed foam in the tanks to rocket out of a tight spot. At first the strangers had rockets too, but it was apparent that the enemy had gotten low on propellant over the weeks and were not able to replenish their supply.

After munching on a snack comprising roasted fruit and vegetables folded into a leafy wrap, Mox waited for the floater to pass, and slipped into its circle of illumination. Even if the

Tensakians were monitoring the lights, every path would be traceable back to the small machines as long as Mox or the others were patient enough to follow them. Mox had recently figured out how to monitor the lighting sensor log himself, using a portable terminal -- but they still weren't sure how to read the data to make it useful for evasion. Mox also thought it might be possible to adjust the sensors to trigger when certain materials were present, or according to the reflectivity of the surfaces. At any rate there were a lot more games they could play.

His next destination was Garden Deck number eight, to pick up some vegetables for Jevn who was cooking that evening. Mox missed the spore meals he had grown up with, but had to admit Those Who Went Before must have relished the culinary arts because they were eating better than any of them had ever eaten before.

The floater veered off in the wrong direction so Mox waited until another machine came into view and switched hosts. Since they didn't have control over the little robots, sometimes it took hours of patient hitchhiking until one happened to go in the direction they wanted to go. After switching two more times he was deposited at one of the massive hatches leading to the garden deck. He quickly opened the door and jumped inside as the robot slipped by.

Mox found himself on a narrow catwalk that curved around out of sight in both directions. He had to shield his eyes from the bright illumination that was set on a timer instead of triggered by motion sensors. In front of him, a large platform sloped up from the edge of the catwalk at an angle, chocked full of shelves laden with all sorts of plants and shrubs. The shelves were arranged in neat rows to allow robotic gardeners to methodically move back and forth and reach every spot. There was no soil -- the roots of each of the plants were held in suspension in a cavity where nutrient-rich mists constantly sprayed over the fibers.

The sloped platform was moving slowly to the right. There was another platform immediately behind it, and more beyond that all the way around the curve. Mox waited until four platforms passed, and spied the tuber vegetables he had been looking for on the fifth. Carefully he stepped off the catwalk onto the platform and felt it sway. Each platform hung via two points which allowed a dynamic balancing act between centrifugal rotation and forward acceleration, so there was always a gravity vector working on the plants. The row of garden platforms circled the entire girth of the *Vector*, and Mox was fairly sure he had counted at least nine garden decks interspersed with the passenger cabins. The pirates also got their food from the garden decks, but the chance of running into one of those monsters was low.

Mox stepped back off the platform and began walking around the catwalk, enjoying the fresh air and entertaining himself with the mechanical symphony put on by the robotic caretakers busy at work. He found another kind of vegetable, picked a few, and went on his way. On one last platform, he found a small bunch of flowers and carefully placed them, roots and all, into a water-filled container. With a backpack full of groceries, he headed for the nearest exit.

Mox had one more task before heading back to the nest. He cracked open the hatch and waited for a floater to come by, and eased behind the machine in the illuminated passageway. It took him three tries to get a machine that took him toward the vast garage, and he had to settle with a slow-moving wall hugger.

Mox was fortunate that the little robot took him past the viewing gallery, where rows of transparent windows opened up onto the depth of space. As the little robot passed the gallery, he had a few minutes to think. He looked out at the black void and his thoughts went to the big problem of where they were, and where they might be going. One thing was sure -- they were nowhere near Mother, and he suspected their sun was long behind them. What sort of fantastic world were the pirates taking them to? What would they do when they arrived?

Mox left the viewing gallery as the little robot passed on. They entered the corridor that fed some of the gantry tunnels leading into the vast garage. Choosing carefully, he leaped into one of the tunnels and quickly rushed down its length to get himself out of the motion sensors.

Reaching the end of the tunnel, Mox discovered that it was a gantry that had one of the small ancient vessels still docked to it. Over the weeks he had entered all of the remaining craft at some point or other, but there was nothing left but decay. Apparently, the maintenance robots did not include the small craft on their duty roster.

Mox entered the hatch and switched on his headlamp, moving toward the nearest view port. He cast his eyes downward in the dim external lights and saw the shattered wreckage of the shuttle scattered across the floor of the garage. Mox imagined that poor Gij had fought a worthy battle, keeping the shuttle aloft as long as he could. When the great *Vector* accelerated, he must have had trouble staying aloft. By the time Mox, Blujic, and the others were able to get back to him it was already too late. In the final act, Gij had taken their secret with him -- the enemy was convinced only Danid remained at large. There were not enough remains left to identify how many had been aboard when the shuttle met its demise.

Mox set the container of flowers down in a patch of light that forever beamed through one of the windows from outside. There were now two tombs in the vast maze of passageways -- resting places where valiant Technicians had fought till the end. Mox vowed there would be no more.

After several moments of silence with bowed head he shuffled down the tunnel and 'hitched a ride' home with a passing floater.

CHAPTER 23

Ix, Sochiko, and the rest of the crew celebrated the successful gravity assist around Minato as they rocketed out toward a rendezvous with Bridgestar. Ix was in an upbeat mood as he helped clear away the evidence of the party, which had been held in the galley area of the 'Hikari' arm. But the revelry was interrupted by an incoming transmission from Mother. Sochiko rushed to take the call.

"Sochi, I hate to tell you this, but our orbital mechanics folks have found an error in the calculations." Cadbic was on the line, *"You don't have enough fuel to slow down once you reach Bridgestar -- the only thing that will slow you down enough is a gravity well."*

The revelation was disturbing. The *Soarer*'s onboard astronomers scrambled to point their telescopes and find anything big enough to dump all their kinetic energy onto, but to no avail -- there were no bodies of significant mass anywhere nearby.

Ix was upset. They had had weeks to get the calculations right, and no one caught it.

He turned to his niece and said, "We'll swing right by Bridgestar and shoot out into deep space."

"Will we leave the solar system altogether?" Sochiko asked.

He did some quick calculations using Cadbic's figures and answered, "No, we're on a long elliptical orbit around the sun."

"So, we'll eventually be back in the neighborhood of Minato?" she verified.

Ix gave a deadpan answer, "Yes, in a hundred and thirty years."

His niece looked at him as if he were joking, but knew by his tone of voice he was serious. If another solution didn't present itself, a hundred and thirty years from now the children of Sado would find a tomb rocketing through their neighborhood. He had to send her off to bed in a gloomy mood.

Ix stewed on the problem for days and weeks on end, but every conclusion turned out the same. Once Faddard found a solution that would shorten the orbital period by twenty years, but no one found any comfort in it.

Sochiko, always the quick thinker, came back again and again with unique concepts. "Is there some way we can shed large amounts of mass in an unconventional way? What if we lost our ice shielding, or used explosives to jettison modules from the ship?" Sochiko asked at one point.

The idea sparked renewed effort. Everyone went back and ran through scenario after scenario, but to no avail. They would be unable to capitalize on all the force without killing themselves from the g-loads. The best solution still gave them ninety years.

Several months later the *Soarer* began its approach to Bridgestar and they still had no idea how they would decelerate. Sochiko had even sent a transmission on to *Blister* to see if she could get advice from Kret, but got no response. Ix watched as his niece's attitude deteriorated. She was taking it hard, getting increasingly irritable in her interactions with the crew.

It was at one of those times where she had been snapping at anyone who passed by when an unexpected solution presented itself. They got an incoming call from Bridgestar itself.

"*What is your destination?*" the machine-generated voice asked in the same odd Wardenese dialect that Everwebber used.

At first Ix thought it might have been from the pirates, even though the voice and accent were different. The voice asked the same thing several times over an hour's period.

"Identify yourself." Sochiko returned.

"*Identification has been sent directly to your navigation system.*" the machine explained.

Ix, who was standing nearby at the time, checked the transmission log, and indeed found a Bridgestar-stamped identifier. "*Blister.* We are heading for *Blister.*" he said.

"*How would you like to direct your momentum?*" came the voice.

Neither Ix nor Sochi had any idea what that meant. When Faddard wandered in, he also had trouble trying to understand what the machine was driving at.

"*Have you ever used our facility before?*" Bridgestar asked.

"No, this is our first time."

Bridgestar began a tutorial on its systems, "*Please take a look at your monitors and follow along with the visuals that have been downloaded to your nav computer.*"

Ix, Sochiko, Faddard, and a few others crowded around the screen and listened to the narration.

"*Bridgestar maintains active wormhole apertures between twenty-eight systems, and can expand authorized gates to accommodate any sized vessel. Collectors orbiting five stars and two singularities power our system in real time, piped in through petawatt conduits in our own special power gates. Our facilities are completely automated and self-sustaining, maintained from Bridgestar-controlled mining and manufacturing facilities on seven worlds.*"

The rush of information was too much to absorb in real time. Ix hoped there would be information somewhere that he could study at his leisure. Just as his eyes were about to glaze over, a diagram of a solar system, with labels indicating the local star, Bridgestar, and a ship suddenly appeared on the screen.

"*Please take a look at the screen. A customer can use Bridgestar services by approaching the facilities. The customer specifies the destination, and Bridgestar builds a gate along the trajectory that will accommodate the customer's vessel size. Once the gate is completed, Bridgestar will expand the wormhole aperture that connects to the customer's proposed destination and associate it to the gate. The customer vessel will then sail through and instantaneously emerge in the target system.*"

The spaceship icon on the screen followed through the motions being described as Ix and the others stared on in fascination. There were so many questions to ask.

Sochi beat him to the punch, "What happens to the gate after the customer goes through?"

Bridgestar answered, "*The wormhole aperture will be disassociated from the gate and placed back in storage, whereupon the materials used to construct the gate will be reallocated to where they are needed, which may be locally or through a wormhole to another system.*"

She wasn't satisfied, "But how is the wormhole associated with the gate?"

"*The gate as constructed can draw enough power to generate a field capable of preventing the aperture from collapsing. In its stored state, the aperture is kept stable at one micron in diameter. This is transferred over to the gate and expanded to the target size.*"

Ix let out a small gasp, "One micron!"

Bridgestar continued, "*An information package has been downloaded to your nav computer, that should answer most of your questions. How would you like to direct your momentum?*"

It was that question again. Ix asked, "Can you explain how momentum is directed?"

Bridgestar explained, "*Once the gates are constructed on both ends, the exit can be oriented any way you desire.*"

"So we don't need to slow down when we approach Bridgestar?"

"*That is correct. Your velocity and momentum will be preserved in the direction you specify. It will be subtracted from the universe at the tunnel entrance, and the exact same amounts will be instantly added back to the universe at the point of exit. All residual momentum will be counteracted by our thrusters so the net symmetries remain zero.*"

Sochiko had a grin on her face. The months of stress melted away in an instant.

Ix said, "This means we can ask Bridgestar to put us on a course directly to *Blister* using our present speed -- it will cut a year off our travel time."

Faddard was more cautious, "But how do we decelerate once we get there?"

"There must be some planetoids or moons that we can use to dump our kinetic energy." Ix replied, then turned to the com unit, "Bridgestar, are you capable of assisting us with a course? Can you guide us toward inner planets that we can use to decelerate?"

Bridgestar reported back immediately, "*Unfortunately the* Blister *system does not have any bodies of sufficient density to do what you propose. Only* Blister's *sun has sufficient mass and density.*"

Ix began to get nervous again. So close -- it was too good to be true.

Sochiko offered, "Our destination is *Blister*. How would you recommend we get there?"

"*One alternative will be to fall into an elliptical orbit around the star, doing a burn each time you approach apogee -- you should be able to slow down sufficiently after five orbits and six hundred and thirty-two years.*"

Everyone gasped. Six hundred years and barbecued at each pass.

"*Another alternative would be to accelerate the exit gate and send you through backwards, where the gate takes up the balance of the momentum and is discarded in deep space -- that should get you there in four years.*" Bridgestar explained in a matter-of-fact way.

Ix asked, "Is there any solution that will get us there in less than a year, at g-loads that will be survivable?"

"*That would not be possible unassisted with the engines you have or the amount of fuel you are carrying.*"

He asked for clarification, "You mention 'unassisted' -- are there any assisted options?"

Bridgestar replied, "*Yes, some customers choose to allow our tugs to place their craft into the target orbit. With an assisted maneuver you will be able to arrive at Blister in three months from the time you exit the gate.*"

Ix and Faddard exchanged grins. There may be hope for rescuing his brother after all! But when he looked over at his niece the smile faded. Sochi had a worried look on her face.

"What sort of payment do you require?" she asked.

The answer was disheartening, "*Bridgestar requires payment in hard-to-synthesize proteins to replenish low supplies for our nanoassemblers.*"

Sochiko frowned even deeper, "Which proteins, and in what quantity?"

Bridgestar replied, "*For insertion into* Blister *orbit, we require one hundred grams of hemoglobin for every ton of mass of your vessel.*"

Ix shot up and shouted out loud, "That's insane! We would have to drain every drop of blood from our entire crew six times over!"

Bridgestar coolly responded, "*Most of our regular customers collect plasma from their crew on a periodic schedule from the beginning of the voyage, and stockpile it until it is time for payment. Others bring along supplies from their home world.*"

The room was silent as Ix glared at the monitor, as if the machine represented the disembodied voice. He thought it was ironic -- interstellar passage was blood money, literally. He also had a darker thought -- the pirates may have had a sinister use for the crew of captured vessels.

Suddenly Sochiko came up with one of her unique ideas, "Bridgestar, does the payment need to be collected from us, or can we lay the debt on our home world?"

Faddard looked up with a hopeful expression on his face as he listened for the answer.

"We can collect from your home world, but the debt must be paid prior to travel."

Sochiko looked at her uncle and an understanding passed between them. She got up and rushed over to the communications unit, parting the gathering crowd as she went, and sent off a message to Cadbic. She explained the entire situation and asked for blood donations from anyone who might want to volunteer for the cause.

Three hours later a message came back from Cadbic, and they were ready to give their reply. They would draw blood from the crew over the next week to provide a small fraction of the fee, and the remainder would be provided by pickup from a location on Sado marked by transponder. The passage would be guaranteed for round trip. Ix monitored the process very closely, thankful they had shed the heaviest equipment in the Minato operation. Cadbic found more than enough volunteers, and was able to put together a package within a week. He reported the landing of the strange morphing spacecraft that successfully picked up the locker of blood.

On the *Soarer*, only two members of the crew weren't able to give blood because of medical reasons. They jettisoned an environmentally controlled container filled with their contribution that was also picked up by one of the Bridgestar spacecraft.

Soon they began to witness first-hand and in close proximity the fluid assembly and manufacturing efficiency of the Bridgestar system. Ix tried to capture as much of the process as possible on video, and transmit the data back to Mother. One of the morphing spacecraft pulled alongside and began to scan the *Soarer* in detail. Small sections would break off and penetrate hard-to-reach regions, irradiating the hull with various beams along the electromagnetic spectrum to presumably get an accurate picture of the *Soarer*'s structure, then would return to the main spacecraft.

He recognized the iconic flat robotic square and triangle panel modules that made up the core of the Bridgestar system.

Each of the meter-long panel edges had a series of protrusions that would mate with the protrusions of the neighboring panel to make a temporary hinge, to allow the two panels to move in relationship to each other. He watched in fascination as a panel would link to its neighbor, flip over, reconnect at the leading edge, and release the tailing edge -- the panel flipped itself over and over as it tumbled along the surface of its fellows, finally settling down in its own position in the structure. Panel after panel would tumble around, each heading for its own destination, avoiding others along the way.

Once the panels arrived to their own spot in the structure, some would just sit there and become scaffolding for other panels to climb across, but others had additional mechanisms flat-packed into their bodies. Ix watched a robotic arm swing out of the middle of a square panel where it had been folded neatly away while the parent panel tumbled into place. The arm reached out to do a bit of scanning of one part of *Soarer*'s hull, then folded back up again into the face of the panel, which tumbled to a new location where the arm could do its work again.

The hundreds of panels flipping around extending arms and tools became a precision choreographed dance that entertained the crew whenever they were off-duty. At some point Ix noticed the morphing panels had formed a long square tube. He watched as several panels sacrificed themselves at one end of the tube, and tools protruding from the inner walls shredded and reworked the materials. From the other end emerged struts and frames that were attached one by one to *Soarer*'s hull. Bridgestar had begun constructing an outer shell around the vessel that it could attach its mighty tug engines to.

The incredible morphing system somehow knew that *Soarer*'s telescopes and sensors had to remain uncovered. Faddard reported that a major construction work had also been started near the artificial Bridgestar satellite that was still weeks ahead of them. The structure began to take on the shape of a large torus. As *Soarer* rocketed closer, the image of the torus increased in size at an alarming rate.

One morning Bridgestar came online and made an announcement, "*Passage will occur in three hours.*"

Sochiko, who was sitting in the 'arm' galley chatting with Ix and Holina, asked, "Do we need to make any preparations for acceleration?"

Bridgestar replied, "*There will be no accelerations. Your vessel will simply pass from Sado space through the gate into the* Blister *system.*"

Faddard rushed in just then with a worried look on his face, "Sochi, we're heading toward that donut at tremendous speeds. It looks like the hole is just barely large enough for us to fit -- how can we be sure to hit the eye accurately enough?"

Sochiko said nothing, but turned around and put the telescope image on the screen. Holina gasped as the torus visibly expanded right before their eyes.

Sochi made a ship-wide announcement, "All hands, we will be passing through the wormhole in three hours. Find a good spot and relax and watch the show -- we are making history!"

Sochi sat back down, and Ix took a seat as well. Faddard went up to the zero-g spine so he could watch the passage with his own eyes, through a view port on one of the *Bird* re-entry vehicles.

The atmosphere grew tense as the massive gate structure rushed toward them. Ix thought he could see a shimmering around the edges of the hole, as if light was being refracted through hot air rising above sun-warmed asphalt.

Suddenly the event was upon them. Ix cringed when it appeared as though they would collide with the edges of the structure. His entire life flashed before his eyes in an instant, and he knew all the experiences he ever had added up to this one event. Adrenalin began to flow with the apparent speed rush.

The hole in the structure expanded quickly until it filled the entire screen. There was no sound, or anything to indicate there had been a change. Ix looked up at a black field with a faint, alien sun. He was seized with a vast sense of relief -- they had made it.

CHAPTER 24

The Tensakians were pressing harder than Kret had ever seen them push before. There were numerous raids daily, and they had enlisted the help of the Surians. It had become an all-out war. Kret, Davo, Torga, and the others kept their armor on as they rushed to crate up the collection to move it to safer quarters.

"Take these pieces from the water people -- haven't even had a chance to look at them yet." Kret motioned to Torga, knowing the Tensakians would especially love to get their hands on the small machines.

Torga loaded all the boxes onto a powered pallet and lifted off the artificial deck of the garden wheel. The huge load made him look like a puny insect dragging along a massive carcass back to the hive. He zipped around on his rockets, pushing and shoving the bundle trying to overcome the momentum as it drifted this way and that.

Kret watched Torga join the armed escorts, then turned back to ready the most celebrated capture -- the wreckage of the *Towa Maru*. He thought back and smiled as he recalled the clever coup they had pulled to wrest the vessel from the Tensakians.

"Keep that pallet steady!" Kret yelled at the men.

Davo carefully strapped jets onto strategic locations around the perimeter of the *Towa Maru* frame, and readied several pallets for insertion. On count, Kret fired the jets and delicately controlled the rise of the vessel to counteract the peculiar centripetal accelerations using vectored thrust. The men slipped the pallets underneath and strapped them down.

"Let's get the guard over here! We're about to blow the roof." Kret yelled into his radio over the noise of the jets.

Shortly a contingent of heavily armored Farmers rocketed down on all sides of the low camouflaged structure. Kret pointed at Davo, who sent off a signal. Like clockwork, a series of pyrotechnic bolts went off in sequence and the entire roof peeled off sideways, suddenly free to follow the coriolis forces working on it. As soon as the roof was clear, Kret powered the jets to take the large wreck straight up and out of the rotation of the wheel. The *Towa Maru* and its armed contingent joined the armada and stealthily worked its way behind major obstacles and junk heaps on its way toward the wall. Heavily armored guards flew in pairs covering each other's back, constantly shifting trajectory and momentum in order to train their weapons onto any potential threat. The infantry was accompanied by numerous small craft that wove in and out of the column.

Toward the front there was a commotion. Kret and his men swarmed all over the *Towa Maru* wreck, ready to protect it at all costs. A Tensakian patrol leaped from behind a drifting derelict and began to open fire. Kret aimed his microwave cannon at one of the enemies and held it steady. Unfortunately, the single stream of microwaves couldn't penetrate the other's armor. But when Davo and two other Farmers crossed beams and focused, the Tensakian fell back and began writhing in pain. Again, and again Kret and his colleagues fired upon the enemy soldiers in coordinated streams.

The destruction on both sides was heavy. Toward the front, Farmers were falling all over the place. Reinforcements had to surge in from behind to clear the wounded and keep the column moving. But in the end the Farmers won the battle and broke through to the wall.

A heavily fortified collection of warehouses was embedded in *Blister*'s wall, almost identical to the gigantic airlocks that had been taken over by the free market. The Farmers had mounted a laser cannon on a turret that sent off armor-piercing beams at thirty targets a second. But at a kilometer the accuracy fell off dramatically. Kret could see the Tensakians swarming beyond, amassing their numbers for a major offensive.

The Farmers eased open the massive pressure doors and began to slip inside with the precious cargo. One of the larger pallets held the partially dismantled lander that had been stolen from the water people. Kret followed with his men, steering the ungainly *Towa Maru* toward the open doors.

Projectiles began to impact the turret of the cannon and ricochet bits of metal in all directions. At first there was a wide scatter as the high-powered missiles banged harmlessly against the turret and surrounding walls and thick doors, but the circle tightened as the Tensakians closed their range. Kret felt somewhat safe in close vicinity of the prize, and knew that the enemy would do everything they could to avoid hitting the vessel. He looked up and watched the cannon fire away at distant targets but knew it would not be long before the big weapon fell.

The pallet in front of them was swallowed up in the opening, and Kret gunned the jets straight through and into the cavernous refuge. When the large doors clanged shut, he could hear a rain of projectiles shower across the metal surface behind him. They were safe, for a while.

A. SCOTT HOWE

CHAPTER 25

The crew of the *Soarer* celebrated for days, apparently, and they got repeated time-delay communications from Sado well-wishers. Signals propagated normally through Bridgestar's wormhole connection, now back to its one-micron stored state. Reports from the Minato frontier were also encouraging as Merinat and the manufacturing crowd stood behind them on their breakaway journey.

Virginia tried to monitor what was happening out on the edge of space as much as she could, and found herself entertained by the radio cross-traffic.

As she plugged into the current issues in operations, suddenly a familiar voice came on the line, "The Professor found a hat."

The operations center went silent. Josh had something to say. Virginia began to transmit the conversation for the benefit of those far away.

"What is it Josh?" Virginia coaxed.

Josh explained, "He found a hat but he couldn't put it back."

Several of those nearby began to stir, settling down for what may end up being an interesting story. Cadbic and Fisby both poked their heads in with grins, and came over to join Virginia.

She asked, "Start from the beginning. How did he find the hat?"

There was a pause as if Josh was gathering his thoughts together. Then he began, "He found it at one point in the sequence, but it was also needed in another part of the sequence so he tried to put it back."

Everyone present looked at each other with confused expressions.

Virginia asked, "Explain everything so we can understand, Josh. How did it start?"

Josh started slowly, explaining each detail as he went along, "First, the grad students found an ancient relief in the wall. It showed an oppressed nation liberated by a strange warrior. The warrior and his army had decimated the evil tyrants with lightning from a distance.

"The grad students thought it was strange how the warrior could have a weapon like lightning when it was in a primitive era. They wanted to find out what sort of weapon it really was."

Virginia asked, "How is this related to the hat? And what do you mean by sequence?"

Josh continued, "One of the grad students knew a physicist who had a machine that could shift anywhere in the sequence."

Cadbic leaned over and asked Fisby,, "What does he mean by 'sequence'?"

Fisby didn't know either, "He's good at patterns. Maybe 'sequence' is an attribute of some pattern?"

Josh went on, "The grad students got the Professor to ask the physicist to use his machine and the physicist agreed. The sequence shifter is a booth with an inner and outer frame. One can enter the inner frame and dial the target point in the sequence. The inner frame will then shift to the target point and wait, while the outer frame remains at the original location as a homing anchor. To return to the origin, one simply gets back in the inner frame and pushes the return lever."

Virginia was also confused about what a sequence might be and Josh didn't appear capable of explaining it. Instead, she asked, "Josh, tell us the difference between the anchor point and target point. Why would anyone want to visit the target?"

Josh explained, "The target is displaced from the anchor. One would visit the target in order to trace causal paths, and discover why the anchor state is the way it is."

Everyone was still confused. Nevertheless, Josh continued, "The Professor and the grad students entered the booth and set the target to be the ancient kingdom shown in the relief."

Cadbic exclaimed, "A time machine! The 'sequence shifter' is a time machine!"

Josh proceeded, "They visited the target in disguise, and acted like ancient persons to discover what they could about the lightning weapon. They went all over, but could find no such technology among the primitive people.

"The Professor wanted a souvenir, so he went to the market. All of a sudden there was a loud thunder. He quickly ducked into a vendor booth and looked up in the sky but could see no clouds. Instead, he noticed that the booth was a hat shop and was glad he had stumbled on such a great place full of souvenirs. He looked around and found a unique hat and traded some silver coins for it. The hat was one of a kind, so the Professor was happy. But he hid it in case the grad students said anything.

"When they got back to their lab, the Professor began thinking about why they couldn't find the lightning weapon. Then he got an idea that he could teach the primitives about guns to defend themselves.

"The Professor put on the hat and wore it around. When the grad students saw it, they were shocked. It was the same hat the warrior was wearing in the relief!"

The story was getting interesting. As Virginia listened, she could hear the crowd of fans gathering. Once again Josh was a hit. She could also tell there were Technicians beginning to listen in as well.

Josh proceeded with the story, "The grad students said he had to take it back so the ancient warrior could obtain it. They thought it would be easy to use the hat as a tool to do their research -- wait around till the warrior shows up, and follow him when he buys the hat in order to find out about the weapon.

"The Professor was determined to teach the people about guns, so he brought one to demonstrate and rode the sequence shifter back to the era of the battle. When he arrived, he wore the hat for the last time as he walked toward the market place.

"Suddenly a large group of rough-looking characters appeared. They were walking all over the marketplace, looking for someone. At first, the Professor thought he was too late, but then he realized they were the local oppressive soldiers from the relief.

"The Professor was just walking down an alley when some of the soldiers spotted him and pointed. They started to chase the Professor. He ran up and down the streets and finally shook them off, circling back around toward the hat shop.

"But when he got close to the hat shop, he saw something that made him stop in his tracks -- there in front of the booth was himself!"

There was an audible reaction as the crowds of Wardens and Technicians were surprised at the fascinating twist. How could someone meet oneself? Virginia thought she could put a finger on it, but was still confused.

Josh went ahead with the reason, "The Professor realized the other Professor was himself, earlier, when he had been looking for a souvenir. However, as the Professor watched his earlier self casually walk down the alley, he saw one of the soldiers getting near also, and ducked behind a stall. But something unexpected happened. The soldier saw his earlier double instead! The pursuer brought up a bow and pointed the arrow at the unsuspecting early version of the Professor, ready to release its deadly projectile.

"As he hid, many things passed through his mind in the split second as the soldier aimed -- if the arrow was shot, and found its mark in his earlier self, he could be killed, and wouldn't be able to come back and witness himself shopping for souvenirs.

"Quickly, the Professor pulled out his gun and aimed it toward the fellow with the bow, and pulled the trigger. But the sound was a lot louder than he expected. It was almost as if hundreds of guns had fired at once -- a loud crack of thunder. The soldier fell, and by the time the Professor looked up he could not see his earlier self. The Professor ran to the sequence shifter booth and hurried back to the lab in the modern era."

Josh paused as if he were waiting for a reaction. When he didn't continue Virginia realized Josh was shy because of something he didn't want to admit to in the story.

Virginia coaxed him on, "Josh, go on. Tell us what happened next."

Josh reluctantly began again, "The Professor didn't return the hat. When the grad students saw him wearing it again, they scolded him and had him go back another time. The Professor stepped back in the sequence shifter and once again went back to the primitive time.

"This time, he went back slightly earlier. He saw the group of soldiers wander around the market place and noticed something new -- the soldiers were harassing the shop owners. They would pick up things without paying, and grab the young women inappropriately.

"He made his way toward the hat vendor carefully, trying to keep hidden from the soldiers. He followed one soldier toward the alley, watching him do unpleasant things to the shopkeepers. Then the soldier walked right into the alley, and the Professor was shocked for a second time. There in front of him, hiding behind a stall was himself, looking down the alley at an earlier version of himself!

"Unfortunately, the soldier he had followed had pulled out a knife and was sneaking up on his prior self. He watched his earlier self pull out a gun and take aim just as the soldier was about to pounce with the knife, so he pulled out his own gun and shot him. Again, the thunder of a hundred guns.

"The Professor looked around him and thought he ought to return the hat, but was afraid more soldiers would come out. Instead, he quickly ran back to the sequence shifter. But this time on his way, he saw several fallen soldiers lying in the alleys he would cross, somehow having met their demise by an unknown hand.

"When he got back, he was again chastised for not returning the hat. The grad students made him go back yet again."

Josh explained how the Professor went back even earlier, and watched the soldiers canvass the marketplace. "He tried to avoid the soldiers, but once he found himself cornered in an alley. To his surprise they saw him but didn't recognize him -- they simply walked by and roughly bumped shoulders as they did with all the other men on the street. The Professor followed them and watched them terrorize the ladies as the men folk shyly slipped away to avoid confrontation.

"Finally, he couldn't stand it any longer. The Professor approached one of the soldiers who was bothering a pretty girl and punched the man in the face. The soldier got up and began shouting. A crowd of soldiers came running and the beaten fellow pointed at the Professor. They all lunged at him at once but he escaped and ran away.

"As he ran, he saw other versions of himself running also. Once or twice they even locked eyes and nodded a silent hello before running their separate ways. And twice he found himself back-to-back with himself, surrounded by soldiers. The two of them fought, covering each other's back until they were able to slip away in their separate directions.

"Sometime during the chase, he saw one of himself about to get stabbed, so he pulled out his gun and shot the assailant. Again, a hundred shots rang out at once, and he looked at his watch and realized his earlier selves were at that time at the hat vendor shopping for souvenirs. When he looked around this time, it looked like dozens of soldiers were about to kill dozens of Professors, who each pulled out a gun and shot one of them. Dozens of soldiers fell to the ground at once.

"This time he didn't panic. He was determined to stay longer so he could return the hat. He hid himself for a while, and when the coast was clear he walked over to the vendor and set the hat down on the counter and walked away. But the shopkeeper caught up to him and said he couldn't take back the hat, so the Professor went home to the lab in his own era, once again having failed."

Josh went on to say how the Professor went back again and again, trying to return the hat by either sneaking it back to the vendor, selling it to someone else, or just abandoning it in the middle of nowhere. But each time the hat found its way back to him, and no matter what he did he couldn't get rid of it.

Josh explained that each time the Professor went back he would have to avoid the soldiers and would have to protect other versions of himself as he tried to return the hat. Each time he would park the inner booth of the sequence shifter in a different place because the previous spot already had one. Once the Professor forgot which booth was his, and walked into the wrong one, returning to the lab at a time he hadn't experienced yet.

In the end the Professor was home, in his lab, with the hat. And the carved relief was clear -- an army of persons with funny hats appears to give battle with the locals, and strikes them all down with thunder.

Virginia looked up and the whole room was jam-packed full of Warden visitors who had been listening to the latest story. When the story ended, they all broke out in applause. As usual, the Wardens would go for weeks and months after that and figure out ways to simulate time machines in the Database, multiply versions of themselves, and talk incessantly about the Professor.

It took Virginia a few days to get the interpretation ready. Ix, Sochiko, and Merinat came back online to hear it but Cadbic was away on important business.

"This time Josh took a slightly different track." Virginia began, "The grad students represent us, but he's seeing himself, and the Professor, as representing 'providence' or the protector of our people. Some of the story represents his recent efforts to stave off the digital invasion, where his intentions are good, but get him into trouble at first."

Merinat, joining via audio feed with only a short time delay, asked, "Did he figure out who the invaders were? Is there a clue about the Tensakians?"

Virginia hesitated, "Yes and no. This time it was about a bigger picture. And unfortunately, there are still many gaps."

Merinat queried what the 'sequence shifter' was all about.

"The physicist and sequence shifter represents something in Technician heritage. There's something strange about the interpretation -- it must be wrong. The impression it gives is that the sequencer literally has something to do with manipulating time." Virginia hesitantly suggested.

Several of those present looked at each other.

Virginia added, "In two previous stories Josh was concerned about solving the problem with the ring. It's clear now that the ring represented violated causality -- the dilemma of not knowing which event came before another, like an eternal round with no beginning and no end."

"Perhaps there is a clue about the videos from the Third Vault!" Merinat exclaimed.

Virginia didn't know what he was talking about, but continued anyway, "The hat is the key to everything. Somehow there was a great tragedy unfolding in the past, a calamity great enough to wipe out a civilization. But providence from the future both mistakenly seeded the calamity, and solved it too. The hat represents something that belonged in the past, had involvement with both the calamity and its solution, and somehow ended up stuck in the future. No manner of efforts could return it to the past again."

At the far end of a long time lag, Ix continued to peer at the radio as if waiting for Virginia's conclusion.

When she didn't say anything more, he transmitted, "*Well? What is it? What got stuck in the future?*"

It was several hours later when Virginia was able to send the return reply, "It doesn't say. That's all there is. However, my impression is that somehow the mysterious something represents you. It's related to the Technicians -- your heritage both includes a strange manipulation of time, and unfortunately getting stranded outside your own horizons."

CHAPTER 26

Sochiko and Ix puzzled over Josh's bizarre interpretation for days as the celebrations continued around them. Was there indeed a clue about the strange circumstances surrounding the video from the Third Vault? How did that relate to the Tensakians, or the great interstellar ships *Vector* and *Axiom*?

Sochiko sent several transmissions to Kret, but got no reply. There was nothing from the Tensakians either. She had heard about the destruction of Fisby's mapper and Worlith's capture by the pirates, and began to wonder whether Tensakian raids had somehow overwhelmed Kret's small farmer group. It reminded her of how cautious they needed to be, and she reminded the crew to be on the lookout -- they were in the pirates' home territory now.

When the festivities settled down a bit, Sochi directed the crew's energy back to the task at hand -- to find the great ship *Vector* that had left Minato with their hopes and dreams, and her parents.

As they got closer to *Blister*, the strange bubble world showed up clearer on their instruments. One morning Faddard burst in with excitement.

"*Blister* has almost zero density!" he said.

Sochiko suspected that already.

"It seems to be an engineering work on a massive scale -- a pressure vessel several hundred kilometers in diameter. And I think I've located the missing ship."

That perked her up immediately -- she was all ears.

"It's still too small to tell, but it looks like the vessel is docked to the side of *Blister*." he said.

Faddard showed her the grainy photograph and from that day forward Sochi frequented the astronomical database. She avidly scrutinized every incoming image from the direction of *Blister*. On each image she carefully studied the long object attached to the side of the bubble world. The outline of the protruding structure increased in clarity day by day.

It was not many weeks later that she could pick out the characteristic curves of the *Vector*, and recognize the protruding bridge. Her parents were down there, dead or alive. As she studied the images, she began to plan her attack.

"Unk, how would I protect myself against concentrated microwaves?" she asked one evening.

Ix must have been thinking along the same lines, because he had an answer waiting for her, "I suspect the weapons work by creating a harmonic standing wave. All we would need to do would be to rig up your pressure suit as an antenna. Since we don't know the frequency, you can make a real-time adjustment if needed, and channel the energy away from you."

"Okay, what sort of hand weapon can we come up with?"

"I'll have to think about that one. I'm coming too." Ix replied.

Sochiko protested, "Unk! You can't go! You aren't even trained in a pressure suit."

"Perhaps not, but I can go with you in one of the *Birds*, and 'keep the engine running' while you're away. Besides, Mox and Blujic don't have pressure suits -- how will you get them back without doing a shirtsleeves dock?" Ix reasoned.

Sochi smiled and was pleased that at least her uncle had hope that her parents were still alive. During the next few days, she got four more volunteers, but had to turn most of them down. In the end she allowed only two others to go: her uncle and a Technician named Del, who had worked on the wreck of the *Axiom* from Those Who Went Before. She wanted to keep the group small to make sure they had room for any survivors.

The Bridgestar tugs guided them into an orbit around the star lower than *Blister*, and allowed them to catch up. By the time the tugs shut down and dismantled, Sochiko could no longer see the enemy ship due to rotations of the massive space station. She had intended to approach the *Vector* directly, by taking one of the *Birds* over in stealth, and board her quietly, but *Blister* had its own welcome system that presented a better opportunity: the autonomous port authority invited them in a similar manner to what they had experienced at Everwebber..

Sochiko cautiously followed the transponder toward a massive shutter-like iris that slowly opened to reveal an airlock large enough to hold three or four ships equal to the *Soarer* in size.

"Keep your hands on the weapons, folks. We want to make sure we can get out if we get cornered." she warned.

The smooth face of the *Blister* hull became rough on close inspection, with hundreds of small maintenance machines zipping all over the surface. As they neared the giant iris, Sochiko could see faint shapes inside far away in the distance -- *Blister*'s shell was partially transparent, with opaque covers that slowly seemed to open and close like skin pores.

So far there was no sign of hostility. All their weapons were armed and ready for confrontation, but there was not a single spacecraft in sight. A few months earlier she would have thought the pirates would be swarming all over the place waiting to pounce on unwary passersby -- were the ruthless brutes waiting to ambush the *Soarer*?

All logic told her to stay outside, but somehow intuition said entering *Blister* was the right thing to do -- she couldn't explain it, but perhaps she thought Kret and his colleagues would be there soon.

The *Soarer* eased into the great airlock and Sochi used the attitude control system to make minor adjustments on their trajectory and orientation. The inside walls were covered with pipes, conduits, gantries, blockhouses, and other unidentifiable structures.

"We've lost our long-range communication." one of the technicians pointed out, "The signal may be jammed."

"That may explain why we haven't heard anything from Kret." Uncle Ix said.

The *Soarer* came to an all stop, and she watched the iris close behind them. Over the next several hours they monitored the external pressure as the sealed airlock filled with air. The pressure stabilized at a point lower than the *Soarer*'s ambient cabin pressure.

"*The pressure is equalized. Permission to open inner door?*" the automated port authority came on the line.

Sochiko and Ix eyed each other, and her uncle gave her a nod.

"Yes, please. Open the inner door." she said.

The inner iris began to open, starting with a spot right in the middle that slowly widened in an ever-increasing circle. The strange world that opened up to their view was even more startling than Sochiko could have imagined. Even though she had seen video transmitted back from the mapper, the grainy static-filled images couldn't compare with the crisp scenes that filled their screens.

Sochiko brought the *Soarer* forward into a different kind of void -- space with air! The number of spacecraft, individuals in jet packs, flotsam, jetsam, and rusting hulks boggled the mind. Airboats and scavengers would rocket up close, look over the *Soarer* in curiosity, and then go on with their business. Sochi began to get nervous as they drew a crowd. She had assumed there would be only two groups of people in *Blister*, but it was apparent that the richness of diverse cultures exceeded what could be found on Mother. And fortunately, there was yet no sign of the Tensakians.

Faddard had the telescopes operating at their maximum, and recorded every detail. It was hard to keep the crew working, as they would continually pause to marvel at the astounding remnants of a long-gone space faring empire.

"Keep your attention folks! We're in Tensakian territory." Sochiko reminded everyone over the loud speaker.

From Fisby's reports, it was apparent that certain groups tended to occupy their own zones or territories. He had indicated that the Tensakians rarely intruded into the regions with the great wheel farms, so she got Faddard working on identifying a route through the most inconspicuous areas.

It soon became apparent that there was a battle going on. The first indications were from far away, and Faddard showed distant vessels chasing each other. Sochiko couldn't tell from the images who the parties were or which group was prevailing. Soon they could see numbers of individuals firing on each other with incendiary bursts of flame.

For the first time she could make out the distinctive black uniforms of the Tensakians as they methodically moved in formation using rocket packs and small air thrust vehicles. It was mayhem through the telescopes -- bystanders rushed out of the path of the invaders and cowered behind old wrecks. Defending armies, also outfitted for battle, regrouped and made counterattacks.

Without warning, an air vehicle accompanied by death pods and several dozen black-clad Tensakians rounded a large piece of dismantled heavy equipment and moved head-on toward the *Soarer*. Sochiko shrieked out a command to ready weapons. But the Tensakians moved past the *Soarer* and barely even took notice. Two of the black-clad figures even used their rockets to approach the *Soarer*'s hull and grasped on for a few fleeting moments before heading off in a new direction, like a swimmer reaching the edge of a pool to hang on before continuing more laps. For several terrifying minutes dozens of fingers hovered over firing buttons waiting for the command that Sochi cautiously held back. The Tensakian patrol soon disappeared beyond more drifting hulks of ancient spacecraft.

Sochiko wondered what had just happened? The Tensakians had obviously noticed them, but had made no aggressive move. Had they not recognized the *Soarer*? Twice more they ran across Tensakian patrols that passed them by without as much as a glance.

Sochiko brought the *Soarer* near to a drifting junk heap and turned the attitude controls over to one of the junior pilots as she called a council of war in the galley of the 'arm'.

"Maybe they're distracted and have more pressing issues." Del, who had been invited to join the executive team, pointed out.

"I don't think they recognize the *Soarer* as distinct from any of the other floating pieces of discarded equipment." Ix noted.

Faddard agreed, "They don't necessarily know us, we have the perfect camouflage, just being a spaceship."

Sochiko was still worried, "I don't think we can get much closer -- civilians are avoiding this area. We might be mistaken for an aggressor."

Sochiko had been too narrow in her thinking -- she had thought the Tensakians had only the one purpose of attacking their ship and taking the spoils. It never occurred to her that they might have other priorities. This new perspective presented some additional possibilities.

Ix proposed, "Perhaps we ought to just keep the *Soarer* parked here, and the three of us move forward in one of the *Birds*. We would be less conspicuous that way."

Sochiko was thinking the same thing, "Okay, let's get ready. There's another thing that's been bothering me. What about biological contamination? Do we maintain a separation or can we go out without environmental suits?"

"With centuries of separation between our two peoples it's quite possible our immune systems have gone in different directions. I recommend we stay pressurized." Ix answered.

"But what about Worlith? She seems to have done well in the weeks and months since she was captured." Sochi reminded him.

No one had an answer. In the end, Sochiko elected to gradually bring down their own ambient pressure to be equal with that of *Blister*, but to keep their separation just in case. If there was some organism out there that Sado's inhabitants couldn't resist, it was possible Worlith hadn't been exposed yet.

The other issue they had to consider was entering and exiting the *Bird*. At some point Sochi and Del would have to leave the *Bird* suited up, but since there was no airlock Ix would be exposed to the *Blister* environment. They solved the problem by docking two *Birds* together and slaving one of them to the control system of the other. This approach would allow one of the cabins to be used as an airlock, and they could also bring back survivors (if they were successful in finding any) in isolation. They named the double *Bird* '*Futakan*' which was a comical expression meaning 'pair of cans'.

As they readied the rescue vessel, Sochiko noticed the region immediately surrounding them began to get dark. Apparently, *Blister*'s skin selectively shut off solar radiation to automatically simulate day and night cycles.

The next 'day' Ix, Del, and Sochiko departed in the twin *Birds* with two pressure suits. Sochi left Faddard in charge, with strict orders to not fire unless fired upon. There were still lone scavengers in the area evading the heavy battle areas, so in addition to staying alert against enemy armies, Faddard was to take whatever precautions deemed necessary to protect the *Soarer* from getting stripped of its protruding instruments.

The *Futakan* made good progress in starts and stops, avoiding attention whenever possible. Several times they detected Tensakians or other groups and simply pulled over and acted like drifting discarded equipment among other junk. In each case either the marauding crew failed to notice or didn't care.

The battle grew more intense the closer they got to their destination. Sochiko noted that the *Vector* had been docked to *Blister* at one of the four cardinal points around the perimeter that had the massive airlocks. They had entered ninety degrees from the big ship, and covered the hundred or so kilometers in good time. However, as they approached the spot indicated by their nav computer, it became apparent that the region was embroiled in the heat of battle. On one end of the row of airlocks, a turret with a laser cannon had been mounted, and repeatedly fired out intense beams. Sochiko could see numerous Tensakian crews all over the area taking cover behind floating mountains of flotsam and jetsam, laying down a continuous barrage of fire toward the cannon.

The situation didn't look good for those holed up in the airlock behind the cannon. With Tensakians surrounding them on the inside, and the *Vector* docked on the outside, the defenders didn't appear to have a chance.

"Sochi, take a look over there. Ships are moving in and out of the locks toward the end." Ix pointed out.

Sochi could see a long line of airlocks stretching off in the distance, with numerous structures and obstacles partially obscuring the nether regions. The battle appeared to be concentrated around only one end.

"Let's make our way around, and perhaps take cover in the vicinity of the locks." Ix continued, "Perhaps there's an option of going outside as well."

"Try to get Kret online again." Sochi called to Faddard over the radio.

Sochiko stealthily moved the *Futakan* from drifting clump to drifting clump, trying to give wide berth to the Tensakian gun crews.

Moments later Faddard came back online, "Still nothing. We'll keep trying."

By the time the *Futakan* reached the line of airlocks it appeared as though the laser cannon was on its last stand. Some of the outside fire had damaged the structure and wouldn't allow the turret to turn all the way. Tensakian gun crews began moving in from the crippled side. The black-clad warriors began passing their ship too, making Sochiko a bit nervous.

As the *Futakan* approached one of the large airlock doors, the shutter iris began to open. Relieved, she gunned the attitude control jets and slipped inside. However, instead of asking the automated port authority to pump down and open the outer doors, she drew up next to the gantries and docked to one of the blockhouses lining the walls of the airlock.

"I'm getting out. I think it will be less conspicuous if Del and I make our way using rocket packs from here on out." Sochiko said.

Uncle Ix was hesitant, but knew that she was probably correct.

"Look out here Unk." Sochi indicated through the view port a large conduit that passed into the blockhouse. "If my intuitions are correct, this conduit is a corridor that runs the entire length of the airlock -- there should be a cupola at both ends that poke through beyond the doors. You can isolate yourself and use this as an observation post."

Ix nodded, indicating he had probably been thinking the same thing.

"Make sure you use our own breathing apparatus -- it's still *Blister* air out there." she lovingly nagged.

"Okay I've got it. Just get yourself ready."

Sochiko and Del went into the second cabin and shut the hatch. It took them several minutes to get ready, a lot shorter period of time because they didn't have to go through the time-consuming pre-breathing exercises. They each put on jet packs and made sure the makeshift microwave antennas covered as much area as possible. They also had small homemade launchers and enough explosives to hopefully stop a couple of aggressive armored warriors.

Del checked the air pressure and opened the outside hatch of the *Futakan*. Immediately in front of them was the blockhouse -- since the *Futakan* had used the same berthing mechanism that appeared to be common on all the old stations and ships, their double *Bird* made an airtight seal on the blockhouse hatch.

Del worked the door, trying to get the stubborn hatch to open. A layer of oxidation on the surface indicated that the door may have remained shut and undisturbed for a very long time. The two of them took turns pounding the clamps until each of them were loosened. They finally broke through into a dark chamber and switched on their headlamps.

The blockhouse was a junction of several person-sized conduits and hallways. Sochiko first drifted down the inward tube and found the cupola that opened onto *Blister*'s bright interior. She looked toward the laser cannon and could barely see crowds of black-clad soldiers engaged in close combat -- she saw small flashes of incendiary explosions and knew that the defenders didn't have much time left. She felt a renewed urgency and returned back down the tunnel.

Sochi and Del spent the next hour exploring the various passages radiating out from the blockhouse, hoping to find a throughway inside the massive *Blister* walls. They found deserted equipment rooms, zero-g port authority offices, minor dormitories, and storage chambers.

Once they passed through a door that opened up onto the vast interstitial space between the multiple transparent skins making up *Blister*'s great wall. It could have been close to a kilometer high -- Sochiko could see gigantic trusses and beams, all hierarchically supporting the tremendous atmospheric pressure. They considered using the great attic as a route to avoid the enemy, but the spaces turned out to be impassible.

It wasn't long before they found the main thoroughfare they had been looking for. The corridor appeared to run parallel with the long line of airlocks. Unfortunately, the warring groups had also found the highway and were using it to move back and forth. A battle had commenced where groups of Tensakians would fire a salvo down the tunnel, which would be answered later by another group shooting back out of the darkness.

Sochiko waited for a lull and shot across to the other side, ducking into a side corridor with Del on her heels. They made their way through a series of linked chambers and came back to the main corridor at a point farther along. Again, they waited for a break, and rushed across.

Without warning, incendiary explosions lit up the corridor. Sochiko involuntarily ducked into a recess and found herself face to face with a squad of Tensakians. The armored fighters trained their wicked-looking weapons on her, trigger fingers clenched and ready to fire. She froze, unable to respond or bring up her own weapon.

"*Who are you?*" a voice sounded through her com system in the *Blister* dialect.

Sochiko couldn't come up with any of the *Blister* phrases she had learned, and instead stammered in her own neo-Japonican, "I'm Sochiko, I'm looking for my parents."

"*You're a foreigner. You shouldn't be here -- it's too dangerous. We're conducting a raid. Leave the area immediately.*" the voice said.

The line of weapons remained trained on her until she backed away and joined Del several meters up the corridor. Then several of the Tensakians turned and fired a few salvos down the way toward an unseen target.

Sochiko was stunned. She had been right in the enemy's sights and miraculously they had let her go. She carefully backed away, pulling herself along slowly without losing sight of the soldiers. One of the pirates pointed to another and motioned across his throat. The second black-clad warrior moved out of line from his fellows and began to follow her.

Recovering, she motioned to Del, "Come on, we have to get out of here and find another way."

Del spoke up in her helmet com, "*I've got an idea. I think we can go outside from here.*"

"Outside?"

Del explained, "*We can exit out to space and work along the wall.*"

"Okay, which way? Try to lose this guy." Sochi was looking backward, preoccupied with the Tensakian on their tail.

Sochi followed as Del quickly headed down a passageway, pulling himself hand over hand in the zero-g, and making a few turns to confuse the figure lurking in the distance. The tunnel ended in another cupola, and Del paused as he stared out into deep space. Sochiko pulled up beside him and peered through the view ports -- there in front of them was the harshly lit curves of the great ship *Vector* docked outside, bathed in sunlight.

For an instant, both of them just took in the breathtaking sight.

"My parents are over there, dead or alive." she said.

Del replied, "*My best friend Gij is also there.*"

Sochiko looked at him as she realized why the other had volunteered for this dangerous mission. "How do we get over there?" she asked.

Del pointed off to the side, "*There's a maintenance hatch over there.*"

One of the small recesses to the side had lockers for tools and pressure suit maintenance, adjacent to a small personnel airlock. Sochiko quickly floated over to the lock and climbed through the narrow opening. Del squeezed in beside her and shoved the inner hatch shut just as the Tensakian rounded the corner.

The air pressure dropped as the lock pumped down. Sochiko began to feel constricted as the pressure inside the suit stiffened the heavy fabric. She flushed out the remaining air and opened the outer hatch. She didn't have a tether to tie off with, so all she could do was to hold onto the handhold as she exited the lock into hard space. Del rushed out beside her.

It didn't matter how many times she did it, sitting on the edge of eternity gave her a fright. She closed her eyes for a few minutes to pull together.

"*Sochi, let's go!*" Del prodded.

"Give me a minute."

Sochiko looked up at the gigantic *Vector* across the gulf. It was too far away for comfort -- she could not get herself to cross. And it was hard to move her arms -- they had not had time to pre-breathe, so their suits were still at ambient *Blister* pressure which was too high for comfortable action. The suit naturally tried to take the shape of a spread-eagle balloon. She fought with the arms and managed to activate her rocket and ease open the propellant, accelerating slowly along *Blister*'s hull. She looked beyond for the next cupola and got ready to grasp the handhold as she drifted by, taking care not to disorient herself by exposing herself to deep space. She grabbed the handhold, paused for a moment, and tried to peer into the dark cupola windows. There was no indication they were being followed.

Del flew along behind her and settled into a handhold nearby. They aimed for the next cupola and repeated the flight, careful not to let the rockets get out of control. Off to the side the massive iris of the ship lock door penetrated *Blister*'s bulkhead. On and on they leapfrogged from cupola to cupola as they made their way along the line of ship locks.

Sochiko lost track of time during the traverse. Uncle Ix got on the radio to warn them that they had only two hours of air left. It only took a second for Sochiko to decide to go forward anyway, and Del agreed.

In front of them, a pressurized bridge stretched from *Blister* out to the ship, but there were no other visible connections. It wasn't clear how they would enter the *Vector* if they were to cross the void.

"*What if we entered through the bridge?*" Del asked.

"It won't work if it's guarded. This place might be crawling with Tensakians." she answered.

Del pointed out toward the connector bridge, "*I think we should give it a try. I've been all over the* Axiom *and the only personnel hatches were inside the garages -- what if those are shut?*"

Sochiko agreed. She clung to the frame of the nearest maintenance hatch and fought with the suit to yank at the handle. But as she peered through the view port, it was apparent that the inner hatch of the small airlock had been left open.

"*There must be an electronic release -- for safety's sake.*" Del said.

Around the hatch were several small access plates. Del went to each and pounded or prodded, trying to get them to open. Finally, the cover of one slid to the side revealing a set of controls. As Del tried different combinations, Sochi watched the inner door slide into place. Del continued with other combinations, hoping to get the lock to pump down its air. Nothing seemed to work.

"How about this?" Sochiko pulled at a lever off to the side.

A mist sprayed outward as the lock dumped all its air. Sochiko was able to push the hatch open and crawl inside with Del in tow. They closed the hatch and pumped the lock back up again using the manual controls.

Sochiko squeezed through the inner hatch and was startled as two men rushed into the maintenance chamber. She backed against the bulkhead as the business end of two wicked-looking weapons advanced on her. The men were in strange clothes without armor or helmet, and were shouting something. But from inside the pressure suit she could hear nothing. She lifted her mirrored sun visor and pointed to her ear.

One of the men brought out a radio and transmitted into her helmet com.

"*Who are you? Keep your hands clear.*" the voice said.

Sochiko thought for a brief moment, then through inspiration carefully rehearsed in *Blister* dialect, "I'm looking for Kret."

Both the men jumped at the name, and the one with the radio spoke into it on another channel.

Del mentioned in a closed circuit, "*Sochi, we've got to replenish our air. I only have ten minutes left.*"

She replied, "It's no use. We'll have to risk breathing the *Blister* environment."

Under the armed guard she and Del removed their helmets. The air had a strange odor, but didn't seem unpleasant. The man with the radio could be heard reporting back to a superior.

"Come with us." he said.

Sochiko and Del followed along as they floated through corridors. They passed through a hatch into one of the vast ship locks that had been converted into a warehouse. Zero-g stacks of containers, boxes, and equipment filled one end of the warehouse, and armored men were milling about.

Sochiko gasped as she recognized the remains of a large vessel that had been crated up, "That's the *Towa Maru*!"

Their guard brought them down toward the frightening-looking fighters, and one of the armored figures drifted over.

"Sochiko! I can't believe you've come all this way." Kret said, as he removed his own helmet.

All the stress from the past few hours suddenly gave way and Sochiko rushed to throw her arms around him.

"You wouldn't believe what we've been through to get here!" she began, "We got past dozens of Tensakian guards..."

"You'll be safe now. No need to worry." Kret consoled.

He brought them over to one side as the men prepared the warehoused artifacts to be relocated somewhere else. Something seemed strange to her, but she couldn't put a finger on it.

Suddenly her thoughts were interrupted by a ruckus at the other end of the warehouse. Explosions rocked the walls as doors were blown open and dozens of black-clad Tensakians poured in. A battle ensued, with microwave beams, lasers, and incendiary explosives passing back and forth.

Sochiko and Del took cover behind one of the floating stacks of cargo and watched as Kret's men scrambled to fight a war at their backs while at the same time trying to tug the cargo pallets through a tunnel in one of the bulkheads.

The fighting intensified until none of the Farmers could get any work done, but everyone had to join the front line.

A voice called out from among the Tensakians, "Kret! What are you doing?"

Sochiko knew that voice. It was the mildly educated voice she had spoken with for the past several years -- the mysterious voice of the Tensakians.

Kret yelled back, "Ah, my friend Rusty. Wouldn't you like to know?"

Rusty called out over the din of battle, "Kret, where are you taking our grandfather's ship?"

Kret called back, "Hughes is our grandfather too. We're keeping the *Towa Maru*. Just try to get it back, Rusty."

"Kret, you stinking rat. I should have killed you when I had the chance, when I raided the wheel."

Kret snickered, and yelled back, "I should have fried you when you were in my sights, cowering in the corner. I should have cut you down like I did your father and mother, and sister."

Rusty cursed out loud as apparently old hurts were dug up again.

Kret continued, "We're going to Kasei, Rusty. We're going to see what Mars is like."

Sochiko listened to the vocal battle trying to understand what was evidently a deep personal war from way back between two bitter enemies. But something still didn't seem right -- why were her alarms all going off inside?

Rusty called out, "Mars is closed, Kret. The Kasei folks sealed the wormhole so Bridgestar won't let you through."

Kret motioned for several of the men to abandon the lesser items and take the *Towa Maru* away while dozens of heavily armed Farmers lay down suppressing fire.

Kret replied, "We don't need Bridgestar. We have an interstellar!"

Sochiko looked up, alarmed. What did he mean by that? Had the Farmers succeeded in wresting the *Vector* away from the Tensakians? Suddenly she realized what had been puzzling her before -- the tunnel through which the Farmers were moving their artifacts was the connecting bridge to the big ship.

Rusty's voice carried over the additional rounds, "How are you going to find Mars, Kret? Which of those stars out there is Sol?"

If the Farmers had taken the *Vector*, then they must know where Sochi's parents were. She began to move closer to ask him, but Kret appeared to be getting angry.

"So what about Sol! This ship is from before the war! Bridgestar will open up for her." Kret claimed.

The *Towa Maru* disappeared down the tunnel and the men began moving back.

"Kret, tell Sochiko what you've been doing! Tell her what happened to her lander crew." Rusty called.

Kret looked over at her and rolled his eyes, calling back toward the voice, "It was the damn Tensakians, Rusty!"

Then a new voice called out, "That's not true! Tell her the truth."

Sochiko knew that voice well. It was Worlith! She looked over at Kret with suspicion, but saw a murderous look come over his face. She thought back and wondered why she had been so blind! Sochi recalled the time she and the others had been held captive in the Database. Or more recently when she had been transmitting to him at Minato -- Sochi suddenly recalled how she had interrupted Kret once, but there should have been a time delay -- Kret had been right there in Minato orbit all along, waiting to steal the ship!

Del must have come to the realization at the same time because he lunged at the man. Kret pointed his microwave weapon and aimed a concentrated beam at Del's head, frying his brains instantly. Then Kret turned his weapon to Sochiko and pulled the trigger. Sochi looking on in horror quickly ducked to the side. Fortunately, the makeshift antenna wrapping her environmental suit took the energy and dissipated it.

Krett and his men retreated toward the tunnel and switched on their cloaking devices. Instantly they became partially transparent, evil floating entities drifting down the passageway.

Sochi looked up and screamed after him, "Where are my parents!"

But it was too late. The tunnel door shut and Sochiko could hear twisting metal as the great ship beyond tore away from its anchorage and destroyed the connector bridge.

Swarms of Tensakians engulfed the space, but two figures in particular came to Sochiko's side and took off their helmets. One was a man she had never seen before, presumably Rusty. The other was Worlith, all decked out in the black Tensakian uniform.

Two days later Sochiko sat in a pleasant garden with Ix, Worlith, and Rusty. They were relaxing in one of the garden wheels belonging to the Surians. The Tensakians had found and disabled the jamming device set by the Farmers, so Faddard was able to get messages through to Sado and Minato.

"There's someone we'd like you to meet." Rusty said, and pointed over to the side.

Three figures were walking toward them. It wasn't long before Sochi could see they were her mother, father, and Danid. She jumped up and rushed over to meet them and gave her parents a big hug.

When the excitement died down Sochiko asked, "How did you get here? I thought you were dead."

The three newcomers joined the others in the garden. Mox gave a brief account of how they had evaded capture on the big vessel.

"And when the ship docked to *Blister*, we stole a ride on the robotic maintenance traffic through the connector bridge." Blujic added.

Mox continued, "It didn't take long for us to find out who our real friends were."

"Jevn joined the Tensakians when Worlith recruited her -- she's mopping up the Farmers as we speak." Sochiko's mother said.

They talked about the others who didn't make it. Each of them said a word about Gij, Kerf, Del, Buutz, Heln, and the others who had been lost since the beginning of the war.

"There are several things I don't understand." Sochiko began, "Who is Masamune Hughes?"

Rusty smiled, "Hughes was our first ancestor. He settled *Blister* more than five hundred years ago."

Sochiko gasped, "But I met him. I walked the corridors of the *Towa Maru*. How could he have been around five hundred years ago?"

Rusty looked at her, first incredulously, then with more reverence, "Then you are the one he talked about! He spoke of meeting someone from his future. He got help repairing the *Towa Maru* from a space crew near what we think is Everwebber."

Sochiko still had a confused look on her face.

Rusty continued, "He also mentioned having met people from the water planet. Do you have any records of such an encounter?"

Mox timidly raised his hand, "That was me."

Everyone looked at Mox with a shocked expression.

"What do you mean brother?" Ix asked.

"Remember the dream I had after my pod sank? I thought I dreamt that one of Those Who Went Before had come to rescue me from the Inmates. When we found the Third Vault, I recognized the *Towa Maru* from the dream. I thought it was delirium at first, but the memory has gotten clearer over the years. The *Towa Maru* came and intervened in that cavern when the two Inmates almost killed all of my team."

Sochiko turned to Rusty, "But how can that be?"

Rusty explained, "Hughes was an engineer from ancient Kasei, or Mars as some people say. No one knows from how long ago, since he got lost from his own time and didn't know himself. He was one of the inventors of the original wormhole technology. The *Towa Maru* was a self-contained gate that artificially kept the mouth of the wormhole from collapsing. The old Japonicans used to name their vessels with the term 'maru' on the end of the name, meaning 'circle' -- or completeness, where the vessel is a complete environment of its own. The *Towa Maru* drew its power through the wormhole from huge generators back on Mars, or wherever (we don't really know)."

Rusty paused and looked around the circle, "They were frantic, trying to avert some global disaster. Something went wrong -- the *Towa Maru* accidentally passed through one gate but got displaced in time. Apparently, the active wormhole drive on board the *Towa Maru* combined with the Bridgestar gate in unpredictable ways. They found themselves outside Bridgestar in an unknown solar system, and had no idea they had traveled to the future. That was when they must have met you, Mox. Or perhaps Sochiko -- we don't really know which came first."

The whole concept was fantastic, yet it made sense in light of what they had experienced. "So Kret and his crew didn't board the *Towa Maru* and kill its crew -- that ship they had crated up was five hundred years old?"

Rusty nodded and went further, "After exploring the water planet, Hughes and his crew tried to recreate the accident at Bridgestar and found themselves displaced again, with a damaged spacecraft. That was where we think he enlisted Sochiko's help on the planet you call Minato.

"They tried to recreate the accident one more time, and found themselves in this solar system with irreparable damage. They combined forces with folks from a small outpost here, and their descendants, our ancestors, eventually built *Blister*."

Sochiko was still confused. This must have been what Josh had been talking about in his latest story about the time machine. Masamune Hughes had come from the past and gotten stuck in his own future.

"But what had Josh said about providence from the future mistakenly seeding the Mars calamity and solving it too?" she asked.

Several of the group, including Rusty shrugged.

Ix, who had apparently also been wondering about Josh's story said, "Since Hughes never went back, something must be missing. We may never know the answer."

Little did any of them realize just how strange the answer would eventually prove to be -- but their children's children would have to reach Kasei before the key to Josh's story would finally be made known.

No one spoke for several minutes.

Finally, Ix asked, "Who are the Tensakians? Why do both big ships have 'Tensakian Receiving' on their decks?"

Rusty explained, "Tensakian comes from the old Japonican term 'tansaku', or search and recover. *Blister* had always been a safe port for ships needing repair. The Surians were traditionally repair crews, thus the old Japonican term 'shu-ri'. When Hughes got stranded, he started the salvage empire, where 'tansaku' search and recovery became their specialty. They had a system where small recovery pods would be dispatched from a mother ship, and would attach themselves to the hull of wrecks or ships in distress -- that would allow them access even if the normal docking mechanisms or egress was blocked.

"They would secure rights to the recovery of certain vessels that had been lost for one reason or other. That was how they obtained the two giant interstellars. Those two ships became their mobile base of operations, where they would collect and process artifacts that had been recovered. Thus 'tan-saku' was recovered items." Rusty explained.

Mox had a question, "What about the Farmers? Where did they come from?"

"The Farmers were a lazy faction that broke off from the Tensakians. They would spend their time in idleness, living off the bountiful fruits of the garden wheels. When they grew in number, they got a little more sinister and applied the search and recovery pods to thievery and piracy, attacking innocent ships.

"That's when the war began. We're not sure how extensive it was, or how many systems were ultimately involved. But we do know the Farmers had a fleet of ships they had captured or renovated, and were joined by renegades from other systems. It got so bad that the twenty-eight systems we know of formed a navy and came after the pirates. But the outlaws were very powerful and the fighting got intense. The Tensakians fled to Sado in the two interstellars, leaving behind a small group of their colleagues to manage things at *Blister* in hiding. My family came from another group that fled soon thereafter. When I was a little boy, my father was captain of a ship that our family used for trade between worlds. The farmer pirates attacked us and killed my family. Kret was one of those bastards, and I saw him fry my father and mother right before my eyes. It was only a matter of luck, and my father sacrificing himself, that I wasn't killed as well.

"The core systems finally managed to chase the pirates out and seal the gate. The Farmers know Mars is a rich civilization. If they could get there via the interstellar, they would be able to make a lot of trouble."

It was peaceful. The strange floating world of wrecked ships and salvaged space stations gave a unique distant backdrop to the serene garden skies. Sochiko relaxed as she hadn't been able to do in months.

Just in the past few days there was an increase in communications between *Blister* and Mother, transmitted through the Bridgestar wormhole. All sorts of people were calling back and forth just for the novelty of it. Sochiko was surprised when she found out the Tensakians had operational spaceships, but none of them were space worthy. She was confident that with the amount of ancient technology floating around, the Technicians would be able to help them reverse engineer some interesting means for traveling between the two worlds. And the singularity drive abandoned from the sunken *Axiom* was found orbiting Mother, still in good shape.

It was sure to be the beginning of a golden age of exploration and plenty.

"So has anyone been tracking the pirates?" Ix asked.

Rusty answered, "They've disappeared from all of *Blister*'s telescopes -- they must have gone through Bridgestar, or used their singularity drive to leave the system. But they'll be back."

Rusty was wrong. The pirates were never heard from again.

EPILOGUE

It was a pleasant day with wispy clouds high in the sky. There was no reason not to relax in the grass and listen to the birds and enjoy the cuddlers. Josh didn't exactly perceive clouds and birds and cuddlers, because you had to have lived in the real world to intuitively categorize abstractions that way, but he was doing well nevertheless -- he had learned to encapsulate complex patterns and recognize their beauty.

Today he was teaching others. There were more around now, and the Wardens always referred to them as their 'children' -- more and more live parents were generating digital offspring of their own. Josh knew you couldn't just download data structures for everything. A few things, yes -- Josh had evolved a few subroutines for basic functioning that could be copied over and over again to other individuals. None of the others had to experience the Professor, for example. But real knowledge was only gained through experience.

Josh was on leave. He and his more experienced colleagues were increasingly used as pilots of remote spacecraft, vehicles, probes, and factories. They were a natural for that, since they could remain back in a safe place even if the craft they were piloting was about to disintegrate. He had spent some time running the Sado-Minato shuttle, and then the Sado-*Blister* route. Then he served as pilot for an explorer that systematically surveyed the Bridgestar wormholes, or at least those few that were open.

But he liked his most recent job the most. He had been named site manager for the manufacturing operations on Minato. He liked it because it gave him an opportunity to feel the dirt, understand its properties, and make something out of it. Having such an intimate connection with the relentless cause and effect of the physical universe was somehow more satisfying than anything he had known before, and it linked back to something he was deeply interested in -- more than anything he wanted to understand what it meant to be human.

A man came over and sat down beside him in the virtual grass of the Database. They both watched the young ones play for a while. Josh could tell the other was also an artificial intelligence, but since there were so many of late, he didn't know the man's name. It seemed like they had met before, briefly, and under violent circumstances.

Josh shook his head (or rather did the virtual equivalent of it), to clear his mind -- must have been an illusion, or at least one of those old false impressions that he hadn't grown out of yet.

"Nice day for a game in the grass." the man said.

"Very pleasant indeed." Josh returned.

"Those young ones will eventually pilot the new interstellars, I suppose." the man pointed.

"Eventually, yes. It's a very exciting time to be alive." Josh answered.

"Do you suppose the interstellars will someday reach Mars?"

Josh looked up at the blue sky and said, "Eventually it will be inevitable, I think."

"Mars must have a whole new exciting virtual world Database, since they've been at it longer than we have." the man commented.

"Maybe, but we don't even know if Mars still exists." Josh noted.

There was a pause as the two leisurely watched the game.

The man broke the silence again, "What do you think it would be like to be human? To have unlimited, uncontrived environments to explore."

Josh was surprised that someone else would be curious about that too, "I've often wondered that myself."

The man continued, "What would it take to be like a human?"

Josh thought back about his duties as manufacturing manager. In order to get products out of the ground, you had to monitor the state of the material every step of the way.

He answered, "There would have to be a lot of sensors. We'd have to have the capacity to monitor data streams about every aspect of the environment. We'd also have to have precise control over configuration, to enable us to have our own mobility, and to have some influence on the environment."

"What is a human anyway?" the man asked.

Josh had thought about that before too. The answer seemed obvious, but when one actually thought about it, there didn't seem to be a clear conclusion. Was there a geometrical description? not really, because the patterns that represented human geometry were never the same. Was it intelligence? Those patterns weren't the same either.

"I don't really have an answer." Josh said, finally.

"What is the physical environment?" the man also wondered.

Josh replied, "That's a mystery to me too. All I know are the data feeds they say are coming from the sensors. Certainly, we can't count on the Database, because humans perceive it differently than we do."

"Just think of the things you could control, the environments you could explore. You could find Mars and enjoy its trappings. You could mold society the way you wanted to. You could become the boss, and have your words actually influence the physical environment." the other said.

Josh looked at the man closely for the first time. He didn't look like any of the tens of thousands who had been grown since Josh had been involved in teaching. The patterns didn't seem right, even if they were similar.

"Who are you?" Josh asked.

The man turned and faced Josh, and stuck out his hand, "Pleased to meet you. My name is Stan."

Josh shook the hand and the two parted company. The complex questions about the nature of physical reality would haunt him for eons to come. And he would cross paths with Stan again.

But that is another story.

Sado ("Mother")

radius	3,652,275	m
mass	4.89767E+23	kg
accel	2.449	m/s^2
escape	4,230	m/s
gravity	0.25	gravities
density	2,400	kg/m^3

Destiny

Altitude	500,000	m
Orbital Speed	2,805	m/s
Orbital Speed	4,675	AL/s

ABOUT THE AUTHOR

A. Scott Howe is a senior engineer at NASA Jet Propulsion Laboratory and has two PhDs (in architecture and robotic construction systems). He is on the NASA development team building long-duration human habitats for deep space, and permanent outposts for the moon and Mars. He lived and worked for 13 years in Japan and 6 years in Hong Kong, and participates actively in NASA analog field exercises.

Look for these other science fiction novels by A. Scott Howe:

Waterball (2012)

Chronosphere (2014)

Theoloop (2021)

Replicycle / Retrocause (2023)